APR 2013

Roseville Public Library
Roseville CA 95678

P9-DFR-758

BW

BY ELIZABETH STROUT

Amy and Isabelle
Abide with Me
Olive Kitteridge
The Burgess Boys

The Burgess Boys

The Burgess Boys

A Novel

ELIZABETH STROUT

RANDOM HOUSE

NEW YORK

The Burgess Boys is a work of fiction. Names, characters, places, and incidents are the products of the author's imagination or are used fictitiously. Any resemblance to actual events, locales, or persons, living or dead, is entirely coincidental.

Copyright © 2013 by Elizabeth Strout

All rights reserved.

Published in the United States by Random House, an imprint of The Random House Publishing Group, a division of Random House, Inc., New York.

RANDOM HOUSE and colophon are registered trademarks of Random House, Inc.

LIBRARY OF CONGRESS CATALOGING-IN-PUBLICATION DATA
Strout, Elizabeth.
The Burgess boys : a novel / Elizabeth Strout.
p. cm.
ISBN 978-1-4000-6768-8
eBook ISBN 978-0-8129-8461-3
1. Brothers—Fiction. I. Title.
PS3569.T736B87 2013
813'.54—dc23   2012035132

Printed in the United States of America on acid-free paper

www.atrandom.com

6 8 9 7

Book design by Dana Leigh Blanchette
Title-page photograph: © iStockphoto.com

To my husband,
Jim Tierney

The Burgess Boys

Prologue

My mother and I talked a lot about the Burgess family. "The Burgess kids," she called them. We talked about them mostly on the telephone, because I lived in New York and she lived in Maine. But we talked about them also when I visited her and stayed in the hotel nearby. My mother had not been in many hotels, and it became one of our favorite things: to sit in a room—the green walls stenciled with a strip of pink roses—and speak of the past, those who had left Shirley Falls, those who had stayed. "Been thinking about those Burgess kids," she'd say, pulling back the curtain and looking toward the birch trees.

The Burgess kids had a hold on her, I think, as a result of the fact that all three had suffered publicly, and also my mother had taught them years before in her fourth-grade Sunday-school class. She favored the Burgess boys. Jim, because he was angry even back then and trying to control it, she felt, and Bob because his heart was big. She didn't care much for Susan. "Nobody did, far as I know," she said.

"Susan was pretty when she was little," I remembered. "She had those curls and big eyes."

"And then she had that nutty son."

"Sad," I said.

"Lots of things are sad," my mother said. My mother and I were both widowed by then, and there would be a silence after she said this. Then one of us would add how glad we were that Bob Burgess had found a good wife in the end. The wife, Bob's second and we hoped his last, was a Unitarian minister. My mother did not like Unitarians; she thought they were atheists who didn't want to be left out of the fun of Christmas, but Margaret Estaver was from Maine, and that was good enough. "Bob could have married someone from New York after living there all those years. Look what happened to Jim, marrying that snob from Connecticut," my mother said.

We had talked about Jim a good deal, of course: how he'd left Maine after working homicides in the attorney general's office, how we'd hoped he would run for governor, the puzzle of why he suddenly hadn't, and then we—naturally—talked about him the year of the Wally Packer trial when Jim was on the news each night. The trial was back when they were first allowing trials to be televised, and in another year O. J. Simpson would eclipse many people's memory of the Packer trial, but until then there were Jim Burgess devotees across the country who watched with amazement as he got an acquittal for the gentle-faced soul singer Wally Packer, whose crooning voice (*Take this burden from me, the burden of my love*) had swept most of our generation into adulthood. Wally Packer, who had allegedly paid to have his white girlfriend killed. Jim kept the trial in Hartford, where race was a serious factor, and his jury selection was said to be brilliant. Then, with eloquent and relentless patience, he described just how deceptive the fabric could be that wove together—or in this case, he claimed, did not weave together—the essential components of criminal behavior: intent and action. Cartoons ran in national magazines, one showing a woman staring at her messy living room with a caption that said, "If I intend this room to be clean, when will it become clean?" Polls indicated that most people believed as my mother and I did, that Wally Packer was guilty. But Jim did a stunning job and became famous as a result. (A few magazines listed him as one of the Sexiest Men of 1993, and even my mother, who loathed any mention of sex, did not hold this against him.) O. J. Simpson reportedly wanted Jim on his "Dream Team"; there was a flurry of talk about this on the networks, but with no comment from the Burgess camp it was decided that Jim was "resting on his laurels." The Packer trial had given my mother and me something to talk about during a time when we were not pleased with each other. But that was in the past. Now when I left Maine I kissed my mother and told her I loved her, and she told me the same.

Back in New York, calling from my twenty-sixth-floor apartment one evening, watching through the window as dusk touched the city and lights emerged like fireflies in the fields of buildings spread out before me, I said, "Do you remember when Bob's mother sent him to a shrink? Kids talked about it on the playground. 'Bobby Burgess has to see a doctor for mentals.'"

"Kids are awful," my mother said. "Honest to God."

"It was a long time ago," I offered. "No one up there went to a psychiatrist."

"That's changed," my mother said. "People I go square-dancing with, they have kids who see therapists and they all seem to be on some pill. I must say, no one keeps quiet about it either."

"So you remember the Burgess father?" I had asked her this before. We did this kind of thing, repeated the stuff we knew.

"I do. Tall, I remember. Worked at the mill. A foreman, I think. And then she was left all alone."

"And she never married again."

"Never married again," my mother said. "I don't know what her chances were back then. Three little kids. Jim, Bob, and Sue."

The Burgess house had been about a mile from the center of town. A small house, but most of the houses in that part of Shirley Falls were small, or not big. The house was yellow, and it sat on a hill with a field on one side that in spring was so richly green I remember wishing as a child I could be a cow so I could munch all day on the moist grass, it seemed that scrumptious. The field by the Burgess place didn't have cows, or even a vegetable garden, just that little sense of farmland near town. In the summer Mrs. Burgess was sometimes in the front yard, dragging a hose around a bush, but since the house was on a hill she always seemed remote and small, and she didn't answer my father's wave whenever we drove by, I assume because she didn't see it.

People think of towns as bubbling with gossip, but when I was a child I seldom heard grown-ups talking about other families, and the Burgess situation was absorbed the way other tragedies were, like poor Bunny Fogg who fell down her cellar stairs and didn't get discovered for three days, or Mrs. Hammond getting a brain tumor just as her kids left for college, or crazy Annie Day who pulled her dress up in front of boys even though she was almost twenty and still in high school. It was the children—we younger ones especially—who were gossips, and unkind. The grown-ups were strict in setting us straight, so if a child on the playground was overheard saying that Bobby Burgess "was the one who killed his father" or "had to see a doctor for mentals," the offender was sent to the principal's office, the parents were called, and snacks were withheld at snack time. This didn't happen often.

Jim Burgess was ten years older than I, which made him seem as far away as someone famous, and he kind of was, even back then: He was a football player and president of his class, and really nice looking with his dark hair, but he was serious too, I remember him as someone whose eyes never smiled. Bobby and Susan were younger than Jim, and at different times babysat for my sisters and me. Susan didn't pay much attention to us, although one day she decided we were laughing at her and she took away the animal crackers that my mother always left for us when my parents went out. In protest, one of my sisters locked herself in the bathroom, and Susan yelled at her that she'd call the police. What happened is not anything I remember except there were no police, and my mother was surprised to see the animal crackers still there when she got home. A few times Bobby babysat, and he would take turns carrying us on his back. You could tell you were clinging to someone kind and good, the way he kept saying, turning his head partway, "You okay? You all right?" Once, when one of my sisters was running in the driveway and tripped and skinned her knee, we could see that Bobby felt terrible. His big hand washed it off. "Ah, you're a brave girl. You'll be all right."

Grown, my sisters moved to Massachusetts. But I went to New York, and my parents were not happy: It was a betrayal to a New England lineage that stretched back to the 1600s. My ancestors had been scrappy and survived a great deal, my father said, but they had never stepped into the cesspool of New York. I married a New Yorker—a gregarious, wealthy Jewish man, and this exacerbated things. My parents did not visit often. I think the city frightened them. I think my husband seemed a foreigner and that frightened them, and I think my children frightened them; bold and spoiled they must have appeared, with their messy rooms and plastic toys, and later their pierced noses and blue and purple hair. So there were years of bad feelings between us.

But when my husband died the same year my last child left for college, my mother, widowed herself the year before, came down to New York and stroked my forehead as she had done when I was little and sick with a bug, and said she was sorry I had lost both father and husband within such a short time. "What can I do for you?"

I was lying on my couch. "Tell me a story," I said.

She moved to the chair near the window. "Well, let's see. Susan Burgess's husband's left her and moved to Sweden, I guess he had ancestors there calling to him, who knows. He came from up north in that tiny town of New Sweden, remember. Before he went down to the university. Susan still lives in Shirley Falls, with that one son."

"Is she still pretty?" I asked.

"Not a bit."

And so it began. Like a cat's cradle connecting my mother to me, and me to Shirley Falls, bits of gossip and news and memories about the lives of the Burgess kids supported us. We reported and repeated. I told my mother again about the time I had come across Helen Burgess, Jim's wife, when they lived, as I once did, in the neighborhood of Park Slope in Brooklyn: The Burgesses moved there from Hartford after the Packer trial, Jim taking a job with a large firm in Manhattan.

My husband and I one night found ourselves dining near Helen and a friend in a Park Slope café, and we stopped near Helen's table as we were leaving. I'd had some wine—I suppose that's why I stopped—and I said to her that I'd come from the same town Jim had grown up in. Something happened to Helen's face that stayed with me. A look of quick fear seemed to pass over it. She asked my name and I told her, and she said Jim had never mentioned me. No, I was younger, I said. And then she arranged her cloth napkin with a little shake, and said, "I haven't been up there in years. Nice to meet you both. Bye-bye."

My mother thought that Helen could have been friendlier that night. "She came from money, remember. She'd think she was better than someone from Maine." This sort of remark was one I had learned to let go; I no longer bothered myself with the defensiveness of my mother and her Maine.

But after Susan Burgess's son did what he did—after the story about him had been in the newspapers, even in *The New York Times,* and on television too—I said on the phone to my mother, "I think I'm going to write the story of the Burgess kids."

"It's a good one," she agreed.

"People will say it's not nice to write about people I know."

My mother was tired that night. She yawned. "Well, you don't know them," she said. "Nobody ever knows anyone."

Book One

1

On a breezy October afternoon in the Park Slope neighborhood of Brooklyn, New York, Helen Farber Burgess was packing for vacation. A big blue suitcase lay open on the bed, and clothes her husband had chosen the night before were folded and stacked on the lounge chair nearby. Sunlight kept springing into the room from the shifting clouds outside, making the brass knobs on the bed shine brightly and the suitcase become very blue. Helen was walking back and forth between the dressing room—with its enormous mirrors and white horsehair wallpaper, the dark woodwork around the long window—walking between that and the bedroom, which had French doors that were closed right now, but in warmer weather opened onto a deck that looked out over the garden. Helen was experiencing a kind of mental paralysis that occurred when she packed for a trip, so the abrupt ringing of the telephone brought relief. When she saw the word PRIVATE, she knew it was either the wife of one of her husband's law partners—they were a prestigious firm of famous lawyers—or else her brother-in-law, Bob, who'd had an unlisted number for years but was not, and never would be, famous at all.

"I'm glad it's you," she said, pulling a colorful scarf from the bureau drawer, holding it up, dropping it on the bed.

"You are?" Bob's voice sounded surprised.

"I was afraid it would be Dorothy." Walking to the window, Helen peered out at the garden. The plum tree was bending in the wind, and yellow leaves from the bittersweet swirled across the ground.

"Why didn't you want it to be Dorothy?"

"She tires me right now," said Helen.

"You're about to go away with them for a week."

"Ten days. I know."

A short pause, and then Bob said, "Yeah," his voice dropping into an understanding so quick and entire—it was his strong point, Helen thought, his odd ability to fall feetfirst into the little pocket of someone else's world for those few seconds. It should have made him a good husband but apparently it hadn't: Bob's wife had left him years ago.

"We've gone away with them before," Helen reminded him. "It'll be fine. Alan's an awfully nice fellow. Dull."

"And managing partner of the firm," Bob said.

"That too." Helen sang the words playfully. "A little difficult to say, 'Oh, we'd rather go alone on this trip.' Jim says their older girl is really messing up right now—she's in high school—and the family therapist suggested that Dorothy and Alan get away. I don't know why you 'get away' if your kid's messing up, but there we are."

"I don't know either," Bob said sincerely. Then: "Helen, this thing just happened."

She listened, folding a pair of linen slacks. "Come on over," she interrupted. "We'll go across the street for dinner when Jim gets home."

After that she was able to pack with authority. The colorful scarf was included with three white linen blouses and black ballet flats and the coral necklace Jim had bought her last year. Over a whiskey sour with Dorothy on the terrace, while they waited for the men to shower from golf, Helen would say, "Bob's an interesting fellow." She might even mention the accident—how it was Bob, four years old, who'd been playing with the gears that caused the car to roll over their father and kill him; the man had walked down the hill of the driveway to fix something about the mailbox, leaving all three young kids in the car. A perfectly awful thing. And never mentioned. Jim had told her once in thirty years. But Bob was an anxious man, Helen liked to watch out for him.

"You're rather a saint," Dorothy might say, sitting back, her eyes blocked by huge sunglasses.

Helen would shake her head. "Just a person who needs to be needed. And with the children grown—" No, she'd not mention the children. Not if the Anglins' daughter was flunking courses, staying out until dawn. How would they spend ten days together and not mention the children? She'd ask Jim.

Helen went downstairs, stepped into the kitchen. "Ana," she said to her housekeeper, who was scrubbing sweet potatoes with a vegetable brush. "Ana, we're going to eat out tonight. You can go home."

———•———

The autumn clouds, magnificent in their variegated darkness, were being spread apart by the wind, and great streaks of sunshine splashed down on the buildings on Seventh Avenue. This is where the Chinese restaurants were, the card shops, the jewelry shops, the grocers with the fruits and vegetables and rows of cut flowers. Bob Burgess walked past all these, up the sidewalk in the direction of his brother's house.

Bob was a tall man, fifty-one years old, and here was the thing about Bob: He was a likeable fellow. To be with Bob made people feel as if they were inside a small circle of us-ness. If Bob had known this about himself his life might have been different. But he didn't know it, and his heart was often touched by an undefined fear. Also, he wasn't consistent. Friends agreed that you could have a great time with him and then you'd see him again and he'd be vacant. This part Bob knew, because his former wife had told him. Pam said he went away in his head.

"Jim gets like that too," Bob had offered.

"We're not talking about Jim."

Waiting at the curb for the light to change, Bob felt a swell of gratitude toward his sister-in-law, who'd said, "We'll go across the street for dinner when Jim gets home." It was Jim he wanted to see. What Bob had watched earlier, sitting by the window in his fourth-floor apartment, what he had heard in the apartment down below—it had shaken him, and crossing the street now, passing a coffee shop where young people sat on couches in cavernous gloom with faces mesmerized by laptop screens, Bob felt removed from the familiarity of all he walked by. As though he had not lived half his life in New York and loved it as one would a person, as though he had never left the wide expanses of wild grass, never known or wanted anything but bleak New England skies.

"Your sister just called," said Helen as she let Bob in through the grated door beneath the brownstone's stoop. "Wanted Jim and sounded grim." Helen turned from hanging Bob's coat in the closet, adding, "I know. It's just the way she sounds. But I still say, Susan smiled at me once." Helen sat on the couch, tucking her legs in their black tights beneath her. "I was trying to copy a Maine accent."

Bob sat in the rocking chair. His knees pumped up and down.

"No one should try and copy a Maine accent to a Mainer," Helen continued. "I don't know why the Southerners are so much nicer about it, but they are. If you say 'Hi, y'all' to a Southerner, you don't feel like they're smirking at you. Bobby, you're all jumpy." She leaned forward, patting the air. "It's all right. You can be jumpy as long as you're okay. Are you okay?"

All his life, kindness had weakened Bob, and he felt now the physicality of this, a sort of fluidity moving through his chest. "Not really," he admitted. "But you're right about the accent stuff. When people say, 'Hey, you're from Maine, you can't get they-ah from he-yah,' it's painful. Painful stuff."

"I know that," Helen said. "Now you tell me what happened."

Bob said, "Adriana and Preppy Boy were fighting again."

"Wait," said Helen. "Oh, of course. The couple below you. They have that idiot little dog who yaps all the time."

"That's right."

"Go on," Helen said, pleased she'd remembered this. "One second,

Bob. I have to tell you what I saw on the news last night. This segment called 'Real Men Like Small Dogs.' They interviewed these different, sort of—sorry—faggy-looking guys who were holding these tiny dogs that were dressed in plaid raincoats and rubber boots, and I thought: This is news? We've got a war going on in Iraq for almost four years now, and this is what they call news? It's because they don't have children. People who dress their dogs like that. Bob, I'm awfully sorry. Go on with your story."

Helen picked up a pillow and stroked it. Her face had turned pink, and Bob thought she was having a hot flash, so he looked down at his hands to give her privacy, not realizing that Helen had blushed because she'd spoken of people who did not have children—as Bob did not.

"They fight," Bob said. "And when they fight, Preppy Boy—husband, they're married—yells the same thing over and over. 'Adriana, you're driving me fucking crazy.' Over and over again."

Helen shook her head. "Imagine living like that. Do you want a drink?" She rose and went to the mahogany cupboard, where she poured whiskey into a crystal tumbler. She was a short, still shapely woman in her black skirt and beige sweater.

Bob drank half the whiskey in one swallow. "Anyways," he continued, and saw a small tightening on Helen's face. She hated how he said "Anyways," though he always forgot this, and he forgot it now, only felt the foreboding of failure. He wasn't going to be able to convey the sadness of what he had seen. "She comes home," Bob said. "They start to fight. He does his yelling thing. Then he takes the dog out. But this time, while he's gone, she calls the police. She's never done that before. He comes back and they arrest him. I heard the cops tell him that his wife said he'd hit her. And thrown her clothes out the window. So they arrested him. And he was *amazed*."

Helen's face looked as if she didn't know what to say.

"He's this good-looking guy, very cool in his zip-up sweater, and he stood there crying, 'Baby, I never hit you, baby, seven years we've been married, what are you doing? Baby, pleeeease!' But they cuffed him and walked him across the street in broad daylight to the cruiser and he's spending the night in the pens." Bob eased himself out of the rocking chair, went to the mahogany cupboard, and poured himself more whiskey.

"That's a very sad story," said Helen, who was disappointed. She had hoped it would be more dramatic. "But he might have thought of that before he hit her."

"I don't think he did hit her." Bob returned to the rocking chair.

Helen said musingly, "I wonder if they'll stay married."

"I don't think so." Bob was tired now.

"What bothered you most, Bobby?" Helen asked. "The marriage falling apart, or the arrest?" She took it personally, his expression of not finding relief.

Bob rocked a few times. "Everything." He snapped his fingers. "Like that, it happened. I mean, it was just an ordinary day, Helen."

Helen plumped the pillow against the back of the couch. "I don't know what's ordinary about a day when you have your husband arrested."

Turning his head, Bob saw through the grated windows his brother walking up the sidewalk, and a small rush of anxiety came to him at the sight of this: his older brother's quick gait, his long coat, the thick leather briefcase. There was the sound of the key in the door.

"Hi, sweetheart," said Helen. "Your brother's here."

"I see that." Jim shrugged off his coat and hung it in the hall closet. Bob had never learned to hang up his coat. What is it with you?, his wife, Pam, used to ask, What is it, what is it, what is it? And what was it? He could not say. But whenever he walked through a door, unless someone took his coat for him, the act of hanging it up seemed needless and . . . well, too difficult.

"I'll go." Bob said. "I have a brief to work on." Bob worked in the appellate division of Legal Aid, reading case records at the trial level. There was always an appeal that required a brief, always a brief to be worked on.

"Don't be silly," said Helen. "I said we'd go across the street for supper."

"Out of my chair, knucklehead." Jim waved a hand in Bob's direction. "Glad to see you. It's been what, four days?"

"Stop it, Jim. Your brother saw that downstairs neighbor of his taken away in handcuffs this afternoon."

"Trouble in the graduate dorm?"

"Jim, stop."

"He's just being my brother," Bob said. He moved to the couch, and Jim sat down in the rocking chair.

"Let's hear it." Jim crossed his arms. He was a large man, and muscular, so that crossing his arms, which he did often, seemed to make him boxy, confrontational. He listened without moving. Then he bent to untie his shoes. "Did he throw her clothes out the window?" he asked.

"I didn't see anything," Bob said.

"Families," Jim said. "Criminal law would lose half its business without them. Do you realize, Helen, you could call the police right now and accuse me of hitting you and they'd take me away for the night?"

"I'm not going to call the police on you." Helen said this conversationally. She stood and straightened the waistband of her skirt. "But if you want to change your clothes, go. I'm hungry."

Bob leaned forward. "Jimmy, it kind of shook me up. Seeing him arrested. I don't know why. But it did."

"Grow up," Jim said. "Sheesh. What do you want me to do?" He slipped off a shoe, rubbed his foot. He added, "If you want, I'll call down there tonight and make sure he's all right. Pretty white boy in the pens."

In the next room, the telephone rang just as Bob said, "Would you, Jim?"

"That'll be your sister," said Helen. "She called before."

"Tell her I'm not home, Hellie." Jim tossed his sock onto the parquet floor. "When was the last time you spoke to Susan?" he asked Bob, slipping off his other shoe.

"Months ago," said Bob. "I told you. We argued about the Somalis."

"Why are there Somalian people in Maine anyway?" Helen asked as she walked through the door to the next room. Calling over her shoulder, "Why would *any*one go to Shirley Falls except in shackles?"

It always surprised Bob when Helen talked like this, as though her dislike of where the Burgesses came from required no shred of discretion. But Jim called back to her, "They are in shackles. Poverty's a shackle." He tossed the second sock in the direction of the first; it landed on the coffee table, hanging from its corner.

"Susan told me the Somalis were invading the town," Bob continued. "Arriving in droves. She said three years ago just a few families were there and now there's two thousand, that every time she turns around a Greyhound bus unloads forty more. I said she was being hysterical, and she said women were always accused of being hysterical and regarding the Somalis I didn't know what I was talking about since I hadn't been up there in ages."

"Jim." Helen returned to the living room. "She really wants to speak with you. She's all upset. I couldn't lie. I said you'd just come home. I'm sorry, honey."

Jim touched Helen's shoulder on his way by. "It's okay."

Helen bent to pick up Jim's socks, and this made Bob wonder whether, if he had hung up his coat like Jim did, Pam might not have been so mad about his socks.

After a long silence they heard Jim quietly asking questions. They could not make out the words. There was another long silence, more quiet questions, remarks. Still, they could not hear the words.

Helen fingered her small earring and sighed. "Have another drink. It looks like we may be here awhile." But they could not relax. Bob sat back on the couch and peered through the window at the people walking home from work. He lived only six blocks from here, on the other side of Seventh Avenue, but no one would joke about a graduate dorm on this block. On this block, people were grown-ups. On this block, they were bankers and doctors and reporters, and they carried briefcases and an amazing variety of black bags, especially the women. On this block, the sidewalks were clean, and shrubs were planted in the little front gardens.

Helen and Bob turned their heads as they heard Jim hang up.

Jim stood in the doorway, his red tie loosened. He said, "We can't go away." Helen sat forward. Jim took his tie off with a furious pull and said to Bob, "Our nephew's about to be arrested." Jim's face was pale, his eyes had become small. He sat on the couch and pressed his hands to his head. "Oh, man. This could be all over the papers. The nephew of Jim Burgess has been charged—"

"Did he kill someone?" Bob asked.

Jim looked up. "What's wrong with you?" he asked, just as Helen was saying cautiously, "Like a prostitute?"

Jim shook his head sharply, as though he had water in his ear. He looked at Bob and said, "No, he didn't kill someone." He looked at Helen and said, "No, the person he didn't kill was not a prostitute." Then he gazed up at the ceiling, closed his eyes, and said, "Our nephew, Zachary Olson, has thrown a frozen pig's head through the front door of a mosque. During prayer. During *Ramadan*. Susan says Zach doesn't even know what Ramadan is, which is completely believable—Susan didn't know what it was until she read about this in the paper. The pig's head was bloody, starting to melt, it's stained their carpet, and they don't have the money to buy a new one. They have to clean it seven times because of holy law. *That's* the story, you guys."

Helen looked at Bob. Puzzlement came to her face. "Why would that be all over the papers, Jim?" she finally asked, softly.

"Do you get it?" Jim asked, just as quietly, turning to her. "It's a hate crime, Helen. It's like if you went over to Borough Park, found an Orthodox Jewish temple, and forced everyone in there to eat ice cream and bacon before they could leave."

"Okay," said Helen. "I just didn't know. I didn't know that about Muslims."

"They're prosecuting it as a hate crime?" Bob asked.

"They're talking about going after it every way they can. The FBI's already involved. The attorney general's office might go in for a civil rights violation. Susan says it's on national news, but she's so nuts right now it's hard to know if that's true. Apparently some reporter from CNN happened to be in town, heard it reported locally, loved the story, sent it out nationally. What person *happens* to be in Shirley Falls?" Jim picked up the remote control for the television, aimed it, then dropped it onto the couch next to him. "I don't want this right now. Oh, man, I do not want this." He ran both hands over his face, his hair.

"Are they holding him?" Bob asked.

"They haven't arrested him. They don't know Zach did it. They're out looking for some punk, and it's just idiot little nineteen-year-old Zach. Zach, Son of Susan."

"When did this happen?" Bob asked.

"Two nights ago. According to Zach, which means according to Susan, he did this alone as a 'joke.'"

"A joke?"

"A joke. No, sorry, a 'dumb joke.' I'm just reporting, Bob. He bolts, no one sees him. Ostensibly. Then he hears it all over the news today, gets scared, and tells Susan when she comes home from work. She's flipped *out*, of course. I told her to take him in right now, he doesn't have to make a statement, but she's too scared. She's afraid they'll lock him up for the night. She says she won't do anything till I get there." Jim slumped back into the couch, then sat forward again immediately. "Oh, man. Oh, *shit*." He stood up quickly and walked back and forth in front of the grated windows. "The police chief is Gerry O'Hare. Never heard of him. Susan says they dated in high school."

"He dumped her after two dates," Bob said.

"Good. Maybe he'll be nice to her. She did say she might call him in the morning and tell him she'll bring Zach in as soon as I get there." Jim reached out to hit the arm of the couch as he walked past it. He sat back down in his rocking chair.

"Does she have him a lawyer?" Bob asked.

"I have to find one."

"Don't you know someone in the AG's office?" Helen asked. She picked a piece of lint from her black tights. "I can't think there'd be a lot of turnover up there."

"I know the attorney general himself," Jim said loudly, rocking back and forth, holding the arms of the rocking chair tight. "We were prosecutors together years ago. You met him at a Christmas party once, Helen. Dick Hartley. You thought he was a moron and you were right. And no, I can't contact him, Jesus. He's sticking his nose in the case. Totally a conflict. And strategically suicide. Jim Burgess can't just go barreling in, good God." Helen and Bob exchanged glances. After a moment Jim stopped rocking and looked at Bob. "Did he kill a prostitute? What was *that* about?"

Bob held up a hand in a gesture of apology. "Zach's a bit of a mystery, is all I meant. Quiet."

"The only thing Zach is, is a moron." Jim looked at Helen. "Honey, I'm sorry."

"I'm the one who said 'prostitute,'" Helen reminded him. "So don't get mad at Bob, who's right, you know, Zach has always been different, and frankly it is the kind of thing that happens in Maine, a quiet guy living with his mother killing prostitutes and burying them in some potato field. And since he didn't do that, I don't know why we have to give up a vacation, I really don't." Helen crossed her legs, clasped her hands over her knees. "I don't even know why he has to turn himself in. Get him a Maine lawyer and let *him* figure it out."

"Hellie, you're upset, and I get it," Jim said patiently. "But Susan's a mess. And I'll get him a Maine lawyer. But Zach has to take himself in because—" Here Jim paused and looked around the room. "Because he did it. That's the first reason. The other first reason is that if he goes in right away and says, 'Oh, stupid me,' they'll probably be easier on him. But the Burgesses aren't fugitives. That's not who we are. We don't hide."

"Okay," said Helen. "All right."

"I kept telling Susan: They'll charge him, set bail, get him right back home. It's a misdemeanor. But she's got to get him in there. The cops are under pressure with the publicity." Jim spread his hands as if he were holding a basketball in front of him. "The immediate thing is to *contain* this."

"I'll go," Bob said.

"You?" Jim said. "Mr. Scared-to-Fly?"

"I'll take your car. I'll leave early in the morning. You guys go wherever you're going. Where are you going?"

"St. Kitts," said Helen. "Jim, why don't you let Bob go?"

"Because . . ." Jim closed his eyes, bowed his head.

"Because I can't do it?" Bob said. "It's true she likes you better, but come on, Jimmy, I'll go. I want to." Bob had a sudden feeling of drunkenness, as if the earlier whiskey had just kicked in.

Jim kept his eyes closed.

"Jim," Helen said. "You need this vacation. You're seriously over-worked." The urgency in her voice made Bob's heart ache with a fresh loneliness: Helen's alliance with Jim was strong—and not to be assaulted by the needs of a sister-in-law whom Helen, after all these years, barely knew.

"Fine," Jim said. He picked his head up, looked at Bob. "You go. Fine."

"We're one mess of a family, aren't we, Jimmy?" Bob, sitting next to his brother, put his arm over Jim's shoulder.

"Stop it," said Jim. "Would you stop? Jesus Christ almighty."

Bob walked back home along the darkened streets. As he got closer to his building, he saw from the sidewalk that the television was on in the apartment below his. He could just make out the form of Adriana sitting alone and staring at the TV. Had she no one who could spend the night with her? He might knock on her door, ask if she was all right. But he pictured himself, the big gray-haired man who lived above her, standing in her doorway, and thought she would not want that. He climbed the stairs to his place, tossed his coat onto the floor, and picked up his phone.

"Susie," he said. "It's me."

———◆———

They were twins.

Jim had his own name right from the start, but Susie and Bob were

The Twins. Go find the twins. Tell the twins to come and eat. The twins have chicken pox, the twins can't sleep. But twins have a special connection. They are, fingers crossed, like this. "Kill him," Susan was saying now, on the telephone. "String him up by his toenails."

"Susan, take it easy, he's your kid." Bob had switched on his desk lamp and stood looking over the street.

"I'm talking about the rabbi. And the queer-o woman minister of the Unitarian church. They've come out with a statement. Not only has the *town* been damaged by this, but the whole state. No, excuse me. The whole country."

Bob rubbed the back of his neck. "So, Susan. Why did Zach do this?"

"Why did he do it? When was the last time you raised a child, Bob? Oh, I know I'm supposed to be sensitive about that, never mention your low sperm or no sperm or whatever it is, and I never have. I've never said a word about why Pam might have left, so she could have children with someone—I can't believe you're making me say all this, when I'm the one in trouble."

Bob turned away from the window. "Susan, do you have a pill you can take?"

"Like a cyanide tablet?"

"Valium." Bob felt an inexpressible sadness go through him, and he wandered back toward the bedroom with the phone.

"I never take Valium."

"Well, it's time to start. Your doctor can phone in a prescription. You'll be able to sleep tonight."

Susan didn't answer, and Bob knew that his sadness was a longing for Jim. Because the truth (and Jimmy knew it) was that Bob didn't know what to do. "The kid's safe," Bob said. "No one's going to hurt him. Or you." Bob sat down on his bed, then stood up again. He really had absolutely no idea what to do. He wouldn't sleep tonight; not even a Valium, and he had plenty, would get him to sleep, he could tell. Not with his nephew in trouble, and that poor woman below him watching TV, and even Preppy Boy in jail. And Jimmy headed off to some island. Bob walked back to the front of the apartment, switched off his desk lamp.

"Let me ask you something," his sister was saying.

In the darkness, a bus pulled up across the street. An old black woman sat looking out the bus window, her face implacable; a man toward the back nodded his head, maybe listening to earphones. They seemed exquisitely innocent, and far away—

"Do you think this is a movie?" his sister asked. "Like this is some boondocks of a town and the farmers are going down to the courthouse and demand his head on a stick?"

"What are you talking about?"

"Thank God Mommy's gone. She'd die all over again. She would." Susan was crying.

Bob said, "This will blow over."

"God's teeth, how can you say that? It's on every news station—"

"Don't watch," Bob told her.

"Do you think I'm crazy?" she asked.

"A little bit. At the moment."

"That's helpful. Thank you. Did Jimmy tell you a little boy in the mosque fainted, the pig's head scared him so much? It'd begun to thaw, so it was bloody. I know what you're thinking. What kid stores a pig's head in his mother's freezer without her knowing, and then does something like this? You can't deny you're thinking that, Bob. And it makes me crazy. Which you just called me a moment ago."

"Susan, you've—"

"You expect certain things with kids, you know. Well, you don't know. But car accidents. The wrong girlfriends. Bad grades, that stuff. You don't expect to have anything to do with friggin' mosques, for crying out loud."

"I'm driving up there tomorrow, Susan." He had told her this when he first called. "I'll take him in with you, help contain this. Don't you worry."

"Oh, I won't worry," she said. "Good night."

How they hated each other! Bob cracked open the window, shook out a cigarette, then poured wine into a juice glass and sat down in the metal foldout chair by the window. Across the street, lights were on in different apartments. There was a private show up here: the young girl who could be seen in her bedroom walking around in her underpants and no top. Because of how the room was laid out, he never saw her breasts, just her bare back, but he got a kick out of how free she seemed. So there was that—like a field of bluets in June.

Two windows over was the couple who spent a lot of time in their white kitchen, the man reaching into a cupboard right now—he seemed to be the one who cooked. Bob didn't like to cook. He liked to eat, but as Pam had pointed out, he liked the stuff that kids ate, things without color, like mashed potatoes or macaroni and cheese. People in New York liked food. Food was a very big deal. Food was like art. To be a chef in New York was like being a rock star.

Bob poured more wine, settled himself at the window again. What-*ever*, as people said these days.

Be a chef, be a beggar, be divorced a zillion times, no one in this city cared. Smoke yourself to death out the window. Scare your wife and go to jail. It was heaven to live here. Susie never got that. Poor Susie.

Bob was getting drunk.

He heard the door open in the apartment below him, heard footsteps down the stairs. He peered out the window. Adriana stood beneath a streetlamp, holding a leash, her shoulders hunched and shivering, and the tiny dog was just standing there shivering too. "Ah, you poor things," Bob said quietly. Nobody, it seemed to him in his drunken expansive-ness, nobody—anywhere—had a clue.

———•———

Six blocks away, Helen lay next to her husband and listened to him snore. Through the window in the black night sky she saw the planes on their way into La Guardia, every three seconds if you counted—as her children had when they were young—like stars that kept coming and coming and coming. Tonight the house seemed full of emptiness, and she thought of how her children used to be asleep in their rooms and how safe it had been, the soft buoyancy of nighttime. She thought of Zachary up in Maine, but she had not seen him for years and could only picture a skinny pale boy, a motherless-seeming child. And she did not want to think of him, or a frozen pig's head, or her grim sister-in-law, because she saw how the incident was an irritant rubbing already against the fine fabric of her family, and she felt right now the small pricks of anxiety that precede insomnia.

She pushed on Jim's shoulder. "You're snoring," she said.

"Sorry." He could say that in his sleep. He turned over.

Wide awake, Helen hoped her plants wouldn't die while she and Jim were gone. Ana was not particularly good with plants. It was a feel, and you had it or you didn't. Once, years before Ana, the Burgess family had gone on vacation and the lesbians next door had let the lavender petunias that filled Helen's window boxes die. Helen had tended those plants every day, snipping off the sticky dead heads, watering them, feeding them; they were like sweet geysers gushing forth from the front windows of the house, and people commented on them as they walked by. Helen told the women how much attention was needed for any flowering plant in the summertime and they said yes, they knew. But then, to return from vacation and find them shriveled on the vine! Helen had cried. The women moved soon after, and Helen was glad. She'd never been able to be nice to them, not really, after they had killed her petunias. Two lesbians named Linda and Laura. Fat Linda and Linda's Laura is how they'd been spoken of in the Burgess home.

The Burgesses lived in the last of a row of brownstones. On their left was a tall limestone, the only apartment building on the block. Co-ops now. The Linda-Lauras had lived in the street-level co-op and then sold it to a banker, Deborah-Who-Does (short for Deborah-Who-Knows-Everything, as opposed to the Debra in the building who didn't know everything), and her husband, William, who was so nervous he had introduced himself as "Billiam." The kids would sometimes call him that, but Helen asked them to be kind because Billiam had, years ago, been in the Vietnam War, and also, his wife, Deborah-Who-Does, was a terrible nuisance and Helen thought it had to be awful living with her. You couldn't step out into the back garden without Deborah-Who-Does stepping out into hers, and in two minutes she'd be mentioning that the pansies you were arranging wouldn't last on that side of the garden, that the lilies would need more light, that the lilac bush Helen planted would die (it had) because there was so little lime in the soil.

Debra-Who-Doesn't, on the other hand, was a sweet woman, tall and anxious, a psychiatrist and a bit dippy. But it was sad: Her husband was cheating on her. It was Helen who had discovered this. Home alone during the day, she heard through the walls the most appalling sexual sounds. When Helen peeked out the front window she saw Debra's husband emerge down the front steps with a curly-haired woman behind him. Later, she saw them together in a local bar. And once she had heard Debra-Who-Doesn't say to her husband, "Why are you picking on me tonight?" So Debra-Who-Doesn't-Know-Everything didn't know everything. In this way, Helen didn't always care for living in the city. Jim yelled like a crazy person when it was basketball season. "You dumbfuck asshole!" he'd yell at the TV, and Helen worried the neighbors would think he was yelling at her. She had considered mentioning it to them in a laughing way, and then decided that in issues of veracity the less said the better. Not that she'd be lying.

Still.

Her mind raced and raced. What had she forgotten to pack? She didn't want to think of herself dressing one night to meet the Anglins for dinner and finding she'd not packed the right shoes—her outfit ruined just like that. Tucking the quilt around her, Helen realized that tonight's telephone call from Susan was still here in the house, dark and formless and bad. She sat up.

This is what happened when you couldn't sleep, and when you had an image in your mind of a frozen pig's head. Helen went into the bathroom and found a sleeping pill, and the bathroom was clean and familiar. Back in bed she moved close to her husband and within minutes felt the gentle tug of sleep, and she was so glad she wasn't Deborah-Who-Does, or Debra-Who-Doesn't, so glad she was Helen Farber Burgess, so glad she had children, so glad to be glad about life.

———◆———

But such urgency in the morning!

On a day when Park Slope opened with its Saturday's munificence—children on the way to the park with soccer balls in netted bags, their fathers watching the traffic lights and hurrying the kids along, young couples who arrived at the coffee shops with hair still wet from showering after morning love, people who, having dinner parties that night, were already near Grand Army Plaza at the end of the park in order to browse the farmers market for the best apples and breads and cut flowers, their arms laden with baskets and paper-wrapped stalks of sunflowers—in the midst of all this, there were of course the typical vexations found anywhere in the country, even in this neighborhood where people, for the most part, exuded a sense of being exactly where they wanted to be: There was the mother whose child was begging for a Barbie doll for her birthday and the mother said no, Barbie dolls are why girls are skinny and sick. On Eighth Street there was the stepfather grimly trying to teach the recalcitrant boy how to ride a bicycle, holding on to the back of the bike while the child, white-faced with fear, wobbled and looked at him for praise. (The man's wife was finishing her chemo for breast cancer, there was no getting out of any of it.) On Third Street a couple argued about their teenage son, whether he should be allowed to stay in his room on this sunny autumn day. So there were these disgruntlements—and the Burgesses were having problems of their own.

The car ordered to take Helen and Jim to the airport had not shown up. Their bags were on the sidewalk, and Helen was directed to stay with them while Jim went in and out of the house, on his cell phone to the car service. Deborah-Who-Does stepped out onto the sidewalk and asked where they were headed off to on this nice sunny day, it must be wonderful taking so many vacations. Helen had to say, "Excuse me, please, I need to make a call," taking her own cell phone from her bag and pretending to call her son, who (in Arizona) would still be sound asleep. But Deborah-Who-Does was waiting for Billiam, and Helen had to fake a conversation into her phone because Deborah kept smiling her way. Billiam finally appeared and off they went down the sidewalk holding hands, which Helen thought was showy.

Meanwhile, Jim, pacing around the foyer, noticed that both car keys were hanging on the key holder by the door. Bob had not taken the key last night! How was he going to drive the car to Maine without the goddamn car key? Jim yelled this question to Helen as he joined her on the sidewalk, and Helen said quietly that if he yelled like that any more she would move into Manhattan. Jim shook the key in front of her face. "How is he supposed to *get* there?" he whispered fiercely.

"If you would give your brother a key to our house, this wouldn't be an issue."

Approaching around the corner, driving slowly, was a black town car. Jim waved his arm above his head in a kind of backward swimming motion. And then finally Helen was tucked into the backseat, where she smoothed her hair as Jim, on his cell phone, called Bob. "Pick up the phone, Bob." Then: "What happened to you? You just woke *up*? You're supposed to be on your way to Maine. What do you mean you were awake all night?" Jim leaned forward and said to the driver, "Make a stop at the corner of Sixth and Ninth." He sat back. "Well, guess what I have in my hand? Take a guess, knucklehead. The key to my car, that's right. And listen—are you listening? Charlie Tibbetts. Lawyer for Zach. He'll see you Monday morning. You can stay through Monday, don't pretend you can't. Legal Aid doesn't give a crawling crap. Charlie's out of town for the weekend, but I thought of him last night and spoke to him. He should be the guy. Good guy. All you have to do in the next couple days is keep this *contained*, understand? Now get down to the sidewalk, we're on our way to the airport."

Helen pushed the button that lowered the window, put her face to the fresh air.

Jim sat back, taking her hand. "We're going to have a terrific time, sweetheart. Just like the farty-looking couples in the brochures. It'll be great."

Bob was in front of his building wearing sweatpants and a T-shirt and grimy athletic socks. "Hey, slob-dog," Jim called. He tossed the car key through the open window, and Bob caught it in one hand.

"Have fun." Bob waved once.

Helen was impressed at how easily Bob caught the key. "Good luck up there," she called.

The town car rounded the corner, disappeared from sight, and Bob turned to face his building. When young, he had run into the woods rather than watch the car that took Jim off to college, and he wanted to run there now. Instead, he stood on broken cement next to metal garbage bins, and shards of sunlight stabbed his eyes while he fumbled with his keys.

Years earlier, when Bob had been newer to the city, he had gone to a therapist named Elaine. She was a large woman, loose-limbed, as old as he was now, which of course back then had seemed pretty old. He had sat in the midst of her benevolent presence, picking at a hole in the arm of her leather couch, glancing anxiously at the fig tree in the corner (a plant that looked fake except for its marked and sad leaning toward the tiny sliver of light that came through the window, and its ability to grow, in six years' time, one new leaf). Had Elaine been here on the sidewalk right now, she would have told him, "Bob, stay in the present." Because dimly Bob was aware of what was happening to him as his brother's car turned the corner, *left him,* dimly, he knew, but—oh, poor Elaine, dead now from some awful disease, and she had tried so hard with him, been so kind—it did no good. The sunlight shattered him.

Bob, who was four years old when his father died, remembered only the sun on the hood of the car that day, and that his father had been covered by a blanket, also—always—Susan's little-girl accusing voice: "It's all your fault, you stupid-head."

Now, standing on the sidewalk in Brooklyn, New York, Bob pictured his brother tossing him the car key, watched the town car disappear, thought of the task that was waiting, and inside him was the cry *Jimmy, don't go.*

Adriana stepped through the door.

2

Susan Olson lived in a narrow three-story house not far from town. Since her divorce seven years earlier she had rented the top rooms to an old woman named Mrs. Drinkwater, who came and went with less frequency these days, and who never complained about the music coming from Zach's room, and always paid her rent on time. The night before Zach was to turn himself in, Susan had to climb the stairs, knock on the old woman's door, and explain to her what had happened. Mrs. Drinkwater was surprisingly sanguine. "Dear, dear," she said, sitting on the chair by her little desk. She was wearing a pink rayon robe, and her stockings were rolled to right above her knees; her gray hair was pinned back, but much of it was falling down. This is how she looked if she wasn't dressed to go out, which was a lot of the time. She was thin as kindling.

"You need to know," Susan said, sitting down on the bed, "because after tomorrow you might get asked by reporters what he's like."

The old lady shook her head slowly. "Well, he's quiet." She looked at Susan. Her glasses were huge trifocals, and wherever her eyes were, you could never quite see into them directly; they wavered around. "Never been rude to me," she added.

"I can't tell you what to say."

"Nice your brother's coming. Is it the famous one?"

"No. The famous one is off vacationing with his wife."

A long silence followed. Mrs. Drinkwater said, "Zachary's father? Does he know?"

"I emailed him."

"He's still living in . . . Sweden?"

Susan nodded.

Mrs. Drinkwater looked at her little desk, then at the wall above it. "I wonder what that's like, living in Sweden."

"I hope you sleep," Susan said. "I'm sorry about this."

"I hope *you* sleep, dear. Do you have a pill?"

"I don't take them."

"I see."

Susan stood, ran a hand over her short hair, looked around as though she was supposed to do something but couldn't remember what.

"Good night, dear," said Mrs. Drinkwater.

Susan walked one flight down and knocked lightly on Zach's door. He was lying on his bed, huge earphones over his ears. She tapped her own ear to indicate that he should remove them. His laptop lay on the bed beside him. "Are you frightened?" she asked.

He nodded.

The room was almost dark. Only one small light was on, over a bookshelf that had stacks of magazines piled on it. A few books lay scattered below. The shades were drawn, and the walls, painted black a few years earlier—Susan had come home from work one day and found them that way—were empty of posters or photographs.

"Did you hear from your father?"

"No." His voice was husky and deep.

"I asked him to email you."

"I don't want you to ask."

"He's your father."

"He shouldn't write me because you tell him to."

After a long moment she said, "Try and get some sleep."

At noontime the next day she made Zach tomato soup from a can and a grilled cheese sandwich. He bent his head close to the bowl and ate half the sandwich with his thin fingers, then pushed back the plate. When he looked up at her with his dark eyes, for a moment she saw him as the small child he'd once been, before his social ungainliness had been fully exposed, before his inability to play any sport had hindered him irredeemably, before his nose became adult and angular and his eyebrows one dark line, back when he had seemed a shy and notably obedient little boy. A picky eater, always.

"Go shower," she said. "And put on nice clothes."

"What's nice clothes?" he asked.

"A shirt with a collar. And no jeans."

"No jeans?" This was not defiant, but worried.

"Okay. Jeans without holes."

Susan picked up the phone and called the police station. Chief O'Hare was in. Three times she had to give her name before they let her talk to him. She had written down what she would say. Her mouth was so dry her lips stuck to each other, and she moved them extra to get the words out.

"Any minute now," she concluded, looking up from the notebook paper she'd written on. "I'm just waiting for Bob." She could picture Gerry's big hand holding the telephone, his face without expression. He had added a great deal of weight over the years. Sometimes, not often, he came into the eyeglass store at the mall across the river where Susan worked and he'd wait while his wife's glasses were fixed. He'd nod to her. He was not pleasant, or unpleasant; she'd have expected it that way.

"Yuh. Susan. The way I see it is, we got a situation here." His voice over the phone was tired, professional. "Once we know who the perp is, I'd be wrong not to send someone to get him. Lot of publicity with this."

"Gerry," she said. "Dear God. Please do not send a cop car. Please do not do that."

"Here's what I think. I think we're not having this conversation. Old friends. That's what we are. I'm sure I'll see you soon. Before the day is over. That's it."

"Thank you," she said.

———◆———

Bob drove comfortably in his brother's car, the motion steady beneath him. Through the windshield he saw signs for shopping outlets, or lakes, but mostly there were the trees of Connecticut always moving closer, then whizzing by, then gone. Traffic moved quickly and with a sense of community, as though all drivers were tenants in this fast forward-moving form. The image of Adriana appeared in Bob's mind. I'm scared, she had said to him, standing by the doorway in a maroon sweat suit, her streaky blond hair moving in the breeze. She had a throaty voice he'd not heard before—she had never talked to him before. Without makeup she looked much younger; her cheekbones were pale, her green eyes, rimmed with red, were large and questioning. But the fingernails were bitten, and this broke his heart. He thought: Almost, she could have been my daughter. For years Bob had lived with the shadow of his not-children appearing before him. Earlier in his life it might have been a child on a playground he passed by, yellow-haired (as Bob had once been), playing hopscotch tentatively. Later a teenager—boy or girl, it happened with each—on the sidewalk laughing with a friend. Or, these days, a law student interning in his office might reveal a sudden aspect of expression that would cause Bob to think: This could have been my kid.

He asked if she had family nearby.

Parents in Bensonhurst who managed apartment buildings. Shaking her head, she wasn't close to them. But she had a job in Manhattan as a paralegal. Except how would she work, feeling so— And she made a circular motion by her ear. Her lips were very pale. Work will help, he told her. You'll be surprised.

I won't always feel this way?, she asked.

Oh no. No. (But he knew: The end of a marriage was a crazy time.) You'll be all right, he told her. He told her that many times, as the shivering dog sniffed the ground; she had asked him many times. She said she might lose her job; a woman was coming back from maternity leave and it was a very small office. He gave her the name of Jim's law firm; the place was big, they hired frequently, she was not to worry. Life had a way of working out, he said. But do you really think so?, she asked, and he said he did.

The pinkish-tinted buildings of Hartford passed by, and Bob had to slow the car and concentrate. Traffic was picking up. He passed a truck; a truck passed him. And then as he finally drove into Massachusetts, his thoughts, as though waiting, turned to Pam. Pam, his dearly loved ex-wife, whose intelligence and curiosity were matched only by her conviction that she had neither. Pam, whom he had met walking across the campus of the University of Maine more than thirty years ago. She had come from Massachusetts, the only child of older parents who, by the time Bob first greeted them at graduation, appeared worn out by their chaotic daughter (the mother, though, still living, bedridden, in a nursing home not far from this turnpike, no longer knowing who Pam was, or Bob either, should he choose to visit, which he had in the past). Pam, full-figured when she was young, intense, bewildered, always ready to laugh, always tumbling from one enthusiasm to the next. Who could say what anxiety drove her? He recalled her squatting one night to pee between two parked cars in the West Village, drunk and laughing, after they'd moved to New York. Here's to the women's movement, a fist in the air. Equal pissing rights! Pam, who could swear like a sailor. His dearly loved Pam.

And now, seeing a sign for Sturbridge, Bob's mind went to his grandmother, who used to tell stories of their English ancestors arriving ten generations earlier. Bob, sitting in his child's chair: "Tell me the part about the Indians." Oh, there were scalpings, and a little girl kidnapped, taken off to Canada, and her brother, though it took him years in his raggedy clothes, went and rescued her, brought her back to their coastal town. Back then, his grandmother said, women made soap out of ashes.

They used daisy root for earaches. One day his grandmother told him how thieves would be made to walk through the town. She said if a man stole a fish he had to walk around town holding the fish, calling out, "I stole this fish and I am sorry!" While the town crier followed, beating a drum.

Bob's interest in his ancestors was over with that story. Forced to walk through the town yelling, "I stole this fish and I am sorry!"?

No. The end.

And the beginning of New Hampshire, with its state liquor store right off the turnpike, autumnal clouds low in the sky. New Hampshire, with its archaic legislature of hundreds of people, and still that license plate LIVE FREE OR DIE. The traffic was bad; people were getting off at the traffic circle to make their way to the foliage in the White Mountains. He stopped to get coffee and call his sister. "Where are you?" she said. "I'm losing my mind. I can't believe you're so late, except I can."

"Oy. Susan. I'll be there soon."

The sun was already on its ride down. Back in the car, he left behind Portsmouth, gussied up for years now, the way so many of these coastal towns were; all that urban renewal started in the late seventies when they got their cobblestone streets back, their old houses fixed up, lampposts from the olden days and lots of candle shops. But Bob remembered when Portsmouth was still a tired naval town; and a deep tremor of nostalgia passed through him as he recalled the potholed, unpretentious streets, the large windows of a department store, long since gone, where the displays had seemed to change only from summer to winter, mannequins waving eternally with a handbag hanging from a broken wrist, an eyeless woman standing next to a happy eyeless man, a garden hose at his feet—they did have smiles, those mannequins. All this Bob remembered, for he and Pam had stopped here on their way to Boston in the Greyhound bus, Pam, swaybacked in her wraparound skirt.

A million years ago.

"Stay in the present," Elaine would say, and so now he was on his way to the unlovely Susan. Family is family, and he missed Jimmy. Bob's ancient inner Bobness had returned.

———•———

They sat on a cement bench in the lobby of the Shirley Falls police station. Gerry O'Hare had nodded to Bob as though he had seen him yesterday—though in fact it had been years—and then taken Zach through a door to an interview room. An officer brought coffee in paper cups to Bob and Susan; they thanked him, and held the cups tentatively. "Does Zach have friends?" Bob asked when they were alone. He asked this quietly. It had been more than five years since Bob had been to Shirley Falls, and the sight of his nephew—tall, skinny, blank-faced with fear—had startled him. And so had the sight of his sister. She was thin, her short wavy hair mostly gray now; she was strikingly unfeminine. Her plain-featured face looked so much older than he had expected that he could not believe they were the same age. (Twins!)

"I don't know," Susan answered. "He stocks shelves at Walmart. Sometimes—hardly ever—he drives over to West Annett to see a guy he works with. But no one comes to the house." She added, "I thought they'd let you go in with him."

"I'm not registered to practice here, Susan. We went through this." Bob looked over his shoulder. "When did they build this place?" The old Shirley Falls Police Department had been housed in City Hall, which was a spread-out big building at the bottom of the park, and Bob remembered it as having an openness; you walked in and there were cops behind a desk. This was not like that. This had a small lobby facing two darkened windows, and they'd had to press a doorbell-type thing in order to get someone to even step up to one of them. Bob felt guilty just being here.

"Five years ago maybe," Susan said vaguely. "I don't know."

"Why did they need a new police station? The state's losing population, getting poorer every day, and all it does is build new schools and municipal buildings."

"Bob. I don't care. Frankly. About your observations on Maine. Besides, this city's population is growing—" Susan's voice dropped to a whisper. "Because of *them*."

Bob drank his coffee. It was bad coffee, but Bob was not particular about his coffee—or his wine—the way so many people were these days. "Say you thought it was a dumb joke and you'll have a lawyer on Monday. They might try to get you to say more than that, but don't." Bob had told this to Zachary. Zachary, so much taller than the last time Bob had seen him, so skinny, so *scared*-looking, had just stared at him.

"Any idea why he did this?" Bob tried to ask the question gently.

"None." After a moment Susan said, "I thought maybe you could ask him."

This alarmed Bob. He didn't know what to do about kids. Some of his friends had kids he loved, and Jim's kids he loved very much, but not having kids made you different. He didn't see how he could explain that to Susan. He asked, "Is Zach in touch with his father?"

"They email. Sometimes Zach seems . . . well, not happy, but less *un*happy, and I think it's because of whatever Steve's written him, but Zach won't talk to me about it. Steve and I haven't spoken since he walked out." Susan's cheeks grew pink. "Other times Zach gets really down, and I think that's related to Steve too, but I don't *know*, Bob, okay?" She squeezed her nose, sniffed hard.

"Hey, don't panic." Bob looked around for a paper napkin or a Kleenex, but there was nothing. "You know what Jimmy would say, don't you? He'd say there's no crying in baseball."

Susan said, "What in hell, Bobby?"

"That movie they made about women's baseball. It's a great line."

Susan leaned forward to place her cup of coffee on the floor beneath the bench. "If you're playing baseball. My son's in there getting arrested."

A metal door opened, slammed shut. A policeman, short, and with a sprinkle of dark moles on his young face, walked into the lobby. "All set, folks. They're transporting him over to the jail. You can follow him there.

They'll book him and call the bail commissioner, and you can take him back home."

"Thank you." The twins said this in unison.

The late afternoon light was fading and the town seemed twilight-gray and somber. Following the cruiser they could just make out Zach's head in the backseat. They drove toward the bridge that would take them across to the county jail. "Where is everyone?" Bob asked. "Saturday afternoon and the town is dead."

"It's been dead for years." Susan leaned forward as she drove.

Glancing down a side street Bob saw a dark-skinned man walking slowly, his hands in the pockets of his open coat, which seemed too big for him. Under the coat he wore a long white robe that went to his feet. On his head was a squarish cloth hat. "Hey," Bob said.

"What?" Susan looked at him sharply.

"Is that one of them?"

"One of them? You're like a retarded person, Bob. Living in New York all these years, and you haven't seen a *Negro*?"

"Susan, relax."

"Relax. Hadn't thought of that. Thanks." Susan pulled into a spot near the police car, which had driven into a large parking area behind the jail. They had a brief glimpse of Zach in handcuffs. He seemed to fall against the cruiser once he stepped out, then the officer guided him toward the building.

"Right behind you, buddy," Bob called out, opening the car door. "Got you covered!"

"Bob, stop," said Susan.

"Got you covered," he called again.

Again they sat in a small lobby. Only once did a man in dark blue clothes step out, to tell them that Zach was being booked, fingerprinted, and that they had put in a call to the bail commissioner. It might take awhile for him to show up, the man said. How long? He couldn't say. And so brother and sister sat. There was an ATM, and a vending machine. And, again, the darkened windows.

"Are we being watched?" Susan whispered.

"Probably."

They sat in their coats, looking straight ahead. Finally Bob asked quietly, "What's Zach do other than stock shelves?"

"You mean, does he drive around and rob people? Is he addicted to child porn? No, Bob. He's just—Zach."

Bob shifted in his coat. "You think he has any connection to a skinhead group? White supremacy group, anything like that?"

Susan looked at him with surprise, and then squinted her eyes. "No." Adding in a softer tone, "I don't think he has a real connection with anybody. But he isn't like that, Bob."

"Just checking. It's going to be okay. He might have to do community service. Take a diversity class."

"Do you think he's still in handcuffs? That was terrible."

"I know it," Bob said, and he thought about how the sight of his Preppy Boy neighbor being led across the street felt as if it had happened years ago. Even his morning talk with Adriana seemed not believable, it was so far away. "Zach's not in cuffs now. That's just procedure. To escort him here."

Susan said tiredly, "Some of the local clergy want to have a rally."

"A rally? About this?" Bob rubbed his hands across his thighs. "Oy," he said.

"Could you not say 'Oy'?" Susan asked angrily. "Why do you *say* that?"

"Because for twenty years I've worked for Legal Aid, Susan, and lots of Jewish people work for Legal Aid, and they say 'Oy' and now I say 'Oy.'"

"Well, it sounds affected. You're not Jewish, Bob. You're as white as they come."

"I know that," Bob agreed.

They sat in silence. Bob finally said, "When is this rally?"

"I have no idea."

Bob dropped his head, closed his eyes.

After a few minutes, Susan asked, "Are you praying, or are you dead?"

Bob opened his eyes. "Remember how we took Zach and Jim's kids to Sturbridge Village when they were little? The smugness of those toady women who guide you around dressed up with those dumb hats that cover their heads? I'm a self-loathing Puritan."

"You're a self-loathing weirdo," Susan answered. She was agitated, craning her neck to peer through the darkened window of the entrance. "What's taking so long?"

And it was long. They sat there for almost three hours. Bob stepped outside once to have a cigarette. The sky had grown dark. By the time the bail commissioner showed up, Bob's weariness seemed like a large wet coat he was wearing. Susan paid the two hundred dollars in twenties, and Zach came through the door, his face as white as paper.

As they got ready to leave, a uniformed man said, "A photographer's out there."

"How can that be?" Susan asked, alarm springing through her voice.

"Don't freak. Come on, kiddo." Bob steered Zach toward the door. "Your Uncle Jim loves photographers. He'll be jealous if you take over as family media hog."

And Zach, perhaps because he found it funny, perhaps because the tension of the day was coming to an end—in any case, the boy smiled at Bob as he stepped through the door. A sudden flash of light met them in the chilly air.

3

That first gentle assault of tropical breeze—it had touched Helen as soon as the airplane door opened. Waiting for the car to be packed, Helen felt bathed by the air. They drove by houses with flowers tumbling from their windows, golf courses green and combed, and in front of their hotel was a fountain, its gentle water rising to the sky. In their room a bowl of lemons sat on the table. "Jimmy," Helen said, "I feel like a bride."

"That's nice." But he was distracted.

She crossed her arms, her hands touching her opposite shoulders (their private sign language of many years), and then her husband stepped forward.

During the night she had bad dreams. They were vivid, terrifying, and she struggled to wakefulness as the sun crept through the opening of the long curtains. Jim was leaving to play golf. "Go back to sleep," he said, kissing her. When she woke again happiness had returned, bright as the sun that now sliced through the drapes. She lay flattened by happiness, running a leg across the cool sheet, thinking of her children, all three in college now. She'd write an email: Dearest Angels, Dad's playing golf and your old mother is about to get some sun on her blue-veined ankles. Dorothy's glum, as I feared she would be—Dad says the older girl, Jessie (Emily, you never liked her, remember?), is really giving them trouble. But no one mentioned it last night at dinner, and so I was polite and didn't brag about *my* darlings. Instead we talked about your cousin Zach—more on *that* later!—miss you, and you, and you—

Dorothy was reading by the pool, her long legs stretched before her on a chaise. "Morning," she said, and did not look up.

Helen moved a chair to get the best of the sun. "Did you sleep well, Dorothy?" She sat down and took lotion and a book from her straw bag. "I had nightmares."

Moments passed before Dorothy looked up from her magazine. "Well, that's a shame."

Helen rubbed lotion on her legs, arranged her book. "Just so you know, don't feel bad about dropping out of the book club."

"I don't." Dorothy put her magazine down and gazed over the brilliant blue of the pool. She said meditatively, "A lot of women in New York are not stupid until they get together and then they are stupid. I really hate that." She glanced at Helen. "Sorry."

"Don't be sorry," said Helen. "You should say whatever you want."

Dorothy chewed on her lip, staring back toward the expanse of blue water. "That's nice of you, Helen," she finally said, "but in my experience people don't really want someone to say whatever they want."

Helen waited.

"Therapists don't," Dorothy said, still looking straight ahead. "I told the family therapist I pitied Jessie's boyfriend, and I do—she's completely controlling—and the therapist looked at me like I was the worst mother in the world. I thought, Jesus, if you can't speak the truth in a shrink's office, where can you? In New York, raising children is a horrendously competitive sport. Really fierce and bloody." Dorothy took a long drink from her plastic cup of water and said, "What do they have you reading this month?"

Helen brushed her hand over the book. "It's about a woman who used to clean houses, and now she's written a book about everything she found when she snooped." In the heat, Helen flushed. The writer had found handcuffs, whips, nipple clamps—and things Helen hadn't known existed.

"Don't read such a silly thing," Dorothy said. "That's what I mean— women telling women to read stupid books when there's a whole world out there. Here, read this article. It's related to your sister-in-law's crisis that Jim was talking about last night." She stretched out her long arm and handed Helen a section of newspaper from where it lay on the plastic table beside her, adding, "Though, as you know with Jim, he thinks any crisis is all his."

Helen rummaged through her straw bag. "Well, it's like this." She glanced up from her bag and held up a finger. "Jim left Maine." She held up two fingers. "Bob left Maine." Three fingers. "Susan's husband left her *and* Maine." Helen returned to her bag and found her lip balm. "So Jim feels responsible. Jim has a keen sense of responsibility." Helen touched her lips with lip balm.

"Or guilt."

Helen thought about it. "No," she said. "Responsibility."

Dorothy turned the page of her magazine and did not answer. So Helen—who would have liked to talk, she felt the bubbles of chattiness rising inside her—felt compelled to pick up the newspaper and read the article assigned to her. The sun grew hotter, and perspiration formed in a line above her upper lip no matter how many times Helen wiped her finger over it. "Goodness, Dorothy," she finally said, because the article was really disturbing. And yet she felt that if she put it down, Dorothy would see her as a (stupid) superficial woman who had no concern for the world beyond her own. She read on.

The article was about refugee camps in Kenya. Who was in those camps? Somalis. And who knew? Not Helen. Well, now she knew. Now she knew that some of those people living in Shirley Falls, Maine, had first lived for years in dreadful conditions, hardly believable. Helen, squinting, read how the women, in order to gather firewood, had to wander away from the camp, where bandits might rape them; some of these women had been raped several times. Many of their children died of starvation right in their arms. The children who lived did not go to school. There were no schools. The men sat around chewing leaves—*khat*—which kept them high, and their wives, of which they could have up to four, had to try to keep the family alive with the little bit of rice and drops of cooking oil they received from the authorities every six weeks. There were photographs, of course. Skinny tall African women balancing wood and huge plastic water jugs on their heads, ripped tarps and mud huts, a sick child with flies near his face. "This is terrible," she said. Dorothy, nodding, kept reading her magazine.

And it was terrible, and Helen knew she was supposed to feel terrible. But she did not understand why these people, who had walked for days to get out of their violent country, should make it to Kenya and end up in such hellacious distress. Why wasn't someone taking care of this? Helen did wonder that. But mostly she didn't want to read it, and that made her feel she was a bad person, and here she was on a lovely (expensive) vacation and she did not want to feel like a bad person.

Fatuma walks for three hours to get firewood. She always goes with other women, but they know they are not safe. Safe is not a word spoken here.

And then for Helen, with the heat banging down on her, sunlight shrieking across the bright blue pool, there was a sudden and unexpected feeling of vast indifference. This loss—for it was a loss not to care about the warmth, the bougainvillea, to have this morning dissolve into merely waiting for Jim to return from golf—the loss was enough to feel, in another moment, something close to anguish, and then it rocked back into place: indifference. But it had done damage; Helen shifted on her chair, crossed her ankles—for in that moment of almost anguish her own children seemed lost to her; some brief spasm of her mind caused her to envision herself in a nursing home, her grown children visiting with crisp solicitude while she said, "It all goes so fast"—meaning life, of course—and seeing the look of sympathy on their faces as they waited for enough time to pass so they could leave, their own urgent lives pulling them. They won't want to be with me, Helen thought, as this very-real-feeling-moment knocked around in her head. Never had she thought this before.

She watched the fronds of a palm tree swirl gently.

Just a silly wives' tale, women in her book group had told Helen when she fretted about her son—her last child—heading off to college in Arizona. Empty nest is freedom, they told her. Empty nest invigorates women. It's the men who start to crack up. Men in their fifties have a hard time.

Helen closed her eyes against the sun and saw her children splashing in the play pool in their yard in West Hartford, the moist skin of their little limbs pure as they crawled in and out; saw them as teenagers moving down the sidewalk in Park Slope with their friends; felt them curled up next to her on the couch on the nights when the family gathered to watch their favorite TV shows.

She opened her eyes. "Dorothy."

Dorothy turned her face toward Helen, the black sunglasses aimed at her.

"I miss my kids," Helen said.

Dorothy turned back to her magazine and said, "You're not singing to the choir, I'm afraid."

4

The dog was waiting at the door, wagging her tail anxiously, a German shepherd with white on her chin. "Hey, pooch." Bob rubbed the dog's head, and stepped into the house. The house was very cold. Zach, who had said nothing on the ride home from jail, went immediately up the stairs. "Zach," called Bob, "Come talk to your uncle."

"Leave him alone," Susan called back, following her son. A few minutes later she came down the stairs wearing a sweater with reindeer across the front. "He's not eating. They put him in a cell, and he's half dead with fear."

Bob said, "Let me talk to him." He added, more quietly, "I thought you wanted me to talk to him."

"Later. Just leave him. He doesn't like to talk. He's been through a lot." Susan opened the kitchen door and the dog came in, looking guilty. Susan poured dry dog food into a tin pan, then went into the living room and sat on the couch. Bob followed her. Susan pulled out a bag of knitting.

So there they were.

Bob had no idea what to do. Jim would know what to do. Jim had children, Bob did not. Jim took charge, Bob did not. He sat with his coat on and looked around. Dog hair was scattered along the mopboards.

"You have anything to drink, Susan?"

"Moxie."

"That's it?"

"That's it."

So they were at war, as they had always been. He was captive in his coat, freezing cold, and with nothing to drink. She knew it, and kept him that way. Susan never drank, as their mother had not. Susan probably thought that Bob was an alcoholic, and Bob thought he was almost, but not quite, an alcoholic, and he thought there was a big difference between the two.

She asked if he wanted food. She said she thought she had a frozen pizza. Or a can of baked beans. Hot dogs.

"No." He was not going to eat her frozen pizza, or her baked beans.

He wanted to tell her that not even remotely was this how people lived, that this is why he had not come here for the last five years, because he couldn't stand it. He wanted to tell her that people came back to their house after a tense day, had a drink, made warm food. They turned up the thermostat, spoke to each other, called friends. Jim's kids were always running up and down the stairs: Mom, have you seen my green sweater; Tell Emily to give me the hair dryer; Dad, you said I could stay out till eleven; even Larry, the quietest one, laughing, Uncle Bob, remember that tepee joke you told me when I was real young? (At Sturbridge Village, wriggling themselves into the stocks and pillories: Take a picture, take a picture! Zachary, so skinny that both legs fit into one ankle hold, quiet as a mouse.)

"Will he go to jail, Bobby?" Susan stopped knitting and looked at him with a face that seemed suddenly young.

"Ah, Susie." Bob took his hands out of his pockets, leaned forward. "I doubt it. It's a misdemeanor."

"He was so *scared* in that cell. I've never seen him so scared. I think he would die if he had to go to jail."

"Jim says Charlie Tibbetts is great. It's going to be all right, Susie."

The dog came into the room, looking guilty again, as if eating her dog food was something she should be beaten for. She lay down and put her head on Susan's foot. Bob could not remember seeing such a sad dog. He thought of the tiny yapping dog that lived below him in New York. He tried to think of his apartment, his friends, his work in New York—none of it seemed real. He watched while his sister started knitting again, then said, "How's your job?" Susan had been an optometrist for years, and he realized he had no idea what it was like for her.

Susan pulled slowly on the yarn. "We baby boomers get older, there's always business. I've had a few Somalians come in," she added. "Not many, but a few."

After a moment, Bob asked, "What are they like?"

She gave him a glance as though it might be a trick question. "A little secretive, in my opinion. They don't make appointments. Wary. They don't know what a keratometer is. One woman acted like I was putting a spell on her."

"I don't know what a keratometer is."

"Nobody does, Bob. But they know I'm not putting a spell on them." Susan's knitting needles began to move quickly. "They might try and negotiate the price, which blew me away the first time it happened. Then I heard that's what they do, barter. No credit cards. They don't believe in credit. Excuse me. They don't believe in *interest*. So they pay cash. I don't know where they get it." Susan shook her head at Bob. "Look, they kept coming and coming and there was hardly enough money, well, there wasn't enough money, and so the city had to get more from the Feds, and really, Shirley Falls, when you consider how unprepared it was, has been great to them. It gives every liberal in town a great cause, which they need, of course—as you know yourself, being a liberal, they always need a cause." She stopped her knitting. Her face, as she looked up, had a faint overlay of childlike bewilderment and so once again seemed young. "Can I say something?" she asked.

He raised his eyebrows.

"What I want to say, what I notice, and it puzzles me, are the people in town who are so *happy* to let everyone know they're helping the So-malians. Like the Prescotts. They used to own a shoe shop up in South Market, maybe it's gone out of business now, I don't know. But Carolyn Prescott and her daughter-in-law are always taking these Somalian women shopping and buying them refrigerators and washing machines or a whole set of pots and pans. And I think, is there something wrong with me that I don't want to buy a Somalian woman a refrigerator? Not that I have the money, but if I did." Susan gazed off into space, then started knitting again. "But I don't feel like dragging these women around buying them things and then telling everyone I did it. It makes me cyni-cal, that's all." Susan crossed her ankles. She continued, "I have this friend, Charlene Bergeron, who got breast cancer, and people offered to help with her kids, take her to treatments. But then her husband di-vorced her a few years later. And zip. Zero. Nothing. No one stepped forward to help her at all. And it hurts, Bob. That's how it was for me, back when Steve left. I was scared to death. I didn't know if I'd be able to keep this place. Nobody offered to buy me a refrigerator. Nobody of-fered to buy me a *meal*. And I was dying, frankly. I was lonelier than I bet these Somalians are. They have family crawling all over them."

Bob said, "Oh, Susie. I'm sorry."

"People are funny, that's all." Susan rubbed her nose with the back of her hand. "Some say it's no different from when the city was filled with French Canadian millworkers speaking French. But it *is* different, be-cause what nobody talks about is that they don't want to be here. They're waiting to go home. They don't want to become part of our country. They're just kind of sitting here, but meanwhile they think our way of life is trashy and glitzy and crummy. It hurts my feelings, honestly. And they just completely stick to themselves."

"Well, Susie. For years the French Canadians stuck to themselves too."

"It's different, Bob." She gave a yank on the yarn. "And they're not called French Canadians anymore. Franco-Americans, please. The So-malians don't like being compared to them. They claim they're entirely different. They're *incomparable*."

"They're Muslim."

"I hadn't noticed," she said.

When he stepped back inside from having a cigarette, Susan was taking hot dogs from the freezer. "They believe in clitoridectomies." She ran water into a pot.

"Oy, Susan."

"Oy, yourself. God's teeth. Do you want one of these?"

He sat in his coat at the kitchen table. "It's illegal here," he said. "It has been for years. And they're Somalis, not Somalians."

Susan turned and held the fork by her chest. "See, Bob, this is why you liberals are morons. Excuse me. But you are. They have little girls here bleeding like crazy, brought in to the hospital because they're bleeding so hard at school. Or the family saves up the money and has them sent back to Africa to have it done there."

"Don't you think we should ask Zach if he's hungry?" Bob rubbed the back of his neck.

"I'm going to take these up to his room."

"People don't say 'Negro' anymore, either, Susan, you should know. Or 'retarded.' Those are things you really should know."

"Oh, for crying out loud, Bob. I was making fun of you. Craning your neck the way you did." Susan peered into the pot on the stove, and after a moment she said, "I miss Jim. No offense."

"I'd prefer it myself, if he were here."

She turned, her face pink from the steam of the boiling water. "One time, right after the Packer trial, I was at the mall and I heard this couple talking about Jim, saying he went from being a prosecutor to a defense attorney just so he could take on a big-profile case and make money. It killed me."

"Oh, they're idiots, Susie." Bob waved a hand. "Lawyers switch all the time. And he was already doing defense work at that Hartford firm. It's all defense work. Defend the people or defend the accused. That case fell into his lap and he did a great job with it. Whether or not people think Wally was guilty."

Susan said earnestly, "But I think most people who remember Jim still love him. They get a kick out of it when he shows up on TV. He never sounds like a Mr. Know-It-All, that's what people say. And it's true."

"It is true. He hates showing up on TV, by the way. He does it because the firm tells him to. During the Packer trial I think he loved the publicity, but I don't know that's true anymore. Helen likes it. She always lets everyone know when he's going to be on TV."

"Well, Helen. Sure."

It united them, their love for Jim. Bob took advantage of this to stand up and say he was going out to get some different food. "That spaghetti place still open?" he asked.

"It is, yeah."

The streets were dark. He was always surprised how dark the night was outside the city. He drove to a small grocery store and bought two bottles of wine, which you could do in a grocery store in Maine. He bought the ones with screw tops. As he drove, not recognizing things the way he'd thought he would, he was careful not to go in the direction of his childhood home. Since his mother's death (years ago, he had lost count of the years) he had not once gone past the house. He pulled up at a stop sign, turned right, and saw the old cemetery. On his left were wooden apartment buildings four stories high. He was nearing the center of town. He drove behind what had once been the main department store, Peck's, before the mall was built across the river. When Bob was small, his clothes for school were bought in the boys' department there. The memory was one of shame and excruciating self-consciousness: the salesman cuffing the bottom of his pants, once putting a tape measure right up the leg and to his crotch; red turtlenecks bought, also navy blue, his mother nodding. The building was empty now, its windows boarded up. He drove past where the bus station had been, where there had been coffee shops and magazine stores and bakeries. And suddenly a black man appeared, walking beneath a streetlamp. He was tall and graceful, his shirt loose-fitting, although perhaps there was a vest over it, Bob couldn't tell. Wrapped around his shoulders was a scarf of black and white with tassels. "Hey, cool," Bob said softly. "Another one." And yet, Bob, who had lived for years in New York, Bob, who'd had a brief career there defending criminals of various colors and religions (until the stress of the courtroom forced him into appellate work), Bob, who believed in the magnificence of the Constitution and the rights of the people, all people, to life, liberty, and the pursuit of happiness, Bob Burgess, after the tall man with the tasseled scarf turned down a side street of Shirley Falls—Bob thought, *ever so fleetingly* but he thought it: Just as long as there aren't too many of them.

He drove further and there was the familiar Antonio's, the spaghetti cafeteria, tucked back behind the gas station. Bob stopped the car in the parking lot. On the glass door of Antonio's was a sign in orange letters. He looked at the clock on the dashboard. Nine o'clock on a Saturday night and Antonio's was closed. He unscrewed the top off a bottle of wine. How could he describe what he felt? The unfurling of an ache so poignant it was almost erotic, this longing, the inner silent gasp as though in the face of something unutterably beautiful, the desire to put his head down on the big loose lap of this town, Shirley Falls.

He drove to a small grocery store, bought a package of frozen clam strips, and took them back to Susan's.

———

Abdikarim Ahmed stepped off the sidewalk and walked in the street so as not to be close to doorways where a person might linger in the darkness. He approached the home of his cousin and saw how the lightbulb over the door was—again—not lit. "Uncle," voices called out to him, and he entered the apartment and continued down the hall to his room, where the walls were covered with Persian rugs; Haweeya had hung them when he moved in months ago. The colors of the wall rugs seemed to move as Abdikarim pressed his fingers hard against his forehead. Bad enough that the man arrested today was unknown to the village. (It was assumed he would be one of the men who lived nearby, one of those who drank beer in the morning on the front steps, thick arms tattooed, driving loud trucks with bumper stickers reading WHITE IS MIGHT, THE

REST GO HOME!) Yes, bad enough that this Zachary Olson had a job, lived in a good house with his mother, who also had a job. But what continued to frighten Abdikarim, what made his stomach sick and his head squeeze with pain, was what he had seen the night it happened: The two police-men, who arrived soon after the imam called, had stood in the mosque in their dark uniforms and belts of guns, had stood, glanced down at the pig's head, and laughed. Then said, "Okay, folks." Filled out forms, asked questions. Became serious. Took pictures. Not everyone had seen them laugh. But Abdikarim, standing close to them, moist beneath his prayer robe, had seen this. Tonight the elders asked him to describe for Rabbi Goldman what he had seen, and so he had acted it out: the grins, the talking into the hand radios, the exchange of glances between the two policemen, their quiet laughter. Rabbi Goldman shook his head in sorrow.

Haweeya was standing in his doorway rubbing her nose. "Are you hungry?" she asked, and Abdikarim said that he had eaten at the home of Ifo Noor. "Is there more trouble?" she asked softly. Her children ran down the hall to her, and she spread her long fingers over her son's head.

"No, everything is the same."

She nodded, her earrings swinging, and ushered her children back to the living room. Haweeya had kept them inside most of the day, having them memorize again their lineage, their great-grandfather, great-great-grandfather, and so on, far, far back; Americans seemed to have little concern for their past family. Somalis could recite back many genera-tions, and Haweeya did not want her children to lose that. Still, keeping them inside all day had been hard. No one liked to go so long without seeing the sky. But when Omad arrived home—he was a translator at the hospital—he said they would go to the park. Omad and Haweeya had been in-country longer than others, they were not so quick to be afraid. They had survived the very bad parts of Atlanta, where people took drugs and robbed others right in their own buildings; Shirley Falls was safe and beautiful compared to that. So this afternoon, tired from the fast, and from the clear fall air that—Haweeya did not understand why—made her nose drip and eyes itch, she'd watched the children run after falling leaves. The sky was almost blue.

After she cleaned the kitchen and washed the floor, Haweeya returned to Abdikarim. She had great affection for this man, who had come to Shirley Falls a year ago only to find that his wife Asha—sent earlier, with the children—no longer wanted him. She had taken the children and moved to Minneapolis. This was a source of shame. Haweeya understood that; everyone did. It was America that Abdikarim blamed for teaching Asha such foolhardy independence, but Haweeya thought that Asha, years younger than her husband, was born to do what Asha wanted to do; some people were like that. An added sadness: Asha was the mother to Abdikarim's one living son. Of other children born to other wives, only daughters remained. He had losses, as many people had.

He was seated on his bed now, his fists pressed into the mattress. Haweeya leaned against the doorjamb. "Margaret Estaver telephoned this evening. She told me not to be worried."

"I know, I know." Abdikarim raised a hand in a gesture of futility. "According to her he's Wiil Waal: 'Crazy Boy.'"

"Ayanna says she's keeping her children home from school on Monday," Haweeya whispered, and then sneezed. "Omad told her they're as safe in school as anywhere, and she said, 'Safe where they're kicked and punched when the teacher looks away?'"

Abdikarim nodded. At Ifo Noor's tonight there had been talk of the school and the teachers promising to be more vigilant now that the pig's head had been rolled into the mosque. "Everyone promises," Abdikarim said, as he stood. "Sleep with peace," he added. "And get that lightbulb fixed."

"Tomorrow I'll buy a new one. I'm driving to Walmart." She smiled at him playfully. "Hoping Wiil Waal has not returned to work there." Her earrings moved as she walked away.

Abdikarim rubbed his forehead. At Ifo Noor's tonight, Rabbi Goldman sat with the elders and asked them to practice the true peacefulness of Islam. This was insulting. Of course they would do that. Rabbi Goldman said that many townspeople supported their right to be here, and after Ramadan the town would show this with a demonstration. The elders did not want a demonstration. To gather people in a crowd was not good. But Rabbi Goldman of the wide heart said it would be healthy for the town. Healthy for the town! Each word was like a hit with a stick saying this was not their village, their town, their country.

Abdikarim, standing by his bed, squeezed his eyes in anger, because where were the Rabbi Goldmans of America when Abdikarim's eldest daughter had first stepped off a plane in Nashville with her four children and no one to meet them, and the moving stairs called an *escalator* were so frightening they could only stare at them and get pushed aside by others who pointed and laughed? Where were the Rabbi Goldmans of America when a neighbor brought Aamuun a vacuum cleaner and Aamuun did not know what it was and never used it and the neighbor told people in town the Somalis were ungrateful? Where were the Rabbi Goldmans and the Minister Estavers when little Kalila thought the ketchup dispenser at Burger King was where she could wash her hands? And when Kalila's mother saw the mess her daughter had made she slapped her, and a woman came up to them and said, In America we don't beat our children. Where was the rabbi then? The rabbi could not know what it was like.

And of course the rabbi could not know, back in his own safe house now with his worried wife, that as Abdikarim sat down heavily on the bed, it was not fear that rose in him with most prominence but the un-curling of remembered shame from this evening, when he had put a piece of *mufa* in his mouth and experienced the feral, furtive pleasure of its taste. In the camps he had been hungry constantly, it was like a wife, the companionship of this ceaseless exhausting need. And now that he was here it was exquisitely painful to notice the animal craving he still felt for food; it debased him. The need to eat, excrete, sleep—these were the needs of nature. The luxury of their naturalness had long ago been taken away.

Fingering the tapestry of his bedcover, he murmured, "Astaghfirullah," *I seek forgiveness,* because the violence in his homeland felt to him to be the fault of his people for not living the true life of Islam. As he closed his eyes, he recited his final Alhamdulilah of the day. *Thank you, Allah.* All good came from Allah. The bad from humans who allowed the sprig of evil in their hearts to blossom. But why this was so, the evil unchecked like malignancy—this was the question Abdikarim always walked into. And always the answer: He did not know.

———◆———

That first night, Bob slept on the couch with all his clothes on, even his coat, it was that cold. It was not until the light began to come through the window blinds that he finally dozed, and he woke to hear Susan yelling, "Yes, you're going to work. You're the one who did this stupid, stupid thing! You damn well go earn that two hundred dollars I spent so you could be free. *Go.*" Bob heard Zach murmur briefly, heard the back door close, and in a few minutes a car drove away.

Susan appeared, hurled a newspaper across the room at him. It landed on the floor by the couch. "Nice job," she said.

Bob looked down. On the front page was a large photo of Zach leaving the jail, grinning. The headline read NO JOKE.

"Oy," Bob said, struggling to sit up.

"I'm going to work." Susan called this to him from the kitchen. He heard cupboard doors slam. And then the back door slammed and he heard her drive off.

He sat with just his eyes moving about the room. The drawn blinds were the color of hard-boiled eggs. The wallpaper was a similar color, with a series of swooping long-beaked birds that were thin and blue. There was a wooden hutch that had Reader's Digest Condensed Books along its top shelf. There was a wing chair in the corner with its arms worn so the upholstery had rips. Nothing in the room seemed designed for comfort, and he felt comfortless.

A motion on the stairway caused a rush of fear to pass through him. He saw the pink terry-cloth slippers, then the skinny old woman aiming her huge glasses at him. She said, "Why are you sitting there in your coat?"

"I'm freezing," Bob said.

Mrs. Drinkwater walked down the rest of the stairs and stood holding the banister. She looked around the room. "It's always freezing in this house."

He hesitated, then said, "If you're too cold, you should tell Susan."

The old lady moved to sit down in the wing chair. She pushed at her big glasses with a bony knuckle. "I wouldn't want to complain. Susan doesn't have much money, you know. She hasn't had a raise at that eye shop for years. And the price of oil." The old lady twirled a hand above her head. "Mercy."

Bob picked the newspaper off the floor and put it on the couch next to him. The picture of Zach stared up at him, grinning, and he turned the paper over.

"It's on the news," Mrs. Drinkwater said.

Bob nodded. "They're both at work," he told her.

"Oh, I know, dear. I came down to get the paper. She leaves it for me on Sundays."

Bob leaned forward and handed her the paper, and the old lady continued to sit in the chair with the paper on her lap. He said, "Ah, so listen, does Susan yell at him a lot?"

Mrs. Drinkwater looked around the room, and Bob thought she wasn't going to answer. "Used to. When I first moved in." She crossed her legs and rocked one ankle up and down. Her slippers were huge. "Of course her husband had just run off back then." Mrs. Drinkwater shook her head slowly. "Far as I could tell, the boy never did anything wrong. He's a lonely boy, isn't he."

"Always has been, I think. Zach's always seemed, well, fragile— emotionally. Or just immature. Or something."

"You think your children will be like the ones in the Sears catalog." Mrs. Drinkwater rocked her foot harder. "But then they aren't. Though I admit, Zachary seems more alone than most. Anyways, he cries."

"He cries?"

"I hear him in his room sometimes. Even before this pig's head stuff. I feel like a tattletale, but you're his uncle. I try to mind my own business."

"Does Susan hear him?"

"I don't know, dear."

The dog came to him, sticking her long nose into his lap. He stroked the rough hair of her head, then tapped the floor so she would lie down. "Does he have *any* friends?"

"Never seen any come to the house."

"Susan says he put the pig's head there by himself."

"Maybe he did." Mrs. Drinkwater pushed at her huge glasses. "But there are plenty others who'd have liked to. Those people, the Somalians, they're not welcome here by everyone. I don't mind them myself. But they wear all that stuff." Mrs. Drinkwater spread a hand in front of her face. "You just see their eyes peeking out." She looked around the room. "I wonder if it's true, what they say—they keep live chickens in their cupboards. Mercy, that seems strange."

Bob stood up, felt for his cell phone in his coat pocket. "I'm going out to have a cigarette. If you'll excuse me."

"Of course, dear."

Standing under a Norway maple whose yellow leaves arched over him, Bob lit a cigarette, squinted at his phone.

5

Jim, sunburned and glistening, stood in their room demonstrating to Helen why his golf game had been a success. "It's all in the wrist, see." He bent his knees slightly, crooked his elbows, swung an invisible golf club. "See that, Hellie? See what I just did with my wrist?"

She said that she did.

"It was great. Even the dickwad doctor with us had to agree. He was from Texas. Short disgusting little prick. Didn't even know what Texas Tea was. So I told him." Jim pointed his finger toward Helen. "I said it's what you guys use to kill people now that you've stopped frying them faster than potato chips. Sodium thiopental, pancuronium bromide, potassium chloride. He didn't say a thing. Dickwad. Just got a little smile on his face." Jim wiped a hand across his brow, then settled into position for another make-believe swing. Behind him the glass door to the patio was partly open and Helen walked past her husband and the bowl of lemons on the table to close it. "See that? Nice! I told the putz," Jim continued, wiping his face with his golf shirt, "if you guys believe in the death penalty, a prima facie indicator that civilized society's become cor-

rupted by inhumanity, why don't you at least *train* your Neanderthal
executioners to administer Texas Tea properly? Instead of jabbing mus-
cles and making that last poor fuck they executed just lie there— You
know what kind of doctor he was? A dermatologist. Face-lifts. Butt-tucks.
I'm going to get in the shower."

"Jim, Bob called."

Jim stopped walking toward the bathroom, turned around.

"Zach's back at work. He got two hundred dollars bail. And Susan
was at work too. Zach doesn't get arraigned for a few weeks and Bob said
Charlie Tibbetts could do that with a ticket. I think. I didn't understand
that part, I'm sorry." Helen started to open the bureau drawer to show
Jim the little gifts she had bought to send the children.

"It's how they do it up there," Jim said. "An arraignment calendar.
Does Zach have to make an appearance?"

"I don't know. I don't think so."

"How did Bob sound?"

"Like Bob."

"What does that mean, 'Like Bob'?"

At the tone of his voice, Helen closed the bureau drawer and turned
to face him. "What do you mean what does that mean? You asked how
he sounded. Like Bob. He sounded like Bob."

"Sweetheart, you're making me a little crazy here. I'm trying to figure
out what's going on in that hellhole, and to say he sounded like Bob isn't
helpful. What do you *mean* when you say he sounded like Bob? Did he
sound upbeat? Did he sound serious?"

"Please don't cross-examine me. You're the one who was off enjoying
yourself on the golf course. I was stuck with grumpy old Dorothy, who
forced me to read about refugee camps in Kenya and that is *not* fun, like
playing golf. And then *my* cell phone rings—you know, Beethoven's
Fifth that the kids fixed on my phone for Bob—so I knew it was Bob
calling, and I had to sit there and talk to him like I was your secretary
because he knew enough not to bother you."

Jim sat down on the bed and stared at the rug. Helen recognized this
look. They had been married for many years. Jim very seldom got angry

with Helen and she appreciated that, because she always took it as a sign of respect. But when he looked as though he was trying to be reasonable in the face of her silly behavior, it was hard for her to take.

She tried being funny now. "Okay, strike that. Not responsive." Her voice did not sound humorous. "Irrelevant," she added.

Jim kept looking at the rug. Finally he said, "Did he, or did he not, ask me to call him back?"

"He did not."

Jim turned his face to her. "That's all I needed to know." He stood up and walked toward the bathroom. "I'm going to shower, and I'm sorry you had to be with grumpy Dorothy. I've never liked Dorothy."

Helen said, "Are you kidding? Then why are we here with them?"

"She's married to the managing partner, Helen." The bathroom door closed and in a minute there was the sound of the shower running.

At dinner they sat outside and watched the sun set on the water. Helen wore her white linen blouse and her black Capris and ballet flats. Alan smiled and said, "You girls look very pretty tonight. What do you have planned for tomorrow?" He kept rubbing Dorothy's arm from where he sat next to her. His hand was freckled. His mostly bald head was freckled too.

Helen said, "Tomorrow, while you fellows are playing golf, Dorothy and I thought we'd try breakfast at the Lemon Drop."

"Nice." Alan nodded.

Helen touched her earring and thought: Being a woman sucks. Then she thought: No it doesn't. She sipped her whiskey sour. "Want to try my whiskey sour?" she asked Jim.

Jim shook his head. He was glancing down at the table and seemed far away.

"On the wagon, are we, Jim?" Dorothy asked.

"Jim hardly ever drinks, I thought you knew that," Helen said.

"Afraid of losing control?" Dorothy asked, and a needle of anger entered Helen. But Dorothy said, "Look at that," and pointed. Close to them a hummingbird poked its long beak into a flower. "How sweet."

Dorothy leaned forward, clasping her hands on the arms of her chair. Helen felt Jim squeeze her knee beneath the table, and Helen pursed her lips just slightly in the brief sign of a kiss. The four of them ate dinner leisurely then, silverware clinking softly, and Helen, after a second whiskey sour, even told the story of the night she had danced on a table at a bowling alley after the Wally Packer trial. Helen had bowled one strike after another—unbelievable! And then she drank too much beer and danced on a table.

"Well, I'm sorry to have missed that," said Dorothy.

Alan gazed at Helen with a vacant pleasantness that seemed to go on too long. He reached over and touched Helen's hand lightly. "Lucky Jim," he said.

"Believe it," Jim said.

6

For Bob, it had been interminable—the day vast and empty as he had waited for Jim to call back. Other people would have done something. Bob did realize that. Other people would have gone to a grocery store and made a meal for Susan and Zach to come home to. Or driven over to the coast and watched the surf. Or gone up to a mountain and taken a hike. But Bob—except for his trips to the back porch to smoke—had sat in his sister's living room and skimmed Reader's Digest Condensed Books, and then flipped through a women's magazine she had. He had never read a women's magazine before, and it saddened him, the articles on how to rev up your sex life with a husband you'd had for years (surprise him with sexy underwear), and how to lose weight at work, the exercises to help your flabby thighs.

Susan came home and said, "I didn't expect to see you here. After the mess you managed to make with the morning paper."

"Well. I came up here to help." Bob put the magazine down.

"Like I said, I didn't expect to see you here." Susan let the dog out, took off her coat.

"I have to see Charlie Tibbetts tomorrow morning. You know that."

"He phoned me," Susan said. "He won't get back to town until the afternoon. He's been delayed."

"Okay," said Bob. "I'll see him in the afternoon."

When Zach came through the door, Bob stood up. "Come on, Zachary. Talk to your old uncle. Start by telling me how your day went today."

Zach stood, looking white-faced and frightened. His hair in its buzz cut made his ears seem exceptionally vulnerable, yet the angularity of his face was adult. "Um. Maybe later." He went up to his room, and again, Susan took his food to him. This time Bob stayed in the kitchen, drinking wine from a coffee cup, eating frozen pizza heated in the microwave. He had forgotten how early some people ate dinner in Maine; it was only half past five. All evening Bob and Susan watched TV silently, Susan holding the remote and switching channels when any station was giving the news. The phone never rang. At eight o'clock Susan went to bed. Bob walked out onto the back porch and smoked, then returned inside and finished the second bottle of wine. He did not feel sleepy. He took a sleeping pill, then another. Again, he spent the night on the couch with his coat on, and again, the night was bad.

He woke to the sound of banging cupboard doors, and the morning light was strong from beneath the blinds. He felt the sickness of an early breaking of drugged sleep, and with this came the thought that his sister, in her fury yesterday, had sounded remarkably like their mother, who, when the kids were young, would have spells of loud fury herself (never directed at Bob, but aimed at the dog, or a jar of peanut butter that rolled off the counter and broke, or—mostly, usually—at Susan, who did not stand up straight, had not ironed a shirt properly, had not cleaned up her room).

"Susan—" He was thick-tongued.

She came and stood in the doorway. "Zach's already gone to work, and I'm about to, as soon as I take my shower."

Bob gave a mock salute, stood up, and found his car keys.

He drove carefully, as though he had been ill and housebound for weeks. Seen through the windshield, the world seemed far away. He pulled into a gas station that had a convenience store. Once he was inside, the store tossed into his vision an array of such variety—dusty sunglasses, batteries, locks with keys, candy—that confusion washed through him and he felt almost afraid. Behind the counter stood a young woman with dark skin and large dark eyes. In his stupefied mind she seemed out of place, like she might have come from India, but not quite. In a Shirley Falls convenience store the clerk was always white and almost always overweight; this is what Bob's mind told him he expected. Instead, a tiny snapshot of New York seemed inserted here, where the clerk could have been anyone. But this dark-eyed young woman watched Bob without any hint of welcome and he felt like an intruder. He wandered stupidly through the aisles, so aware of her wariness that he felt he had shoplifted something, though Bob had never shoplifted anything in his life. "Ah, coffee?" he asked, and she pointed. He filled a Styrofoam cup, found a package of powdered doughnuts, and then saw on the floor yesterday's newspapers: his nephew grinning at him. Bob groaned quietly. Passing the cooler he saw bottles of wine, and he stopped and took one, the bottle clinking against the others as he pulled it out to tuck under his arm. He was not staying—he hoped—after seeing Charlie Tibbetts this afternoon, but just in case he was stuck at Susan's again, he felt better knowing he'd have wine. He placed the bottle on the counter with his coffee and package of doughnuts, and asked for cigarettes. The young clerk did not look at him. Not when she dropped the cigarettes on the counter, not when she told him the amount he owed. Silently she pushed forward a flat paper bag and he understood he was to pack the items himself.

In the car he sat, his mouth warm from coffee. White powder from the doughnuts fell onto his coat and smeared into white streaks as he brushed at it. Backing up, the cup in its holder by the gearshift, he became aware of a sound, and there was a small, slow-moving pocket of time before Bob understood that what he heard was human screaming. He turned the car off; it lurched.

He seemed to fumble forever with the door before he could climb out.

A woman wearing a long red robe and a gauzy scarf covering her head and most of her face stood behind the car, crying out at him in a language he didn't understand. Her arms flew up and down, and then she reached and struck his car with her hand. Bob moved toward her and she waved both arms. All of this, for Bob, seemed to happen slowly and in silence. He saw that behind the woman stood another woman, dressed the same way though in darker colors, and he saw her mouth moving, shouting at him, he saw her long and yellow teeth.

"Are you okay?" Bob was yelling this. The women were yelling. For Bob came the sudden sense that he could not breathe, and he tried to indicate this with his hands moving in front of his chest. And now the clerk from the store was there, taking hold of the first woman's hand, speaking to her in the language Bob didn't understand, and only then did Bob realize the clerk must be Somali. The clerk turned to Bob and said, "You were trying to run the car over her. Go away from us, crazy man!"

"I wasn't," said Bob. "Did I hit her?" He was gasping. "The hospital is—" He pointed.

The women spoke among themselves, rapid, foreign sounds.

The clerk said, "She's not going to the hospital. Go away."

"I can't go away," Bob said, helplessly. "I have to go to the police and report this."

The clerk raised her voice. "Why the police? They are your friends?"

"If I hit the woman—"

"You didn't hit her. You tried to hit her. Go away."

"But it's an accident. What's her name?" He went to the car to find something to write on. By the time he was stepping back out of the car the two women in the long robes and long headscarves were running down the street.

The clerk was back inside the store. "Leave," she yelled through the glass door.

"I didn't see her." He raised his shoulders and turned out his palms. A bolt was turned. "Leave!" she said.

Very slowly Bob drove back to Susan's. He heard the shower running. When Susan came downstairs she was in her bathrobe, rubbing a towel over her hair. Bob said, still feeling breathless, watching Susan stare at him, "Ah, so listen. We have to call Jim."

7

Helen sat on the patio of their hotel room holding a cup of coffee. From down below came the sound of the fountain as it splashed; honeysuckle vines covered each patio she could see. Helen stretched her bare feet into a patch of sun and wiggled her toes. Breakfast at the Lemon Drop had been canceled. Alan had phoned earlier to say that Dorothy was choosing to spend the morning resting in her room, Helen should not take offense. Helen did not take offense. She ordered breakfast to be brought up, and ate her fruit and yogurt and roll with a clarity to her gladness. Jim was only going to play nine holes, he would not be gone long. They could be together then; Helen felt the sweet compression of desire waiting within her.

"Thank you so much," she said to the polite man who answered when she called to say her breakfast tray could be removed. She took her straw bag and went down to the lobby, stopping in the gift shop to buy a gossip magazine, the kind she used to read with her girls, cuddled together on the couch looking at the gowns of the movie stars. "Oh, I like that one!" Emily would say, pointing, and Margot would sigh, "But look—that one's reeeeally nice." Helen also bought a women's magazine because on its cover was an article headline "The Joys of Empty Nesting." "Thank you so much," she said to the woman behind the counter, and wandered out through the pathway between flowering trees and rock gardens to the beach, to stick her ankles into the sun.

Looking each other in the eye, the article counseled, that was important in aging relationships. Write a sexy email. Give compliments. Grumpiness is contagious. Helen closed her eyes behind her sunglasses and let her thoughts glide over to the Wally Packer days. What Helen had never told anyone was that those months had taught her what it must feel like to be the First Lady. One had to be ready for a camera click at any moment. One was building an image always. Helen had understood this. She had been excellent at the job. That some in their circle in West Hartford had become cool to her did not bother Helen. With her entire soul she believed in Jim's defense of Wally, and in Wally's right to have that defense. Any photo taken of her—she and Jim in a restaurant, at the airport, stepping from a cab—had, she felt, hit the right note each time, in her variety of tailored suits, cocktail dresses, casual slacks. What easily could have been called a circus was given gravitas by the dignity of Jim and Helen Burgess. Helen felt it then, and she believed it now, remembering.

And the excitement! Helen flexed her ankles. The late nights spent talking with Jim once the kids had gone to bed. Going over what had happened in the courtroom that day. He asked her opinion. She gave it. They were partners, they were in collusion. People said it must be a stress on the marriage, a trial like that, and Jim and Helen had to be careful not to burst into laughter, not to let it show: just the opposite; oh, it was just the opposite. Helen stretched, opened her eyes. She was his one and only. How many times had he whispered this over the last thirty years? She gathered her things and wandered back toward their room. Beside the croquet lawn, water fell gently over a little pile of rocks in a stream. A couple—the woman wearing a long white skirt and a pale blue blouse—was playing croquet, and there was the quiet *thwack* as a ball moved across the green. Along with the tumbling tropical blossoms, the blue sky seemed to whisper to the guests moving about, Now be happy. Be happy, be happy. Helen thought: Thank you, I will.

She heard him before she entered the room. "You're a fucking mental case, Bob!" Her husband was repeating this over and over. "You're a fucking mental case! An incompetent fucking mental case!" She slipped the key into the door and said, "Jim, stop."

Standing by the bed, he turned to her with a face bright red; he waved a hand downward as though he would have hit her had she been closer. "You're a fucking mental case, Bob! An incompetent mental case!" Dark patches of sweat unevenly patterned his blue golf shirt, and drops of sweat ran down his face. He yelled again into the phone.

Helen sat across from the bowl of lemons. Her mouth—like that—was dry. She watched her husband throw the phone onto the bed, and he kept yelling: "A mental case! Oh my God, Bob is a fucking mental case!" A scrap of a memory hurtled across her mind: Bob telling about his neighbor who screamed the same thing over and over to his wife. You're driving me fucking crazy, isn't that what he said? Before he was taken away in handcuffs. And she was married to a man like that.

A queer calmness descended on her. She thought, There is a bowl of lemons right in front of me, and yet the idea that it is a bowl of lemons cannot seem to make it into my mind. And her mind answered back: What do you want me to do, Helen? Stay calm, she told her mind.

Jim was punching a fist into his palm. He walked round and round in circles while Helen sat without moving. Finally he said, "Do you want to know what happened?"

Helen said, "I want you never to scream like that again. Is what I want. And if you do I will walk out of here and fly myself back to New York."

He sat down on the bed and wiped his face with the bottom of his shirt. In a tight, precise voice, he told her that Bob had almost run over a Somali woman. That Bob had caused Zach's smiling face to be plastered on the front page of the newspaper. That Bob had not even *talked* with Zach. That Bob refused to get into a car again, that he was going to fly back to New York and leave their car in Maine, and when Jim asked,

How is the car supposed to get back?, Bob said, I don't know, but I'm not driving it, I'm not getting behind a wheel again, and I'm flying home tonight, this Charlie Tibbetts will have to do his job without me. "Bob is," Jim said, quietly, "a fucking mental case."

"He is," Helen said, "someone who was traumatized at the age of four. I am really surprised, and really put off, that you can't figure out why he would not want to get behind the wheel of a car right now." She added, "But it was incredibly stupid of him to run over a Somalian woman."

"Somali."

"What?"

"Somali. Not Somalian."

Helen leaned forward. "You're correcting me in the middle of this?"

"Oh, sweetheart." Jim closed his eyes briefly, opened them; it seemed a dismissive gesture. "Bob's screwed everything up, and if we have to go up there to help out, it's best if you know what they're called."

"I'm not going up there."

"I want you to go with me."

Helen felt a huge, sudden envy of the couple playing croquet, the woman's long white skirt rising in the breeze. She pictured herself in this room a few hours earlier, waiting for Jim, waiting for the way he would look at her—

He did not look at her. He looked toward the window, and in his profile she saw the light catch the blue of his eye. A slackness invaded his face. "Do you know what Bob said to me when I got an acquittal for Wally?" He turned to Helen briefly, then looked back out the window. "He said, 'Jim, that was great. You did a great job. But you took the guy's fate from him.'"

Sunlight sat flatly in the room. Helen looked at the bowl of lemons, at the magazines the chambermaid had fanned out on the table. She looked at her husband, who was leaning forward now on the edge of the bed, and saw the crumpled moistness of his golf shirt. She was about to say, reaching her arm toward him, Oh, honey, let's try and relax, let's try and still have a good time while we're here. But when he turned to her, such different contortions seem to grip him that she thought if she passed this man on the sidewalk she might not have known it was Jim. She dropped her arm.

Jim stood up. "He said that to me, Helen." His face, unnatural-looking and imploring, gazed at her. He crossed his arms then, his hands touching his opposite shoulders, their private sign language of many years—and Helen either could not, or would not (she never knew which), but she did not stand and go to him.

8

It was absolutely true: Bob was useless. He sat on Susan's couch without moving. "You've always been useless," Susan had shouted before she drove off. The poor dog came and shoved her long nose under Bob's knee. "It's okay," he murmured, and the dog lay down at his feet. His watch said it was midmorning. He made his way carefully to the back porch, where he sat on the steps and smoked. His legs would not stop shaking. A gust of wind sent the yellow leaves of the Norway maple to the ground and then toward the porch. Bob put his cigarette out on the moving leaves, scraped them with his foot while his leg shook, then lit another cigarette. A car slowed by the driveway and pulled in.

The car was small and not new, and low to the ground. The woman behind the wheel seemed tall, and when she opened the door she had to give herself a good hoist to get out. She was about Bob's age and had glasses slipping down her nose. Her hair, different shades of dark blond, was messily pulled back with a clip, and her coat was full and kind of a tweedy black-and-white. She had a familiarity to her that Bob sometimes felt when he saw people from Maine.

"Hi," she said. She pushed her glasses up her nose as she walked toward him. "I'm Margaret Estaver. Are you Zachary's uncle? No, no, don't stand up." To his surprise she sat down on the step next to him.

He put out his cigarette and offered his hand. She shook it, though it was awkward, seated as they were beside each other. "Are you a friend of Susan's?" he asked.

"I'd like to be. I'm the Unitarian minister. Margaret Estaver," she added again.

"Susan's at work."

Margaret Estaver nodded as though she had thought that might be true. "Well, I imagine she doesn't want to see me anyway, but I thought— I thought I'd just come on over. She's probably pretty upset."

"Yuh. She is." Bob was reaching for another cigarette. "Do you mind—I'm sorry—"

She waved a hand. "I used to smoke."

He lit the cigarette, drew his knees up, and put his elbows on them so she wouldn't see that his legs were shaking. He blew the smoke away from her.

"It came to me very clearly this morning," Margaret Estaver said. "I should extend myself to Zachary and his mother."

He looked at her, squinting. Her face had a liveliness to it. "Well, I've messed things up more," he confessed. "A Somali woman thinks I tried to run her over."

"I heard."

"You did? Already?" Fear roared through him again. "I didn't mean to," he said. "I really didn't."

"Of course you didn't."

"I called the police to report it. I spoke to a cop I went to high school with, not Gerry O'Hare, I went to school with him too, but Tom Levesque; he was on duty down at the station when I called. He said not to worry about it." (In fact Tom Levesque had said the Somalis were whackjobs. "Forget it," Tom said. "They're jumpy as shit. Forget it.")

Margaret Estaver stretched her feet out, crossed them at the ankle. She wore backless clogs, dark blue, her socks were dark green. The image settled on Bob's eye quietly as he heard her say, "The woman said you didn't hit her, just that you tried. She's not filing charges, so that's the end of it. A lot of people in the Somali community are distrustful of authorities, as you can imagine. And of course they're feeling pretty sensitive right now."

Bob's legs were still shaking. Even his hand was shaking as he put the cigarette to his mouth.

Margaret's voice continued. "I heard Susan's been raising Zachary alone for a few years. My mother raised me alone, and it's not fun, I know that." She added, "A lot of the Somali women are raising their children without fathers, too. But they tend to have a lot more than one child, and they tend to have sisters or aunts. Susan seems very alone."

"She is."

Margaret nodded.

"She said there's going to be a rally."

Margaret nodded again. "In a few weeks, after Ramadan. A demonstration of support for tolerance. In the park. We're the whitest state in the country, I guess you probably know that." Margaret gave a little sigh and pulled her knees up, leaning forward to hug them; the gesture was youthful and natural, and somehow surprising to Bob. She turned her head to glance at him. "As you can imagine we're a little behind in the diversity field." Her voice had a slight Maine accent, a dry wryness that he recognized.

Bob said, "Well, Zachary's not a monster, but he's a sad kid. Boy, there's no doubt about that. Do you have children?"

"No."

She's gay. Women ministers. This was Jim's voice in his head.

"Me neither." Bob put his cigarette out. "Wanted to, though."

"Me too. Always. Expected to."

Awkward. Jim's sarcastic voice.

Margaret said, a lift of energy in her tone now, "I don't want Susan thinking the demonstration's against her or Zachary. I'm a little concerned how some of the clergy here are getting that mixed up, the 'against' stuff. Against violence, against intolerance of religious differences. And they're right. But the law is there to condemn. The ministry should uplift. Speak out, of course. But uplift. How corny is that?"

Corny.

"I don't think it's corny," Bob said.

Margaret Estaver stood up, and Bob thought the word *overflowing-ness* as he took in her messy hair and big coat. He stood as well. She was tall but he was taller, and he saw the gray roots of her streaked dark blond hair as she bent her head to reach into her pocket. She gave him a card. "Seriously," she said. "You call anytime."

Bob stood for a long time on the back steps. Then he went inside and sat in the cold living room. He thought of Mrs. Drinkwater saying that Zach cried. He thought of Susan yelling. And he thought he should not leave. But darkness rolled through him. *You incompetent mental case.*

When the man on the phone told him how much it would cost to take a taxi all the way from Shirley Falls to the Portland airport, Bob said he didn't care. "As soon as you can," Bob said. "The back door. I'll be standing right there."

Book Two

1

The colors of Central Park were quietly fall-like: the grass a faded green and the red oaks bronzed, the lindens changing to gentle yellow, the sugar maples losing their orangey leaves, one floating here, another falling there, but the sky was very blue and the air warm enough that the windows of the Boathouse were still open at this late afternoon hour, the striped awnings extending over the water. Pam Carlson, seated at the bar, gazed out at the few boats being rowed, everything slow-motion-seeming, even the bartenders, who worked with unhurried steadiness, washing glasses, shaking martinis, sliding their wet hands over their black aprons.

And then—like that—the place filled up. Through the door they came, businessmen shedding their jackets, women flipping back their hair, tourists moving forward with slightly stunned looks, the men holding backpacks that carried a bottle of water in a netted pocket on the side, as though they had hiked a mountain all day, their wives holding a map, a camera, the conferring of their confusion.

"No, my husband's sitting there," Pam said when a German couple started to move the tall chair beside her. She put her handbag on the chair. "Sorry," she added. Years of living in New York had taught her many things: how to parallel park, for example, or intimidate a taxi driver who claimed to be off-duty, how to return merchandise that was supposedly nonreturnable, or to say without apology "This is the line" when someone tried to cut ahead at the post office. In fact, living in New York, Pam thought, poking through her bag for her cell phone to check the time, was a perfect example of what great generals had understood throughout history: that the person who cared the most won. "A Jack Daniel's on the rocks with lemon," she told the bartender, tapping the counter next to her untouched glass of wine. "For my husband. Thanks."

Bob was always late.

Her real husband would not be home for hours, and the boys were at soccer practice. None of them cared that she was meeting Bob. "Uncle Bob," her kids called him.

Pam had come straight from the hospital where she worked twice a week as an intake assessor, and she'd have liked to go and wash her hands now but if she got up the Germans would take her seat. Her friend Janice Bernstein—who had dropped out of medical school years ago—said Pam should wash her hands the minute she left work; hospitals were just petri dishes of bacteria, and Pam agreed completely. In spite of her frequent use of hand-sanitizing lotion (which dried the skin), the thought of this vast array of waiting germs made Pam very anxious. Janice said that Pam was very anxious about too many things, she really should try to control it, not just to be more comfortable but because her anxiety caused her to appear socially eager, and that was not cool. Pam replied that she was too old to worry about being cool, but in fact she did worry about it, and that's one reason it was always nice to see Bobby, who was so uncool as to inhabit—in Pam's mind—his own private condominium of coolness.

A pig's head. Jesus.

Pam shifted on her chair, sipped her wine. "Could you make that a double?" Pam asked, after studying the glass of whiskey set down. Bob had sounded dismal on the telephone. The bartender took back the whiskey, returned to set it down again. "Start a tab, yes," said Pam.

Years ago—when she was married to Bob—Pam had worked as a research assistant to a parasitologist whose specialty was tropical diseases. Pam had spent her days in a lab looking through an electron microscope at the cells of Schistosoma, and because she loved facts the way an artist would love color, because she experienced a quiet thrill at the precision science aimed for, she had loved the days she'd spent in that lab. When she heard on the television about the incident in Shirley Falls, saw the imam walking away from the storefront mosque on a downtown street that looked terribly deserted, all sorts of feelings flooded her, not the least being an almost out-of-body nostalgia for a town that had once been familiar to her, but also—and almost immediately—a concern for the Somalis. She'd right away looked into it: Yes, those refugees who came from the southern regions of Somalia had showed Schistosoma haematobium eggs in their urine, but the bigger problem was—not surprisingly to Pam—malaria, and before they were allowed to come to the United States they were given a single dose of sulfadoxine-pyrimethamine for malaria parasitemia, and also albendazole for intestinal parasite therapy. What concerned Pam more, though, was learning that the Somali Bantu—a darker-skinned group, apparently shunned in Somalia, having come there as slaves from Tanzania and Mozambique a couple of centuries before—showed a much higher rate of schistosomiasis and, according to what Pam had read from the International Organization for Migration, also serious mental health problems of trauma and depression. The Somali Bantu, the Organization said, had certain superstitions: They might burn the skin of areas affected by disease, or pull out the baby teeth of a small child with diarrhea.

Part of what Pam felt when she read that was what she felt now remembering it: *I am living the wrong life.* It was a thought that made no sense. It's true she missed the smells of a lab: acetone, paraffin, alcohol, formaldehyde. She missed the *swoosh* of a Bunsen burner, the glass slides and pipettes, the particular and deep concentration of those around her. But she had twin boys now—with white skin, perfect teeth, no burn marks anywhere—and lab work was a life of the past. Still, the variety of problems, parasitological and psychological, of this refugee population made Pam feel homesick for whatever life she was not having, a life that would not feel so oddly wrong.

These days life was her townhouse, her boys and their private school, her husband, Ted, who ran the New Jersey office of a large pharmaceutical company and so had a reverse commute, her part-time job at the hospital, and a social life that required seemingly endless deliveries from the dry cleaners. But Pam was often homesick. For what? She could not have said, and it made her ashamed. Pam drank more wine, looked behind her, and there stepping through the foyer of the Boathouse bar was dear Bob, like a big St. Bernard dog. He could have been wearing a wooden cask of whiskey around his neck, ready to paw through the autumn leaves to get someone out. Oh, Bobby!

"You would think," she confided, nodding toward the Germans, who had only now stopped hovering nearby, "that after starting two world wars they wouldn't be so pushy."

"That's the dumbest thing ever," Bob said pleasantly. He was watching his whiskey, swirling it slowly. "We've started lots of wars and we're still pushy."

"Exactly. So you just got back last night? Tell me." With her head ducked toward his, she listened carefully, was transported back to the town of Shirley Falls, where she had not been in many years. "Oh, Bobby," she said sadly, more than once, as she listened.

Finally she straightened up. "By God." She got the bartender's attention, indicated another round. "Okay. First of all: Can I ask a stupid question? *Why* did he do this?"

"Very good question." Bob nodded. "I don't know what's behind it. He seems so amazed that it turned out to be serious. Honestly, I don't know."

Pam tucked her hair behind her ear. "All right. Well, second of all, he needs to be on medication. He's crying alone in his room? That's clinical and needs attention. And third of all: Fuck Jim." Pam's husband, Ted, did not like her to swear, and the word felt like a well-hit tennis ball as it left her mouth. "Just fuck Jim. Fuck. Him. I would say the Wally Packer trial spoiled him, but I thought he was an asshole before that."

"You're right." There was no one else Bob would allow to say that about Jim. But Pam had standing. Pam was family, his oldest friend. "Did you just *snap* your fingers at that bartender?"

"I moved my fingers. Relax. So you're going back up there for this demonstration?"

"I don't know yet. Zach worries me. Susan said he was scared beyond reason in that holding cell and she doesn't even know what a holding cell looks like. I think *I'd* die in a holding cell, and you take one look at Zach and realize he's less equipped." Bob put his head back as he drank from his whiskey glass.

Pam tapped her finger on the bar. "Wait. So could he go to jail for this?"

Bob opened his hand upward. "I don't know. The problem could be with the civil rights woman in the state AG's office. I did a little research today. Her name's Diane Dodge. She joined the AG's office a couple years ago after doing civil rights work in all the right places, and she's probably gung ho. If she decides to go ahead with a civil rights violation and Zach's found guilty of it, screws up on any of the conditions, *then* he could go to jail for up to a year. It's not impossible, is what I'm saying. And who knows what the Feds will do. I mean, it's nuts."

"Won't Jim know the woman in the AG's office? He'd know someone there."

"Well, he knows the AG, Dick Hartley. Diane Dodge sounds too young to have been there with him. I'll find out when he gets home."

"But Jim got along well in that office."

"He was headed right to the top." Bob shook his glass and the ice cubes rattled. "Then Mom died and he couldn't leave the state fast enough."

"I remember. It was weird." Pam pushed her wineglass forward and the bartender filled it.

Bob said, "Jim can't go barging in, pulling strings with Dick Hartley, though. That's just not an option."

Pam was rummaging around in her handbag. "Yeah. Still. If anyone can pull strings it's Jim. They won't even know their strings are being pulled."

Bob drank the last of his whiskey and pushed the glass toward the bartender, who placed a new one before him. "How are the kids?"

Pam looked up, her eyes softened. "They're great, Bob. I suppose in another year or so they'll hate me and get pimples. But right now they're the sweetest, funniest boys."

He knew she was holding back. He and Pam had worn themselves down trying for kids, putting off going to a doctor for years (as though they had known it would be the end of them), agreeing in vague conversations that getting pregnant should happen naturally and would, until Pam—her anxiety increasing monthly—suddenly said that such thinking was provincial. "There's a *reason* it's not happening," she cried. Adding, "And it's probably me." Not having his wife's inclination toward science, Bob had silently agreed, only because this aspect of women seemed to him more complicated than issues for men, and in Bob's imprecise imaginings he pictured Pam going in for a tune-up, tubes cleared, the rest cleaned, as though ovaries could be polished.

But it was Bob.

Immediately, this made—and still made—devastating sense to him. When he was small he had heard his mother say, "If a couple can't conceive, then God knows what He's doing. Look at crazy Annie Day, adopted by well-intentioned people"—raising her eyebrows—"but they sure weren't made for parenthood." Oh, that's ludicrous! Pam had shouted this many times during those months they were trying to get used to it: Bob not being able to reproduce. Your mother was smart, Bob, but she wasn't educated, and that's just magical thinking, it's *ludicrous*, crazy Annie Day was crazy from the start.

So it took its toll. It did.

When Pam balked at adoption—"We'll end up with our own crazy Annie Day"—he had been troubled. When she balked at insemination from a donor, he was troubled further. The relentlessness of the situation seemed to finally loosen the weave of their marital fabric. And when he met Ted, two years after Pam moved out (two years during which she had often called him in tears about *stupid* dates with *stupid* men), he saw that Pam, with her strong mind and splintering anxieties, had meant what she said: "I just want to start over."

Pam was twirling a strand of hair around her finger. "So what happened with Sarah? Do you ever see her anymore? Are you guys broken *up* broken up? Or just taking a break?"

"Broken up." Bob drank his whiskey, looked around. "I guess she's okay, I don't hear from her."

"She never liked me."

Bob gave a small shrug to indicate she shouldn't worry about it. In fact Sarah, who in the beginning thought it was so pleasing and civilized that Bob and Pam (and Ted and the boys) all stayed connected—since her own ex-husband was evil—had come to resent Pam tremendously. Even if weeks went by when Bob and Pam didn't speak, Sarah said, "She picks up the phone whenever she wants to be *really* understood. She rejected you, Bob, for a whole new life. But she still depends on you because she thinks you know her so well."

"I do know her so well. And she knows me."

The ultimatum was finally presented. No marriage to Sarah unless Pam was out of the picture for good. The arguments, the talks, the endless distress—but Bob, finally, could not do that.

Helen had said, "Bob, are you crazy? If you love Sarah, stop talking to Pam. Jim, tell him he's crazy to do this."

Jim surprisingly would not tell him that. He said, "Pam is Bob's family, Helen."

Pam nudged him now with her elbow. "What was it? What happened?"

"Strident," Bob said, his eyes going over the people pressed up to the bar. "Sarah became strident. It ended, that's all."

"I told my friend Toni about you and she'd love to have dinner." Pam snapped down a business card she had taken from her bag.

Bob squinted, pulled out his glasses. "Did she seriously dot the *i* with a little smiley face? I don't think so." He slid the card back to Pam.

"Fair." She dropped the card back into her bag.

"I have friends always trying to fix me up, don't worry."

"Dating's awful," Pam said, and Bob shrugged and said it pretty much was.

It was wintry dark by the time they left, Pam stumbling once or twice as they crossed the park to Fifth Avenue; she'd had three glasses of wine. Her shoes were low-heeled and pointy-toed, he noticed. She was skinnier than the last time he'd seen her. "This dinner party I showed up too early for," she was saying, steadying herself on his arm while she shook something from her shoe. "People at the party started talking about another couple who weren't there, saying they had no taste. Meaning bad artwork. I think. I'm not sure. It made me really nervous, Bobby. People could be saying I'm socially eager and have no taste."

He couldn't help it, his laughter burst out. "Pam. Who cares?"

She looked at him and suddenly laughed deeply, her laugh familiar to him from long ago. "Really. Who the *fucking* fuck cares?"

"Maybe people say Pam Carlson is really smart and used to work with a great parasitologist."

"Bobby, nobody even knows what a parasitologist is. You should hear them. A what? Oh, *that.* My mother went to India and got a parasite and was sick for two years, that's what they say. Fuck it." She stopped walking and looked at him. "Have you ever noticed how Asians just go ahead and bump into you, how they don't seem to have any sense of personal space? Boy, that pisses me off."

He took her elbow lightly. "Mention that at your next dinner party. Let me get you a taxi."

"I'll walk you to the subway station, oh, okay." He had already hailed one, and he opened the door now and helped her get in. "Goodbye, Bobby, that was fun."

"You say hi to all the boys." He stood in the street and waved as the taxi sped off into traffic, the busyness of neon lights around him. She turned and waved from the back window, and he kept waving until the taxi drove out of sight.

———

When Bob had returned from Maine, he'd found the apartment below his with its door open, and he'd stopped to look at the place where Adriana and Preppy Boy had lived out their marriage. The landlord was fixing a faucet and he nodded to Bob, but the glimpse Bob had—a space empty of curtains, couches, rugs, whatever it is that people make a life around—struck him with its gone-ness. Dust bunnies had been swept into the center of the living room, and the twilight that showed through the windows was indifferent, stark. The blank walls seemed to say wearily to Bob: Sorry. You thought this was a home. But it was just this, all along.

Tonight as Bob climbed the stairs, he saw that the door of the apartment was again partly open, as though emptiness was not worth concealing or protecting. The landlord was not there, and Bob closed the door quietly, then continued up the stairs. His phone machine was blinking. Susan's voice said, "Call me, *please*."

Bob poured wine into a juice glass and settled himself onto his couch.

Gerry O'Hare had surprised everyone—certainly surprised Susan, who felt personally betrayed—by holding a press conference that morning in the City Chambers of Shirley Falls. An FBI agent stood by his side. "Big old fat thing," Susan said on the phone to Bob. "Standing there all puffed up, loving how important he looks as chief of police." She had not intended to speak to Bob again—she made this clear at the start of the call, but she couldn't figure out how to dial Jim's cell number overseas, didn't have the name of his hotel—

Bob supplied her with both.

She kept right on. "I wanted to turn the TV off, but I couldn't, it was like I was frozen. And now it'll be in the morning papers. You *know* Gerry doesn't give a doughnut's damn about the Somalians, but there he stood going blabby blab—'This is very serious. This will not be tolerated.' He hopes his response shows the Somalian community they can feel safe and confident. Oh, please. And then one reporter said there'd been incidents of tire slashing and window scratching against the Somalians and what did he have to say about that, and Gerry gets all pompous and says the police can't respond to anything if the Somalians don't come forward with their complaints. So you can just *see* that he kind of can't stand them, he's just doing this because the whole friggin' thing's gone out of control—"

"Susan. Have Zach give Charlie Tibbetts permission to talk to me. I'll call him tomorrow." He pictured her, upset in her cold house. It saddened him, but it seemed far away. But he knew very soon it would not feel far away; the murkiness of Susan and Zachary and Shirley Falls would seep into his apartment the way the emptiness below waited to remind him that his neighbors were no more, that nothing lasts forever, there is nothing to be counted on. "It's going to be all right," Bob told Susan, before hanging up.

Later, sitting by the window, he saw the young girl across the street moving about her cozy apartment in her underwear, and nearby the couple in their white kitchen were doing the dishes together. He thought of all the people in the world who felt they'd been saved by a city. He was one of them. Whatever darkness leaked its way in, there were always lights on in different windows here, each light like a gentle touch on his shoulder saying, Whatever is happening, Bob Burgess, you are never alone.

2

It was the laugh. The policemen's casual laugh when they spotted the pig's head on the rug. Abdikarim could not stop hearing it, seeing it. He would wake in the night picturing the two uniformed men, the short one especially, with his small eyes and unintelligent face, the sound of mirth he made before he straightened up and asked sternly, looking around, "Who speaks English? Somebody better speak English." As though they had done something wrong. This thought went repeatedly through Abdikarim's head: But we have done nothing wrong! This is what he murmured now as he sat at a table in his café on the corner of Gratham Street. To have women gaze right at him as they walked by, to have children tugging on the hand of their parent, turning their small heads to stare when they were safely past, to have the thick-armed tattooed men screech their trucks past his café, or high school girls whisper and giggle and cross the street to yell a name— None of these things bothered Abdikarim so much as the memory of the policemen's laughter did. In the mosque one block away—which was only a dark room, rain-stained

and unlovely (but theirs and holy)—he and the others had been treated
as mere schoolboys complaining of a bully.

Abdikarim had walked this morning through the dawn's gray light to
his café after morning prayer. The mosque held within it the presence of
fear; the smell of the cleaning foam used many times in the last few days
seemed itself to be the smell of fear. It had not been easy to pray, and
some men hurried through it to stand watch by the door. The *adano* was
back at work at Walmart as though nothing had happened—news of this
kept going around the village, and there was more trouble than ever with
sleep. The police chief's press conference was baffling too. A reporter
had come to the café yesterday. "Why weren't there any Somalis at the
press conference?"

Because no one had told them about it.

Abdikarim wiped down the counter, swept the floor. The sun rose
yellow between the buildings across the street. With the fast, only
Ahmed Hussein would be in later to eat. He worked nearby in the paper
factory and was allowed to drink tea and eat bites of stewed goat meat
because of his diabetes. At the back of the café behind stringed beads
was a small area where scarves and earrings and spices and teas and
nuts and figs and dates were sold. Throughout the day women would
come in together and buy what they might need for Maghrib tonight,
and Abdikarim went and ran a duster over packages of basmati rice. He
arranged the packages so the counter wouldn't look too barren, then
went back to the front of the café and sat in a chair by the window. The
phone in his pocket vibrated. "Again?" he asked, for it was his sister calling from Somaliland.

"Yes, again," she said. "Why are you still there, Abdi? You're in more
danger than here! No one is throwing pigs' heads here."

"I can't put the shop on my back and walk away," he said with affection.

"The man is out of jail. Zachary Olson— They let him out! How do
you know he's not coming right now to your café?"

Her questions pricked alarm in him. But he said gently, "News trav-
els fast." He added, "I will think about it."

For an hour he sat by the window watching Gratham Street. Two Bantu men, their skin as black as winter night sky, walked past the window and did not look in. Abdikarim rose and moved through his store, touching the scarves, the few packages of bedsheets, some towels. Last night there had been another meeting of the elders, and their voices circled around Abdikarim's head as he made his way to the front of the café.

"He's not in jail. Where is he? Back at work. Home with his mother."

"And his father."

"He has no father."

"A man was with him when he came out of jail. A big man. The man who tried to run over Ayanna, after he bought a bottle of wine in the morning for breakfast."

"I heard women talking in the library. They think there's overreaction to this. They said, 'It's rude to throw a pig's head, yes, but that's all it is.'"

"Forget them, they've not run through Mogadishu with machine guns pointed at them."

"Mogadishu! What about Atlanta? People there would kill us for a dollar."

"Minister Estaver said Zachary Olson's not like that. She said he's a lonely boy—"

"We know what she said."

A headache arrived now for Abdikarim. He went to the door and stood looking out at the sidewalk and the buildings across the street. He did not know how he could ever get used to living here. There was little color anywhere, except the trees in the park in the fall. The streets were gray and plain and many stores were empty, their big windows blank. He thought of the colorfulness of the Al Barakaat open market, the brilliance of the silks and colorful *guntiino* robes, the smells of gingerroot and garlic and cumin seed.

The thought of returning to Mogadishu was like a stick that poked at him with each heartbeat. It was possible peace had come; earlier this year there had been great hope. There was the Transitional Federal Government, unsteady, but there in Somaliland. In Mogadishu was the Islamic Courts Union, and it was possible they could rule with peace. But there were rumors, and who knew what to believe? Rumors that the United States was urging Ethiopia to invade Somalia, to get rid of the Islamic Courts. It did not seem true, but it also seemed it could be true. Only two weeks ago came reports that Ethiopian troops had seized Burhakaba. But then other reports: No, it was government troops who had come to the town. All of it, and all that came before it, caused a heaviness inside Abdikarim. It was a heaviness that grew with each passing month, so that to go or to stay—he could not make the decision. He saw how some of the young people here managed; they laughed, joked, talked with excitement. His eldest daughter had arrived half-starved and knowing no English, and already when she called him from Nashville these days he heard excitement in her voice. He felt too old for the spring of excitement to return to him again.

And he felt too old to learn English. Without that, he lived with the constancy of incomprehension. In the post office last month he had mimed and pointed to a square white box, the woman in her blue shirt repeating and repeating and he did not know and everyone in the post office knew and finally a man came to him and crossed his arms quickly toward the floor, saying, "Fini!" And so Abdikarim thought the post office was finished with him and he must go and he did go. Later he found out the post office was out of the boxes they had sitting on the shelf with price tags on them. Why did they show them if they did not have them to sell? Again, the incomprehension. He came to understand this had a danger altogether different from the dangers in the camp. Living in a world where constantly one turned and touched incomprehension—they did not comprehend, he did not comprehend—gave the air the lift of uncertainty and this seemed to wear away something in him, always he felt unsure of what he wanted, what he thought, even what he felt.

His phone vibrated, startling him. "Yes?" It was Nahadin Ahmed, Ayanna's brother.

"Did you hear? A white supremacy group in Montana heard about the demonstration. They're writing about it on their website."

"What does Imam say?"

"He's gone to the police and asked them not to have the demonstration. The police ignored him, the demonstration excites the police."

Abdikarim unplugged the heater, closed up his café, locked the door, and hurried through the streets back to the apartment where he lived. No one was there. The children were in school, Haweeya was at work, assisting a social service group, Omad was at the hospital in his job as translator. Abdikarim stayed all morning in his room, missing prayers at the mosque, keeping the shades drawn as always. He lay on the bed, and there was darkness inside him and darkness in the room.

———

Susan drove to work wearing sunglasses even when the mornings were overcast. Right after Zachary's picture appeared in the paper, she had pulled up at the traffic light by the overpass that would take her to the mall when a woman she had known casually for years pulled up in the lane beside her and—Susan was certain of this—pretended not to see her, fiddling with her radio until the light changed. Susan had the physical sensation of water draining straight down through her. It was not unlike the feeling she'd had when Steve came home and told her he was leaving.

Now, pulled up at the intersection, looking straight ahead through her sunglasses, thinking of her early morning dream of sleeping in the backyard of Charlie Tibbetts's house, Susan suddenly remembered this: that in the weeks after Zach was born she'd secretly, briefly, fallen in love with her gynecologist. The doctor lived in the Oyster Point section of town in a big house with four children and a wife who didn't work. They were not from Maine, Susan remembered that, and they had seemed— filing into a pew each Christmas Sunday service—as exquisite as a flock of foreign birds. With Zachary strapped into his safety seat, Susan would drive by their house slowly, that was how deep her longing had been for the man who had delivered her baby.

Remembering, Susan felt no embarrassment. It seemed long ago—it was; the doctor would be old by now—and as though it was the behavior of someone other than herself. Perhaps if she was still young she would be driving by the home of Charlie Tibbetts, but there was no sap left in her. The thick sugary pull of life had gone. And yet in her nighttime dream she had been camping out on Charlie Tibbetts's back lawn, and this made sense to her, the desire to be near him. He was fighting for her son, which meant he was fighting for her. For Susan, this was a feeling altogether new, and it added to her respect for Jim. Wally Packer, it seemed to Susan, must have practically fallen in love with him. She had no idea if the two stayed in touch after all these years.

"No," Bob said, when Susan called him from work. There were no customers in the store.

"But don't you think Jim misses him?"

"I don't think it's like that," Bob said. Susan felt ripples of humiliation spread through her. She didn't want to think that she and Zach were just a job.

She said, "Jim hasn't called me at all."

"Ah, Susie, he's tied up playing golf. You should see him at those places. One time Pam and I went with them to Aruba. Sheesh. Poor Helen sits there, soaking up melanomas, and Jim walks around with his mirrored sunglasses, standing by the pool like he's Mr. Cool. He's busy, is what I'm saying. Don't you worry, Charlie Tibbetts is great. I talked to him yesterday. He's asking for a gag order and a change in bail conditions—"

"I know. He told me." But she felt a ridiculous stab of jealousy. "Before you switched to appeals, Bobby, when you were doing courtroom defense work down there, did you like your clients?"

"Like them? Sure, some. A lot of them were dirtbags. And of course they're all guilty, but—"

"What do you mean, they're all guilty?"

"Well, they're guilty of something, Susie. By the time they've come up through the system. Not always the first charge, so you do what you can to get it reduced. You know."

"Did you ever defend a rapist?"

Bob didn't answer right away, and Susan realized he'd probably been asked this question many times. She pictured him at cocktail parties in New York (she didn't know what a cocktail party in New York could look like, so the image was vague and movieish), a skinny pretty woman asking him this same question confrontationally. On the phone Bob said, "I did."

"Was he guilty?"

"I never asked. But he was convicted and I wasn't sorry."

"You weren't sorry?" Susan felt tears inexplicably fill her eyes. She felt the way she had felt for years when she was premenstrual. Crazy.

"He got a fair trial." Bob sounded patient and tired, and that was how Steve used to sound with her.

Susan looked around the store in a kind of panic, untethered. Zach was guilty. He could have a fair trial and go to jail for a year. And it was going to cost a lot of money before they were through. And nobody— maybe Bobby, a little—would *care*.

Bob was saying, "You need intestines of steel for courtroom work. Those of us in appeals here, we're . . . Well, let's just say Jim has insides made of steel."

"Bobby, I'm hanging up."

A group of Somali women had entered the store. In long draping cloaks, everything covered except their faces, they momentarily seemed to Susan to be one entity, a large foreign assault presenting itself to her, a blurry arrangement of dark reds and blues and green head coverings, a splotch of lively peach color; no arms, or even hands, to be seen. But there were the murmurings and sounds of different voices and then the subsequent separating off of one, an elderly woman, short and lame, seating herself in the corner chair, and this clarified to Susan's eye what seemed to be the situation: which was that the youngest one, tall and bright-faced and (to Susan) surprisingly beautiful in a way that seemed almost American, with her dark eyes and high cheekbones, was holding forth a pair of glasses, broken at the hinge, and asking, in poor English, to have them fixed.

Beside the tall young girl stood a darker-faced woman, large and boxy in her robe, her face immobile, watchful, unreadable. She was holding plastic bags through which Susan could see cleaning materials.

Susan picked up the glasses. "Did you purchase these here?" Directing her question to the young girl, whose beauty felt aggressive to Susan. The tall girl turned to the boxy woman; they spoke back and forth quickly.

"Hey?" asked the girl, whose peach-colored headscarf seemed flamboyant, amazing.

"Did you purchase these here?" Susan repeated. She knew they had not, these were drugstore glasses she held in her hand.

"Yeah, yeah," said the girl, and repeated her request to have them fixed.

"Okay," said Susan. Her hands were not steady as she worked the tiny screw. "One minute," she said, and took them in the back room, though it was store policy not to leave the front unattended. When she returned, the women were as she had left them; only the young one seemed to have the energy of youth, touching the frames that were arranged in a stand by the cash register. Susan put the glasses on the counter and pushed them forward. A commotion from the boxy woman made Susan look to her, and she was amazed to see a child's foot exposed as the woman pulled her arm back to reach beneath her robe. The woman bent to put down, then pick up, the bags of cleaning materials, and another bulge on the other side of her was made visible; she had been standing here with two children strapped to her. Silent children. As silent as their mother.

"Do you want to try any of those on?" Susan asked. The tall young girl continued touching the frames without removing them from the stand. None of the women were looking at Susan. They were in the store, but they were far away.

"These are fixed now." Susan's voice sounded too loud to her. "No charge."

The young girl reached beneath her robe, and Susan—as though all her fear had waited for this moment—had the sudden thought the girl was going to draw a gun on her. It was a small purse. "No," said Susan, shaking her head. "Free."

"Okay?" the girl asked, her large eyes looking quickly over Susan's face.

"Okay." Susan held up both her hands.

The girl slipped the fixed glasses into her purse. "Okay. Okay. Thank you."

There was commotion once more as they spoke in their language, hard and brisk to Susan's ear. The babies stirred beneath the mother's robe, and the old woman stood up slowly. As they moved toward the door, Susan realized that the old woman was not old. How she knew this she couldn't have said, but the woman's face had a fatigue so deep it seemed to have cleaned away whatever it was in a face that gave it life; her face, as she walked slowly without a glance at Susan, had left on it only a deep and haunting apathy.

From the doorway of the store Susan watched them walk slowly through the mall. Don't make fun of them, she thought with alarm, because she saw two teenage girls stare at them as they went past. At the same time the absolute foreignness of these draped women gave Susan an inner shuddering sigh. She wished they had never heard of Shirley Falls, and it scared her to think they might never go away.

3

A wonderful thing about New York—if you have the means—is that if you don't feel like preparing food, finding a fork, washing a plate, you certainly don't have to. And if you live alone and don't want to be alone you don't have to be either. Bob often walked to the Ninth Street Bar and Grille, where he sat on a stool, drank beer, ate a cheeseburger, and spoke with the bartender or to a reddish-haired man who had lost his wife in a bicycle accident the year before, and sometimes this man spoke to Bob with tears in his eyes, or they might laugh about something, or the man might wave one hand and Bob understood that it was a night the man had to be left alone. An osmosis of understanding extended among the regulars; people revealed only what they wanted to and it was not much. Conversation was about political scandals, or sports, or sometimes—fleetingly—the deeply personal: Bob knew the details of the wife's freak bicycle accident, but did not know the name of the reddish-haired widower. The fact that Sarah had not accompanied Bob to the place in months was never mentioned. The place was what it intended to be: safe.

Tonight the bar was almost full, though the bartender nodded toward one empty stool and Bob squeezed himself between two other customers. The reddish-haired man was farther away and nodded in greeting by way of the huge mirror they faced. A large television screen in the corner was silently showing the news, and Bob, waiting for his beer to be drawn, glanced up and felt a jolt at the sight of Gerry O'Hare's face, broad, expressionless, next to the grinning photo shot of Zachary. The words at the bottom of the TV went by too fast for Bob to read, but he caught "hoping," "isolated incident," and then "looking," "white supremacy group."

"Crazy world," said an older man seated next to Bob, his face aimed toward the television as well. "Everyone's gone nuts."

"Hey, knucklehead," a voice called, and Bob turned and saw his brother and Helen. They had just entered the place and Helen was seating herself at one of the little tables by the window. Even in the low lighting Bob could see their tans. He got off his stool and went over to them.

"Did you see what was just on TV?" He pointed. "How are you guys? When did you get back? Did you have a nice time?"

"We had a lovely time, Bobby." Helen was opening her menu. "What's good here?"

"Everything's good here."

"You trust the fish?"

"I do, yeah."

"I'm sticking with a burger." Helen closed her menu, shivered, and rubbed her hands together. "I've been freezing ever since we got back."

Bob pulled up a chair and sat down. "I'm not staying, don't worry."

"Good," said Jim. "I'm trying to take my wife out to dinner."

Bob thought their tans looked strange, off-season like this. He said, "Zach was just on TV."

"Yeah, shit." Jim shrugged. "But this Charlie Tibbetts, he's terrific, Bob. Did you see what he did?" Jim opened his menu, glanced at it a few moments, then closed it. "Charlie sailed right in after that stupid press conference O'Hare gave, demanded a gag order and a change in the bail conditions. First he says his client's being prosecuted aggressively and unfairly, that no other misdemeanor's ever been given a press conference, but his greatest line—because the bail conditions say Zach has to stay away from any Somali person—the greatest line, Charlie says to the judge, what was it Helen? He says, 'The bail commissioner made the unfortunate and naïve assumption that all Somalis dress, look, and act alike.' Fabulous. How are you planning to get our car back?"

"Jim, why don't you let your brother enjoy his evening, and we'll enjoy ours, and you two can figure that out later?" Helen turned to the waiter. "The pinot noir, please."

"How is Zach?" Bob asked. "Susan's called me a few times, but she's always vague about how Zach is."

"Who knows how Zach is. He doesn't have to appear for the arraignment, which isn't till November third. Charlie filed a not-guilty plea, had the whole thing moved to Superior Court, and asked for a jury trial. He's good."

"I know. I've talked to him." Bob paused, then said, "Zach cries alone in his room."

"Oh God," said Helen.

"How do you know?" Jim looked at his brother.

"The old lady upstairs told me. Susan's tenant. She says she's heard Zach crying in his room."

Jim's face changed, his eyes seemed smaller.

"She could be wrong," Bob said. "She seems a little wacky."

"Of course she could be wrong," Helen said. "Jim, what are you having to eat?"

"I'll go get the car," Bob said. "I'll fly up and drive it back. How soon do you need it?"

"Soon as you have time, which would be always. Nice how Legal Aid has that strong union. Five weeks vacation, and it's not like anyone there works hard to begin with."

"That's not true, Jim. Some really good people work there." Bob spoke quietly.

"The bartender's waving at you. Go drink your beer." Jim's voice was dismissive.

Bob returned to the bar and understood that his evening was spoiled. He was a knucklehead, even Helen was mad at him. He had gone up to Maine and done nothing except respond like an idiot, panic, and leave their car up there. He thought of the gracious big-boned Elaine, sitting in her office with the fig tree, explaining so patiently the replication of the response to traumatic events, the masochistic tendencies he had because he felt he needed to be punished for a childhood act of innocence. In the mirror he saw the reddish-haired man watching him, and when he caught his eye the man nodded at him. What Bob understood in that brief glance was the unspoken recognition of another guilty person—the reddish-haired man had bought his wife the bike, suggested the ride that morning. Bob nodded back, and drank his beer.

———•———

Pam sat at her favorite Upper East Side salon watching the head of a Korean woman bent over her feet, worrying as she always did that the utensils had not been sterilized properly, because once you got a nail fungus you almost never got rid of it, and the girl, Mia, whom Pam preferred, was not in today; this one, scrubbing gently at Pam's toes, spoke no English. There had been miming, and Pam asking too loudly, "Clean? Yes?," pointing to the metal box, before she finally relaxed and settled into her thoughts, which she had been having for days now, about her past life with the Burgess family.

At the start, she had not liked Susan. But this was because they were young—children, no older than the sons of Pam's friends who had just left for college—and Susan's unrelenting disdain for Bob had been taken personally by Pam. It was back at a time in her life when Pam wanted everyone to like everyone. (She especially wanted everyone to like her.) It was also at a time when people on the Orono campus of the University of Maine would speak a greeting when they passed someone on the walkways that wound around the buildings and beneath the trees, even if the people did not know each other. Though many students did know Bob, and this was because of his friendliness and also because some had known Jim, who was gone by then but had been president of the student government and was one of the university's very few graduates ever to get into Harvard Law School—let alone receive a full scholarship to go there—which heightened his renown. Awareness of the Burgess boys was as common as the oaks and maple trees the students walked under, holding their books. (A few elms remaining, too; sick, though, with their top leaves wilting.) Being with Bob and his loping easiness was the safest Pam had ever felt, and an enthusiasm for college life—for life, period—opened and unfolded within her. This exuberance was insulted each time Susan pretended not to see them, when she walked around to a different doorway, should they be headed into the student union at the same time. Thin, Susan was, back then, and pretty, turning her face away. Or in Fogler Library, Susan was capable of walking right past Bob and not even glancing at him. "Hey, Suse," Bob would say. Nothing. Nothing! Pam was appalled. It did not seem to bother Bob. "She's always been that way."

But after weekends and holidays spent at the Burgess home in Shirley Falls, where Pam's future mother-in-law, Barbara, greeted her in what Pam understood was a welcoming manner (mostly conveyed by making sardonic jokes at others' expense and glancing at Pam with a granite-faced inclusion), Pam began to feel sorry for Susan. This was surprising to Pam, perhaps her first understanding of the prismatic quality of viewing people. She felt she had been seeing only the front of Susan and had missed entirely the large white light of motherly disapproval that shone behind her. It was Susan who was most often the recipient of her mother's so-called jokes, it was Susan who set the table silently while her mother said to Bob, who had made the dean's list and Susan had not, "Oh, Bobby, of course you did, I always knew you were smart." It was Susan who was wearing her long hair parted in the middle "like some foolish flower-child hippie," it was Susan, with her slender waist and straight hips, who was told that someday she would, like all women, turn Crisco: fat in the can.

Pam's own mother had never been scornful of her, but she did seem uncertain of her parental duties and carried them out from a distance, as though Pam—a girl who spent hours of her youth reading in the local library, and gazing at magazine ads hinting at lives lived *out there*—had still required too much from her. Pam's father, quiet and receding, seemed even less qualified to escort his daughter through the ordinary obstacles of growth. It was to escape this arid atmosphere that Pam spent most of her holidays at the Burgess home, that small yellow house on a hill not far from the center of town. The house was smaller than the one Pam had grown up in, though not much smaller. But the rugs were worn, and the dishes were cracked, and the bathroom had tiles missing; these things had troubled her. Again, that sense of discovery: Her boyfriend and his family were poor. Pam's father had his own small stationery supply business and her mother gave piano lessons. But their house in western Massachusetts was always fresh-looking, and out by farmland, safe and open; Pam had never thought once about it. When she saw the Burgess home with its discolored linoleum floor curling up in the corners, the window casings that were so old and warped they were stuffed in the winter with newspaper, the one bathroom whose toilet was lined with a rust-colored stain, and the shower curtain so faded she was not sure if it had once been pink or red—she thought of the family in her hometown who were the only really *poor* family she had known: They had rusted cars all over their lawn, the kids showed up at school dirty, and Pam was taken aback: Who was this Burgess boy she had fallen for? Was he like *that*? On the campus in Orono he had seemed no different from anyone else, wearing the same blue jeans every day—but lots of kids back then wore the same jeans every day—his dorm room messy and, his half, sparse—but lots of boys' dorm rooms were messy and sparse. Except Bob was more *there* than other boys, more easygoing; she had not known that he and his unpleasant sister came from this.

It did not last long, that reaction. Bob brought with him into every

room what it was that made him Bob. And so the house became—
quickly—one of comfort. At night she could hear his easy voice speaking
quietly to his mother, for they often stayed up late, mother and son, talking. She heard them many times say the word "Jim," as though his presence remained in the house, the way his presence lingered on the Orono
campus.

"Jim-this, Jim-that" is what Pam intended to say when she finally met
him. He was sitting at the kitchen table on a Friday afternoon in November when it was already dark outside, and he seemed too large for
the house, slouched back on the chair, his arms crossed. Pam only said,
"Hello." He stood up and shook her hand, and with his free hand pushed
at Bob's chest. "Slob-dog, how are you," he said, and Bob said, "Harvard
man, you're home!"

Pam's first feeling was relief that she was not attracted to her boyfriend's older brother, because she saw that many girls probably were.
He was too conventionally handsome for her taste, his dark hair, perfect
jaw; but also, he was hard. Pam saw this and it frightened her. No one
else seemed to see it. When Jim teased Bob (as sharply as Barbara would
tease Susan), Bob laughed, and received it. "When we were kids," Jim
told Pam that first night, "this guy"—nodding toward Bob—"drove me
nuts. Nuts. Hell, you still drive me nuts."

Bob shrugged happily.

"Like what would he do?"

"Whatever I ate, he wanted to eat the same thing. 'Tomato soup,' he'd
say, when Mom asked what he wanted for lunch. Then he'd see I had
vegetable soup, and he'd say, 'No, that's what I want.' Whatever I wore,
he wanted to wear the same thing. Wherever I went, he wanted to go
too."

"Wow. How terrible." Pam was being sarcastic, but it was one pebble
thrown against a thick windshield; Jim was impermeable.

Those years that Jim was in law school he came back frequently to
visit his mother. All three kids, Pam saw, were loyal to their mother. Both
Susan and Bob worked in the dining hall at school, but they would swap
shifts with people and hitch rides with anyone headed down the turn-

pike to Shirley Falls. This was touching to Pam, and made her feel guilty about her long absences from her own home, but the Burgess home is where she went whenever Bob, and Susan too, decided they should be there. Susan had not yet met Steve, and Jim had not met Helen, so Pam, looking back on it, felt that not only was she in love with Bob, but that she was almost his sibling as well; for those were the years when they became her family. The prickliness of Susan softened. Often they all played Scrabble at the kitchen table, or just talked, squished together in the living room. Sometimes the four of them went bowling and came back to tell Barbara how Bob almost beat Jim. "But he didn't," Jim said. "Never has and never will." One freezing cold Saturday, Pam and Susan carefully ironed their long hair, laying it on the ironing board in the glassed-in porch of the little house, and Barbara yelled at both of them that they could have burned the house down. While the Burgesses seemed to have no knowledge of, or interest in, food (there were meals of scrambled hamburger covered with an unmelted sheet of orange cheese, or a tuna casserole made with canned soup, or a chicken roasted without any spices, not even salt), Pam discovered that they loved baked goods, and so she made banana bread and sugar cookies, and sometimes Susan stood in the small kitchen and helped her, and whatever was baked was eaten hungrily, and this touched Pam as well—as though these kids had been starved all their lives for sweetness. Barbara was not sweet, but Pam appreciated a fundamental decency in her that all three kids, for all their differences, seemed to share.

Jim talked about his law classes while Bobby leaned forward and asked questions. Jim was drawn to criminal law from the beginning, and he and Bob spoke about the rules of evidence, the hearsay exceptions, the procedural aspects of trying a case, the role of punishment in society. Pam had already established her own interest in science and she saw society as one large organism working with its million, billion cells heaving itself alive. Criminality was a mutation that interested Pam, and she joined tentatively in these discussions. Jim was never condescending to her, as he could be to Bob or Susan; his sparing her always surprised her. There was a strange combination of arrogance and earnestness in Jim that often surprised her. Years later, during the Wally Packer trial, when Pam read an interview about Jim quoting a Harvard classmate as saying that Jim Burgess "had kept himself removed, always seemed unknowable," she understood then what she had not fully understood those years before—that Jim must have felt an outsider at Harvard, and that he returned to Shirley Falls because something compelled him to, not just his mother, to whom he was attentive and caring, but perhaps a familiarity of accents and chipped plates and bedroom doors too warped to close. He did not mention any girlfriends during those law school years. But one day, because his grades were perfect and his skills already sharp, he spoke of landing a job at the Manhattan DA's office. He would get trial experience and bring it back to Maine.

"Ouch," Pam said. The Korean woman, massaging Pam's calf muscle, looked up at Pam with apology, spoke a word Pam did not understand. "Sorry," Pam said, waving her hand quickly. "But too hard." A shudder of nostalgia moved through her, and she had to close her eyes against the pale sheet of what could only be boredom that moved toward her. Was it merely youth and new love that had made Shirley Falls seem to Pam a place of miracles? Would she never have that yearning and high-pitched excitement again? Did age and experience just *mute* you?

Because it was in Shirley Falls that Pam had felt first the thrills of adulthood. If college life had brought her into the world of many people and thoughts and facts—which she loved, loving facts—it was Shirley Falls that held the magic of a foreign city, and Pam, on her visits there, had felt dizzily, ecstatically catapulted into being a grown-up. This appeared in the casual act of going by herself (while Bob helped clean his mother's gutters) to a family-owned bakery on Annett Avenue and drinking coffee at a table, the plump women serving her with a wonderful nonchalance, the windows dressed with ruffled pulled-back curtains, the air sweet with the smell of cinnamon, and men in suits walking along the sidewalk on their way to the courthouse or an office, women in dresses heading who knew where, but looking serious about it. Pam could have been in a magazine ad from her childhood library, a smiling young woman drinking coffee, right in the midst of life.

Sometimes, when Bob was studying or playing basketball with Jim at the old high school parking lot, Pam climbed the hill that rose on the edge of the small city, and she would look down over the spires of the cathedral, the river that was lined with the brick mills, the bridge that spanned its foaming water, and sometimes when she climbed back down she would wander into the shops on Gratham Street. Peck's had closed by then, but there were two other department stores in town, and Pam felt a quiet hush of excitement when she strolled through them, touching the dresses, pushing the hangers apart on their metal racks. She'd squirt herself with perfume at the makeup counters, and when Barbara commented, "You smell all Frenchie," Pam said, "Oh, Barbara, I just took a walk through the department store!"

"I guess you did."

The alliance with Barbara was an easy one. Pam understood she had the advantage Susan could not have, which was to share no blood with this woman, and this allowed Pam to go places Susan did not, like the Blue Goose, where a glass of beer was thirty cents and the jukebox played so loud the tables vibrated with the deep strains of Wally Packer and his band singing, *Take this burden from me, the burden of my love . . .* Pam swaying next to Bob, her hand on his knee.

To celebrate the end of finals, or a birthday, or Pam and Bob making the dean's list, they would—all of them—go to Antonio's, the spaghetti cafeteria off Annett Avenue that presented huge platefuls of spaghetti, the order taken by the man who ran the place, who went by the name of Tiny and was obese. When he died after gastric bypass surgery Pam felt terrible, they all did.

During summer Barbara let Pam live in the house. Pam had a job waitressing while Bob worked in the paper factory and Susan worked in the hospital as an assistant in the business office. Pam and Susan shared the room that Jim and Bob had shared growing up, and Bob took Susan's room, Jim sleeping on the couch whenever he came home. "It's nice to have the house full," Barbara said, and for Pam, who had no siblings, those weeks and weekends and summertimes in the Burgess home became something she later understood as having an inexpressibly deep importance and perhaps, too, undermining her marriage to Bob in the years to come. Because she could never stop feeling that Bob was her brother. She had taken his past—his terrible secret, which was never mentioned by anyone else—and benefited from the fact that Bob was their mother's favorite, and as she was the girl he chose to love, Barbara loved her as well. Pam wondered if Barbara, to save herself from the rage she would have felt at Bob after the accident that left her a widow, had decided instead to love Bob the best. In any event, Bob and his past and his present became Pam's past and present, and she loved all that surrounded him, even his sister, who still could not seem to abide Bob, but was friendly enough to Pam.

The Burgesses—the Burgess boys, especially—had their annual town rituals, and Pam went with them to Moxie Day parades with the motley crowd of people that wore bright orange to celebrate the drink that made its identity Maine—St. Joseph's Church had on its billboard: Jesus is our savior, Moxie is our flavor—a drink so bitter that Pam could not stand it, no Burgess could stand it except for Barbara; they would clap at the little floats that went by, the car carrying the local girl crowned "Miss Moxie." These girls more often than not seemed to show up years later in the paper having come to some bad end, either beaten by a husband or robbed by a drug addict, or arrested for some petty crime. But on the day they rode through the streets of Shirley Falls, waving while their ribbon sashes rippled in the breeze, they were applauded by the Burgess boys, even Jim took it seriously, clapping, and Susan would shrug her shoulders, because her mother had long ago not allowed her to compete for such a title.

In July there was the Franco-American Festival, Bob's favorite, and so Pam's too: four nights of concerts in the park and everyone dancing and old mémés and their factory-worn husbands shimmying to the loud music of the C'est Si Bon band. Barbara never joined them, she had little to do with the French Canadians who worked in the mills where her husband had been a foreman, and she had no interest, either, in music or dancing or revelry. But the Burgess kids went, and Jim was drawn to the talk of labor strikes and unions organizing, and the nights of the festival he walked around speaking to many people; Pam could picture him still, listening with his head bent, an arm briefly clapping a shoulder in greeting, already showing signs of the politician he said he later wanted to be.

The color Pam had chosen for her toenails was wrong. She could see that now, gazing down at them. It was autumn; why had she chosen something melon-colored? The Korean woman looked up at her, the tiny brush held above a toe. "It's fine," Pam said. "Thank you."

Barbara Burgess had been dead twenty years, Pam realized, watching her toes become a ghastly ("Frenchie") color. She had not lived to see Jim famous, to see Bob divorced and childless, to see Susan divorced and her son so nutty. Or to see Pam sitting and getting her toenails painted orange in a city she had visited only once, when Jim worked for the Manhattan DA. How Barbara hated New York! Pam's lips moved, remembering; she and Bobby had come to live here by then, and poor Barbara could barely leave their apartment. Pam had entertained her by making fun of Helen, who was recently married to Jim and was doing her best to please her new mother-in-law, offering to take her to the Metropolitan Museum, or to a matinee on Broadway, or to a special café in the Village. "What does he *see* in her?" Barbara had asked, lying on the bed staring up at the ceiling fan.

"Normalcy." Pam lay next to her, staring up as well.

"She's normal?"

"Connecticut normal, I think."

"Wearing white loafers is Connecticut normal?"

"Her loafers are beige."

The next year Jim moved with Helen to Maine, and Barbara had to get used to her; they lived an hour away, in Portland, so it was not so bad. Jim was an assistant attorney general in charge of the criminal division and right away had a reputation for toughness and decency and always handled the press well. To family, he was open about his intentions of entering politics. He would run for the State Legislature, become the attorney general, eventually win the governorship. Everyone thought he could do it.

Three years into this, Barbara became sick. Illness made her tender-hearted and she told Susan, "You've always been a good kid. All you kids were good." Susan wept silently for weeks. Jim entered and left the hospital room without looking up. Bob was stunned, and his face often held the expression of a very young child. Remembering this, Pam had to wipe her nose. The strangest part of it was that a month after Barbara's death, Jim and Helen and their new baby moved to a fancy house in West Hartford. Jim told Bob he never wanted to see Maine again.

"Oh, thank you," Pam said. The Korean woman was holding forth a tissue, her face expectant. "Thank you so much." The woman nodded quickly, then wrapped a strip of cotton around Pam's toes.

———•———

The tree-lined streets of Park Slope had enough leaves swooping along their sidewalks that little children played in the rustling piles, holding up armfuls and letting them fly off in the wind while their patient mothers looked on. But Helen Burgess found herself irritated by people who stopped, or moved in such a rambling way that her own walking rhythm was disturbed. She found herself sighing in long lines at the bank, saying to the person in front of her, "Honestly, why don't they have more people working the windows?" She stood in the express checkout lane at the grocery store counting the number of items of the customer before her, and had to really stop herself from saying, "You have fourteen items there, and the sign says ten." Helen did not like to be this way, it was not who she thought of herself as being, and she traced it back in her mind and realized this: The day after they had returned from St. Kitts, Helen was alone, unpacking, when she suddenly flung a black ballet flat across the bedroom. "Damn you!" she said. She picked up a white linen blouse and could have ripped it in half. Then she sat on the bed and wept because she did not want to be a person who threw shoes or swore at people even if they weren't around. Helen found anger unbecoming, and had taught her children to never hold a grudge and also not to let the sun go down on a disagreement. That Jim was often angry was mostly lost on Helen, partly because his anger was seldom directed at her and because it was her job to calm him down, and she did that job well. But his anger in the hotel room had distressed her. It was Susan she was swearing at as she unpacked, she realized, and the batty son, Zach. And Bobby as well. They had robbed her of a vacation. They had robbed her of a time of intimacy with her husband. That moment of finding her husband so *unappealing* had not faded as it should have, and this unsettled Helen, at the same time causing her to worry—to believe—he found her unappealing as well. Both aspects made her feel terrible. Old, she felt. And snappish. Which was unfair because that's not who she was. Helen, in her heart, knew a happy marriage had a happy sex life (it was like having a special secret, just the two of them), and while she never would have discussed such a thing, what she'd read about the cleaning woman finding nipple clamps and other things had wiggled its way into her worries. She and Jim had never needed anything except each other. This is what Helen thought. But how did she know what other people did? Years ago, in West Hartford, there had been a man who took his little girls to the same nursery school Helen's girls went to, and the man would sometimes look at her with a grim severity. She never spoke to him. At the time she felt he saw in her what she felt existed in her, which was an everglade of brutish sexuality. The everglade was far away, and being Helen she never went near it. It came to her now, at times, the realization that it was too late in her life for any of that to be discovered. And all of it was foolishness, because she would not trade her life for any other. But it did bother her—it really did—how in St. Kitts, Jim had become withdrawn, playing golf for hours, going to the gym. And now here she sat, back home on the edge of the empty nest that nobody except her seemed to worry about.

The surprising thing about this feeling was that it didn't go away. As the days passed, and she mailed the gifts to her kids—a T-shirt and cap to her son in Arizona with a warning to please wear the cap, he was not used to such sun, a sweater to Emily in Chicago, a pair of earrings to Margot in Michigan—as she paid the bills that had piled up, sorted out the winter clothes that had been in storage, her anger at the Burgesses would flower again. You took something from me, she would think. You did.

"That's ridiculous," she said one night to Jim. He had just told her that he might be asked to speak at the tolerance rally in Maine. "What in the world good would that do?"

"What do you mean, what good would it do? The question is whether I *want* to, but if I did, obviously the presumption is that it would do good." Jim ate his grapefruit without putting his napkin in his lap, and Helen saw that his feelings were hurt.

"Thank you, Ana," she said as the lamb chops were placed on the table. "We're all set now. Would you dim the light on your way out?" Short, sweet-faced Ana nodded once, touched the light panel, and left the room. Helen said, "This is the first I've heard of this crazy idea. Who hatched it up, and why didn't you tell me?"

"I just found out today. I don't know who hatched it up. The idea just appeared."

"Ideas don't just appear."

"Yeah, they do. Charlie says my name comes up a lot in Shirley Falls—in a good way—and the people pulling this rally together thought it might help everyone feel cozy if I showed up and—without mentioning Zach, of course—said how proud I am of Shirley Falls."

"You hate Shirley Falls."

Jim said pleasantly, "You hate Shirley Falls." When Helen didn't respond to this, Jim added, "My nephew is in trouble."

"He got himself in trouble."

Jim picked up a lamb chop with both hands as though it was a cob of corn; he looked at her while eating. She glanced away and saw his reflection in the windowpane; it was dark by dinnertime now.

"Well, I'm sorry," Helen continued. "But he did. You and Bob act like there's a government conspiracy against him, and what I don't understand is why he's not expected to be held accountable."

Jim put his lamb chop down and said again, "He's my nephew."

"Does that mean you're going?"

"Let's talk about it later."

"Let's talk about it now."

"Look, Helen." Jim wiped at his mouth with the napkin. "The AG's office is thinking about filing a civil rights violation against Zach."

"I know that, Jim. Do you think I'm deaf? Do you think I don't listen to you? Do you think I don't listen to Bob? It seems it's all that's talked about these days. Every night the phone rings: Help! The change in bail conditions was denied. Help! The motion for a gag order was denied. All procedural, no worries, yes, Zach will have to appear, get him a sports coat, blah, blah, *blah*."

"Hellie." Jim put a hand over hers for a moment. "I agree with you, sweetheart. I do. Zach should be held accountable. But he's also a nineteen-year-old kid who apparently has few if any friends and cries at night. And has a very tense mother. So if there's anything I can do to help this thing die down and go away—"

"Dorothy says you have a guilty conscience."

"Dorothy." Jim picked up his second lamb chop and ate it noisily. Helen, who long ago recognized this as a sign of Jim's poor upbringing (and detested it), had also learned that Jim was more apt to eat noisily when he was tense. Jim said, "Dorothy is a very skinny, very rich, and very unhappy woman."

"She is," Helen acknowledged. Adding, "Don't you think there's a big difference between feeling guilty and feeling responsible?"

"Yes."

"You're just saying that. You don't have any interest in whether there's a difference."

"My interest is in seeing you happy," Jim said. "I think my idiot sister and ridiculous brother managed to screw up our nice vacation. I wish it hadn't happened. But the reason—if they do go ahead and ask me—that I would go, if I *do* go, is because from what Charlie understands it's an assistant AG, Diane something, in charge of the civil rights division who wants to pursue this. But moron Dick Hartley would have to back her, being her boss, and of course he'll be speaking at the rally too. So it gives me a chance to schmooze with him, reminisce about the old days—who knows? If everything's all peaceful and happy he may call Princess Diana into his office Monday morning and say, Drop it. And if that happens, there's a better chance the U.S. attorney will say, Yeah, fuck it. Leave it alone as a misdemeanor, goodbye."

"Why don't we go to the movies this weekend?" Helen asked.

"We can do that," Jim said.

So it seemed to begin: the business of Helen hating the sound of her own voice, its undercurrent of unpleasantness, and trying to get back to what she thought of as herself. Each time, like tonight, she hoped it was merely one incident, related to nothing else.

4

The day before Zach was to make a court appearance—where Charlie would ask again for a change in bail conditions and also a new gag order—Susan sat in her car on the edge of the mall's large parking lot. It was her lunch break, and the tuna sandwich she had made that morning sat on her lap in a baggie. Her cell phone was on the seat next to her, and she glanced at it many times before picking it up and poking at the numbers. "What is this regarding?" asked a woman's voice that Susan didn't recognize.

Susan opened the car window a crack. "Can I just speak to him please? I've known him forever."

"I'll need to pull your chart, Mrs. Olson. When were you last in?"

"Oh, for God's sakes," Susan said. "I don't want an appointment."

"Is this an emergency?" asked the receptionist.

"I need something to help me sleep," Susan said, squeezing her eyes shut and pressing her fist to her forehead, because in her mind she might as well have just taken a bullhorn and announced to the entire community that Zachary Olson's mother was asking for sleeping pills.

Maybe she'd been hooked all along, people would say. No wonder she didn't know what her son was doing.

"You can discuss that with the doctor when you see him. How's next Thursday morning?"

Susan called Bob in his office, and Bob said, "Ah, Susie, don't you hate that? Call a different doctor, say you're dying with a sore throat and fever and they'll see you right away. Make the fever high. Adults aren't supposed to have high fevers. Then when you see the doctor, tell him why you came."

"Just *lie?*"

"Be pragmatic, is what I'm suggesting."

By the end of the day Susan had a bottle of tranquilizers and a bottle of sleeping pills. She had driven two towns over so no one in the pharmacy would know she was using these things. But when it came time to take one, the black of the sleep she imagined sinking into felt like death and so she called Bobby again.

He listened. "Take them now, while we're on the phone," he suggested. "I'll keep talking until you get sleepy. Where's Zach?"

"In his room. We already said good night."

"Okay. You'll be all right. Zach doesn't have to say anything tomorrow except whatever Charlie tells him to say, it should take five minutes and then you'll be out of there. Now you relax, and I'll talk you to sleep. So I spoke to Jim and guess what? He's coming up with me for the tolerance rally. He's going to speak. He'll do his politician's come-to-Jesus thing—I'm joking, he's not going to say a word about Jesus, of course, God, can you imagine? He'll speak after Dick Hartley, who will bore people into sleep, you could buy a bottle of that, Susie, and Jim will say, Dickie, you're amazing, make the guy feel good, then Jim will try not to upstage him, which of course he can't help but do. Jim will speak better than the governor, did you know the governor was coming? Jim will speak better than anyone. And we'll make sure Zach is safe and then we'll drive the car back to New York. Did you take the pill? Drink half a glass of water, you want to get it all the way down. Yuh, at least half a glass.

"Turns out," Bob continued, "that City Hall in Shirley Falls—hey, that almost rhymes, City Hall in Shirley Fallzzzz—is sick of all the publicity this thing's getting. According to Jim, according to Charlie, inner feuds are developing. Between the police, the city council, and the clergy— Anyways, you're not to worry about it, Suse, that's my point. Just like you said, it gives every liberal a cause—which is good for them, especially up there in Maine. Like doing calisthenics, breathe in, breathe out, we are the righteous, the mighty, mighty righteous. How're you feeling, Susie, sleepy at all?"

"No."

"Okay. Don't worry. Want me to sing to you?"

"No. Are you drunk?"

"Not that I'm aware of. Want me to tell you a story?"

And so Susan fell asleep listening to the time Jim got fired as a crossing guard in fourth grade for throwing a snowball and the other crossing guards went on strike and the principal had to give Jim his job back and it was the first time Jim understood the strength of labor unions—

5

Helen, raking leaves in their back garden a few days later, said, "She acts like a sleeping pill is heroin. It's insane."

"It's Puritan." Bob shifted his weight on the wrought-iron bench.

"It's insane." Helen stopped raking and tossed the rake onto the pile of leaves.

Bob glanced at Jim, who stood by the back door, his arms crossed. Beside Jim was the large barbecue grill, now zipped inside its black tarp covering. The grill, which had been new that summer and seemed to Bob to be the size of a small boat, was protected also by the wooden deck above it, whose steps down to the garden were covered with scattered leaves. A pair of hedge clippers leaned against the bottom step. Where Bob sat, the brick walkway and the circular area around the bird-bath had the trim look of someone with a new haircut, but the rest of the garden still had leaves from the plum tree covering the ground, and there was the pile where the rake lay now, its prongs upward. Children's voices could be heard in another back garden; there was the sound of a ball bouncing. It was Saturday afternoon.

"Well, it seems insane," Bob finally said. "But it comes from our Puritan ancestors. Who were kind of insane, when you think of it. Too insane to stay in England. Puritans have a lot of shame," he added. "You have to understand."

"Not my ancestors," Helen said, surveying the pile of leaves. "I'm one quarter German, two quarters English—not Puritan—and one quarter Austrian."

Bob nodded. "Mozart, Beethoven, that's good stuff, Helen. But we Puritans didn't believe in music or theater because it 'excites the senses.' Remember, Jimmy? Aunt Alma used to tell us that stuff? Nana too. They loved our history. I don't love our history. Let's say I am profoundly uninterested in our history."

"When are you going back to your graduate dorm?" Jim put his hand on the knob of the back door.

"Jim, stop it," said Helen.

"As soon as I finish this whiskey your wife was hospitable enough to pour for me." Bob emptied the glass in one swallow. It stung throughout his throat, his chest. "I believe we were celebrating Zach living through his court appearance and Charlie's success in getting better bail conditions and the gag order."

"You sang Susan to sleep?" Jim crossed his arms again. "You two hate each other."

"I talked Susan to sleep. And I know. That's what made it extra nice. Very nice when good things happen to bad people. Or good people. Any people." He stood, hitched his coat on over his shoulders.

"Thanks for stopping by," Jim said evenly. "Come by my office next week and we'll plan the rally deal then. They keep postponing it, but it looks like it will happen soon. Plus, jerkoid, I need my car back."

Bob said, "I've apologized a thousand times. And I've gathered information to help with your fancy speech."

"I'm not going," Helen said. "Jim wants me to, but I'm not."

Bob looked back at her. Helen was taking off her gardening gloves. She tossed them onto the pile of leaves and brushed back her hair, which had a leaf caught in it. Her quilted jacket was unbuttoned, and when she put her hands on her hips the jacket opened on both sides of her.

"It's not a situation she feels requires her presence," Jim said.

"That's right," Helen said, moving past them to go inside. "I thought I'd leave this one to the Burgess boys."

6

The police chief, Gerry O'Hare, was also taking a sleeping pill. He opened the bottle by his bed, dropped one into his mouth, and swallowed. His sleeplessness was not from anxiety, but from a sense of being energized. He'd had a meeting at City Hall that afternoon with the mayor, the girl from the AG's office, city council members, clergy, and the imam, whom he'd been sure to invite since the Somalis were pissed off they didn't get asked to the press conference right after the incident. Gerry was reporting this to his wife, who was already in bed. He'd told those people gathered that he knew his job, and that job was to keep the community safe. He'd said (stealing some thunder, he suspected, nodding to his wife meaningfully, from some of the flaming liberals there, like Rick Huddleston and Diane Dodge) that studies showed racial violence went down when the community responded against it. Incidents left unacknowledged only gave permission to those citizens intent on committing racial crimes. His patrolmen, he added, had been given photographs of Zachary Olson so they could spot him if he showed up within two miles of the mosque on Gratham Street.

The meeting went on for almost three hours, and plenty of tension zigzagged through that room. Rick Huddleston (who only had the job of heading the Office of Racial Anti-Defamation by being rich enough to create the office) had to gas on, of course, about every incident unreported—"I'm not interested in unreported incidents, I said 'unacknowledged incidents,'" Gerry had interrupted—and Rick continued, unstoppable, unflappable, about the vandalizing of Somali store windows, tires slashed in their neighborhoods, racial slurs hurled at women across a parking lot, school reports of taunting as well as physical assaults by kids. "I'm not going to stand here and pretend, as some of you may be pretending," Gerry said, "that there aren't real divides in the Somali community itself. We know some of these slurs have been instigated by ethnic Somalis against the Bantu Somalis, or against those of a different clan." And then Rick Huddleston exploded. Yale-educated prissy Rick Huddleston, who, Gerry told his wife, brought such ferocity to the prosecution of bias-related crimes because he, in spite of the very pretty Mrs. Huddleston and three pretty prissy little daughters, was probably a closet queer. Rick exploded and accused Gerry of not providing ample protection to the Somali community in the past, which was why, Rick said, pink-faced, putting down his water glass so hard that water slopped over onto the conference table, *why* this incident had garnered so much press, locally, nationally, and even (as though Gerry was an imbecile who might not read a paper or watch the news) internationally.

A councilman rolled his eyes. Diane Dodge, plain as custard, nodded at what had just been said. And then Rick couldn't help himself, he whipped out his handkerchief and carefully mopped up the water so the conference table could retain its luster, even though (Gerry winked at his wife) that conference table was as old as his grandfather's casket and made of pressed plywood. Dan Bergeron, councilman, spat forth the idea that all the publicity was the fault of the Washington-based Council on Islam Affairs, who had to grab their fifteen minutes of fame wherever they could find it.

Throughout, the imam sat passively.

"Aren't you scared about violence during the demonstration? What about the white supremacy stuff?" Gerry's wife asked from the bed, where she was smoothing a pungent-smelling cream over her bunions.

"That's a rumor. No one's coming all the way from Montana to squawk about our town. If they wanted to do that they'd have headed to Minneapolis, where there's forty thousand of these guys." Gerry was unbuttoning his shirt, rank with body odor. He walked into the bathroom, squashed the shirt into the hamper.

"Is it true the Burgess boys are coming up?" his wife called.

Back in the bedroom, pulling on his pajamas, Gerry said, "Yep. Jimmy's going to speak. Be all right, I think, as long as he's not too full of himself."

"Well, I'll be curious to see," his wife sighed, picking up her book, settling herself back against the pillows.

7

Jim's office was in a building in Midtown Manhattan. Security required Bob to hand over his driver's license at the desk in the lobby, where he stood patiently while a temporary ID was made for him. It took a little time, because Jim's office had to be notified, and permission had to be given, in order for Bob to proceed. Bob handed the ID to a uniformed man standing by a row of turnstiles, who held it in front of a grid, and blinking red lights turned green. On the fourteenth floor, large panes of a glass wall opened when a young man, unsmiling, pushed a button inside. A young woman arrived to escort Bob to Jim's office.

"Kind of takes the fun out of dropping by," Bob said after the young woman had backed away and left him standing in front of two photographs of Helen and the children.

"That's the point, bozo." Jim pushed back a paper he was reading, took his glasses off. "How was the dentist? You look a little drooly."

"I asked for more novocaine. I think because we weren't allowed any when we were kids." Bob sat on the edge of the chair by Jim's desk, his knapsack bulging behind him. "Today the drilling sent shivers right through me, and I thought, Wait, I'm a grown-up. So I asked for more."

"Amazing." Jim straightened his tie, stretched his neck.

"It was amazing. If you're me."

"And I'm not, praise God. Okay, so it's two weeks away, let's get it planned. I'm busy."

"Susan wants to know if we're staying with her."

Jim opened his desk drawer. "I don't sleep on couches. I especially don't sleep on dog-hairy couches in a house where the thermostat is set at forty-two and a batty old lady lives upstairs wearing a nightgown all day. But you enjoy yourself. You and Susan are tight these days. I'm sure she has plenty of booze in the house. You'll be very comfortable." Jim closed his desk drawer, reached for the sheet of paper he'd been reading. He put his glasses back on.

Bob, looking around the room, said, "I know you know that sarcasm is the weapon of weakness."

Jim kept his eyes on the paper, then moved them to take in his brother. He said slowly, "Bobby Burgess." There was a faint smile to his mouth. "King of the profound."

Bob slid his knapsack off his back. "Are you worse than usual, or have you been a prick this bad all along? Seriously." He stood up and went to sit on the skinny low couch that ran along the wall of Jim's office. "You are worse. Has Helen noticed? I think she's noticed."

Jim put the pen down. He held the arms of his chair and leaned back, looking out the window. His face lost its hardness. He said, "Helen." He sighed and sat forward, put his elbows on his desk. "Helen thinks I'm crazy to go up there. To involve myself in this. But I've thought a lot about it, and it does make a certain sense." Jim looked at Bob and said—suddenly earnest—"Look, I'm still known up there, sort of. I'm still liked up there, sort of. I haven't had anything to do with the state for a long time. So now I come back. And I come back to say, Hey, you guys, here's a state whose population is getting older and poorer and industry is leaving, has left, for the most part. I'll say the vibrancy of society depends on newness, and what a fantastic job Shirley Falls has done in welcoming this newness, let's keep on with it.

"The truth is, Bob, they *need* those immigrants. Maine's been losing its young people—you and I are a perfect case in point. And the truth also is: That's sad. Even before Zach got into this mess, I've been reading the *Shirley Falls Journal* online every day, and Maine is just dying. It's on life support. It's terrible. Kids leave to go to college and never come back, and why should they? There's nothing there for them. The ones who stay, there's nothing there for them either. Who's going to take care of all those old white people? Where are new businesses going to come from?"

Bob sat back on the thin couch. He could hear a fire truck's siren, and the faint honking of horns on the street far below. He said, "I had no idea you still liked Maine."

"I hate Maine."

The fire truck's siren loudened, eventually faded. Bob looked around the office: a plant with skinny fronds that sprayed up like a small foun-tain, the oil painting with wiggles of blue and green paint. He looked back at Jim. "You've been reading the *Shirley Falls Journal* every day? For how long?"

"A long time. I find the obituaries moving."

"Jesus, you're serious."

"Perfectly. And to answer your question, I'm staying at the new hotel on the river up there. If you're not staying with Susan, get your own room. I'm not sharing space with an insomniac."

Bob gazed out at the terrace of a building nearby where trees grew, their leaves still golden, but some branches bare. "We should bring Zach down here," Bob said. "I wonder if he's ever seen trees growing on tops of buildings."

"Do whatever you want with the kid. I wasn't aware you'd even man-aged to have a conversation with him."

"Wait till you see him," Bob said. "He's just, like, I don't know—missing in action or something."

"I look forward to it," Jim said. "And that's sarcasm."

Bob nodded, folded his hands patiently on his lap.

Jim leaned back in his chair and said, "The biggest Somali community in this country is in Minneapolis. Apparently at the community college there's a mess in the bathrooms from Muslims washing their feet before prayer. So they're putting in new foot-washing sinks. Some of the blond folks are fit to be tied, of course, but on the whole, really, Minnesotans are kind of great. Which is why, I imagine, so many Somalis are there. I find it pretty interesting."

"It is interesting," Bob agreed. "I've talked to Margaret Estaver on the phone a few times. She's into it."

"You've talked to her?" Jim seemed surprised.

"I like her. She's comforting, somehow. Anyways, it sounds—"

"Would you stop saying 'anyways'? You get"—Jim sat forward and waved his hand—"I don't know, diminished by it. It makes you sound like a hick."

Bob felt his cheeks grow warm. He waited a long time before he spoke. "Anyway," he said quietly, looking at his hands, "it sounds like the biggest problem up there is that most of the Somalis in town really don't speak English. The few that do end up having to be the liaison between the city and their own population, and they aren't necessarily the elders, who are the guys in their culture who make decisions. Also, there's a big difference between the ethnic Somalis—who are big-time into which clan you come from—and the Bantus, who've just started showing up in Shirley Falls, and they used to be looked down on back in Somalia by the others. So it's not like they're all cozy friends up there."

"Listen to you," Jim said.

"And I agree," Bob continued, "Maine does need them. But these immigrants—secondary migrants, by the way, in this case, they've come from their first place of arrival, so they've lost their initial federal support—they don't want jobs that include food because they have to steer clear of alcohol and pork and anything with gelatin in it. Probably tobacco too. The woman who sold me cigarettes and a bottle of wine near Susan's house was Somali, I figured out later—no headscarf, though—and she pushed forward the bag for me to pack them myself, like she'd been asked to touch turds. They can't get most jobs until they learn some English. A lot of them are illiterate—hey, get this: They never even had a written language of their own until 1972, can you believe it? And if they spent years in the refugee camps, which they have, it was hard, if not impossible, to get any schooling there."

"Will you stop?" Jim said. "You're killing me. Sitting there delivering fragmented facts. And it's not like there were jobs in Shirley Falls to begin with. Usually a migrant population moves because of jobs."

"I think they moved there to be safe. I'm just telling you this for your speech. Terrible, terrible stuff they've been through, whether it kills you or not, you should know it, if you're going to speak. Terrible stuff in So-malia, and then waiting around in the camps. So, you know, just keep that in mind."

"What else?"

"You just asked me to stop."

"Well, now I'm asking you not to stop." Jim stared at the ceiling for a moment, as though needing to control some vast irritation. "But I hope your sources are accurate. I don't give speeches anymore, and I don't relish the idea of falling on my face. Maybe you don't know that about me, but I'm not a fall-on-your-face kind of guy."

Bob nodded. "Then you should know a lot of Shirley Falls citizens think the Somalis are given car vouchers—not true. That they're just sucking up welfare—partly true. And for Somalis it's rude to look some-one right in the eye, so people—and our sister's a perfect example—think they're arrogant, or shifty. They barter, and people don't like that. The locals want them to appear grateful, and they don't especially appear grateful. There've been incidents in the schools, of course. Gym classes have been a problem. The girls don't want to undress and aren't sup-posed to wear gym shorts anyway. They're working it out, you know. Committees on this and that."

Jim held up both hands. "Do me a favor and put this in writing. Email me bullets. I'll think of something 'healing' to say. Now go away. I have work to do."

"What kind of work?" Bob looked around before finally standing up.

"You said you were getting sick of this job. When did you say that? Last year? I can't remember." He hoisted his knapsack onto his shoulder. "But you said you haven't seen the inside of a courtroom in four years. All these big cases get settled. I can't think that's good for you, Jimmy."

Jim looked carefully at the sheet of paper he'd been holding. "What in the *world* makes you think you know squat about anything?"

Bob was walking toward the door, and he turned back. "I'm just saying what you told me at some point. I think you have courtroom talent. I think you should be using it. But what do I know—"

"Nothing." Jim dropped his pen onto his desk. "You know nothing about living in a house for grown-ups, instead of a graduate dorm. You know nothing about tuition for private schools, starting at kindergarten and going through college at *least*. Nothing about housekeepers or gardeners, nothing about keeping a wife in— Just nothing, you cretinized bozo. Look, I'm working. Now go."

Bob hesitated, then held up a hand. "Going," he said. "Watch me go."

8

In Shirley Falls the days were short now, the sun never climbing very high in the sky, and when a blanket of clouds sat over the small city it seemed as though twilight began as soon as people finished their lunch, and when darkness came it was a full darkness. Most of the people who lived there had lived there all their lives, and they were used to the darkness this time of year, but that did not mean they liked it. It was spoken of when neighbors met in grocery stores, or on the steps of the post office, often with an added phrase of what was felt about the holiday season to come; some liked the holidays, many did not. Fuel prices were high, and holidays cost money.

About the Somalis, a few townspeople did not speak at all: They were to be borne as one bore bad winters or the price of gasoline or a child who turned out badly. Others were not so silent. One woman wrote a letter that the newspaper published. "I finally figured out what it is I don't like about the Somalis being here. Their language is different and I don't like the sound of it. I love the Maine accent. People think of us as saying 'You cahn't get they-ah from he-yah.' That will disappear. It scares me to think how this changes our state." (Jim forwarded this in an email to Bob with the subject line Racist White Bitch Clings to Native Language.) Others said to each other how nice it was to see the colorful robes of the Somali women in a town as drab and depressed as Shirley Falls had become; there was a little girl in the library the other day, wearing a burkha, cute as the dickens. Honestly.

But among the leaders of the city was a feeling much grander, and it was the feeling of panic. For the last few years there had been the constant struggle to cope—Somali women showing up almost daily at City Hall, unable to speak English, unable to fill out forms for housing, public assistance, or even to tell the birth dates of their children ("born in the season of the sun," a hard-to-find translator would say, and so one after another of these children had birthdays registered as January 1, the year guessed at). Adult English classes were arranged and at first poorly attended, the women sitting listlessly while their children played in the next room; social workers had struggled to learn the words of Somali (*subax wanaagsan:* "Good morning"; *iska waran:* "How are you?"). There was the scramble to learn who these people were and what they needed, and now, after all that, came the sense of a huge wave spilling over the riverbanks as news reports of the pig's head incident spread across the state, the country, parts of the world. Suddenly Shirley Falls was being portrayed as a place of intolerance, fear, meanspirited. And that was not true.

The clergy, who had been only partly helpful—and this included Margaret Estaver and Rabbi Goldman, three Catholic priests and a Congregational minister—realized a crisis had now really arrived. They rose to it. They tried. City council members, the city manager, the mayor, and of course the police chief, Gerry O'Hare, all of whom had been working in their various ways, understood also that a serious situation was suddenly at hand. Meetings took place at all hours as the Together for Tolerance rally was planned. There was tension—lots of it. The mayor promised that in two weeks, on a Saturday at the start of November, peace-loving people would fill Roosevelt Park.

And then—what was feared, happened. A white supremacy group

called the World Church of the People requested a permit to gather on the same day. Susan was told this by Charlie Tibbetts, and she whispered into the phone, "Dear God, they'll murder him." No one was going to murder Zachary, Charlie said (sounding tired), and certainly not the World Church of the People, who thought Zach was a hero. "That's worse," Susan cried. Then, "Why does the city have to give them a permit, why can't they say no?"

Because this was America. People had the right to convene, and it was better for Shirley Falls to give them a permit, more control could be exerted that way. The permit gave them permission to gather in the Civic Center, which was on the outskirts of town and not near the park. Charlie told Susan this no longer had much to do with Zach. Zach had been charged with a misdemeanor, period, the rest of it would quiet down.

It didn't quiet down. Day after day the newspapers printed editorials from the outraged liberals of Maine, and from conservatives too, who wrote measured suggestions that the Somalis were expected, like every other person lucky enough to live here, to get jobs and training and pay their taxes. And then a letter would be published saying that all working Somalis *were* paying their taxes, and our country was based on the freedom to practice whatever religion was chosen, and so on and so forth. But the sense of purpose was heightened by the knowledge that the rally would be competing with the white supremacy group; a full-court press was on.

A team of civil rights units was sent into the schools. The purpose of the rally was explained. The Constitution of the United States was explained. Attempts were made to explain the history of the Somali troubles. Congregations in all the local churches were asked to help out. The two fundamentalist churches did not respond, but the rest did; there was a growing sense of umbrage: No one told Maine people how to live or what to think; the idea that Shirley Falls was somehow a place to recruit bigots was reprehensible. Colleges and universities got involved, civic organizations, senior citizen groups, all sorts of people seemed to be saying the Somalis could damn well live there just like other groups had before them, the French from Canada, the Irish before that.

What was being written on the Internet was another matter altogether, and Gerry O'Hare perspired as he faced his computer screen, scrolling through various websites. He had never in his life met anyone who said the Holocaust was a beautiful time in history, that ovens should be installed in Shirley Falls and the Somalis escorted in. It made him feel that he knew nothing about the world after all. He had been too young to go to Vietnam, though of course he knew men who had gone and he saw the results; some were right now living down there near the Somalis by the river, unable to keep a job, they were so nerved up. But it's not as though Gerry O'Hare hadn't seen things: children who had spent nights locked inside a doghouse, or had scars from parents who'd held their little hands to a stove, women whose hair had been ripped out by furious spouses, a gay homeless man lit on fire and thrown into the river a few years ago. These things had been hard to see. But it was new, what he saw on the Internet, the cool statements of superiority so deeply believed in, that anyone not white should, as one person had written, "be exterminated as easily as we do rats." Gerry didn't share with his wife the things he read. "Cowards," he did say. "You can be anonymous, that's what's the trouble with the Internet." Each night now Gerry took a sleeping pill. He understood: It was his watch this was happening on. He owed his citizens safety and this meant foreseeing the unforeseeable. The state police were brought in, other police departments in the state were tapped for their services, the plastic shields and sticks came out of storage, training in crowd control went on.

And Zachary Olson came through the back door of his home one morning and began to sob. "Mommy," he cried to Susan, who was getting ready to leave for work. "They fired me! I walked in and they said they fired me, I don't have a job." And he bent and hugged his mother as though he had been given the sentence of death.

"They don't have to tell him why," Jim said when Susan called. "No employer if they know what they're doing ever tells the person why. Bob and I will be there soon."

9

With November came the wind, blowing in spurts of fury, and the air in New York turned chilly but not cold. Helen worked in her back garden, planting her tulip and crocus bulbs. Her irritation with the world had dampened into a cushion of soft melancholy that went with her every-where. Afternoons, she would sweep the front stoop of its leaves, talking to the neighbors who passed by. There was the gay man, precise and pleasant, the tall and stately Asian doctor, the beastly woman who worked for the city and whose hair was too blond, the couple a few doors down expecting their first baby, and of course Deborah-Who-Does and Debra-Who-Doesn't. Helen took time to speak to all of these peo-ple. It steadied her, because this had been the time of day her children would amble home from school, the sound of Larry's key in the grated gate.

Within a year the stately Asian doctor would be dead from a heart attack, the gay man would lose a parent, the expectant couple would have their baby and move to a more affordable neighborhood, but all this hadn't happened yet. The changes that were coming in Helen's own life hadn't happened yet (although she thought they had, Larry leaving her to go to college, thrusting her into the biggest change since her children had been born), and so she swept her front stoop and chatted and went inside and spoke to Ana about going home early, and then the house was hers until Jim came home. She would remember those late afternoons the same way she remembered how, when her children were small, she would linger in the living room for a few moments alone on Christmas Eve, watching the tree with its lights and its presents, feeling so excited and peaceful that tears filled her eyes, and then those Christmases were gone: the children no longer small, Emily perhaps not even coming home this year, going to her boyfriend's family instead—no, it was astonishing to think those Christmases were gone.

But here was her home, with Jim. She walked through it after Ana left, the family room with the original old light fixtures, the mahogany trim gleaming when the afternoon sun slid through the upstairs parlor, the bedroom with the deck through the French doors. The bittersweet that grew along the railing now had orange nutlike berries showing through the curled and cracked encasings, and the vines were brown and lovely where the leaves had fallen off. Later, she would remember how Jim came through the door some evenings that autumn and showed an extra layer of largeheartedness toward her, sometimes throwing his arms around her right out of the blue and saying, "Hellie, you are so good. I love you." It made the ache from her silent home more bearable. It made her feel graceful again. And yet—at times—there seemed a neediness to Jim she felt she'd not noticed before. "Hellie, you'll never leave me, right?" Or: "You'll love me no matter what, right?"

"You silly thing," she'd answer. But there was a visceral recoiling in her when he was like that, and she was privately appalled at herself. A loving wife was loving; that's who she'd always been. He spoke frequently of the Wally Packer trial, repeating to her—as though she hadn't been there—his greatest moments. "Single-handedly I crushed that DA. Folded him up. He never saw it coming." It wasn't the fun kind of reminiscing they had done in the past. But how could she be sure? The emptiness of her big house, as the days grew shorter, disoriented her.

"I need a job," she said at breakfast one morning.

"That's a good idea." Jim did not seem startled by the remark, and this mildly offended Helen.

"Well, it's not that easy," she said.

"How so?"

"Because a hundred years ago when I was—briefly, it's true—a successful accountant, everything wasn't computerized. I'd be lost in that world now."

"You could go back to school," Jim said.

Helen drank her coffee, put it down. She looked around the kitchen. "Let's go walk in the park before you leave for work. We never do that."

Walking, Helen's heart lightened; she took Jim's hand. With her other hand she waved to people from the neighborhood who'd come out early to run their dogs. They all waved back, some calling out a greeting. You have a friendly way, Jim had told her over the years, people are always glad to see you. And this made Helen think of her women friends who used to gather weekly in the kitchen of Victoria Cummings for a glass of wine on Wednesday afternoons: Oh, Helen, you've come! Calling out to her, some clapping their hands at the sight of her. Hey, girls, Helen's here! The Kitchen Cabinet, they called it, two hours of gossip and laughing, and now that poor Victoria was having such a mess in her marriage she'd stopped hosting it, and Helen decided that when she got back to the house she'd telephone each of the women and say that the Kitchen Cabinet would meet at her house instead. Helen was surprised she hadn't thought of this sooner; the world was righted now, women friends cast their own color of sunshine. That funny old lady from exercise class could come too. You lie on the mat, she had said to Helen the first day, and then you pray to God you get up. Over the hill was the wide swath of brown grass and the deep brown of the tree trunks, the glassy surface of the pond they passed. The building tops seen along the edge of the park appeared different from this angle, stately and old. Helen said, "It's like we're in Europe, that's what it looks like. Let's go to Europe this spring. Alone."

Jim nodded absently.

"Are you worried about the weekend?" Helen asked, wifely once more.

"No. It will be fine."

When they returned to their house—Helen having just greeted the too-blond woman walking by with her briefcase—the telephone was ringing. She heard Jim speaking evenly, and then he hung up and yelled, "Shit, shit, shit!" She stood in the living room and waited. "The schmuck lost his job and Susan's surprised. Why *wouldn't* they fire him? Some journalist was probably nosing around and Walmart just had it. Christ, I don't want to go up there."

"You can still say no," Helen said.

"I can't, though. It's the goddamn *love* police."

"So what? You don't live there anymore, Jimmy."

He didn't answer.

Helen walked past him up the stairs. "Well, you do what you think is best." But she felt again the anxiety that something was being taken from her. She called down the stairs, "Just tell me you love me."

"I love you," said Jim.

"Once more with feeling." She peered down over the banister.

He was sitting on the bottom stairs with his head in his hands. "I love you," he said.

10

The Burgess boys rode up the turnpike as twilight arrived. It arrived gently, the sky remaining a soft blue as the trees along either side of the unfolding pavement darkened. Then the sinking sun sent up a spread of lavender and yellow, and the horizon line seemed cracked open to give a peek at the heavens far beyond. Thin clouds became pink and stayed that way, until finally darkness emerged, almost complete. The brothers had spoken little once they pulled out of the airport in the rental car, Jim at the wheel, and for the last many minutes as the sun went down there had been silence between them. Bob was unutterably happy. He had not expected the feeling, which intensified it. He gazed out the window at the black stretches of evergreens, the granite boulders here and there. The landscape he had forgotten—and now remembered. The world was an old friend, and the darkness was like arms around him. When his brother spoke, Bob heard the words. Still he said, casually, "What did you say?"

"I said this is just unbelievably depressing."

Bob waited, then said, "You mean the mess with Zachary?"

"Well, that," said Jim, in a tone of disgust. "Of course. But I meant this . . . place. The bleakness."

Bob stared out the window for some time. He finally said, "You'll cheer up when we get to Susan's. You'll find it very cozy."

Jim looked over at him. "You're joking, right?"

"I keep forgetting," Bob said. "You're the only one in the family al-lowed to be sarcastic. You'll find Susan's house depressing. You'll want to hang yourself before supper is over. Is my guess." To fall so precipitously from this happiness almost gave him vertigo; it affected him physically. In the dark he closed his eyes, and when he opened them Jim was driving with one hand and gazing silently at the black turnpike ahead.

Zach was the one who opened the door. He said in his deep voice, "Uncle Bob, you've come back." His arms made a gesture forward, then returned to his sides. Bob pulled his nephew to him, feeling the boy's skinniness, and also the surprising body warmth of him. "Great to see you, Zachary Olson. May I present the honorable Uncle Jim."

Zach did not move to Jim. He looked at him with his deep brown eyes and said softly, "I've really messed up."

"Who doesn't mess up? You tell me who doesn't mess up," Jim said. "Nice to see you." He clapped the boy on his back.

Zach said, "You don't." He said this earnestly.

"True," said Jim. "Very true. Susan, can you turn the heat up? Just for one hour."

"That's the first thing you have to say?" Susan asked, but there was an almost-jokiness to her voice, and she and Jim hugged lightly by leaning their shoulders forward. To Bob she nodded, and he nodded back.

And then they sat, the four of them in Susan's kitchen, eating maca-roni and cheese. Bob kept telling Susan it was delicious, helping himself to more. Keenly he felt the need for a drink and pictured the bottle of wine he had packed in his duffel bag, which remained in the car. He said, "So, Zach, you're staying with us at the hotel tonight. You'll stay there tomorrow while we're at the demonstration."

Zach looked at his mother, and she nodded. "I've never stayed in a hotel," he said.

"Yes, you have," said Susan. "You just don't remember."

"We've got adjoining rooms," Bob said. "You'll stay in mine and we can watch TV all night if you want. Your Uncle Jim needs his beauty sleep."

"This is good, Susan." Jim pushed back his plate. "Excellent." They were polite, these three siblings who had not eaten together since their mother died. The air was pregnant with it, though, the waiting.

"The weather's supposed to be good tomorrow. I was hoping it would pour," Susan said.

"Me too," Jim said.

"When was I in a hotel?" Zachary asked.

"Sturbridge Village. We took a trip there when you were little, with your cousins." Susan drank from her water glass. "It was fun. You had a good time."

"Let's go," said Bob, who wanted to get to the hotel before the bar closed. He wanted whiskey now, not wine. "Get your coat, kiddo. Maybe a toothbrush."

Fear washed over Zach's face as he stood by the door, and his mother suddenly stood on tiptoe and kissed his cheek.

"We've got him, Suse," said Jim. "He's going to be fine. We'll call as soon as we get to the room."

————•————

They checked into the hotel by the river, where the receptionist seemed not to know who they were, or care. The rooms had two queen-size beds each, and on the walls were different prints of the old brick mills built along the river. Jim, while shrugging from his shoulder his overnight bag, reached for the remote and turned the television on. "Okay, Zachary, let's look for some crap." Jim hung his coat in the closet and lay down on the bed.

Zach sat on the edge of the other bed, his hands in his coat pockets. "My dad has a girlfriend," he said, after a few moments. "She's Swedish."

Bob glanced at Jim. "Oh, yeah?" Jim asked. He was lying with one arm beneath his head. Above him was a print of the mill where their father had been foreman. Jim stared at the television, clicking through channels.

"Have you met her?" asked Bob, sinking into the chair by the phone. He was going to call down and see if they could bring up a couple of whiskeys; that there was no whiskey in the minibar dismayed him.

"How would I meet her?" Zach's voice was deep and sincere. "She's in Sweden."

"Right," Bob said. He picked up the phone.

"I don't think you should do that," Jim said, still gazing at the TV.

"Do what?"

"Call down for booze, which is what I know you're about to do. Why call attention to this room?"

Bob rubbed a hand over his face. "Does your mom know about the girlfriend?" he asked.

Zach shrugged. "I don't know. I'm not going to tell her."

"Nah," said Bob. "Why bother."

"What's this girlfriend do?" Jim asked, holding the remote control as if it were a gearshift next to him on the bed.

"She's a nurse."

Jim switched channels. "That's a nice thing to be, a nurse. Take your coat off, buddy. We're here for the night."

Zach worked his way out of his coat, tossed it onto the floor between the wall and the bed. "She was over there," he said.

"Hang it up," Jim directed, pointing to the closet with the remote. "Over where?"

"Somalia."

"No shit," Bob said. "Really?"

"I'm not making it up." Zach hung up his coat and went back and sat on the bed, looking down at his hands.

"When was she in Somalia?" Jim propped himself on his elbow to look at Zach.

"A long time ago. When they were starving."

"They're still starving. What was she doing there?"

Zach shrugged. "I don't know. She worked in a hospital when the Paki . . . the Portuguese . . . Who was it, the country with the P?"

"Pakistan."

"Yeah. Well, she was there when those guys went over to help guard the food and stuff, and the Salamis killed a bunch of guys."

Jim sat up. "For God's sake, you of *all* people shouldn't be saying 'Salamis.' Can you get that through your head? Give us a little help here. Jesus."

"Stop it, Jim," Bob said. Zach's face had colored and he stared at the fingers he was twisting in his lap. "Zach, listen. The truth about your Uncle Jim is that no one really knows if he's an asshole or not, but he acts like one a lot of the time, to everyone, not just you. Want to go downstairs with me while I find something to drink?"

"Are you *crazy*?" Jim asked. "We went through this. Zach is not leaving this room. And you must have packed some booze, so pull it out and drink it."

"Did she work for a charity?" Bob asked. "Your dad's girlfriend?" He sat on the bed near Zach, gave Zach's shoulders a squeeze. "She must be a nice person. Your mom's a nice person, too."

Zach leaned toward Bob slightly, and Bob kept his arm around his nephew for a moment longer. Zach said, "She had to come home, back to Sweden. All the nurses she worked with did, 'cause when they brought the soldiers to the hospital their nuts had been cut off and their eyes gouged out. And some Salam . . . Somal . . . Somalian women had taken a big knife and cut this one guy to pieces. Dad's girlfriend flipped her shit. All her nurse friends flipped their shit. That's why they went back home."

"Your father told you this?" Jim glanced at Bob.

Zach nodded.

"So you talk to him, then?"

"He emails me." Zach added, "That's practically like talking."

"It is." Bob stood up and jiggled the change in his pockets. "When did he tell you this?"

Zach shrugged. "A while ago. When these guys started moving here. He emailed and said they were kind of crazy."

"Hold on, Zach." Jim switched off the television. He got up and walked to stand in front of Zach. "Your father emailed you and told you to watch out for the Somalis moving here? That they were kind of crazy?"

Zach was looking down at his lap. "Not exactly to watch out—"

"Speak up."

Zach glanced up at Jim quickly; Bob saw that Zach's cheeks were bright red. "Not exactly to watch out for them. Just—" Zach looked down and shrugged. "You know, they might be kind of crazy."

"How often are you in contact with your father?" Jim crossed his arms.

"I don't know."

"I asked you, how often are you in contact with your father?"

Bob said quietly, "Stop it, Jim. He's not on the stand, for God's sake."

Zach said, "Sometimes he emails me a lot, and sometimes it seems like he forgets about me."

Jim turned away and moved about the room. Finally he said, "So I'm guessing you thought your father might be impressed if you threw a pig's head through their mosque."

"I don't know what I thought," Zach said. He brushed a hand across his eyes. "He wasn't impressed," he added.

Jim said, "Well, I'm glad to hear it, because I was about to tell you, your father's a jerk."

Bob said, "He's not a jerk. He's Zach's father. Stop it, for Christ's sake, Jim."

Jim said, "Listen, Zachary, nobody's going to cut your balls off. These guys came here to get *away* from that. They aren't the bad guys." He sat back on his bed and turned the television on again. "You're safe here. Okay?"

Bob rummaged through his duffel bag, brought out the bottle of wine. "It's true, Zach."

Zach asked, "Are you going to tell my mom? What my dad wrote me?"

Jim said tiredly, "You mean, why you did what you did? What would your mom do?"

"Yell at me."

"I don't know," Jim finally said. "She's your mother. She should know stuff."

"Don't tell her about the girlfriend, though. You won't tell her that part, right?"

"No, buddy," said Bob. "She doesn't need to know that part at all."

"Let's forget it for now," Jim said. "We have a big day tomorrow." He eyed Bob, who was opening the wine. "Does your father drink?" Jim asked Zach.

"I don't know. He didn't used to."

"Well, let's hope you didn't get the genes of your Uncle Slob-Dog." Jim flipped through the channels.

"See, Zachary? That's what I said. Your famous uncle. Is he, or isn't he—an asshole. Only his hairdresser knows for sure." Bob, pouring wine into a hotel glass, winked at Zach.

"Wait." Zach looked from Bob to Jim, then back and forth a few times. He said to Jim, "You dye your hair?"

Jim glanced at him. "No. He's making reference to an ad you're too young to remember."

"Phew," said Zach. "Because men dyeing their hair is really lame." He lay down on the bed and put his arm beneath his head, the same way Jim had his.

———

In the morning Bob went downstairs and brought back cereal and coffee. Jim was looking through some papers that Margaret Estaver had sent Bob earlier from the Together for Tolerance Alliance. "Listen to this. Only twenty-nine percent of Americans believe the state has any responsibility for the poor."

"I know," Bob said. "Amazing, right?"

"And thirty-two percent believe that success in life is determined by forces outside our control. In Germany, sixty-eight percent of people think that." Jim pushed the paper aside.

After a moment Zach said quietly, "I don't get it. Is that a good thing, or a bad thing?"

"An American thing," Jim said. "Eat your Froot Loops."

"So it's a good thing," Zach said.

"Remember. Answer just your cell phone, and only if you recognize the number." Jim stood up. "Get your coat, slob-dog."

———◆———

The November sun—not high in the sky, but coming at the town from an angle—sliced across the streets, across the lawns that were still green, fell on half-sunken pumpkins left on stoops from Halloween, shone against the tree trunks and their bare limbs, beamed through the clear air, making mica specks in the old sidewalks glitter. They parked a few blocks away. As they walked around the corner, Bob was amazed to see the sidewalks filled with people moving toward the park. "Where'd they all come from?" Bob said to his brother. Jim said nothing; his face was tense. But the faces around them were not tense. It was notable, the good-natured seriousness of the people they joined. A few carried poster boards with the logo of the rally drawn on them: stick figures holding hands. "You can't take those inside the park," someone said, and the answer was a cheerful "We know." Turning another corner, they saw the park stretched out before them. It was not packed with people, but it was filled with people, most of them near the bandstand. Along the streets nearby were television vans and more people carrying the logo signs. Orange tape barriers were attached to poles along the edges of the park, and police stood every few feet. Their eyes kept moving—watching, watching—but there was an easiness to them as they stood in their blue uniforms. Along Pine Street was the entrance, where a kind of security center had been set up, tables and metal detectors. The Burgess boys held their arms out, were allowed through.

People in down vests and jeans were standing around, old people with white hair and wide hips moved slowly. The Somalis were gathered mostly near the playground. The Somali men wore Western clothes, Bob noticed, a few with smocklike shirts beneath their coats. But the Somali women—many big-cheeked, some thin-faced—wore robes that went to the ground, and some of their head coverings reminded Bob of the nuns that used to walk around this same park when he was a boy. Except they weren't like that, because many of these scarves were flut-tery and bright, as though a new kind of foliage had found its way to the park, orange, purple, yellow. "The mind always wants to find something to snap itself onto, doesn't it?" Bob said to Jim. "Something familiar. So it can say: *like that*. But nothing's familiar about this. It's not like the Franco Festival or Moxie Days—"

"Shut up," Jim said quietly.

A woman was speaking from the bandstand. Her microphoned voice was just finishing, and people clapped politely. The air seemed both fes-tive and restrained. Bob stepped back, and Jim moved toward the band-stand. He was going to speak without notes, as he always did. The woman leaving the bandstand was Margaret Estaver; she disappeared into a group of people, and Bob's eyes scanned the crowd. He had never been struck, as he was today, with how much white people looked alike. *They all look the same.* White-skinned, open-faced, and strikingly plain compared to the Somalis, who were mingling more with the towns-people now, the long robes of the women weaving through the crowd. A few had allowed their children to come, and the boys were dressed like Americans, in pants and T-shirts showing beneath oversize jackets. Bob thought again how unfamiliar it seemed, to see so many people gathered here, but without the music or dancing or stalls of food that he recalled from his youth. And to be here without Pam. Full-bodied youthful Pam, with her full-throated youthful laugh. Pam, now skinny in New York, raising her sons as New Yorkers. (Pam!)

"Bob Burgess." It was Margaret Estaver, who had appeared from be-

hind him. "Oh, that's quite all right," she said when he told her he was
sorry he had missed her remarks. "It's going beautifully. Better than we'd
hoped for." There was a luminescence to her he'd not noticed the day
she sat next to him on Susan's back steps. "Only thirteen people showed
up at the Civic Center for the counterdemonstration. *Thirteen.*" Her
eyes were gray-blue behind her glasses. "They're estimating there's *four
thousand* here. Feel how lovely it is?"

He said he did feel that.

Approached by many people, she was greeting them all, shaking
hands. Like a nice version of Jim, Bob thought, back when Jim considered being a politician in Maine. Someone called out to Margaret, and
she nodded and said, "I'm coming." She waved to Bob, put her fist to her
cheek to mime "Call me," and Bob turned in the direction of the bandstand.

Jim had not yet climbed the stairs. He was standing with a big
shaggy-looking man whom Bob recognized as the attorney general, Dick
Hartley. Jim stood with his arms crossed, glancing down and nodding,
his head tilted toward Dick, who was talking. ("Let people talk," Jim
used to say. "Most, left unchecked, will talk a noose around their neck.")
Jim looked up, grinned at Dick, clapped him on his shoulder, then took
the stance again of looking down, listening. A number of times both
men seemed to chuckle. More clapping on the shoulders, and then Dick
Hartley was being introduced, and he walked up the stairs ungracefully,
as though he had always been a thin man but had now, mid-fifties, found
himself to be much larger and didn't know how to finesse the extra bulk.
He read his speech, flipping his bangs out of his eyes constantly, which
caused him to appear—whether he was or not—uncomfortable.

Bob, who had intended to listen, found his mind drifting. Margaret
Estaver's face returned to him and then, oddly, Adriana's, her exhausted
and wild-eyed look the morning after she had called the police on her
husband. But honestly, it did not seem possible right now, standing in
this park of his childhood, to believe that his life in New York was real,
that the couple across the street in their white kitchen actually existed,
or the young girl who walked around her apartment so freely, or that he

himself had spent so many evenings there looking out the window of his apartment. This image of himself seemed sad to him, but he knew when he sat in Brooklyn and looked out his window it did not seem sad, it was his life. But what seemed most real right now was this park, these familiar-looking pale people, unassuming, not fast-moving; Margaret Estaver, her manner . . . And he wondered fleetingly what it was like for the Somalis, if they lived constantly with the sense of bewilderment he felt this moment, wondering which life was real.

"Jimmy Burgess," Bob heard a woman say quietly. She was white-haired, short, wearing a fleece vest, standing next to a man who was probably her husband, also short, large-bellied, also wearing a fleece vest. "Nice he's come up for this," the woman continued, her eyes watching the bandstand, but her head moving toward her husband's. "Suppose he feels he has to," she added, as though this thought had only now occurred to her, and Bob moved away.

He felt the urge for a cigarette as he watched Jim climb the band-stand stairs, nodding to Dick Hartley, who was about to introduce him. Jim, even from this distance, seemed strikingly natural. Bob rocked back on his heels, his hands in his pockets. What was this thing that Jimmy had? The intangible, compelling part of Jimmy?

It's that he showed no fear, Bob realized. He never had. And people hated fear. People hated fear more than anything. This is what Bob was thinking as his brother began to speak. ("Good morning." Pause. "I've come here today as a former citizen of this town. I've come here as a man who cares for his family, as a man who cares for his country." Pause. Quietly: "As a man who cares for his community.") Standing here, Bob thought, in Roosevelt Park, named for the man who had assured the country that fear was the only thing to be feared, Jimmy had presence because he looked like fear had never tapped his shoulder and never would. ("When I was a child playing in this park—as children are play-ing in this park right now—I sometimes climbed that hill right over there in order to see the railroad tracks and the small railway station below, where hundreds of people had arrived in this town a century

earlier, in order to work, and live, and worship safely. This town grew
and prospered with the help of all who came here, all who lived here.")

You couldn't fake it. It showed in the glance of an eye, in the way you
entered a room, walked up the steps to a bandstand. ("We know that to
watch with indifference as fellow men and women and children experience pain and humiliation is to add to that pain and humiliation. We
understand the vulnerability of those who are new to our community,
and we will not stand by idly while they are hurt.") Bob, watching his
brother, aware that all those in the park—and the park was *packed* with
people now—were listening to him, not moving or strolling or whispering to others, Bob, noticing how all these people seemed wrapped in
some large shawl that Jim drew closer to him, had no idea that what he
felt was envy. He knew only that he stood there feeling very bad, when
before he had felt hopeful at the excitement of Margaret Estaver, glad
for what she was doing and what she felt herself, and now that ancient
recrudescence of dreariness arrived, disgust at his big, slob-dog, incon-
tinent self, the opposite of Jim.

But still. His heart unfolded with love. Look at him, his big brother!
It was like watching a great athlete, someone born with grace, someone
who walked two inches above the surface of the earth, and who could
say why? ("We will come out to the park today, thousands of us, we will
come out to this park today to say that we believe what is true: The
United States is a country of laws and not men and that we will provide
safety to those who come to us for safety.")

Bob missed his mother. His mother, with the thick red sweater she
often wore. He pictured her sitting on his bed when he was little, telling
him a story to get him to sleep. She had bought him a night-light, which
seemed an extravagance back then, the swollen bulb sucked into the
socket above the mopboard. "Sissy," Jimmy said, and soon Bob told his
mother he didn't need the light anymore. "Then I'm leaving the door
open," his mother said. *Sissy.* "In case one of you falls out of bed or needs
me." It was Bob who fell out of his bed, or would wake, yelling, with a
nightmare. Jimmy did his taunting of Bob when their mother was not

there, and while Bob might fight back, in his heart he accepted his brother's scorn. Standing in Roosevelt Park watching his brother speak with eloquence, Bob still accepted it. He knew what he had done. The kindhearted Elaine, in her office with the recalcitrant fig tree, had one day suggested gently that to leave three small kids in a car at the top of a hill was not a good idea, and Bob had shaken his head, no, no, no. More unbearable than the accident itself was to hold his father responsible for it! He had been a small child. He understood that. No malice aforethought. No reckless endangerment. The law itself would not hold a child responsible.

But he had done it.

"I'm sorry," he'd said to his mother as she lay in the hospital bed. Over and over he'd said that. She'd shaken her head. "You've all been such good kids," she said.

Bob's eyes scanned the crowd. Around the edges of the park, policemen stood; even as they stayed watchful, they seemed to be listening to Jim. Over by the playground, Somali children were dancing, spinning around with their hands up. Sunlight fell over all of it, and beyond the park sat the cathedral with its four spires, beyond that was the river, seen from here as a small winding strip, twinkling, between its banks.

The applause for his brother was sustained, steady, a sound that carried itself throughout the park, continued, dipped slightly, came back up, a soft, full sound. Bob watched as Jim stepped from the bandstand, greeted people, nodded, gave Dick Hartley another handshake, shook hands with the governor, who was going to speak next, all the while the applause continuing. But Jim was not eager to stay. Bob could see this from where he stood: Jim's polite responses as he kept walking away. Always on the exit ramp, Susan had once said of Jim.

Bob moved around to join him.

As they walked quickly down the street a young man wearing a baseball cap approached them, smiling. "Hey," said Jim, nodding, still walking.

The young man kept pace with them. "They're parasites," he said.

"They're here to wipe us out and maybe today you didn't see it but we're not gonna let them."

Jim kept walking. The fellow persisted. "The Jews are going, and these niggers are going, you'll see. They're parasites feeding on the globe."

"Lose it, dickwad." Jim kept walking the same pace.

The fellow was no more than a kid. Twenty-two, tops, Bob thought, as the kid kept looking at them eagerly, as though what he had just said would please the Burgess brothers. As though he had not heard Jim call him a dickwad. "Parasites," Bob said. A sudden deep anger pulsed through him. He stopped walking. "You don't even know what a parasite is. My wife used to study parasites, which meant she was studying you. Have you gone past the eighth grade?"

"Cool it," said Jim, still walking. "Let's go."

"We're God's true people. We won't stop. You might think so, but we won't."

"You are," said Bob, "a little piece of coccidiosis, infecting God's intestine, that's what you are. Asexual," he added, over his shoulder, following Jim. "You belong inside the stomach of a goat."

Jim said fiercely, "What's *wrong* with you? Shut up."

The young man came running to catch up. He said to Bob. "You're a fat idiot, but him"—nodding to Jim—"he's dangerous. He works for the devil."

Jim stopped so quickly that the fellow bumped into him, and Jim grabbed his arm. "Did you just call my brother fat, you fucking little punk?"

Fear stunned the kid's face. He tried to free his arm, and Jim gripped it tighter. Jim's lips had gone white, his eyes small. It was amazing, the power of the anger that was there. Even Bob, used to his brother, was amazed. Jim put his face close to the kid's and spoke quietly. "Did you call my brother fat?" The kid looked over his shoulder, and Jim tightened his grip more. "Your little-dick friends aren't around to protect you. I'm asking you one more time: Did you call my brother fat?"

"Yes."

"Apologize."

Tears were in the young man's eyes. "You're breaking my arm. I mean it, you are."

"Jimmy," murmured Bob.

"I said, apologize. I'll snap your neck off so fast you won't even feel it. Painless. You lucky little shit. You can die pain-free."

"I'm sorry."

Immediately Jim let go, and the Burgesses walked to their car, got in, and drove off. Through the window Bob saw the guy rubbing his arm, walking back toward the park. Jim said, "Don't worry, there's just a few. It's over. But stop calling people parasites. Jesus."

There was the sound of cheering from the park. Whatever the governor had to say on the bandstand, people liked it, the day was almost over, Jim's job was done. "Nice speech," Bob said as they drove over the river.

Jim kept glancing in the rearview mirror while he reached into his pocket, flicked open his cell phone. "Hellie? It's done. Yeah, it was fine. I'll talk to you more when we get back to the hotel. You too, sweetheart." He clicked the phone shut, returned it to his pocket. He said to Bob, "Did you see that little worm's cap with '88' on it? That stands for 'Heil Hitler.' Or 'HH.' The letter H being the eighth letter of the alphabet."

"How do you know all that?" Bob asked.

"How do you not," Jim answered.

———◆———

Night arrived with the sense that the day would go down in the history of Shirley Falls, the day four thousand people marched peacefully to the park to support the right of a dark-skinned population to join their town. The plastic shields were put away. There was a tender gravity of solidarity but very little self-congratulation, because northern New Englanders are not like that. But it was big and good and that could not be taken away. Abdikarim, who had attended only because one of Haweeya's sons came running to get him, saying his parents insisted he come to the park, had been puzzled by what he saw: so many people smiling at him. To look him straight in the face and smile felt to Abdikarim to display an intimacy he was not comfortable with. But he had been here long enough to know it was the way Americans were, like large children, and these large children in the park were very nice. Long after he left, he kept picturing the people smiling at him.

That evening men gathered in his café. Mostly they weren't sure what the rally meant. It felt important, and it had been surprising, because how could they have known so many ordinary people would have put themselves in danger today on their behalf? Time would tell what it meant. "But it was amazing," Abdikarim interjected. Ifo Noor shrugged, and repeated that time alone would tell. Then the men talked of their homeland (this is what they always wanted to talk about), and the rumors that the United States was backing warlords in Somalia who were trying to overthrow the Islamic Courts. Roadblocks set up by gangsters, riots started with the burning of tires. Abdikarim listened with a sinking heart. That people in the park today had pleasant faces was a fact entirely separate from the inner lamentation he lived with every day: He wanted to go home. But people there had lost their senses, and he could not go home. A congressman in Washington had publicly referred to Somalia as a "failed state." The men in Abdikarim's café mentioned this with bitterness. For Abdikarim, there were too many feelings for a heart to contain. The humiliation of the congressman's words, the anger at those at home who were shooting and looting and preventing order, the people smiling at them in the park today—and yet the United States was full of lies, a country of leaders who lied. The Alliance for the Restoration of Peace—it was a farce, the men said.

Abdikarim stayed and swept his café when the men finally left. His cell phone vibrated, and he felt his face opening in pleasure at the sound of his daughter's lively voice, calling from Nashville. It's good, very good, she said, having seen on television the gathering in Roosevelt Park. She talked of her sons playing soccer, how they spoke almost flawless English now, and his heart seemed an engine that both raced and stalled. Flawless English meant they could disappear as full Americans, but it gave them a sturdiness too. "They stay out of trouble?" he asked, and she said they did. The oldest boy had started high school and his grades were brilliant. His teachers were surprised. "I'll send a copy of his report card," his daughter said. "And tomorrow I will text you pictures for your telephone. They're very handsome, my sons, you'll be proud." For a long time after, Abdikarim sat. Finally he walked home through the dark, and when he lay down he saw the people in the park, wearing their winter coats, their fleece vests, open-faced, looking pleasantly right at him. When he woke in the night he was confused. There was a tugging on his mind, familiar from long ago. When he woke again he realized he had dreamed of his firstborn son, Baashi, who had been a serious child. Only a few times in the boy's short life had it been necessary for Abdikarim to strike him in order to teach lessons of respect. In the dream Baashi had looked at his father with bewildered eyes.

———

Bob and Jim had endured one more evening at Susan's house. She'd microwaved frozen lasagna, while Zach ate hot dogs from a fork as though eating popsicles, and the dog slept without moving on her dog-hairy bed. Jim had shaken his head once at Bob to indicate they would not tell Susan right now what they had learned about Zach and his father; Jim took a phone call from Charlie Tibbetts in the other room, and when he returned to the kitchen and sat back down he said, "Okay. Word on the street is people liked me, good feelings about seeing me up there, all that." He picked up his fork, moved some food on his plate. "Everyone's happy. Freedom from white guilt makes everyone happy." He nodded toward Zach. "Your ill-conceived behavior will sink back into being exactly what it is, a Class E misdemeanor, and by the time Charlie takes it to trial, months will've passed, he can get all sorts of postponements and that's good. People won't want to go stirring this up. It's a *happy* time now, and they'll want to keep it that way."

Susan blew out a breath. "Let's hope."

"I'm thinking this twat Diane Dodge in the AG's office will stop pushing for the civil rights violation, and even if she does push, Dick Hartley has to agree to it, and he won't. I could see that today. He's a big old stupid thing, and people were happy to see me, and he's not going to rock that boat. Which sounds grandiose, I know."

"Little bit," Bob said, pouring wine into a coffee cup.

"I don't want to go to jail." Zach mumbled the words.

"You won't." Jim pushed back his plate. "Get your coat if you're staying with us tonight. Bob and I have a long ride in the morning."

Back in the hotel room, Jim said to Zach, "What happened to you in that cell while you were waiting for the bail commissioner?"

Zach, who had looked more normal to Bob as the weekend went by, gazed at Jim with a slightly stunned look. "What happened is . . . I, you know, sat."

"Tell me," Jim said.

"It wasn't much bigger than a closet, the cell, and all white and metal. Even what I sat on was metal, and these guards were nearby and kept looking over at me. I asked them once, 'Where's my mother?' And they said, 'Outside, waiting.' They wouldn't talk to me after that. I mean, I didn't try."

"But you were scared?"

Zach nodded. He looked scared again.

"Were they mean to you? Threaten you?"

Zach shrugged. "I was just scared. I was really, really scared. I didn't even know there was a place like that here."

"It's called a jail. They're everywhere. Was anyone else in there with you?"

"Some man's voice kept screaming swearwords. I mean, like crazy. But I couldn't see him. And the guards would shout at him, 'Shut the fuck up.'"

"Did they hurt him?"

"I don't know. I couldn't see."

"Did they hurt you?"

"No."

"You're sure?" In Jim's voice was the fierce timbre of protection that

Bob had heard when they walked away from the rally earlier and the punk kid called Bob a fat idiot. He saw in Zach's face the surprise, the small instinctive motion of yearning as he absorbed it: This man would kill on his behalf. Jim, Bob realized, was the father everyone wanted.

Bob stood up and walked in a big circle around the room. What he felt seemed unbearable, and he did not know what he felt. After a few moments he stopped walking and said to Zach, "Your Uncle Jim will take care of you. That's what he does."

Zach looked from one uncle to the other. "But you take care of me, too, Uncle Bob," he finally said.

"Ah, Zach, you're a mensch. You really are." Bob reached over and rubbed the kid's head. "All I did was come up and get your mother mad at me."

"Mom gets mad a lot, don't take it personal. Anyways, when they let me go from that jail cell and I saw you standing there with Mom, I was, like, totally the happiest ever. What's a mensch?"

"A good guy."

Jim said, "You were so happy to see Bob you got your grinning face plastered all over the papers."

"Jesus, Jim. It's over."

"Can we watch TV?" Zach asked.

Jim tossed Zach the remote control. "You're going to have to get a job. So I want you to be thinking about what that will be. And then you're going to take some courses, study hard, do well, and enroll in Central Maine Community College here. Work toward something. That's how it's done. You belong to society, you give to society."

Zach looked down, and Bob said, "There's time to find a job, get straightened out. Right now, make yourself comfortable. You're in a hotel so pretend it's vacation. Pretend there's a beach outside and not the smelly river that's actually there."

"The river doesn't smell anymore, you retard." Jim was hanging up his coat. "They cleaned it up. You didn't notice? You're so seventies. Jesus."

"If you're so up-to-date," Bob answered, "you'd know the word 'retard' isn't used anymore. Susan used it too, when I first came up here. Man.

I feel like I'm the only one of us who left grade school, moved into the twenty-first century."

"Gag me," Jim said.

Zach fell asleep watching TV, and the soft sound of his snoring came through the open door to the other room, where Jim and Bob now sat on opposite beds. "Let Susan enjoy her relief that this is over. We can tell her later what her son was up to. I told Charlie Tibbetts about it, and it doesn't matter anyway, his defense is that Zach didn't commit a crime," Jim said. "The law says he would have to know the room was a mosque, and that pork was offensive to Muslims."

"I don't know if that's gonna fly. If Zach didn't know it was offensive to Muslims, then why didn't he toss a chicken's head?"

"Which is why you aren't his defense lawyer. Or anyone's defense lawyer." Jim stood up, put his keys and phone on the bureau. "Because when he went out to visit a friend who had a slaughterhouse, they only *had* the heads of pigs. They didn't *have* other heads. Would you leave this to Charlie? Jesus, Bob. You wear me out. No wonder you shit your pants every time you went to court. Of course you switched to appeals. So you could digest your baby food."

Bob sat back, looked for the wine bottle. "What's your problem?" he said quietly. "You did such a good job today." There was a small amount of wine left, and he poured it into a glass.

"My problem is you. You're my problem. Why don't you just let Charlie Tibbetts worry about this?" Jim said. "I got him, you know. You didn't. So leave it alone."

"No one said he wasn't good. I was just trying to understand the defense." A silence sat in the room that felt so momentarily present and pulsating Bob didn't dare disturb it by raising his glass.

"I don't want to come up here again," Jim finally said. He sat back down on the bed, looking at the rug.

"Then don't." Now Bob drank, and in a moment he added, "You know, an hour ago I thought you were the greatest guy in the world. But man, you are difficult. I saw Pam recently and she wondered if the Packer trial had turned you into a prick or if you were always a prick."

Jim glanced up. "Pam wondered that?" His mouth moved in a small smile. "Pamela. The restless and the rich." He suddenly grinned at Bob, his elbows resting on his knees, his hands hanging down. "It's funny how people turn out, isn't it? I wouldn't have predicted Pam would be someone always going after what she doesn't have. But when you think about it, it's been there all along. They say people are always telling you who they are. And I guess she was. She didn't like her childhood, so she took yours. Then she got to New York and looked around and saw people had kids and she'd better get some too, and while she was at it she'd better get some money as well, because New York has a lot of that too."

Bob shook his head slowly. "I don't know what you're talking about. Pam always wanted kids. We always wanted kids. I thought you liked Pam."

"I do like Pam. I used to think it was funny how she loved looking at those parasites under a microscope, and then one day I realized she's kind of a parasite herself. Not in a bad way."

"Not in a bad way?"

Jim waved a hand dismissively. "Well, think about it. Yeah—not in a bad way. But she started practically living with us when you were both still kids. She needed a home so she fed on ours. She needed a nice husband so she fed on you. Then she needed a daddy to have some kids with and so she's over there on Park Avenue feeding off that. She gets what she needs, is what I'm saying. Not everyone does."

"Jim. Jesus. What are you talking about? You married someone rich yourself."

Jim ignored this. "Did she happen to tell you about her little meeting with me after you guys called it quits?"

"Cut it out, Jim."

Jim shrugged. "There's lots of stuff I know about Pam I bet you don't know."

"I said cut it out."

"She was drunk. She drinks too much. You both do. But nothing happened, don't worry. I bumped into her in Midtown after work, oh this was years ago, we went to the Harvard Club for a drink. I thought, well, she's been in the family for years, I owe her that. And after a few drinks, during which she made some rather poor choices in her confessional judgment, she mentioned how attractive she'd always found me. Kind of coming on to me, which I thought was not very classy."

"Oh, *shut* up!" Bob, trying to stand, found his chair falling backward with his large body in it. The sound of it seemed very loud, and he felt the wine spill on his neck, and it was this sensation that was strangely clear to him: liquid running over the side of his neck while he moved one leg in the air. A light went on.

Zach's voice came from the doorway. "You guys, what's happening?"

"Nothing, kiddo." Bob's heart was beating hard.

"We were roughhousing, like when we were kids." Jim held out his hand and helped Bob up. "Just fooling around with my brother. Nothing like a brother."

"I heard someone shout," Zach said.

"You were dreaming," Jim answered, putting his hand on Zach's shoulders and steering him back into the other room. "That happens in hotel rooms, people have bad dreams."

———•———

The next morning Jim was talkative as they drove away from Shirley Falls. "See that?" he asked. They were about to get on the highway. Bob looked to where Jim pointed and saw a prefab building and a large parking lot with yellow buses. "Catholic churches are emptying out, have been for years, and these fundy churches are big-time. They go around in those buses scooping up any old person who can't get to church. They love their Jesus, they do."

Bob did not answer. He was trying to figure out how drunk he'd been last night. He had not felt drunk, but that didn't mean he wasn't. Maybe what he thought he'd heard was not what he'd heard. Also, he kept picturing Susan this morning, standing on the porch waving as they pulled away, but Zach had bent his head down and gone back inside, and Bob kept picturing that too.

"You probably wonder how I know that," Jim went on, merging onto the highway. "You learn all sorts of things reading the *Shirley Falls Journal* online. Okay, be that way." He added, "So I told Susan this morning, when she was outside with the dog, that Zach might have done this to impress his father. Didn't mention the girlfriend. Just that Steve had emailed Zach some vaguely negative things about the Somalis. And you know what she said? She said, 'Huh.'"

"That's what she said?" Bob looked out the window. After a while he said, "Well, I'm worried about Zach. Susan told me he'd soiled himself in the cell that day. That's probably why he didn't come down for dinner when I was up here. He was totally humiliated. He didn't even tell you yesterday when you were asking what happened to him there."

"When did she tell you that? She didn't tell *me* that."

"This morning, in the kitchen. When you were on the phone and Zach had taken his stuff upstairs."

"I've done everything I can," Jim finally said. "Everything to do with this family depresses me profoundly. All I want is to get back to New York."

"You'll get back to New York. Just like what you said about Pam, some people get what they need."

"I was a dickwad. Let it go."

"I can't just let it go. Jimmy, did she really come on to you?"

Jim exhaled through his teeth. "Oh, Christ, who knows? Pam's kind of crazy."

"Who knows? You know. You said it."

"I just told you—I was being a dickwad." Jim paused. "Exaggerating, okay?"

They drove in silence after that. They drove beneath a gray November sky. The bare trees stood naked and skinny as they passed them. The pine trees seemed skinny too, apologetic, tired. They drove by trucks, they drove by beat-up cars with passengers sucking on cigarettes. They drove by fields that were brownish gray. They drove beneath underpasses that spelled out the names of the roads above them: Anglewood

Road, Three Rod Road, Saco Pass. They drove over the bridge into New Hampshire, and then into Massachusetts. It wasn't until traffic came to a halt outside of Worcester that Jim spoke. "What is this shit? Man, what's going on?"

"That," said Bob, nodding to an ambulance coming in the other direction. There was another ambulance, and two police cars, and then Jim said nothing. Neither brother turned his head when they finally passed the accident. It was their bond, and had always been that way. Their wives had learned this silently, Jim's kids, too. It was a respect thing, Bob had told Elaine in her office, and she had nodded knowingly.

When they were almost on the other side of Worcester, Jim said, "I was a shit last night."

"You were." Bob could see in the side mirror the large brick mills receding.

"It messes with my head, going up there. It doesn't mess with your head as bad, because you were Mom's favorite. I'm not whining about that, it's just true."

Bob thought about this. "It's not like she didn't like you."

"Yeah, she liked me."

"She loved you."

"Yeah, she loved me."

"Jimmy, you were like a hero or something. You were good at everything. You never gave her a minute of grief. Of course she loved you. Susie—Mom didn't like her so much. Loved her, but didn't like her."

"I know." Jim let out a big sigh. "Poor Susie. I didn't like her either." He looked in the side mirror, pulled out to pass a car. "I still don't."

Bob pictured his sister's cold house, the anxious dog, Susan's plain face. "Oy," he said.

"I know you want a cigarette," Jim said. "If you can wait till we stop for food, that would be good. Helen will smell it for months. But if you can't wait, open a window."

"I'll wait." This unexpected kindness Jim flicked toward him made Bob garrulous. "When I was up there before, Susan got mad at me for saying 'Oy.' She said I wasn't Jewish. I didn't bother telling her Jews know about sorrow. They know about everything. And they have these great words for it. Tsuris. We have tsuris, Jimmy. I do, anyway."

Jim said, "Susie used to be pretty, do you remember that? Christ, if you're a woman and you stay in Maine you're really at risk. Helen says it's about products. Skin cream. She says Maine women think it's indulgent to use products, so by the time they're forty their faces look like men. It's a credible theory, I guess."

"Mom never *let* Susan feel pretty. Look, I'm not a parent, but you are. Why wouldn't a mother like her own kid? At least say 'Oh you look nice' once in a while?"

Jim waved a hand. "It had something to do with Susie being a girl. She got screwed because she was a girl."

"Helen loves your girls."

"Of course she does. She's Helen. And it's different in our generation. Haven't you noticed—no, I guess you haven't. But our generation, we're like *friends* to our kids. Maybe it's sick, maybe it isn't, who knows. But it's like we decided, well, we're not doing *that* to our kids, we're going to be *friends* with our kids. Honestly, Helen's great. But Mom and Susan, that's what happened back then. Next exit we'll eat."

By the time they reached Connecticut it felt as though they were in a suburb of New York, and Shirley Falls was far behind. "Should we call Zach?" Bob asked, pulling out his cell phone.

"Go ahead." Jim spoke with indifference.

Bob put his phone back into his pocket. Making the call required an effort he couldn't muster. He asked Jim if he should drive for a while, and Jim shook his head and said no, he was good. Bob knew he would do this. Jim never let him drive. When they were kids and Jim got his license, he would make Bob ride in the backseat. Bob thought of this now and did not mention it; everything to do with Shirley Falls seemed far away, unreachable, and best left unreached.

It was dark by the time they approached Manhattan, the lights of the city spread out beside them, the bridges twinkling with magnificence over the East River, the huge red Pepsi sign blinking from Long Island

City. As they slowed to get onto the ramp for the Brooklyn Bridge, Bob could see the spire of the Municipal Building, and also the tall and crowded apartment buildings right there by the Drive, lights on in almost every window, and he felt homesick for it all, as though it no longer belonged to him but was a place where he had lived in the far past. Across the bridge, down Atlantic Avenue, there was the sense of going deep into some country that was both familiar and foreign, and the simultaneousness of these impressions jarred Bob; he was a child now, tired and querulous, and he wanted to be going home with Jim.

"All right, knucklehead," said his brother, pulling up in front of Bob's apartment building. Jim kept his hands on the steering wheel, only raising four fingers in the gesture of a wave, and Bob took his bag from the back and got out. In front of his building he saw big squares of cut-up cardboard moving boxes near the recycling bin. Walking up the stairs Bob saw the bar of light beneath the door of what had recently been the emptied-out apartment of his old neighbors. Tonight he heard the lilting voices of a young couple, heard a baby cry.

Book Three

1

For most of the nineteen years of Zachary's life, Susan had done what parents do when their child turns out to be so different from what they'd imagined—which is to pretend, and pretend, with the wretchedness of hope, that he would be all right. Zach would grow into himself. He'd make friends and take part in life. Grow into it, grow out of it . . . Variations had played in Susan's mind on sleepless nights. But her mind had also held the dark relentless beat of doubt: He was friendless, he was quiet, he was hesitant in all his actions, his schoolwork barely adequate. Tests showed an IQ above average, no discernible learning disorders—yet the package of Zachness added up to not quite right. And sometimes Susan's melody of failure crescendoed with the unbearable knowledge: It was her fault.

How could it not be her fault?

At the university Susan had been drawn to classes in child development. Attachment theories, especially. Attachment to the mother appeared to be more important than attachment to the father, though of course that was important too. But the mother was the mirror the child was reflected in, and Susan had hoped for a girl. (She wanted three girls and then one son, who would be like Jim.) Her own mother had pre-ferred the boys; Susan knew this as clearly as she knew the color red. *Her* daughters would be loved without narrowness. The house would be filled with chatter; they would be allowed makeup as Susan had not been; they would be allowed phone calls with boys, pajama parties, and clothes bought from stores.

She miscarried. "You shouldn't have told people," her mother said. But Susan was showing, and in her second trimester how could she not have told people? "A girl," the doctor said, because she asked. The first night, Steve held her. "I hope the next one's a boy," he said.

They were not toys on a store shelf, one falling and breaking, the next coming home in one piece. No, she had lost her daughter! And she learned—freshly, scorchingly—of the privacy of sorrow. It was as though she had been escorted through a door into some large and private club that she had not even known existed. Women who miscarried. Society did not care much for them. It really didn't. And the women in the club mostly passed each other silently. People outside the club said, "You'll have another one."

The nurse who handed her Zachary must have assumed that Susan was weeping with joy, but Susan was weeping at the sight of him: skinny, wet, blotchy, his eyes closed. He was not her little girl. She panicked at the thought she might never forgive him for this. He lay on her chest with no interest in suckling. On the third day a nurse put a cold face-cloth to his cheek to see if that would rouse him, but he only opened his eyes and looked startled before his tiny face wrinkled with sorrow. "Oh, please," Susan begged the nurse, "don't do that again." Her breasts hard-ened with milk, became infected with their engorgement. She had to stand in blistering hot showers, pressing the milk out. Her skinny, shriv-eled baby boy remained indifferent, lost weight. "Why won't he suck?" Susan wailed, and no one seemed to have an answer. A bottle of formula was produced and Zachary sucked on that.

"He's strange-looking," Steve said.

He seldom cried, and when Susan checked on him in the night she was often surprised to see his eyes open. "What are you thinking?" she would whisper, stroking his head. At six weeks he gazed at her, and gave the smile of someone patient, kind, and bored.

"Do you think he's normal?" she blurted to her mother one day.

"No. I don't." Barbara was holding Zach's tiny hand. He had, at thirteen months, just learned to walk, and he was moving between the sofa and the coffee table. "I don't know what he is," Barbara said, watching him. Adding, "But he's dear."

And he really was: unfussy, quiet, his eyes on his mother. It's not that Susan forgot about the little girl she'd lost—she never forgot—but the love she had for the lost girl seemed to merge with the love she felt for Zach. Sent to preschool, Zach suddenly cried without stopping. "I can't leave him there," Susan said. "He never cries. Something's wrong with that place."

"You'll turn him into a wuss," Steve said. "He'll have to get used to it."

A month later the preschool asked that Zachary leave, his crying was disruptive. Susan found another preschool in a neighborhood across the river, and Zach didn't cry there. But he didn't play with anyone. Susan stood in the doorway and watched the teacher take his hand and lead him over to another little boy, and Susan watched while the other boy pushed her son, who, so skinny, toppled over like a stick.

By elementary school he was teased mercilessly. By middle school he was beaten up. By high school his father left. Before Steve left, there were loud arguments that Zach must have heard. "He doesn't ride a bicycle. He can't even swim. He's a total weenie and you made him that way!" Red-faced, Steve was adamant. Susan believed her husband, and thought that if Zach had turned out differently, his father might have stayed. So that was her fault too. These failures isolated her. Only Zach was present in her quarantine, mother and son knit together by an unspoken sense of bafflement and mutual apology. At times she yelled at him (more often than she knew), and she was always, afterward, sick with regret and sorrow.

"Good," he said, when she asked how it had been at the hotel with his uncles. "Oh, yeah, totally," when asked if they'd been nice to him.

"Talked and watched TV," when asked what they had done. "Stuff," he said, shrugging pleasantly, asked what they had talked about. But when her brothers had left, she felt Zach's mood sink low. "Let's call your uncles, see they got back to New York all right," she suggested, and Zach made no reply.

She called Jim, who sounded tired. He did not ask to speak to Zach.

She called Bob, who sounded tired, and he did ask to speak to Zach. Susan moved into the living room to give Zach privacy. "Good," she heard her son say. "Yeah, it was." Long silence. "I don't know. Okay. You too."

She couldn't help herself. "What did he say?"

"To keep myself busy."

"Well, he's right."

That Jim had told her Zach may have used the pig's head to impress his father was not something Susan wanted to mention now. Zach's current vulnerability kept her from being mad at him, and while she felt mad at Steve (as she almost always did), she was not going to mention that either. She told Zach she would make calls to see where he could volunteer; Uncle Bob was right about staying busy.

She tried: The library. (No, said Charlie Tibbetts, far too many Somalis were in there all the time.) Delivering meals to old people. (They had enough volunteers already.) Working at a food pantry. (No, Somalis showed up there, too.) And so every night when Susan got home, she asked Zach what he had done that day and the answer was that he had done nothing. She told him he should take a cooking class and cook their supper each night. "Seriously?" The quick fear on his face made her say, "No, heavens, I was kidding."

"Uncle Jim said I should take courses. He didn't mean cooking."

"He said to take courses?" She got a catalog from the community college. "You like computers, look at this." But Charlie Tibbetts said there were apt to be Somalis in those classes, wait a semester until the case was disposed of, then Zach would be free to get on with his life. So their life became waiting.

On Thanksgiving, Susan cooked a turkey and Mrs. Drinkwater ate with them. Mrs. Drinkwater had two daughters living in California; Susan had never seen them. A week before Christmas, Susan bought a small Christmas tree at the gas station. Zach helped her put it up in the living room, and Mrs. Drinkwater came downstairs, bringing the angel to place on top. Susan had allowed this each year since the old lady moved in, but she privately didn't care for the angel, which Mrs. Drinkwater said had belonged to her mother, and which had embroidered blue tears running down its tattered face, swollen with cotton batting. "It's nice of you, dear," Mrs. Drinkwater said. "To put that on your tree. My husband didn't like it, so we never used it." She was sitting in the wing chair wearing a man's cardigan over her pink rayon robe, and she had on her terry-cloth slippers, her stockings rolled to the knees. Mrs. Drinkwater added, "This Christmas Eve I'd like to go to midnight mass at St. Peter's. But I'm scared to be in that part of town so late, an old lady alone."

Susan, who had not been listening, had to go back over the words and find any she could remember. "You want to go to midnight mass? At the cathedral?"

"That's right, dear."

"I've never been there," Susan said finally.

"Never? My word."

"I'm not Catholic," Susan said. "I used to go to the Congregational church across the river. It's where I got married. But I haven't been there for a long time." She meant she hadn't been there since her husband left, and Mrs. Drinkwater nodded.

"That's where I was married too," the old lady said. "It's a sweet little church."

Susan hesitated. "Then why do you want to go to mass at St. Peter's? If you don't mind me asking."

Mrs. Drinkwater gazed at the tree, pushed her glasses up her nose with the back of her wrist. "Church of my childhood, dear. Went every week with all my brothers and sisters. Confirmed there." She looked over at Susan, who could not find the old lady's eyes behind the huge glasses. "I was born Jeannette Paradis. And I became Jean Drinkwater because I fell in love with Carl. His mother would have none of it unless I left the Catholic Church completely. So I did. I didn't mind. I loved Carl. My parents wouldn't come to the wedding. I walked myself down the aisle. It wasn't done then. Who walked you down that aisle, dear?"

"My brother. Jim."

Mrs. Drinkwater nodded. "All these years I haven't missed St. Peter's a bit. But now I find myself thinking about it. They say that's what happens as you get older. You think about the things of your youth."

Susan was taking a red ornament from a low branch of the tree and hanging it higher. She said, "I'll take you to midnight mass if you want to go."

But on Christmas Eve, Mrs. Drinkwater was fast asleep by ten o'clock. Christmas passed slowly, the days between that and New Year's interminable. And then it was done. The days, short and cold, gave way to a January thaw. The sun sparkled on the melting snow, tree trunks gleamed from the dripping wet. And even when the world seized back to its frozen self, you could see the days were lengthening. Charlie Tibbetts phoned to say things were going well, delays over at the DA's office meant by the time this went to trial it would be a nonevent. It wouldn't surprise him if the case eventually got settled, a promise from Zach that he would behave, something simple like that. The AG's office had been silent for weeks, the Feds hadn't moved. We have this beat, Charlie said. Just waiting now, for time to go by.

"Are you worried about the case?" Susan asked Zachary that night as they watched TV.

He nodded.

"Don't be."

But two weeks later the Office of the Maine Attorney General filed a civil rights action against Zachary Olson.

2

The family room in Jim and Helen's brownstone lost the day's light faster than the rest of the house; it was on the bottom floor, and the windows' lower sills were level to the sidewalk. Between the windows and the sidewalk was the little front garden with its box shrubs and delicate Japanese maple, the twiggy branches rubbing up against the windows. In the winter Helen was sure to close the shutters of this room early. The shutters were mahogany and very old, folding out from enclosures built into the wall. It was a ritual she had enjoyed for years, as though she were tucking the house in for the night. But this afternoon the task was pleasureless. Helen's mind held a small worry regarding the evening: They were going to the opera with Dorothy and Alan, and yet they had not seen them the entire holiday season. She had not cared until now; her house had been filled with her children at Thanksgiving and Christmas (Emily not going to her boyfriend's family after all), and so those weeks were filled with preparations, then with people. Boots tossed, and scarves, bagel crumbs, high school friends, laundry to be folded, manicures with the girls, and movies at night with the family

snuggled together again in this very room. *Bliss.* Beneath which strummed
a quiet panic: They would never all live at home again. Then they were
gone. The house silent, scarily so. A chill of change hung in the rooms.

Closing the last shutter now, Helen looked down and saw that the
large diamond in her engagement ring was missing. At first her mind had
trouble believing this, she kept looking at the platinum prongs sticking
up in the air, holding nothing. Heat springing to her face, she looked
along the windowsills, opened the shutters and closed them again,
looked along the floor nearby, checked the pockets of everything she'd
been wearing. She called Jim. He was in a meeting. She called Bob, who
was working from home because he needed to concentrate on a complex brief due the next day. Still, he agreed to come over. "Wow," he said,
taking her hand, squinting. "That's kind of sickening. Like looking in the
mirror and seeing one of your front teeth missing."

"Oh, Bobby. You're awfully good." Because it was like that.

Bob was pulling out couch cushions when Jim came home in such a
furious mood that both Helen and Bob had to stop their search. "That
fucking Dick Hartley, that idiot Diane Dodge! Those stupid pukes, that
stupid state, I hate that stupid state!" In this way Bob and Helen learned
of the civil rights violation that had been filed that day.

"Even Charlie was surprised." Susan's voice was panicky as it came
through the speakerphone in Jim's upstairs study, off the bedroom. "I
don't know why they're doing this now. It's been three months. Why'd
they wait so long?"

"Because they're incompetent," Jim said, almost yelling. He sat with
both hands gripping the arms of his tilt-back chair while Bob and Helen
sat nearby. "Because Dick Hartley's a moron, and it took him this long to
let his stupid assistant Lady Diane go forward."

"But I just don't get why they're *doing* it." Susan's voice wavered.

"To look good! That's why." Jim leaned forward so fast his chair gave
a snapping sound. "Because Diane Dodge probably wants to be AG herself one day, or run for governor, or run for Congress, and it better be on
her little liberal résumé how she fought the good fight." He closed his
eyes briefly. "Twat," he added.

"Jim, stop. That's disgusting," Helen said, leaning forward, a hand covering her wedding band protectively. "Susan? Susan? Charlie Tibbetts will take care of this." She sat back, sat forward again, adding, "It's me, Helen."

Her face was flushed and moist. Bob was not sure he'd seen Helen look like this; even her hair seemed distressed into flatness as she pushed it back from her eyes. He told her, "You won't be late, you've got tons of time," because he knew she was worrying about their opera date with the Anglins, he had heard about it as they moved cushions, looking for the diamond that had fallen from her ring.

Helen answered in a low voice, "But now Susan's called with this awful news, Jim will be angry all night and— Oh, it just makes me sick to see this," turning the band on her finger.

"You guys, stop it." Jim waved a hand backward. "Susan, tell me what's going on with the Feds."

In a tremulous voice, Susan said the Feds had indicated to Charlie that their own investigation was still open, and Charlie had heard the Somali community was pressuring the Feds, especially now that the state had gone forward. Or something like that, honestly, she couldn't keep it all straight. They were to be in court a week from Tuesday. Charlie said Zach should show up wearing a suit, but Zach didn't have a suit, she didn't know what to do.

"Susan, listen to me." Jim spoke slowly. "What you *do* is you take your son to Sears and you buy him a suit. What you *do* is you put your big-girl panties on and deal with this shit." Jim reached and switched off the speakerphone, picked up the receiver. "All right, all right, I'm sorry. Hang up, Susan. I'm going to make some calls." He shot his cuff, looked at his watch. "They may still be in their offices."

"Jim, what are you doing?" Helen stood up.

"Sweetheart. Don't you worry about that ring. We're going to get it fixed." He looked over at her. "And we have plenty of time to make it to the opera."

"But it was the original diamond." Tears swam in Helen's eyes.

Jim was punching numbers on his desk phone, and after a few moments he said, "Jim Burgess. I'd very much appreciate it if she would take this call." Then: "Hello, Diane. Jim Burgess. I don't believe we've met. How are you? You have some snow up there, I hear. You're right. I'm not calling about the snow. Yes. That's just what I'm calling about."

"I can't stomach this," Helen murmured. "I'm getting in the shower."

"I understand," said Jim. "I do understand. I also understand this was a silly prank done by a kid. And it's unconscionable—" He gave the phone the finger. "I did say unconscionable, yes. Yes, I'm aware a little boy fainted in the mosque. And Zachary's aware of that too, and it's awful. I know Mr. Tibbetts is representing him. I'm paying Mr. Tibbetts. I'm not calling you as Zachary's advocate, I'm calling you as his uncle. Listen to me, Diane. This is a misdemeanor. Last I checked that's some-thing the *criminal* law takes care of, and it will be tried in a criminal court of law. This is not what that civil rights statute is for and—" He turned to Bob and mouthed "Fucking asshole." "Do you plan on a po-litical career, Ms. Dodge? This smells very political to me. No, I'm clearly not intimidating you, *that's* very clear. Questioning your integrity? I'm trying to have a conversation. If a Somali kid had thrown that pig's head, would you be doing this? Well, that's my point. If Zachary was a transgender bisexual you wouldn't be doing this either. He's being zeal-ously attacked by the state because he's a sad-sack *white* kid. And you know it. Three months go by? Are you trying to torture him? Okay, okay."

Jim hung up, tapping a pencil furiously against his desk. Then he held the pencil in both hands and snapped it in half. "Someone's going to have to go up there." He swiveled his chair around to face Bob. "And it's not going to be me." The sound of the shower could be heard down the hall. "What are you doing here, again?" Jim asked.

"Helen called to see if I'd come look for her diamond."

Jim looked around the room, his eyes running over the bookshelves, the pictures of the children at different ages. Then he shook his head slowly, looking back at Bob. "It's a *ring*," he whispered.

"Well, it's her ring, and she's upset."

Jim stood up. "I kissed Dick Hartley's ass," he said. "He approved this. They're going after my nephew—and the whole reason I went up there was to make sure this idiotic liberal *fascism* wouldn't happen."

"You went up there to support Zach and give it your best shot, and it didn't work out. That's all."

Jim sat back down, leaning forward with his elbows on his knees. He said quietly, "If I could express, if I could put into words, if I could find the way to get it across—how much I hate that state."

"You got it across. Forget it. I'll go up there for the hearing. I have plenty of vacation days saved up. You take your wife to the opera and get her a new ring." Bob rubbed the back of his neck. Two thirds of the family had not escaped, this is what Bob thought. He and Susan—which included her kid—were doomed from the day their father died. They had tried, and their mother had tried for them. But only Jim had managed.

As he stepped past Jim, his brother took hold of his wrist. Bob stopped at the unexpectedness of the gesture. "What is it?" Bob asked.

Jim was looking toward the window. "Nothing," he said. He took his hand away slowly.

Down the hall the sound of the shower stopped. There was the bathroom door opening, and then Helen's voice. "Jimmy? Are you going to be grumpy about this all night? Because it's *Romeo and Juliet* and I don't want to watch that with a grumpy husband on one side of me and a grumpy Dorothy on the other." Bob could hear she was trying to be playful.

Jim called out, "Sweetheart, I'll be good." To Bob, he said quietly, "*Romeo and Juliet*? Christ. That's a little bit of torture."

Bob lifted his shoulders in a slow shrug. "Considering what our president's doing in offshore prisons these days, I'm not sure going to the Metropolitan Opera with your wife can be called torture. But things are relative. I know that." He regretted this, and braced for Jim's response.

But Jim stood up and said, "You're right. I mean, you really are right. Stupid country. Stupid state. See you later. Thanks for helping her look for the ring."

As he walked home from his brother's house, stepping around dogs sniffing the sidewalk while their owners tugged listlessly on leashes, Bob's mind sank deeper and deeper, remembering his days as a criminal lawyer. He used to imagine himself handing to the jury a bubble of doubt, an embolism, to obstruct the steadiness of logic flowing from the facts of a case. And now a bubble of doubt was pulsing through him, doubt that had been growing since Jim handed it to him in Shirley Falls, so that even now, with the report of Zachary's newest danger, Bob moved past people on the sidewalk and thought only of his former wife. On the car ride back to New York, Bob had not been assuaged by Jim's dismissiveness, but he had not pressed him further to explain. He thought that to call Pam a parasite was absurd. To say she was needy and managed to get what she needed was not absurd. But if she had come *on* to Jim, and made "poor choices in her confessional judgment" when talking to him, then what in the world would that mean?

Bob stepped around a dog, the owner tugged the dog away. Terrifying, how the ending of his marriage had dismantled him. The silence—where there had been for so long the sound of Pam's voice, her chatter, her laughter, her sharp opinions, her sudden bursting forth of tears—the absence of all that, the silence of no showers running, no bureau drawers opening and shutting, even the silence of Bob's own voice, for he did not speak when he came home, did not recount to anyone his day—the silence almost killed him. But the actual ending remained a blur, and whatever details seeped through Bob's mind turned away from quickly. It was a bad thing, the ending of a marriage. It was bad, no matter how it happened. (Poor Adriana from downstairs, wherever she might be.)

He thought how Sarah, just last year, had said, "Nobody leaves a long marriage without a third party being involved. She was cheating on you, Bob," and Bob had said quietly that hadn't been the case. (And if it was the case, what did it matter now?) But Jim's hint about Pam's behavior had disrupted Bob. He had not gone to Pam's Christmas party this year, saying he was busy, and went instead to the Ninth Street Bar and Grille.

In the past he would bring her boys Christmas presents, and he thought he should still do that, but he didn't. He also thought he was being ridiculous, and conjured up the image of his long ago and ever lovely therapist Elaine: What is it that's bothering you most about this, Bob? The fact that she's not who I thought she was. And who is it you think she is?

He didn't know.

He turned and stepped into the Ninth Street Bar and Grille, where some of the regulars were already seated on their bar stools. The reddish-haired man nodded to him, just as Bob's cell phone rang. "Susie," Bob said. "Hold on." He ordered a whiskey straight. Then he spoke into the phone again. "I know it's hard. I know. I'll be there for the hearing. Yes, let Charlie rehearse with him, that's how it's done. No, that won't be lying. It's going to be all right." He listened, closed his eyes. He repeated, "I know, Susie. It's going to be all right."

———•———

That Helen found Dorothy to be judgmental and wearisome did not alter the discomfort Helen felt on their way to Lincoln Center as she realized that Dorothy had hardly phoned since their trip to St. Kitts, and it could only be, Helen concluded, that the Anglins were tired of them. Jim said this was not the case, the Anglins were having a bad time with their daughter, the family was in therapy, Alan found it expensive and without results, Dorothy wept through every session.

Helen tried to keep this in mind as she greeted Dorothy, settling into her seat in the box they'd held for years with season tickets. Below them the orchestra was starting the pleasant disharmonious sound of tuning strings and running trills while people continued to fill the hall. There was a lushness to the scene: the huge chandeliers that would soon rise, the heavy curtain crumpled so grandly where its velvety tasseled edge met the stage, the panels that reached high, high, to absorb noise and return noise—all this was familiar to Helen, always enjoyed. But tonight the thought streaked across her mind that she was locked inside a velvet coffin, that operas went on too long, and that they would never leave early because Helen herself had never allowed it, leaving early made you appear a dilettante.

She turned back to Dorothy, who did not look as if she'd been having weekly weeping sessions. Her eyes were perfectly clear and perfectly made up, her dark hair pulled back as always into a knot at the base of her neck. She gave a little tilt of her head as Helen said, "I lost the diamond from my engagement ring today, it's made me positively sick." At intermission Dorothy asked how Larry liked the University of Arizona and Helen said he loved it, he had a girlfriend whose name was Ariel, who sounded nice, but—and granted she hadn't met her—she wasn't *quite* sure she was the girl for Larry.

Dorothy's steady gaze—no smile, no nod—while Helen delivered this seemed to be saying to Helen, Let him marry a kangaroo, who cares, *I* don't, and this, as the music resumed, hurt Helen, because friends faked it with each other all the time, it's how society existed. But Dorothy turned her eyes to the stage and did not move, and Helen crossed her legs, feeling how her black pantyhose had become twisted at the thighs, no doubt from having to pull them up quickly in the stall as the gong rang out its warning. What had the feminists accomplished, she thought, if women still had to wait twice as long in ladies' room lines?

Jim was saying to Alan, "She's good. She's great, actually."

"Juliet?" asked Helen. "You think she's great? I don't think she's great."

"The new paralegal."

"Oh," said Helen vaguely. "Yes, you've said that."

And then the curtain rose again, and on and on it went. Oh, it would take *forever* for Romeo and Juliet to die. Romeo was a pudgy man in baby-blue tights; he could not conceivably attract the attentions of this Juliet, at least thirty-five years old and singing her full-breasted heart out. For the love of God, Helen thought, moving once more in her seat, put that stage prop knife in your chest and die.

As the final clapping dwindled, Alan leaned in front of Jim. "Helen, you're looking lovely as always tonight. I've missed seeing you. We've had a hell of a time on our hands, maybe Jim has told you."

"I'm so sorry about that," Helen said. "I've missed seeing you, too."

When Alan reached and squeezed her hand, Helen was shocked to feel in herself a response fleetingly sensual in its gratitude.

3

The hearing took place in the new addition of Superior Court. Bob was used to old courtrooms that held a tired grandness, and he thought there was a prefab feeling to the shiny wood paneling of this room, as though they had all been asked to gather in someone's renovated garage. Through the window could be seen the low gray clouds that hung over the river, and as people entered the room, a plain young woman wearing oblong glasses silently placed a stack of folders on the plaintiff's table, then walked to the window and looked out. A green blazer covered the top of her beige dress, her shoes were a low-heeled beige patent leather, and for a moment Bob—knowing from newspaper photos that this was the assistant attorney general Diane Dodge—was touched by her un-adorned hesitant flight toward style. No one in New York would dress that way, not in winter, probably not ever, but she did not live in New York. She turned from the window, tight-lipped, and walked back to her table.

Susan had dressed that morning in a navy blue dress, yet she did not take off her coat. Two reporters had been allowed in, and two photographers; they sat with their cameras and bulky coats in the front row. Zach, wearing the suit that Susan had bought him at Sears, his hair newly cut and very short, his face pale as pasta, stood—as they all did—for the entrance of the round-shouldered judge, who took his seat above the bench and in a grave, directorial voice read that Zachary Olson had been charged with violating the First Amendment right to freedom of religion—

And so it began.

Diane Dodge stood, and clasped her hands behind her back. Her voice was surprisingly girlish as she brought forth the testimony of the police officers called to the scene that night. Walking back and forth, she seemed like a high school student with the lead in a play, praised so often that the self she carried on her slender frame seemed infused with unassailable confidence. The policemen answered in flat tones; they were not impressed.

Abdikarim Ahmed testified next. He wore cargo pants and a blue collared shirt and sneakers, and Bob thought he did not look African so much as Mediterranean. But he looked very much a foreigner, and when he spoke his accent was thick and unfamiliar, and his English was poor enough that a translator was needed. Abdikarim Ahmed told how the pig's head came suddenly through the door, a small boy had fainted, the rug had to be cleaned seven times as required by Islamic law, they had no money to replace it. He spoke with little affect, warily and wearily. But he looked at Zach, and he looked at Bob, and he looked at Charlie. His eyes were large and dark, and his teeth were uneven and stained.

Mohamed Hussein testified to the same thing, and his English was better. He spoke with more energy, saying that he had run to the door of the mosque but seen no one.

And were you frightened, Mr. Hussein? Diane Dodge placed a hand below her throat.

"Very frightened."

Did you believe that you were being threatened?

"Yes. Very much. We still do not feel safe. This has been painful. You do not know."

Against the objection of Charlie, the judge allowed Mr. Hussein to speak of the camps of Dadaab, the *shifta,* bandits who came in the night to rob and rape and sometimes kill. The sight of the pig's head in their mosque had made them very afraid, as afraid as they had been in Kenya, as afraid as they had been in Somalia, when doing any daily task could mean the possibility of a surprise attack and death.

Bob wanted to put both hands to his face. He wanted to say, This is awful, but *look* at this boy. He's never heard of a refugee camp. He was teased to death when he was a kid, beaten up on a little playground in Shirley Falls, no bandits around. But to him the bullies were like bandits, and—can't you see he's just a sad-sack kid?

But the Somali men were sad, too. Especially the first guy. After testifying he had taken his seat in the courtroom and not looked around, keeping his head down, and Bob saw the exhaustion in his profile. Margaret Estaver had told Bob that many of these men wanted to work but were too traumatized to work, that they were living in the section of the city where drug dealers and addicts were living, that they had been, right here in Shirley Falls, threatened, attacked, robbed, and the women frightened by pit bulls. She had told Bob this, and said as well that she wished she could do something for Susan and Zach. Bob craned his head around and there she was, standing in the back of the courtroom. Their nod was almost imperceptible, the way it is when you have known someone a long time.

Zachary took the stand.

Diane Dodge scribbled without stopping while Charlie led Zach through the story of going to the slaughterhouse in West Annett with the hopes of becoming friendly with the son of the owner, who had worked at Walmart with him, no, they weren't really friends at this point, no, but back then the guy had said he could drop by. No, he'd never heard about the mad cow disease regulations, he'd had no idea anything with a spine had to be killed in a special way and its head taken to be used for coyote or bear bait; he hadn't known what was slaughtered at the slaughterhouse he went to. He took the pig's head because it was there, he didn't really know why, no, he didn't buy it, the guy let him have it, but he brought it home and put it in his mother's freezer and kind of thought maybe it'd be a Halloween thing or something, and later took it to the mosque as a dumb joke, he didn't know it was a mosque, just that Somali people went in and out of there, and it slipped from his fingers and he was really sorry.

Zach looked sorry. He looked pitiful and young, telling this to Charlie, everything they'd rehearsed. Charlie said, Okay, then, and sat down.

Diane Dodge stood up. A sheen of perspiration glistened on her forehead, she pushed her glasses up her nose. In her high voice, she began. So one day, Mr. Olson, you just decided you would go find yourself a pig's head. You went to a slaughterhouse and there was a pig's head and you decided to take it and now you sit in this court under oath and tell us you don't know why you did that.

Zachary looked terrified. He kept licking his lips, answering, "It was just there."

The judge asked Zach if he would like a glass of water.

"Oh. Ah. No, sir."

Was he sure?

"Um. Okay, sir. Your Honor, sir. Thank you."

A glass of water was handed to him, and after putting it to his lips he didn't seem to know where to place the glass, even though there was room for it on the stand. From the corner of his eye Bob glanced at Susan. She sat, watching her son.

You went to the slaughterhouse of a friend, who is no longer a friend, with the intention of obtaining the head of a pig.

"No, sir. Ma'am. No, ma'am." His hand trembled and the water spilled, which seemed to startle Zach, who looked immediately down at his pants. Charlie Tibbetts rose then, took the glass from Zachary, placed it on the stand to his right, and returned to his seat. The judge nodded just slightly to indicate they could proceed.

You didn't take the head of a sheep, or a lamb, or a cow, or a goat, did you? You took the head of a pig. Is that right?

"There weren't any other heads there, because of mad cow disease, you can't—"

Answer the question yes or no. You took the head of a pig, is that right?

"Yes."

And you don't know why. Is that what we're to believe?

"Yes, ma'am."

Really. We're supposed to believe that.

Charlie stood: Badgering.

Diane Dodge turned slowly in a full circle, and said, You stored this in your mother's freezer.

"Yes, in the basement freezer."

Was your mother aware the pig's head was there?

Charlie stood: Objection, calling for speculation—

So Zachary did not have to answer that his mother had not used that freezer for years, not since her husband left her to go find his roots in Sweden, left her without anyone except this skinny child to cook for, no need for a freezer in the basement now, not like when she was newly married to her young husband from New Sweden, Maine, who these days could not, apparently, so much as telephone his son, could only tap out an email once in a while— Bob opened his hands on his lap, spread his fingers out, taut. Cold Susan had married a cold man, from a landscape stark as hers. And here was little Zach, with his washed ears, saying, "It was thawing in my hand and that's why it slipped. I didn't mean to hurt them."

So you're telling me, you expect me to believe, you expect this court to believe, that you had no idea this pig's head would just roll its way into the mosque? Just walking along Gratham Street one evening, and oh by the way, I thought I'd carry along a frozen pig's head?

Charlie rose: Your Honor, she is—

The judge nodded, held up a hand.

Diane Dodge said to Zach, Is that what you're telling me?

Zach looked confused. "I'm sorry. Can you ask me the question again?"

You did not believe, even though you knew this was a gathering place for Somalis, that it was a mosque, their place of worship, you still did not believe that the pig's head was going to go into the mosque and cause harm?

"I wish I didn't walk to the door. I didn't want to cause anyone harm. No, ma'am."

And you expect me to believe that. You expect this judge to believe that. You expect Abdikarim Ahmed and Mohamed Hussein to believe that. She flung her hand to indicate those sitting in the back of the courtroom. Her green blazer opened briefly, showing the beige dress across her small chest.

Charlie stood: Your Honor—

Counselor, please rephrase the question.

Do you expect us to believe this?

Zach looked puzzled and glanced toward Charlie, who gave the slightest nod.

Answer the question, Mr. Olson.

"I didn't mean to hurt anyone."

And you knew, of course you knew, that this was during Ramadan, the holiest of holidays for those of the Islamic faith?

Charlie rose: Objection, badgering—

You may rephrase the question.

Were you aware that during the time this pig's head *slipped from your fingers into the mosque* that it was the holy season of Ramadan? Diane Dodge poked her glasses up her nose and clasped her hands once more behind her back.

"No, ma'am. I didn't even know what Ramadan was."

And your ignorance included the fact that pork is vile to Muslims?

"I'm sorry. I don't understand the question."

And on and on, until she was done with him, and Charlie was able to ask questions again. He asked his questions quietly, as he had before. Zachary, had you heard of Ramadan at the time of this incident?

"Not then, no, sir."

When did you first hear what Ramadan was?

"Later, after I read about it in the paper. I didn't know what it was before."

And how did you feel when you found out?

Objection: The question is not related to the facts.

The answer is completely related to the facts. If my client is accused of—

You may answer the question, Mr. Olson.

Charlie asked again, How did you feel when you found out it was Ramadan?

"I felt bad. I didn't mean to hurt anyone."

The judge said to Charlie, Move it along, counselor, we've covered this before.

You weren't aware of the regulations regarding mad cow disease specifying particular preparations of slaughter for any animal with a spine?

"I didn't know anything about that. I didn't know a pig didn't have a spine that went up to its head."

Objection. Diane Dodge almost shrieked the word, and the judge nodded.

And what did you think you might do with the pig's head once you took it?

"I thought it might be funny for Halloween. On a front stoop or something."

Your Honor! This is material being repeated! As though its ostensible veracity will *increase* with each telling. Diane Dodge stood with a look of such sneering ridicule on her face that, had Bob been the judge, he would have cited her for contempt. For surely she was contemptuous.

But the judge agreed with her, and finally Zachary was allowed to leave the stand. His cheeks were bright red as he sat at the table next to Charlie.

Recess was called while the judge considered his ruling. Again Bob glanced at Margaret Estaver, again there was a small nod. Bob went with Zachary and Susan and Charlie Tibbetts to sit in a small room off the courtroom. They stayed absolutely silent until Susan asked Zach if he needed anything, and Zachary looked at the ground and shook his head. They returned to the courtroom when an officer rapped on the door.

The judge asked Zachary Olson to stand. Zach rose, his cheeks red as ripe tomatoes, sweat sliding in drops down the side of his face. The judge said he was guilty of the civil rights violation, that he had committed a threat of violence that violated the First Amendment right to freedom of religion, and should he not abide by the injunction, prohibiting him from going within two miles of the mosque, except to see his lawyer, and having no contact with the Somali community, he faced a five-thousand-dollar fine and up to a year in jail. At this point the judge removed his glasses and looked blandly (and therefore almost cruelly) at Zach, and said, "Mr. Olson, in this state right now there are two hundred such orders in effect. There are six people who have violated them. And they are—all—in jail." The judge pointed a finger at Zach, his head thrust forward. "So the next time I see you in this courtroom, young man, you'd better bring your toothbrush. It's the only thing you'll need. Adjourned."

Zach turned to look for his mother. The alarm in his eyes rippled through Bob, who would remember it forever.

And so would Abdikarim.

———◆———

In the hallway Margaret Estaver stood off to one side. Bob touched Zach's shoulder and said, "I'll see you back at the house."

They rode through the streets of Shirley Falls, and finally Bob spoke. "The decision was already written, before any of the testimony was heard. You know that's true. That Diane Dodge just beat up on him."

"She did," Margaret agreed. They were riding along the river, the empty old mills to their right. The sky was a light gray above the empty parking lots.

"She was enjoying it," Bob said. "She loved it." When Margaret didn't respond to this he glanced at her, and she returned the look with a concerned face. "You can see what a sad guy Zach is," Bob added. He moved his feet around two empty soda cans, a wrinkled paper bag. She had apologized earlier for the untidiness of her car.

"He's a heartbreaker." Margaret turned the wheel and drove up past the community college. She said, "I don't know if Charlie told you. About Jim."

"Jim? My brother? What about him?"

"It seems he hurt things. I know he came up here wanting to help. But he spoke so well he made Dick Hartley feel like a fool, and worse—he didn't stick around."

"Jim never sticks around."

"Well." Margaret said the word with a sigh. "In Maine you stick around." Her hair, pulled up messily, had strands that hid part of her face. She said, "The governor spoke after him, if you recall, and it was taken as a sign of disrespect—I'm just telling you what I heard—that Jim walked away right as the governor got ready to speak." Margaret slowed for a stop sign. "And of course," she added in a lower voice, "the governor didn't speak so well."

"Nobody's going to speak as well as Jim, it's what he does."

"I could see that. I'm just saying there was some fallout in Augusta. I know someone in the AG's office up there, and apparently Dick Hartley stewed about this for weeks, and then gave Diane the go-ahead as soon as they felt they could prove the bias part. Jim called Diane himself, is that right? It only made her angrier, of course. I think that's part of what you heard today."

Bob looked out his window at the small houses they were passing, Christmas wreaths still hanging on many doors. "Were there editorials about this in the *Shirley Falls Journal*? Jim reads that online."

"No, this was all internal, I think. And the reality is—well, you saw those men testify, Mohamed and Abdikarim. It was a really distressing thing for them to go through. I know you know all that. But this decision today may nudge the U.S. Attorney's Office along. Some folks in the Somali community are still pushing for them to take action."

"Jesus." Bob gave a small groan. Then he said quietly, "Sorry."

"For what?"

"For saying 'Jesus.'"

"Oh God. You're serious." Margaret looked over at him, rolled her eyes. She made another turn, heading back toward town. "Gerry O'Hare didn't want the AG's office going ahead, he didn't want what happened today. I guess he's known Susan from way back. His feeling's been: Enough. But—" Margaret gave a small shrug. "You've got people like Rick Huddleston at the Office of Racial Anti-Defamation, who doesn't ever want it to drop. And honestly, if it wasn't Zachary, I wouldn't want it dropped."

"But it is Zachary." He could not get over the feeling that he had known her a long time.

"Yes, it is." After a moment, Margaret added, "Oy," with a sigh.

"Did you say 'Oy'?"

"I did. One of my husbands was Jewish. I picked up some expressions. He was very expressive."

They drove past the high school, its playing fields covered with snow. A signboard spelled out GO HORNETS BEAT DRAGONS. "Have you had a lot of husbands?" he asked.

"Two. My first I met in college in Boston, the Jewish one. We're still friends, he's pretty great. Then I came home to Maine and I married a man up here, and that ended quickly. Two divorces by the age of fifty. I imagine it affects my credibility."

"You think so? I don't think so. If you're a movie star you're just getting started with two."

"I'm not a movie star." She pulled into Susan's driveway. Her smile was clear and playful and faintly sad. "Nice to see you, Bob Burgess. Call if there's anything I can do."

To his surprise Susan and Zach were at the kitchen table as though they'd been waiting for him. "We were hoping you'd brought something to drink," Susan said. In her navy blue dress, she appeared grown up, in charge.

"In my duffel bag. Did you look? I got whiskey and wine on my way from the airport."

"That's what I figured," his sister said. "But we don't go pawing through people's private belongings in this house. I'd like a little wine. Zachary said he'd like some too."

Bob poured the wine into water glasses. "Sure you wouldn't like whiskey, Zach? You've had kind of a rough day."

"I think whiskey might make me sick," Zach said. "Once I got sick on whiskey."

"When?" said Susan. "When in the world did that happen?"

"Eighth grade," Zach answered. "You and Dad let me go to that party at the Tafts one night. Everyone was drinking like mad. Out in the woods. I thought whiskey was like beer or something, and I just drank it down. And then I puked."

"Oh, honey," said Susan. She reached across the table and rubbed her son's hand.

Zachary looked at his glass. "Each time one of those photographers clicked his camera I felt like I'd been shot. I mean with a bullet. Click. I hated it. It's why I spilled the water." He looked at Bob. "Did I screw up real bad?"

"You did not screw up," Bob said. "The woman was a pinhead. It's over. Forget it. It's done."

The sun was low now, and it sent a pale blade of light through the kitchen window that fell briefly across the table, then the floor. It was not bad, sitting there with his sister and nephew, drinking wine.

"So, Uncle Bob, do you, like, have a crush on that woman minister or something?"

"A crush?"

"Yeah. 'Cause it kind of seems like you do." Zach raised his eyebrows in a questioning expression. "I don't know if old people get crushes or not."

"Well, they do. Do I have one on Margaret Estaver? No."

"You're lying." Zachary suddenly grinned at him. "Never mind." He drank more wine. "I just wanted to come home. The whole time I was in there I kept thinking, I want to go home."

"Well, now you're home," Susan said.

4

There were Saturday evenings, like this one, when Pam, with her conge-
nial husband, stepped off an elevator into the foyer of an apartment
where globes of yellow light and fabulous shadows played throughout
the rooms beyond, when leaning to kiss the cheeks of people she barely
knew, taking a glass of champagne from a tray held forward, stepping
farther and seeing the paintings lit upon walls of dark olive or deep red,
a long table set with crystal, and turning to look down upon an avenue
that stretched triumphantly right to the horizon, a jubilance of red tail-
lights merging as they moved away, then turning back to the women
wearing their silver and gold necklaces down the fronts of their black
dresses, standing in their wonderful well-fitting shoes—Pam would
think, as she did now, This is what I wanted.

What she meant, exactly, she could not have said. It was simply a
truth that clamped down on her with gentle snugness, and gone, gone,
gone were those needling thoughts that she was living the wrong life.
She was calm with a completeness that seemed almost transcendent,
this moment that spread before her with the assuredness of itself. Cer-

tainly nothing in her past—the long bike rides on the farm roads of her childhood, the hours spent in the cozy local library, the creaking-floored dormitory in Orono, the tiny home of the Burgess family, not even the excitement of Shirley Falls that had seemed the start of adult life, or the apartment she had shared with Bob in Greenwich Village, though she had liked that apartment very much, the noise on the streets at all hours, the comedy clubs and jazz clubs they had gone to—nothing had indicated to her that she would want this and get this, right here, this particular kind of loveliness so gracefully and astonishingly taken for granted by the people who spoke to her with nodding heads. The host was saying that he and his wife had bought the bowl in Vietnam, eight years ago. "Oh, did you love it?" Pam asked. "Did you love Vietnam?"

"Oh, we did," said the wife, stepping closer to Pam, and including those around her as she swept them with her gaze. "We did love it. We loved it to death. And honestly, I'd been the one who hadn't wanted to go."

"It wasn't, you know, creepy?" Pam had met, a few times, the woman asking this question. She was married to a famous newsman, and her Southern accent, Pam had noted before, increased as she drank. Her clothes—as was the case tonight, she wore a high-collared white buttoned blouse—were not stylish, but rather seemed worn in order to retain the ladylike Southern primness and good manners instilled in her years ago. Pam felt a tenderness toward her, at the recalcitrance she displayed in moving away from her buttoned-up past.

"Oh, no, it's beautiful. It's a beautiful country," the hostess said. "You'd never know—well, you know. You just wouldn't know those awful things went on there."

Moving into the dining room, escorted to her seat—far away from her husband because the rules required mixing (she wiggled her fingers to him from across the long table)—Pam suddenly remembered that it was Jim Burgess who had said to her years ago, when she and Bobby first spoke of moving here, "New York will kill you, Pam." She had never forgiven Jim for that. He had failed to see her appetite, her adaptability, her desire—perpetual—for change. New York had been very different back then, of course, and of course she and Bob did not have much money.

But Pam's determination was almost always stronger than her disappointments, and even when that first apartment, so tiny that they had to wash the dishes in the bathtub, had lost its initial charm, and the subways were really frightening, Pam had still ridden them; the screeching of them as they pulled into their stations she had taken in stride.

The man next to her said that his name was Dick. "Dick," Pam said, and immediately thought it sounded as though she had implied something. "How nice to meet you," she said. He nodded once, with exaggerated politeness, and asked how she was. Pam was—in fact—on her way to being drunk. Because she did not eat as she used to, because she was getting older, which affected metabolism, she could no longer drink as much as she once had. Her desire to explain this to Dick made her understand that she was on her way to being drunk, perhaps already there, and so she merely smiled at him. He asked her, politely, and this time without the camouflage of exaggeration, if she worked outside the home, and she explained about her part-time job, and how she used to work in a lab, and that perhaps she didn't seem like a scientist, people had said that to her, that she didn't seem like a scientist, whatever that meant, and she thought if she didn't seem like a scientist it's because she was *not* a scientist, but she had been an *assistant* to a scientist, to a parasitologist—

Dick was a psychiatrist. He gave a pleasant raise of his eyebrows and placed his napkin into his lap. "Hey, by all means," Pam said. "Let it rip. Analyze me all you want. Doesn't bother me a bit."

She waved again at her husband, who was sitting down toward the end of the long table next to the what's-her-name woman from the South in her white buttoned-up blouse, while Dick was saying he didn't analyze people per se, but rather their desires. He was a consultant to marketing firms. "Really?" Pam asked. Another night this might have caused Pam to suddenly lurch toward that dreadful thought: I am living the wrong life. Another night she might have asked this Dick if he had taken the Hippocratic Oath, she might have asked pointedly if he was using his skills as a physician to help people *consume,* but the evening was a lovely one, and she thought certain aspects could just stay away, as though there were only so many times her cells could rise up in outrage and this would not be one of them; she didn't, she realized, care at all what Dick did for a career, and when he turned to speak to the person on his other side, Pam looked around the table and imagined the sex lives (or not) of some of these people. She thought she captured the surreptitious glance given from one jowly man to a thick-waisted woman who returned to him a steady private gaze, and she found it thrilling that no matter what people looked like they still had a desire to undress and cling to each other—the pull of biology that had long outworn its use, for these women were past the time of childbearing. . . . Yes, Pam, halfway through her slippery salad, had already drunk too much.

"Wait, what?" she said, putting her fork down, because someone farther down the table had said something about a pig's head going through a mosque in a small Maine town.

The person, a man Pam had not met before, repeated this to her. "Yes, I heard about that," Pam said. She picked up her fork; she would not claim Zachary. But the back of her scalp flared in warmth as though she were in danger.

"A fairly aggressive thing to do," the man said. "They had a civil rights hearing, there was a piece in the paper."

"I went to camp in Maine," Dick said, and his voice felt too close, as though he was speaking right into her ear.

"They had a civil rights hearing?" Pam asked. "Was he found guilty?"

"He was, yes."

"What does that mean?" Pam asked. "Is he going to jail?" She remembered how Bob said Zach was crying alone in his room. Anxiety flashed through her: Bob had not come to her Christmas party. "What month is this?" she asked.

The hostess laughed. "I get like that too, Pamela. Sometimes I can't even remember the *year.* It's February."

"He only goes to jail if he violates the sanctions," the man said. "Essentially the sanctions are just to stay away from the mosque and not trouble the Somali community. It seemed to me the state was choosing to send a message."

"Maine's a funny place," someone else mused. "You never know which way it's going."

"Look," said the thick-waisted woman who had gazed steadily at the jowly man. The woman wiped her mouth carefully with her large white napkin, and people had to wait politely to see what she would say. She said, "I agree it was an aggressive act on the part of the young man. But the country is scared." She put both fists down quietly on the table and looked one way, then the other. "Just this morning I was walking along the river by Gracie Mansion and there were New York City helicopters and patrol boats circling and I thought, Dear God, I suppose any minute we could be hit again."

"It's only a matter of time," someone said.

"Of course it is. The best thing to do is forget about it and live your life." A man sitting down by the Southern what's-her-name said this with a tone of disgust.

"How people react to a crisis has always fascinated me," Dick said.

But Pam was pulled away now from the foolish splendor of the evening; the dark presence of Zachary—oh, Zachary, so skinny and dark-eyed, such a sad sweet child he had been!—his presence had come into the room, unfelt by all but her, of course; she was his *aunt*. And she sat there denying him. Her husband would say nothing, she knew this; a glance in his direction showed him to be chatting to his seatmate. She was alone among these people, and the Burgess family expanded before her. "Oh," she almost said out loud, remembering going up to visit Zach when he was newly born, the oddest-looking baby she'd ever seen. And poor Susan, a quiet wreck—he wouldn't nurse, or something. Pam and Bobby had stopped visiting so much after a while, it was just too depressing, Pam said, and even Bobby agreed. Helen really agreed. Pam watched her salad plate get taken away, replaced by a dish of mushroom risotto. "Thank you," she said, for she always thanked servers. Years back, when she had first entered this life through her new marriage, she had arrived at a party like this one and shaken the hand of the man who opened the door. "I'm Pam Carlson," she said, and he looked faintly put out with her, and asked if he could take her coat. That was the butler,

her friend Janice said. Pam had told Bobby about that. He'd been wonderful, of course, his halfhearted shrug.

"I'm reading an amazing book by a Somali woman," someone was saying now, and Pam said, "Hey, I'd like to read it." To hear her own voice
helped push Zachary's presence from her. But oh, here came the sadness—
she placed her hand over her wineglass to refuse more wine—her previous
life, twenty years with the Burgess family, you couldn't live a life for such
a long time and think it would just disappear! (She had thought you could.)
It wasn't just Zach, it was Bob, his kind and open face, the blue eyes, the
deep smile lines that sprang around them. Until the day she died, Bob
would be her home—and how awful, she had not known! She did not turn
to look at her current husband now, it would not matter if she looked at
him or not, at such moments as this one he was not really any more familiar to her than anyone else in this room, all slipping away from her with the
ease of vast indifference, because they were hardly real and meant almost
nothing to her at all, there was only the deep metallic magnet of the presence of Zachary and Bob—and Jim and Helen, all of them. The Burgess
boys, the Burgesses! Her mind filled with the image of little Zachary at
Sturbridge Village, his cousins calling to him to come do this, come do
that, and the poor little dark-haired creature looking like he just didn't
know how to have fun, and Pam had wondered that day if he was autistic,
although apparently they'd had him tested for everything, Pam, already
knowing that day in Sturbridge that she would leave Bob, though he did
not know and he held her hand as they walked the kids to the snack bar,
it made her heart ache horribly to recall— She turned her head. From
down at the end of the table the man who had been contemptuous
about the threat of terror was saying, "I'm not going to vote for a woman
president. The country's not ready for that, and I'm not ready for that."

And the Southern what's-her-name woman, her face bright red, said
suddenly and amazingly, "Well, then fuck yew, just fuck yew!" She banged
her fork down on her plate, and a fabulous silence fell over the room.

In the taxi, Pam said, "Oh, wasn't that *fun*?" She would call her friend
Janice first thing in the morning. "Do you think her husband was embarrassed? Who cares, it was wonderful!" She clapped her hands and added,

"Bob didn't come to our Christmas party this year, I wonder what's up with that." But she no longer felt sadness about it, the pressure of sorrow that had overtaken her at the table, the longing for all the Burgess kids, and the sense of the irreplaceable familiarity of her old life—that had passed the way a cramping of a stomach muscle passes, and the absence of its pain was glorious. Pam looked out the window and held her husband's hand.

———•———

Midtown was a crowded place at lunchtime, sidewalks overflowing with pedestrians who moved through the traffic-jammed crosswalks, some on their way to a restaurant to maybe make a deal. There was an added urgency today, because just that morning the world's largest bank had reported the first mortgage-related loss at well over ten billion dollars, and people didn't know what that meant. There were opinions, of course, and bloggers writing that people would be living in their cars by the end of the year.

Dorothy Anglin was not worried about living in a car. She had enough money that if she lost two thirds of it she could still live exactly how she was living, and sitting in this trendy café on Fifty-seventh Street near Sixth Avenue, with a friend she had met at a fundraiser for an art-in-the-schools program, her thoughts were, as they always were these days, on her daughter, and not on the program they were discussing, and not on the financial situation the country might be facing. She was nodding vaguely to give the appearance of listening when she looked over and saw Jim Burgess sitting at a table with his new paralegal. She made no mention of this to her friend, but she watched the two of them carefully. Dorothy recognized the young woman; they had spoken one day when Dorothy stopped by the office. Dorothy thought of her as a shy girl, long-haired and thin-waisted. They were sitting at a table near the back, and neither—it seemed to Dorothy—had seen her. She watched while the girl put a large cloth napkin to her face, as though she needed to hide a smile. A bottle of wine sat in its cooler next to the table.

Jim leaned forward, then he sat back, folding his arms, cocking his head as though waiting for an answer. The napkin to her mouth again. They may as well have been peacocks with their feathers spread out. Or dogs sniffing each other's behinds. (Helen, Dorothy thought, Helen, Helen, Helen. Poor stupid Helen. But she did not think it with deep feeling, they were just words that slipped over her mind.) They rose to leave, and Jim touched the girl's back lightly as he ushered her from the table. Dorothy put the menu straight up in front of her face, and when she put it down she saw them on the sidewalk, laughing and walking with ease. No, they had not seen her.

Classic: He was old enough to be her father.

That's what Dorothy thought as she pretended to listen to her friend across the table. This friend's daughter had also behaved badly in high school but was now doing well at Amherst, and this was supposed to make Dorothy feel better about her own daughter. But Dorothy could not stop thinking of what she had seen. She could, she supposed, call Helen and say casually, Oh, I saw Jim with the paralegal, isn't it nice they get along? She wasn't going to do that.

"It's all right," Alan said as he and Dorothy were getting ready for bed. "They've been working on a case together, and doing a good job. I don't think Adriana has much money. I see her eating lunch from a plastic container at her desk most days. I'm sure Jim was thanking her by treating her to a nice meal."

"They had a bottle of wine at the most expensive place on Fifty-seventh Street. Jim doesn't even drink when he's on vacation." Dorothy added, "I hope he didn't charge it to the firm."

Alan scooped up his dirty socks from the floor. Walking toward the hamper, he said, "Jim's having a hard time these days, ever since his nephew got in trouble up there. He's really bothered by it. I can see it."

"How can you see it?"

"Honey, I've known the man for years. When he's relaxed or in fight mode, he talks. He opens his mouth and words come out. But when he's preoccupied, he's silent. And he's been pretty silent for months now."

"Well, he wasn't silent today," Dorothy said.

5

Abdikarim tried to stay awake because nighttime brought dreams that pinned him to the bed as though boulders had rolled on top of him. Every night now the dream was the same: His son Baashi looking at him with bewilderment as the truck came slowly and then fast, screeching to the door of his shop in Mogadishu. On the back of the truck were boys, a few not even as old as his son. Abdikarim saw the quick, youthful motions of legs and thin arms as they jumped from the truck, the heavy guns strapped over their shoulders, balanced in their hands. The silent (in the dream) smashing of the counter, the shelves, the abrupt horrendous chaos, the surging wave of hell cresting over them. Evil had come to them, why had he thought it would not?

Abdikarim had had many nights, fifteen years' worth of nights, to think about this, and always he arrived at the same thought. He should have left Mogadishu earlier. He should have put the two worlds of his mind into one. Siad Barre had fled the city, and when the resistance group split into two, Abdikarim's own mind seemed to split into two. When the mind occupies two worlds it cannot see. One world of his mind had said: Abdikarim, there is violence in this city, send your wife and young daughters away—and he had done that. The other world of his mind had said: I will stay and keep my shop, with my son.

His son, tall, dark-eyed, looking at his father, terrified, and behind him the street, and the walls becoming upside down, dust and smoke and the boy falling, as though his arms had been pulled one way, his legs another— To shoot was bad enough to last this lifetime and the next, but not bad enough for the depraved men-boys, who had burst through the door, the splintered shelves and tables, who swung their large American-made guns. For some reason—no reason—one had stayed behind and smashed the end of his gun down onto Baashi repeatedly, while Abdikarim crawled to him. In the dream he never reached him.

Shouts brought Haweeya running down the hallway, and she murmured to Abdikarim, made him a cup of tea. "Don't be sorry, Uncle," she said, because Abdikarim always apologized on those nights his shouting woke her.

"That boy," he told her one night. "Zachary Olson. He is cutting my heart."

Haweeya nodded. "But he'll be punished. The U.S. attorney is getting ready to punish him. Minister Estaver knows this."

Abdikarim shook his head in his darkened room, sweat coming from his face down onto his neck. "No, he cuts my heart. You didn't see him. He's not what we saw in the newspaper. He's a frightened . . ." finishing softly: "child."

"We live now where there are laws," Haweeya said soothingly. "He's frightened because he broke the law."

Abdikarim continued to shake his head. "It is not right," he whispered, "for anyone, with laws or without, to continue making fear."

"And so he'll be punished," she repeated patiently. He took the tea and drank only a little, and told her to go back to bed. He did not return to sleep but lay damp on his bed, and the longing in his heart was what it always was, to return to the place his son had fallen. The very worst moment of his life, and his deepest longing was to return to that moment, to touch the wet hair, to hold those arms—he had loved no one as much, and even in the horror, or perhaps because of the horror, to hold his broken son had been as pure as the sky had been blue. To lie down on the spot his son had last been, to press his face into whatever dirt or rubble had been replaced a hundred times in the years since, was, it felt at these moments, all he wanted. Baashi, my son.

In the dark he lay on his bed and pondered the DVD he had taken from the library when he first came to Shirley Falls. *Moments in American History,* but the only moment Abdikarim watched, repeatedly for weeks, was the assassination of the president, because of the pink-suited wife climbing over the back of the car to try to reach the piece of her husband she saw flying away. Abdikarim did not believe what was said of this famous widow: that she cared only about money and clothes. It was recorded, and he saw. She had felt in her lifetime what he had felt in his. Though she had died (living to be as old as Abdikarim was now), he thought of her as his secret friend.

In the morning, instead of walking from the mosque to his shop on Gratham Street after prayers, Abdikarim walked up Pine Street to the Unitarian church, looking for Margaret Estaver.

———•———

A month passed by. It was the end of February now, and while there was still snow on the ground in Shirley Falls, the sun was higher in the sky and caused, for a few hours some days, the snow to soften and trickle and twinkle beneath the yellow light that warmed the sides of buildings and made the parking lot at the mall have small rivulets of water running at its edge. Often now when Susan left work at the end of her day and walked across the large expanse of pavement, the air still held the open light of spring. On one of these afternoons her cell phone rang as she got into her car. Susan was not as used to cell phones as other people were; it still surprised her when it rang, and she always felt she was talking into something as insubstantial as a graham cracker. She took it from her bag quickly, and heard Charlie Tibbetts's voice say that at the end of the week the Feds were going to charge Zachary with a hate crime. They'd stalled because of the issue of showing intent, but they thought they had a case now. An inside source had told him this. His voice sounded weary. "We'll fight it," he said. "But it's bad."

Susan put her sunglasses on, then pulled out of the parking lot so slowly that a car honked behind her. She drove past the strip of pine trees, pulled up to the intersection, continued past the hospital and the church and the old wooden houses, and pulled into her driveway.

Zach was in the kitchen. "I can't cook," he said. "But I can use the microwave. I bought you frozen lasagna and me macaroni and cheese. And we can have applesauce. That's almost like cooking." He had set the table, seeming pleased with this accomplishment.

"Zachary." She went to hang up her coat, and as she stood at the door of the closet tears fell down her face; she rubbed them off with her glove. Only after she saw that he had eaten his food did she tell him about Charlie's call. Then she watched as he stared at her. He stared at the walls, the sink, and then back at her. The dog began to whine.

"Mommy," Zach said.

"Now, it's going to be all right," Susan said.

He looked at her with his mouth partly open, and slowly shook his head.

"Honey, I'm sure your uncles will come back up for this. You'll have plenty of support. Look, you managed last time."

Zach kept shaking his head. He said, "Mom, I've researched this online. You don't know." She could hear the stickiness of his mouth gone dry. "It's so much worse." He stood up.

"What is, honey?" She said this calmly. "What is it I don't know?"

"The federal hate charges. Mom."

"Tell me." Beneath the table she shoved the poor dog hard because she wanted to shriek at the whimpering animal pressing her nose into Susan's lap. "Sit down, honey, and tell me."

Zach stayed standing. "Like, ten years ago this guy—somewhere, I can't remember—he burned a cross on a black guy's lawn and he went to prison for eight years." Zach's eyes had become spidery-red, and moist.

"Zachary. You did not burn a cross on a black man's lawn." She spoke quietly, precisely.

"And some other guy yelled at a black woman and threatened something, and he went away for six months. Mom. I—I can't." His thin shoulders lifted. Slowly he sat back down.

"It's not going to happen, Zachary."

"But how can you say that?"

"Because you didn't do those things."

"Mommy, you saw that judge. He said bring your toothbrush next time."

"They all say that. They say it to a kid with a speeding ticket, they say it to scare young people. It's stupid. Stupid, stupid."

Zachary crossed his long arms on the table and put his head down.

"Jim will help Charlie take care of this," Susan said. "What's that, honey?" because her son had mumbled something into his folded arms.

Zachary raised his head and looked at her sorrowfully. "Mom. Haven't you noticed? Jim can't do anything. And I think he pushed Bob over, or something, the last night at the hotel."

"He pushed Bob?"

"It doesn't matter." Zach sat up straighter. "It doesn't matter. Mom, don't worry about me."

"Honey—"

"No, really." Zach gave a little shrug as though his earlier fear had simply slipped away. "It doesn't matter. Really."

Susan got up to let the dog out. Standing in the open doorway, with her hand on the doorknob, she felt in the air the faint moistness of the faraway but approaching spring, and for a moment she was caught inside the sudden absurdity that keeping the door open would keep them free. To click it shut would seal them up eternally. Closing the door firmly, she turned back to the kitchen. "I'm going to do the dishes. You find something to watch on TV."

"What?"

She repeated what she'd said, and her son nodded, said quietly, "Okay."

It was hours before she realized she had not let the dog back in. But the dog was there, on the back porch, and her fur was cold as she lay down at Susan's feet.

6

"Helen," Jim had said that morning, sitting on the edge of the bed. "You are so good." He pulled on his socks. Walking past her to the dressing room, he placed his hand on her head. "You're a good person. I love you," he said.

She almost said, "Oh, Jimmy, don't go to work today," turning to watch him as he walked to the dressing room, but she did not say it, because she had woken feeling like an anxious child, and if she spoke like one, she would feel worse. So she had gotten up, put on her bathrobe, and said, "Let's go to the theater this weekend. Let's go see something small, maybe off-off Broadway."

"Sure, Hellie." He called this from the dressing room; she heard the hangers move on the rod. "Find something, and we'll go."

Still in her bathrobe she sat at the family computer in the room off the kitchen and scrolled through all the plays in New York. Feeling her appetite for this run down, she chose a Broadway play instead, about a family in Alaska that was, as the advertisement said, merrily dysfunctional. Then she got dressed and remembered an elderly aunt from her

past who had said to her one day, I'm not hungry anymore, Helen. A few
months later the poor woman was dead. Helen's eyes filled, remembering this, and she went to the phone and made an appointment with her
doctor for a checkup. Helen didn't think she was not hungry for food,
but she did think there was some appetite that was missing. The doctor
could see her on Monday; there'd been a cancellation. This made her
feel efficient, and when she hung up she remembered how kind Jim had
been this morning, and it warmed her, as though she had received a
pleasant gift and had forgotten. She would go into Manhattan for the
day. She picked up the phone and called two women from the Kitchen
Cabinet. One was off to have a dental implant, the other was having
lunch with an elderly mother-in-law, but their responses—Oh, *Helen,*
how I wish I were free!—gave her a sense of buoyancy.

On the sidewalk in front of Bloomingdale's, Helen heard a plump
woman on a cell phone saying, "I got these pillows for the front room,
and they're just the right color," and then Helen was filled with a sudden
warmth of nostalgic joy—as though she had come across the first crocus
of the season. This plump woman, big bags banging softly against her
big thighs, was happily inside her life. It was the luxury of the ordinary,
and it reminded Helen of what she had missed without knowing it, but
it was here: her Kitchen Cabinet friends who wanted to be with her, her
loving husband, her healthy children, no, she had not lost anything.

As she sat in the café on the seventh floor of Bloomingdale's, having
an early lunch of cinnamon squash soup, her cell phone went off. "You're
not going to believe this," Jim said. "Zach has disappeared. He's gone."

"Jimmy, he can't be just gone." She was struggling to hold the thin
phone and also wipe at her mouth with a napkin, she felt the soup on
her lip.

"Sure he can, and he is." Jim did not sound angry. He sounded distraught. Helen was not used to her husband sounding distraught. "I'm
catching a plane this afternoon."

"Can't I come with you?" She was already motioning to the waitress
for the check.

"If you want. But Susan's in real trouble. He left a note. It said, 'Mom, I'm sorry.'"

"He left a *note*?"

She found a taxi, and all the way down the FDR and across the Brooklyn Bridge she kept thinking of Zachary leaving a note. Of Susan— she couldn't picture Susan—pacing the floor, calling the police? What did a person do in these circumstances? A person phoned Jim, that's what. (Truthfully, in Helen, as the taxi swayed and bounced up Atlantic Avenue, there was a tiny sliver of something that was sharp and thrilled. Already she was telling the story to her children: Oh, it was awful, your father was so upset, we didn't know, and I raced back and we got a plane.)

7

Charlie had told her not to do it yet, and Jim had told her the same, but as Susan waited for her brothers to arrive she picked up the phone and called Gerry O'Hare. It was near suppertime, and she was ready to hang up if his wife answered, but Gerry answered. And so Susan blurted out that Zachary was missing. "Gerry. What do I do?"

"Tell me how long he's been gone."

She didn't know. He'd been there when she left at eight, or at least his car had been. But when she came home at eleven, because business was slow and the boss said she could have extra time for lunch, she came into the kitchen and found the note on the table and it said, "Mom, I'm sorry." And his car was gone.

"Are things missing? Are clothes missing?"

"A few clothes, I think, and his duffel bag, and his cell phone. His computer is missing, and his wallet. He has a laptop. You don't commit suicide and take your laptop, do you? Have you ever had someone do that?"

Gerry asked if there were signs of forced entry, and she said no. She said her tenant, Jean Drinkwater, had been in her rooms upstairs and hadn't heard anything.

"Do you keep the doors locked during the day?"

"We do."

"I can send someone over to look around but—"

"Oh, don't do that. I just want to know—I'm waiting for my brothers, they'll be here soon—I just want to know if someone takes their computer if they're going to hurt themselves."

"There's no way of knowing, Susan. Was he depressed?"

"Scared." Now she faltered. She assumed Gerry must know the Feds were going to move by the end of the week, but all she wanted was for someone to tell her that her son was alive. And no one could tell her that.

Gerry said, "We have an adult male who, far as we know, left his house with his car and a few things. There's nothing to suggest foul play. In a missing person case, we won't even file a report on it for twenty-four hours."

She knew this from Charlie and Jim. "I'm sorry to bother you," she said.

"You're not bothering me, Susan. You're being a mother. Your brothers will be there soon? You won't be alone tonight?"

"They just pulled in. Thank you, Gerry."

Gerry stood for a long time in his living room, until his wife called to him to say that supper was on the table. In all his years as a policeman he had never understood—why would he understand?—how it was that some things happened to some people and not to others. Gerry's own sons had turned out well. One was a state trooper and the other was a high school teacher, and who could say why he and his wife had had this luck? The luck could end tomorrow. He had watched people's luck end with one phone call, one knock on their door. Any police chief knew how quickly luck could end. He went into the dining room and held the chair out for his wife.

"What are you doing?" she asked, playfully. She surprised him by putting both arms around his neck, and for a moment they hummed their favorite song, a Wally Packer song from their early days together, *I've got this funny little feeling you're gonna be mine. . . .*

———

The Burgess kids sat at the kitchen table, going over what had happened. Helen sat there too, and felt out of place. The dog kept putting her head onto Helen's lap, and when Helen thought no one was looking she pushed the dog away hard. The dog whined, and Susan snapped her fingers and said, "Lie down." Susan's hands were shaking and Bob told her to take a tranquilizer and she said she had already taken one. She said, "All I want is to know he's alive."

"Let's take a good look," said Jim. "Come on." The brothers went upstairs with Susan to Zach's room. Helen stayed where she was with her coat still on, the house was cold. She heard them walking about above her, heard the murmur of their voices. They stayed up there a long time, closet doors opening, drawers opening and shutting. On the kitchen counter was a magazine called *Simple Meals for Simple Folks* and Helen eventually flipped through it. Each recipe was written with cheerfulness. Put butter and brown sugar on those carrots and your kids will never know they're eating something good for them. She sighed and put it down. The curtains at the window above the sink were a burnt orange color with small ruffles on the bottom, and another ruffle that went all the way across the top. It had been a long time since Helen had seen curtains like that. She sat with her hands in her lap feeling the absence of her engagement ring, which was now at the jeweler's. There was only the simple band on her finger, and it felt odd. She remembered that she had not canceled her doctor's appointment for Monday and wondered if she ought to switch her watch to her other wrist to remind herself to call first thing in the morning, but she just sat, and then the brothers and Susan came back downstairs.

"I think he's run away," Jim said. Helen did not answer. She didn't know what to say to this. It was decided that Bob would stay at the house for the night, Helen and Jim would go to the hotel.

"Have you let Steve know?" Helen asked Susan, standing up, and Susan looked at her as though she had not noticed Helen had been there all this time.

"Of course," she said.

"What did he say?"

"He was nice. Very worried," Jim answered.

"Well, that's good. Did he have any suggestions?" Helen pulled on her gloves.

"It's not like he can do anything from over there." Jim again answered for his sister. "There's printed-out emails from him upstairs, telling Zach to go to school, find an interest, a hobby, that kind of stuff. All set?"

Bob said, "Susie, can you turn the heat up since I'm staying?" and Susan said she would.

As they drove over the bridge to the hotel, Helen asked, "Where would he run away to?"

"We don't know, do we."

"But what's the plan, Jimmy?"

"We wait."

Helen thought how sinister the inky river seemed on both sides of them, how black the night was here. "Poor Susan." She meant this. But she thought the words sounded false, and Jim made no reply.

———•———

The next afternoon there was a wedding at the hotel. The day was sunny and the sky was blue. The snow sparkled, and the river sparkled, as though diamonds had been openhandedly flung throughout the air. On the hotel's large terrace next to the river, the wedding party was lined up for photographs, people laughing as though it were not cold. Helen could see this, but not hear it, since she was standing high up on a balcony and the sound of the river drowned everyone out. The bride wore a white fluffy jacket over her white gown. She was not young, Helen noticed. This must be a second wedding. If so, it was ridiculous for the bride to be wearing a traditional gown, but nowadays people did what they wanted, and also this was Maine. The husband was chubby, happy-looking. Helen felt the faintest stirrings of jealousy. She turned to go back into the room.

"I'm going over to the house. Are you coming?" Jim sat on the bed scratching his feet. He had just showered after working out at the gym in the hotel, and now he was scratching his bare feet furiously. He had been scratching his feet, it seemed to Helen, since they had arrived.

"If I thought it would help I would go, of course," said Helen, who had endured the entire morning at her sister-in-law's house. "But I can't see that my presence makes much difference."

"Suit yourself," said Jim. There were flakes of white skin on the carpet.

"Jimmy, stop. You're tearing your feet apart. Look at that mess."

"They itch."

Helen sat down in the chair by the desk. "How much longer are we going to be here?"

Jim stopped scratching his feet and looked at her. "I don't know. As long as it takes to see what's happening. I don't *know*. Where are my socks?"

"On the other side of the bed." Helen did not want to touch them.

He leaned around, put them on methodically. "She can't be left alone right now. We have to ease her through this, whatever this is. Or turns out to be."

"She should have asked Steve to fly over here. He should have offered." Helen got up and moved back toward the terrace. "People are getting married down there. In the middle of winter. Outside."

"Why would Susan ask Steve to come over here? She hasn't seen him in seven years, he hasn't seen his son in seven years. Why should Susan put up with him now?"

"Because. They have this child together." She turned to face her husband.

"Hellie, you're making me a little crazy here. I don't want to fight with you. Why are you making me fight with you? My sister's going through just about the worst thing a parent can go through, not knowing where her *kid* is, not even knowing if he's alive."

"That's not your fault," Helen said. "And it's not my fault either."

Jim stood up, slipped his loafers on. He patted his pockets for the car keys. "If you don't want to be here, Helen, go home. Get a flight out tonight. Susan won't care. She won't even notice." He zipped up his coat. "I mean it. It's okay."

"I'm not going to go and just leave you here."

She spent the afternoon bundled up, walking along the pathway by the river. The sun was still bright on the snow and also on the water. She stopped when she saw what appeared to be a war memorial. She had never noticed it before, but she had not been to Shirley Falls in more years than she could remember. There were large slabs of granite, upright, in a large circle. Peering closely she was dismayed to see that one was for a young woman recently killed in Iraq. Alice Rioux. Twenty-one years old. Emily's age. "Oh, little sweetie pie," Helen whispered. Sorrow expanded around her in the sunshine. She turned and headed back to the hotel.

The chambermaid startled Helen, standing outside their room with her cart of towels: She wore a robe that went from head to toe and only her face showed, round brown cheeks and bright dark eyes, which meant she must be a Somali, because Helen could think of no other black Muslims up here in Shirley Falls, Maine. "Hello!" Helen said this brightly.

"Hello." The girl—or she could be a middle-aged woman, how was Helen to know, the face was unreadable to her—stepped back with a gesture of shyness, and when Helen entered her room it had already been made up. She'd remember to leave a nice tip.

Bob showed up around five—probably, Helen thought, in order to drink and take a break from his sister's despair. "Come in, come in," she said. "How's your sister?"

"The same." Bob took a tiny bottle of scotch from the minibar.

"I'll join you," Helen said. "Don't let Susan come to the hotel. The chambermaid is a Somalian person, I think. Somali. Sorry." Helen gestured to indicate the top-to-bottom covering she had seen the person wearing.

Bob glanced at her with a slightly quizzical look. "I don't think Susan's mad at them."

"She's not?"

"She's mad at the district attorney and the assistant U.S. attorney and the AG's office, the press—you know, the whole nine yards. Look, do you mind if I turn on the news?"

"Of course not." But she did mind. She felt self-conscious sitting there with her hotel-room glass of whiskey, startled to hear that the market yesterday had dropped four hundred and sixteen points and she not able to say anything about it because it would be disrespectful to the Burgesses' crisis with Zach, and sad too, that a blast in Iraq had killed eight U.S. troops and nine civilians, for she now connected this to the marker she had seen by the river, oh, there were so many dying everywhere, what was to be done, nothing! She was ripped away from all that was familiar (her children, she wanted them small again, moist from their baths)— "I think I may go home tomorrow," she said.

Bob nodded, and kept looking at the television set.

———◆———

Afternoon light over the river had become muted behind a layer of light clouds, and the gray carpet of the hotel room seemed a deeper shade of the pale gray sky, the railing of the little balcony seen through the window a sturdy fine line of a deeper shade still. Jim looked exhausted. That morning he had driven Helen to the airport in Portland, and by the time he'd returned Susan had made the decision to file a missing person report with the police. "There's no warrant for his arrest yet with the Feds," she argued, and this was true. "And his bail conditions and the civil rights injunction only require that he stay away from the Somali community," she insisted.

"Still," Bob said patiently, "I don't know that we want to put him in the system as a missing person right now."

"But he *is* missing," Susan cried, and so they went with her to the police station and filed the report. The description of Zach's car—his license plate number appearing on a computer screen—went into the report, of course, and knowing that the police were now on the lookout for it squeezed Bob with an added layer of fear, and also hope. He pictured Zach in some tiny motel room, his duffel bag of clothes on the floor, Zach lying on the bed listening to music off his computer. Waiting.

Jim and Bob drove Susan back to her house. Jim stayed behind the wheel of the car in the driveway. "Suse, you hang on for a little bit. Bob and I've got some work calls to make at the hotel. We'll be back soon, in time for dinner."

"Mrs. Drinkwater is making dinner. But I can't eat," Susan said as she got out of the car.

"Then don't eat. We'll see you really soon."

Bob said, "He took his clothes, Susie. It's going to be all right." Susan nodded, and the brothers watched while she went up the porch steps.

Back in the hotel room, Bob flung his coat on the floor beside the bed. Jim still had his coat on, and now he reached into his pocket and tossed a cell phone onto the bed. He looked at Bob and nodded toward the phone.

"What?" said Bob.

"It's Zach's."

Bob picked up the phone, looked at it. "Susan said his cell phone and computer were gone."

"The computer's gone. I found the cell phone in his room, in a drawer next to his bed. Under some socks. I didn't tell Susan."

Bob felt pinpricks beneath his arms. He sat down slowly on the other bed. "Maybe it's an old phone," he finally said.

"It's not. The calls on it are recent, made in the last week. Mostly to Susan at work. The last call on it was to me the morning he disappeared."

"You? At your office?"

Jim nodded. "Directory assistance right before that. Probably asking for the number to the law firm. Though he could have googled that, I don't know why he didn't. Anyway, I didn't get the call, and he didn't leave a message with the receptionist. I called her driving back from Portland this morning and she remembered someone had called for me and wouldn't give his name and hung up when she asked what the call was referring to." Jim rubbed his face with both hands. "I yelled at her. Which was stupid." He walked over to the window, his hands in his pockets. He swore quietly.

"Do you think his computer really is gone?" Bob asked.

"Seems to be. And the duffel bag. I guess. Susan would know about the duffel bag, I wouldn't." He turned back from the window. "Don't you have some booze, slob-dog? I'd really go for some sauce right now."

"At Susan's. But there's the minibar."

Jim opened its fake-wood-paneled door, twisted the caps off two small bottles of vodka, poured them into a glass, and drank it down like it was water.

"Jesus," Bob said.

Jim grimaced, breathed out loudly. "Yeah." He opened the minibar again and brought out a can of beer, the small curl of foam appearing as he pulled back the tab.

"Jimmy, take it easy. You should eat something if you're going to do that."

"Okay." Jim said this agreeably, sitting in the chair with his coat still on. He leaned his head back, swallowing. He held out the can as an offer to Bob. Bob shook his head. "Really." Jim grinned tiredly. "When have you ever rejected booze?"

"Whenever things are seriously bad," Bob said. "I didn't touch the stuff for a year after Pam left." Jim gave no answer, and Bob watched as his brother drank steadily from the beer can. "Don't leave," Bob told his brother. "I'm going downstairs to find you something to eat."

"I'll be here." Jim smiled again, drinking down the beer.

———◆———

Susan sat on the couch watching television. It was the Discovery Channel, and dozens of penguins waddled across a long stretch of ice. Mrs. Drinkwater sat in the wing chair. "Cute little devils, aren't they?" she said. She picked idly at the pocket of the apron she wore.

After many moments, Susan said, "Thank you."

"I haven't done anything, dear."

"You're sitting with me," Susan said. "And cooking," she added.

One by one the penguins slipped off the ice into the water. From the kitchen came the smell of the chicken Mrs. Drinkwater had put into the oven earlier. Susan said, "Everything feels not real. Like I'm dreaming."

"I know, dear. Good your brothers are here. Did your sister-in-law go?"

Susan nodded. Moments went by. "I don't like her," Susan said. More moments went by. "Are you close to your daughters?" Susan asked this still watching the television. When there was no answer, she looked over at Mrs. Drinkwater. "I'm sorry. It's not my business."

"Oh, it's quite all right." Mrs. Drinkwater took a balled-up tissue and dabbed at her eyes beneath her huge glasses. "I had some trouble with them, truth be told. The oldest, especially."

Susan looked back at the television. The penguins' heads were bobbing around in water. "If you don't mind talking, it helps me," Susan said.

"Oh, certainly, dear. Annie smoked those marijuana cigarettes. Hell broke loose over that, I sided with Carl. Annie was seeing a boy who got drafted. Vietnam time, the start of it, you remember. This boy went to Canada to escape the draft, and Annie went with him. When they broke up, she wouldn't come home. She didn't want to live in a country as corrupt as our own, this is what she said." Mrs. Drinkwater paused. She gazed at the tissue in her hand, tried to spread it open on her lap, then balled it up again.

Susan said to the television, "He took clothes. You don't take clothes if you're not going to wear them." She added without expression. "Did you go visit her?"

"She wouldn't have us." Mrs. Drinkwater shook her head.

The penguins were slipping back up onto the ice, using their flippers, their flat feet holding them upright, their eyes bright as their little bodies glistened with water.

"Annie had romantic ideas about Canada," Mrs. Drinkwater said. "Never cared how her great-grandfather came from there, had to leave his farm because he went bankrupt. The creditors were just the devils themselves, you know. Annie thought she knew all about corruption. I told her, 'Hah!'" Mrs. Drinkwater's foot in its terry-cloth slipper bounced up and down.

Susan said, "I thought you said she lives in California. I thought you said that once."

"She does now."

Susan stood up. "I'm going to rest upstairs until my brothers come back. Thank you, though. You've been good to me."

"I've been a silly chatterbox." Mrs. Drinkwater waved a hand in front of her face in a gesture of embarrassment. "I'll call up to you when they get here." Mrs. Drinkwater stayed in the chair, plucking at her apron, ripping the tissue into little pieces. The television stopped showing penguins and showed rain forests instead. Mrs. Drinkwater looked at it while her mind went round and round. She thought how crowded her childhood home had been with all her brothers and sisters. She thought how her aunts and uncles would talk of going home to Quebec, but they never did. She thought of Carl and the life they had made. About her girls she did not like to think. She could not have predicted, no one can ever predict anything, that they'd have been raised at a time of protests and drugs and a war they seemed to feel no responsibility for. She pictured a dandelion gone by, the white, almost airless pieces of her family scattered so far. The key to contentment was to never ask why; she had learned that long ago.

The rain forest glittered green. Mrs. Drinkwater rocked her foot and watched.

———◆———

Bob returned to the hotel room with two sandwiches. "Jimmy?" he called. The room was empty. In the bathroom the light was on over the sink. "Jimmy?" He tossed the bag of sandwiches onto the bed next to Zach's cell phone.

His brother was on the balcony, leaning against the wall of the hotel, as though he could be fainting.

"Oy," Bob said. "You're drunk."

"I'm not, actually." Jim spoke quietly, and the sound of the river was loud.

"Jim, come inside." A sudden breeze moved over them.

Jim raised an arm, sweeping it slightly through the air, toward the river and the city beyond, where church spires could be seen above rooftops and trees. "None of what's happened was supposed to be this way." He dropped his arm back to his side. "I was going to defend the people of this state."

"Oh Christ, Jim, it's not the time for self-indulgence."

Jim turned his face toward Bob. He looked very young and tired and puzzled. "Bobby, listen. Any minute a state trooper's going to call to say some farmer found Zach hanging from the rafters of some barn or tree. I have no idea if he took his computer. Duffel bag? Big deal." Jim tapped a thumb lightly on his own chest. "And kind of? In a way? I guess I kind of killed him." He wiped at his face with his sleeve. "I upstaged Dick Hartley, yelled at Diane Dodge. I made everything worse by being a tough-guy show-off."

"Jim, that's the stupidest thing. We don't *know* he's dead—and whatever's happened it's not your fault. For crying out loud."

"He called me at my big bloated law firm, Bob, where he couldn't even get through to me, they take themselves so seriously." Jim turned back toward the river, shaking his head slowly. "I was considered the best criminal defense lawyer in the country once. Can you believe that?"

"Jim, stop."

Jim looked perplexed. "I was supposed to stay here and take care of everybody."

"Yeah? Who says? Now come inside and eat something."

Jim waved the question away, looked at the river, put his hand on the rail. "Instead I ran off and got famous. Everyone wanted my opinion, a talk show here, speech there. Gobs of money offered, which I was glad for so I wasn't dependent on Helen's money. But honestly, I just wanted to defend people nobody would defend." He stood there, watching the river. He said, "And it's all gone to crap." He turned his face toward Bob, and Bob was startled to see that the eyes of his brother were wet. "White-collar crime?" Jim asked. "Defend people who've made millions on their hedge funds? It's *crap,* Bob. And now I come home from work and the house is empty and the kids—God, the kids were everything, and their friends—and now the house is quiet, and I'm *scared,* Bobby. I think about death a lot. Even before this latest trip up here. I think about death and feel like I'm grieving for *myself,* and— Ah, Bobby, man, things are kind of out of control."

Bob took hold of his brother's shoulders. "Jimmy. You're scaring me here. And you're drunk. Right now we deal with Susan and Zach. You're going to be all right."

Jim pulled away, leaned against the wall again, closed his eyes. "You're always saying that to people. But nothing's going to be all right." He opened his eyes, looked at Bob, closed them again. "You poor dumb fuck."

"Cut it out." Bob felt a rip of anger come to him.

Jim's eyes opened again. His eyes seemed colorless, just a faint blue glistening beneath the slits. "Bobby." It was almost a whisper. Tears began to slide down Jim's face. "I'm a sham." He wiped his bare hands across his face as a gust of wind came furiously around the corner of the hotel. The shrubs down below rattled and bent.

"Come inside," Bob said gently. He took his brother's arm, but Jim shook him away. Bob stepped back and said, "Look, you didn't know he called you."

"Bob, I killed him."

The wind swooped and ripped back, so that Bob's coat sleeves rippled like canvas sails. Bob folded his arms across his chest, pressed the toe of his shoe against the bottom railing of the balcony. "How did you kill him? Giving a speech at a peace rally? Defending him zealously?"

"Not Zach."

Bob's foot appeared wide to him as he looked down at it. "Who, then?"

"Our father."

The words seemed conversational, and also as though Jim was waiting for them to begin the Lord's Prayer together. Our father who art in heaven. It took Bob a minute. He turned to face his brother. "No, you didn't. I was the one sitting up by the gears, we all know that."

"You weren't, though." Now Jim's face seemed very old and creased in its wetness. "You were in the backseat. So was Susie. You were four years old, Bob, you don't remember a thing. I was eight. Almost nine. By then you remember some things." Jim stayed leaning against the wall, looking straight ahead. "The seats were blue. You and I had a fight about sitting in the front seat, and before he walked down the driveway he said, Okay, Jimmy in the front seat this time, twins in the back. And I moved over behind the wheel. Even though we'd been told a million times we couldn't ever sit behind the wheel. I pretended I was driving. I pushed in the clutch." Jim shook his head almost imperceptibly. "And the car went down the driveway."

"You're drunk," Bob said.

"I pushed you into the front seat before Mom even came out of the house. Way before the police came, I'd climbed in the back. Eight years old. Almost nine years old, and I was able to be that sneaky. Isn't that amazing, Bobby? I'm like that movie, *The Bad Seed*."

Bob said, "Why are you making this up, Jim?"

"I'm not making it up." Jim raised his chin slowly. "And I'm not drunk. I don't get that, I just drank all that shit."

"I don't believe you."

Jim's exhausted eyes looked at Bob with pity. "Of course not. But, Bobby Burgess, you never did it."

Bob looked down at the river as it moved thunderously past. The boulders along the riverbank seemed large and stark. But it was all un-real, distorted, quiet. Even the noisy river seemed quiet, like Bob was swimming underwater and the sound was muffled. "But why would you say all this now?" He kept looking at the river, and the empty terrace below.

"Because I couldn't stand it."

"Fifty years later, you can't stand it? Jimmy, this doesn't make any sense. I don't believe you. No offense, but you're kind of cracking up right now, and we're up here to help Susan. It's not like it doesn't suck enough. Jesus, Jimmy, come *on.*" The brothers stood facing each other, and the wind swept over them, huge and cold. No more tears came from Jim. He looked gray and sick and old. Bob said, "So you're kidding, right? This is just your idea of the motherfucker of sick jokes. 'Cause you're really making me scared."

Quietly, Jim said, "I'm not kidding, Bobby." He slumped down until he was sitting on the balcony cement, his back against the wall. His knees were bent and his hands hung over them. "Do you know what it's like?" he asked, looking up at Bob. "Watching the years go by, watching myself never say anything. When I was a kid I kept thinking, Today I'll tell. I'll come home from school and I'll tell Mom, just say it. Then when I was a teenager I thought I'd write it down, slip it to Mom before school so she'd have all day to think about it. When I was at Harvard I still thought, I'll send her a letter. But a lot of days I'd think, No, I didn't do that." Jim shrugged, straightened his legs out. "Just didn't do it. That's all."

"You didn't."

"Oh Christ, will you stop?" Jim pulled his knees back to his chest, looked up at his brother. "I'm begging you. You remember what I said that day we found out Zach had thrown the pig's head? I said, he has to turn himself in because he did it. No Burgess runs away, we're not fugi-tives. That's what I said. Can you *believe* it?"

Bob said nothing. But he could hear now the sound of the falls as the river thundered over them. And then he heard from within the room the telephone start to ring. Bob stumbled inside, tripping over the door casing.

Susan was sobbing. "Slow down, Susie, I can't make out what you're saying."

Jim, who had followed Bob into the room, took the phone out of Bob's hand, the old take-charge Jim. "Susan. Slow down." He nodded, glanced at Bob, gave a thumbs-up.

Zachary was in Sweden with his father, he had telephoned Susan just a few minutes ago. His father had said he could stay as long as he wanted, and Susan could not stop her sobbing; she had thought he was dead.

Back at the house, even Mrs. Drinkwater's cheeks glistened as she moved about the kitchen in her apron. "She'll be able to eat now," the old lady said to Bob, nodding as though they shared a secret.

Susan's eyes were so swollen they were practically shut, and her face was shiny, and her happiness so unguarded that she hugged her brothers, Mrs. Drinkwater, and the dog, whose tail thumped vigorously. "He's alive, he's alive, he's alive. My son, Zachary, is alive." Bob could not stop his own face from smiling. "Oh, I'm too happy to eat," Susan said, walking around the table, patting the back of the chairs. "He kept apologizing for scaring me, but I said, Honey, I don't care about anything as long as you're safe."

"She's going to crash," Jim said later, on their way back to the hotel. "She's higher than a kite because he's not dead. In a little while she'll realize he's gone."

"He'll come back," Bob said.

"Wanna bet?" Jim stared over the steering wheel.

"Let's worry about that later," Bob said. "Let her be happy. God, *I'm* happy." Although sitting in the car next to Bob was the terrible conversation earlier on the hotel balcony; it was like a creepy little child poking at him in the dark, saying, Don't forget, I'm here. But it did not seem real. With the excitement of Zach's safety, it did not seem real, or relevant. It did not belong in the car, or in Bob's life.

Jim said, "I'm sorry, Bob."

"You were upset. It's understandable. Don't worry."

"No, I'm sorry about—"

"Jim, stop. It just isn't true. Mom would have figured it out. Even if it was true, which it's not, who cares? Stop feeling so bad. It scared me to see you feeling so bad. Everything's all right."

Jim didn't answer. They drove over the bridge, the river below them black in the night.

"I cannot stop smiling," Bob said. "Zachary's alive and with his father. And Susan, to see her like that— Well, I cannot stop smiling."

Jim said quietly, "You're going to crash too."

Book Four

1

In Brooklyn, Park Slope had spread its edges in every direction. Seventh Avenue was still its main street, but two blocks down Fifth Avenue was starting to open one trendy restaurant after another; boutiques sold fashionable blouses and yoga pants and jewelry and shoes with prices you might expect to find in Manhattan. Fourth Avenue, that wide mess of traffic and grit, now had, surprisingly and suddenly, large-windowed condos among the old brick dwellings; diners appeared on corners, and people walked on Saturdays up to the park. Babies were pushed in strollers as spiffy as sports cars, with fast-turning wheels and adjustable tops. If the parents held inner worries or disappointments, you didn't glimpse it in their flash of healthy teeth and toned limbs as the more enthusiastic ones made a day of walking across the Brooklyn Bridge, or rollerblading across it—there it was, the East River, and the Statue of Liberty, the tugboats, the enormous barges; life churning on and on, miraculous, amazing—

It was April, and while the days were often chilly, there was an exuberance to the forsythia that opened in front gardens, to the skies that

sometimes stayed blue all day, because March had had its times of record cold and a downpour of record rain, and then later the worst snow
of the winter. But here was April, and even with reports that the housing
bubble had started to deflate, nothing in Park Slope seemed to be shrink-
ing at all. Those who strolled about the Brooklyn Botanic Garden, pointing at the sloping hill of daffodils and calling to their children, seemed
content, unworried. The Dow Jones Industrial Average, after skidding
around chaotically, reached another record high.

Bob Burgess did not—especially—notice any of this: the financial
markets, the forecasts of doom, the forsythia along the wall by the library,
the rollerblading young people who whizzed past him. If he appeared
dazed, he was. It's said that amnesiacs not only lose the ability to remember the past but are unable to imagine the future, and in some ways it
was like this for Bob. His incredulousness at discovering that his past
might not be his past seemed to affect his ability to understand what lay
ahead, and he spent a great deal of time walking the streets of New York.
Motion helped. (This is why you didn't find him sitting in the Ninth
Street Bar and Grille, and also, he had stopped drinking.) On weekends
he could be found walking through Central Park in Manhattan, drawn to
it because it wasn't as familiar as Prospect Park in Brooklyn, and he was
aware of the many tourists he passed, with their cameras and maps and
different languages, their walking shoes, their tired children.

"E' bellissimo!" Bob heard a woman exclaim as she entered the park,
and he saw for a moment through different eyes the boulevard of trees
with its row of large trunks, the bicyclists, runners, ice cream stands,
very different from the Central Park Bob had first known when he
moved here years ago with Pam. There were Korean brides standing
bare-shouldered, shivering, while their photographs were taken. There
was the young woman near the steps to the lake who every weekend
sprayed herself gold and, wearing a leotard, tights, and toe shoes, stood
on a box, struck a pose and didn't move, while tourists took pictures and
kids stared and reached for the hands of their parents. How much
money she earned Bob couldn't imagine; the white bucket in front of
the box on which she stood would fill with bills, maybe some fives,

perhaps—he didn't know—a twenty. But the silence she endured those hours seemed to match the silence Bob carried within himself.

He carried also a disquieting idea, which was that he was a stranger now to the place that had been for so long his home. He was not a visitor; neither did he feel himself to be a New Yorker. New York, he thought, had been, for him, like an amiable and complex hotel that housed him with benign indifference, and his gratitude was immeasurable. New York had also shown him things; one of the biggest was how much people talked. People talked about anything. The Burgesses did not. It had taken Bob a long time to understand that this was a cultural difference, and certainly after half a lifetime in New York he talked more than he used to. But not about the accident. Which in Bob's mind did not even have a name. It was just that thing that sat beneath the Burgess family, murmured of briefly, long ago, in the office of the kindhearted Elaine. To have Jim raise it after all these years (to claim it as his own!) was disorienting in its awkwardness, impossible to comprehend. Walking through the park, he felt he'd been asleep for years and had now wakened to a different place and time. The city seemed rich and clean and filled with young people, who thundered past him in their running tights as he strolled around the reservoir.

What he faced was this: He didn't know what to do.

Flying back from Shirley Falls two months ago, he and Jim had spoken of Zach and his father, and what would happen if Zach did not return when the Feds came forward with their charges; they spoke of the misdemeanor trial now scheduled for June, how the jury selection would matter the most. It wasn't until they were in the taxi on the way back to Brooklyn that Bob finally said, "So, Jim—all that stuff you said. You were just upset, right? Like saying that crap about Pam last fall. Just being weird, fooling around."

Jim turned and looked out the window as they sped down the expressway. Lightly he touched Bob's hand, then took his hand away. He said quietly, "You didn't do it, Bobby."

They were silent after that. The taxi went to Bob's place first. As Bob got out, he said, "Jimmy, don't worry about it. None of it matters now."

And yet he had moved as though in a trance up the tilting staircase in the narrow hallway, past the door to where his neighbors had once carried out their altercations. His own place appeared slightly unbelievable to him. But there were his books, his shirts in the closet, a rumpled towel by the bathroom sink. Bob Burgess lived there, of course he did. Still, the sense that it was unreal was frightening.

As those first days went by, anguish came to meet him. His mind, jumpy and distracted, told him, It's not true, and if it is, it doesn't matter. But this gave him no relief because the constant repetition of these thoughts told him otherwise. One night, smoking out his window, he drank far too much wine far too quickly—glass after glass—and it came to him with clarity: It was true, and it mattered. Jim, knowingly and deliberately, had wrongly incarcerated Bob in a life that wasn't his. And the memories came spilling in: Jimmy, as a young boy, saying as Bob ran up to him, "The sight of you makes me *sick*. Go away." Their mother's soft chastisement, "Now, Jimmy, you be good to him." His mother, with almost no money, taking Bob to sit in the office of the psychiatrist, who offered him candy from a bowl that sat on his desk. Back home, outside their mother's hearing, Jimmy's taunts, "Bobby the baby, slob-dog-animal-burper-pig."

In his state of drunken clarity, Bob saw his brother as someone unconscionable enough to be almost evil. Bob's heart beat fast, pulling on his jacket. At his brother's house Bob would yell with open-throttled rage, right in front of Helen if he had to; he did not even take the time now to lock his own door behind him. On the bottom step in the narrow hallway of his building, Bob fell, and, lying there, a vast puzzlement came to him. He said quietly, "Come on, Bob, stand up." And yet he could not seem to do that. He wondered if one of the tenants—they were all so young in this building—might come out and find him like this. Only by turning his shoulders repeatedly and pushing hard against the gritty carpet of the stair was Bob finally able to stand. He returned to his apartment, pulling on the railing.

He stopped drinking after that.

Days later, when his telephone rang and his brother's name appeared—then, like that, the world became right. What was more natural than JIM appearing on his phone?

"Hey, listen," Bob started to say. "Listen, Jim—"

"You won't believe this," Jim interrupted. "Are you ready? The U.S. Attorney's Office just told Charlie his client was no longer under investigation. Amazing! I guess all that mad cow disease shit gave them pause and they can't establish intent. Or they got tired. Isn't that great?" Jim's voice was loud with gladness.

"Ah, yeah, it's great."

"Susan's hoping he'll come home right away, but I guess he doesn't feel like it. Likes being over there with his father. He'd better get back in time for his little misdemeanor trial, which Charlie keeps getting postponed. He's good, Charlie. Man, is he good. Bozo, you still there?"

"I'm here."

"You're not saying anything."

Bob glanced around his apartment. His couch looked small. The rug in front of the couch looked small. That Jim should speak with such familiarity, as though nothing had changed between them—it confused Bob. "Jim. You know. You got me kind of weirded out. Up there. The things you said. I still don't know if you were kidding."

"Ah, Bob." Spoken as though Bob were a small child. "I'm calling with good news. Let's not spoil this moment with all that."

"All that? But *that* is my life."

"Come on, Bobby."

"Look, Jim. I'm just saying I wish you hadn't shoved that crap on me when it isn't true. Why would you do that?"

"Bob. Jesus Christ almighty."

Bob closed his phone; Jim did not call back.

A month passed without the brothers speaking. Then one sunny, windy day, when bits of trash whipped along the sidewalk and people clutched their coats, Bob, returning to his office after lunch, felt relief come to him with a thought he'd had before but that only now seemed clear. He telephoned Jim at work. "You're older, but it doesn't mean you remember, Jim. It doesn't mean you're right. One thing criminal lawyers know is how unreliable memory is."

Jim sighed loudly. "I wish I hadn't told you."

"But you did tell me."

"Yeah, I did."

"But you could be *wrong*. I mean, you have to be. Mom knew it was me."

A silence. Then quietly, "I do remember, Bob. And Mom thought it was you because I made it that way. I explained that to you."

A chill went through Bob, a dropping of his stomach.

Jim said, "I was thinking. Maybe you should see someone. When you first moved here you had that therapist, Elaine. You liked her. She helped you."

"She helped me with my past."

"You should find another one. Someone who could help you again."

"What about you?" Bob asked. "Are you seeing someone? You were a *mess* up there. You don't need help with your past?"

"I don't, really, Bob. It's the past. It's not getting redone. We've lived our lives— And honestly, Bobby? In a way, and I don't mean to be callous here, but in a way, what difference does it make what happened? You said that yourself. We've all arrived at this point, so, you know, we go on."

Bob didn't answer.

"Well, Helen misses you," Jim finally said. "You should stop by the house sometime."

Bob didn't stop by. Without telling Jim, he packed his few things and moved to an apartment on Manhattan's Upper West Side.

———◆———

An uneasiness was following Helen, as though a shadow walked behind her, and if Helen stopped moving, the shadow just waited. The source of this, she could only think, tracing it back repeatedly, was Zach's abandonment of his mother. Why this should affect her so much or, more accurately, why it should be affecting Jim so much, she did not understand. "It's good he's with his father, don't you think?"

Jim said, "Of course. Everyone should have a father." It was unpleasant, how he said it.

"And those federal charges weren't brought. I should think you'd be really happy."

"Who's not happy, Helen?"

"Where's Bobby these days?" Helen asked. "I called him at work, and he got all vague the way he does, and said he's busy."

"He's hung up over some stupid girl."

"That's never stopped him from coming here." Helen added, "You were wrong to say he didn't have to give up Pam. It's perfectly reasonable Sarah wanted him to stop that. *I* wouldn't want to marry a man who was always talking to his ex-wife."

"Well, you don't have to, do you?"

"Jimmy, why are you in such a bad mood all the time?" Helen was plumping up a pillow on the bed. "Ana has her sloppy days."

Jim moved past her into his study. "Work's getting to me."

She followed him. "How, Jim? You don't have to stay at that firm. We have plenty of money. Except if you listen to the news it sounds like this country's in for some trouble."

"We have three kids in college, Helen. And there may be graduate school."

"We have the money."

"You have the money. You've kept it separate from the day we met, and I don't blame you one bit. But don't say *we* have the money. Even though *we* do because of what I make."

"Jim, for heaven's sake. This is important. If you really don't like what you do—"

He turned. "Well, I really don't like what I do. And it shouldn't be a surprise, Helen, I've told you this before. I dress up in a fancy suit to go meet a fancy client. A drug company indicted for filling their pills with poisonous crap wants to know they can hire the great Jim Burgess. Who isn't great anymore. It all gets settled, anyway. But still, there I am, on the side of a company who feeds crap pills to—to people in Shirley *Falls,* for all I know! Come on, Helen, for the love of God, this isn't new. Don't you listen to me?"

Helen's face grew warm. "Okay. All right. But why are you being rude?"

Jim shook his head. "I'm sorry. Oh, Helen. God. I'm sorry." He touched her shoulder, gently pulled her toward him. She felt his heart beating, saw through the French doors a squirrel run across the railing of the deck, the faint sound of its feet rapid, familiar. Why are you being rude? Her words bumped against some memory. (Months later she placed it. Debra-Who-Doesn't saying to her husband, Why are you picking on me tonight?)

2

Up in Shirley Falls, spring was slower to arrive. Nights were cold, but the way the dawn light cracked open along the horizon, bringing a gentle moistness that lightly touched the skin, spoke of a full-throated summer to come, and it was painful, all the promise in the air. Abdikarim, who performed his morning prayer while it was still dark, could feel the aching sweetness of this season as he walked through the streets to his café. Morning, for Susan, a few neighborhoods away, was when she had to learn all over again that Zachary was gone. Waking, she had to settle the waves of terror that lapped through her some nights with dreams she could not remember but that left her nightgown damp. On these mornings she left the house early, driving to Lake Sabbanock, where she could walk for two miles without seeing anyone except an occasional ice fisherman with a truck to pull his shack to the banks of the still partly frozen springtime lake, and she would nod and keep walking, always with her sunglasses on, walking to calm that terror, and also the sense of having done something so wrong that only on this muddied path could she feel unobserved in her sense of shame, deep enough that had she been among others they would have pointed at her, knowing her as an outcast, a criminal. She had done nothing, of course. The ice fisherman would not be notifying the police of her presence; no one would be waiting for her at the store to say, "Come this way, Mrs. Olson." But her dreams told her otherwise: She had entered (most likely long ago) some territory of danger where her life would rattle with unraveling; her husband would leave her, her son would leave, hope itself would leave, casting her so far outside the boundaries of ordinary life that she roamed the land of the unspeakably lonely whose presence society could not abide. The two facts—her son was alive, and federal charges, amazingly, would not be brought—were not diminished as much as occluded by the sadness of her nighttime dreams that lingered in the mornings. A little bit she was aware of the beauty she walked by, the sunlight sparkling off the quiet lake, the bare trees—it was beautiful, she was not unaware of this, but it was futile, and far away. Mostly she looked down at the muddy roots in front of her; the path, uneven with its little use, required concentration to maneuver. Perhaps it was the concentration that allowed her into the day.

Years before, when she'd met her future husband at the university—she a senior and he a freshman from the small mill town of New Sweden hours north—she had been surprised to find he practiced transcendental meditation, though it was newly popular back then. For thirty minutes in the morning and the evening, she was not to disturb him, and she never did, except late one Saturday morning when she walked into his room and found him sitting cross-legged on the bed staring vacantly. "Oh, sorry," she gasped, and walked out, though the image of him embarrassed her deeply, as though she had walked in on his private handling of himself—which many years later she would do. But early in their marriage, he offered to tell her—this, a gift of intimacy; he wasn't supposed to ever tell—the word he repeated during his meditation, a word he'd paid a guru to give him, a word the guru said he'd matched Steve's "energies" to. The word was "Om."

"'Om'?" she said.

He nodded.

"That's your private word?"

Stepping into her car now, the seat warmed from the sun, she thought how perhaps she had not understood at all, that to stare into space thinking "Om" was not so different from her walking and thinking only of the step in front of her. Perhaps Steve still did his meditation. Maybe Zachary did it now. She could email and ask. But she would not. Their emails were hesitant, polite. Mother and son, who had never written to each other before, had to learn a new language, and a shyness was evident for both of them.

———

Because of the missing person report filed with the police, a small newspaper article had appeared reporting the disappearance of Zachary Olson. Shortly after, the report came that Zachary was discovered to be living abroad. There was confusion about this from some people in town, as though Zachary, by leaving, had succeeded in avoiding what he should be forced to face. Charlie Tibbetts, breaking his own gag order, made a statement to the press, explaining that Zachary had not, as some said, jumped bail: His bail was for the Class E misdemeanor trial, and the conditions never required that he remain in the country. Charlie also released the information that his client was no longer under investigation by the U.S. Attorney's Office, and that decision should be respected.

The police chief Gerry O'Hare stated his concern: to keep the community safe. He would continue, he said, to encourage any report by any citizen that caused them to feel otherwise. (To his wife, he confessed relief. "I just hope the kid gets back here for the misdemeanor trial. Or if he doesn't, he stays over there for good. We dodged a bullet with this one, the town did great, and we sure don't need another ruckus." His wife said it would break Susan's heart if the boy never came home, but there'd been something unhealthy about mother and son, didn't Gerry think? Always joined at the hip.)

The newspaper articles had appeared in February, and by April the name Zachary Olson was almost never mentioned anymore. It's true that some of the elders of the Somali community remained angry; earlier they had gone to Rick Huddleston at the Office of Racial Anti-Defamation, and Rick Huddleston was furious, but there was nothing to be done. Abdikarim was not furious. For him, the tall, skinny, dark-eyed boy he had seen in court on the day of the hearing was no longer a source of alarm, no longer was he Wiil Waal, "Crazy Boy," but simply *wiil,* boy. A boy Abdikarim's heart now leaned toward; even in the court-room that day it had started, his heart, leaning across the courtroom to this tall, skinny boy. Abdikarim had seen newspaper photographs of him. But when he saw him in real life, first standing by his lawyer, and then sitting in the witness seat, spilling his glass of water, Abdikarim had felt quietly amazed. He was reminded of how he had imagined snow. Cold and white and covering the ground. But it had not been like that. It was silent and intricate and full of mystery as it fell from the sky that night he had first seen it. And here was this boy, living, breathing, his dark eyes defenseless, assailable, and he was not what Abdikarim had imag-ined at all. Whatever caused the boy to roll a pig's head through the mosque would remain a puzzlement to Abdikarim, but he knew now it had not been an act of evil. He understood that others—his niece, Haweeya—were not impressed by the fear so apparent in this boy. (But Haweeya had not seen him.) So Abdikarim kept silent, though he be-lieved the fear went deep into the bowels of the boy, and his heart, ach-ing and tired, had leaned across the courtroom to him.

It was from Margaret Estaver that Abdikarim learned the boy was living in Sweden with his father, and the knowledge made his body warm with gladness. "Good, very good," he told the minister. Many times a day he thought of this, the boy living with his father in Sweden, and each time his body was made warm with gladness.

"It is good. A fine situation. *Fiican xaalad.*" Margaret Estaver smiled broadly as she said this. They were on the sidewalk by her church. In the basement of her church was the food pantry. Mostly it was Somali Bantu women who lined up twice a week for the boxes of cereal, and crackers, the heads of lettuce, the potatoes, the paper baby diapers. Abdikarim did not speak with them, but sometimes if he was walking by the church and saw Margaret Estaver he stopped and spoke with her. She was learning bits of the Somali language, and her willingness to be strikingly wrong opened his heart with tenderness. It was because of her that he had started to try to increase his English.

"Can he return here?" he asked the minister.

"He can, of course. And he should, before the misdemeanor trial. Otherwise he'll be in more trouble. He's supposed to be here," Margaret said, seeing the confusion on the man's face, "when the court date arrives."

"Explain, please," Abdikarim said. After listening, he said, "And what would happen to make those charges gone, same as the federal charges?"

"The federal charges were never brought, so they didn't have to be dismissed. What it would take for the district attorney to drop the misdemeanor charge, I don't know if that can happen."

"Can you find out?"

"I'll try."

Otherwise, Abdikarim spent the days in his café, or on the sidewalk in front of it, talking with the group of Somali men who gathered there. As the weather became warmer they could stand outside longer; they preferred to be outside. There was fighting in Mogadishu, and it was all the men talked of. A family who had been in Shirley Falls for two years—exhausted with homesickness—had packed their things and returned to Mogadishu in February. Recently no word had come from them, and now what was feared was learned to be true: They had been killed in the fighting. The other week, when the insurgents had fired at the government, and also at the presidential palace and the Ministry of Defense, where the Ethiopians were based, the Ethiopians had fired in return—wildly, savagely, and without discrimination—killing more than a thousand people, even their animals. News of this came through cell phones, and news came through the Internet, which could be checked in the Shirley Falls town library, and it came through the daily broadcasts from the shortwave radio station 89.8 FM from Garowe, the capital of Puntland. The men spoke worriedly of something else: The United States was supporting Ethiopia. The president, the CIA—weren't they involved? They had to be. Claiming Somalia was harboring terrorists. Islam was a religion of peace, and the men on the sidewalk in front of Abdikarim's café were defensive and ashamed.

Abdikarim listened, and felt what the men felt. But he thought he might be getting senile, because tucked now in his heart was something private, and if it was not hope, it was close enough to be hope's brother. His country was ill, having a seizure. Those who should be helping were treacherous, underhanded. But in the years to come, and he understood he would not live to see it, his country would again be strong and good. "Understand this fact," he said to the men. "Somalia was the last African country to get the Internet, but in seven years its access has the highest growth and also we have the cheapest cell phone calling rates. Look at this street, if you want proof of the intelligence of Somalis." He thrust out his arm, indicating the new businesses that had sprung up during the winter here in Shirley Falls. A translation service, two more cafés, a store that sold phone cards, a place for classes in English.

But the men turned away. They wanted to go home. Abdikarim understood that very well. It's just that he could not seem to stop what felt to be an opening in his soul as the horizon itself stayed open those extra moments each day.

3

Pam's life was ruled by so many appointments and errands and parties and playdates that she did not, as she told her friend Janice, have time to think. But now she was having insomnia, which gave her lots of time to think, and it was driving her insane. Hormones, Janice told her. Get your hormone level checked and take some. But Pam had already taken a frightening amount of hormones in order to conceive her boys. She was well aware of the risks she'd incurred; she would not be adding more. So she lay awake at night and at times there was a curious peacefulness to this, the darkness warm as though the deep violet duvet held its color unseen, wrapping around Pam some soothing aspect of her youth, as her mind wandered over a life that felt puzzlingly long; she experienced a quiet surprise that so many lifetimes could be fit into one. She couldn't name them so much as feel them, the soccer field of her high school in autumn, her first boyfriend's thin torso, the innocence unbelievable to her now, and the sexual innocence in some ways being the smallest part of innocence, there was no way to name the slender, true, and piercing hopes of a young girl in a rural town of Massachusetts so long ago—and then Orono and the campus and Shirley Falls and Bob, and Bob, and Bob, the first infidelity (there it was, all innocence gone, the fearsome freedom of adulthood, to enter the complications of all that!) and then a new marriage and her boys. Her boys. Nothing is what you imagine. Her mind hovered above this simple and alarming thought. The variables were too great, the particularities too distinct, life a flood of translations from the shadow-edged yearnings of the heart to the immutable aspects of the physical world—this violet duvet and her slightly snoring husband. Sometimes, to help herself make sense of this, she would picture meeting the boyfriend from high school now—at a diner near her mother's nursing home, perhaps, leaning across the counter, his eyes quiet with curiosity—and telling him. Well, this, and this, and this have happened. It would not be accurate as told. She thought nothing could be told and be accurate. Feeble words dropped earnestly and haphazardly over the large stretched-out fabric of a life with all its knots and bumps— What words would she use to spread her experience before him? That he would have his own experience did not interest her as much, she was aware of that. Horribly—but freely, because she was alone in her violet darkness—she saw that it was not another's experience she wanted to touch and turn and mold and devour, it was her own.

Her mind grew weary, ran down.

Then she would try not to picture her skeletal mother in the nursing home, the clouded confused eyes, unknowing, as Pam thought, Mom, Mom. Or, turning over, tugging the duvet, she tried not to picture those two (young) mothers at school who were never pleasant when she chatted with them, waiting on the sidewalk for the last bell to ring, and why was that? What did they have against her?

And so on.

Reading was the best thing to do when her mind became this way, and so she clicked on her tiny book light and started the book about Somalia that had been mentioned at that splendid dinner party where the Southern woman lost it. At first the book was dull, but then it picked up and Pam became horrified. It was incredible, all she didn't know about lives so utterly different from her own. Her plan was to call Bob about it in the morning, but it was that morning when she found out that her job at the hospital was getting phased out, and then Pam had a run of real panic.

Somehow—and it probably had to do with long-ago fantasies—she took hold of the idea that she would become a nurse. So for a few weeks Pam looked into nursing courses, picturing herself filling syringes and taking blood and holding some old woman's bruised arm in an emergency room, having doctors glance at her respectfully; she saw herself (and maybe she'd finally look into Botox) speaking to young parents who were frightened out of their wits, like those mothers at school who weren't nice to her. She imagined herself striding through the swinging doors of an operating room, authoritative in all her gestures. (She wished nurses were still required to wear white uniforms and caps instead of the frumpish things they wore these days, all kinds of silly sneakers were allowed, and always those baggy pants.) She pictured herself administering blood transfusions, holding a clipboard, lining up a row of meds.

I can't think of anything worse, Janice told her. Nurses work like mad, on their feet for twelve hours. What if you made a mistake?

Stupidly, that hadn't occurred to her. Of course she would make a mistake. Except surely people with less intelligence than she were nurses, she saw them all the time at the hospital, gum-snapping, heavy-lidded—ah, but with the confidence of youth. No exchange rate for the confidence of youth.

But really, what it came down to after those silly weeks of worry—and there was no way around this, even if she went to school part-time—was that she would miss her boys. She would miss helping with their homework (though it always bored her to death), she'd miss staying home with them when they were sick, or had a snow day, and she'd have to study during their holidays. Also, unlike her former sister-in-law, Helen, Pam had trouble keeping help, which she would need a lot of if she tried to do the nursing thing. She went through babysitters and housekeepers at a stunning rate. She was apt to be overfriendly, and then was disappointed when they took advantage of her. She fired them with little notice, handing them money and shaking her head when they took umbrage at this surprise. No, it was not going to work. As consolation, she had her hair cut in a new way, and then was not pleased with the angle at which it now fell across her forehead.

She called Bob at his office and explained her dilemma. "I don't know, Bob. Maybe I didn't even really want to be a nurse. Maybe I just wanted to study the stuff. Anatomy. Like when I was in college."

There was a long silence and then he said, "Pam, I don't have a lot to say. Take an anatomy class if you want."

"Wait, Bobby. Are you mad at me?" Pam had honestly missed the possibility of this. For years she had called Bob whenever she wanted, he always treated her decently and listened patiently; she had come to expect nothing else. She said, "You know, you never came over at Christmas, which hurt the boys' feelings, and it's been just ages since I've seen you. And I guess now that I think about it, when I've called, well, I'll be honest, you've been curt. Are you back with Sarah? I know she didn't like me."

"I'm not back with Sarah, no."

"Then what's the story? What did I do?"

"I'm just busy, Pam. A lot of stuff going on."

"At least tell me this. Is Zachary still with this father? What happened with the charges?"

"The U.S. attorney never went ahead with it."

"Wow. So he ran away for nothing."

"I don't know that living with his father is nothing."

"Okay, that's true. How's Susan?"

"She's Susan."

"Bob, I wanted to tell you about that book I was going to read by that Somali woman. Because now I've read it, or most of it, and it's kind of disturbing."

"Tell me about the book, Pam. Then I have a meeting in a few minutes. We've got a young lawyer here who needs some guidance."

"Okay, okay. I have stuff to do too. But the writer is very specific about how in Somalia to be a woman is pretty insane. You have a child out of wedlock and your life is over. I mean, over. You can just die in the street. No one will care. And that other stuff, good God, they take these five-year-olds, and they *cut* it right off, Bob, then sew it up. The girls can barely pee. Get this: They're taught if they hear a girl peeing too hard they get to make fun of that girl."

"Pam, this makes me sick."

"Me too! I mean, you want to respect their way of life, but how can you respect that? There's controversy in the medical community, of course, because some of these women like to be sewn up again after they have a baby and Western doctors aren't so keen on doing that. Honestly, Bob. It's a little crazy. The woman who wrote the book—I can't pronounce her name—there's a death threat against her, no surprise, for telling the truth. Why aren't you saying anything?"

"Because, first of all, Pam, when did you get like this? I thought you were concerned about them, their parasites, their trauma—"

"I *am*—"

"No, you're not. That book is the right wing's dream. Do you not get that? Do you read the paper at all anymore? And second of all, I saw some of these so-called crazy people in the courtroom at Zach's hearing. And guess what, Pam? They're not crazy. They're exhausted. And partly they're exhausted by people like you reading about the most inflammatory aspects of their culture in some book club, and then getting to hate them for it, because deep down that's what we ignorant, weenie Americans, ever since the towers went down, really want to do. Have permission to hate them."

"Oh, for Christ's sake," Pam spat out. "I can't believe it. You Burgess boys. Defense attorneys for the whole crappy world."

———◆———

Bob's new apartment was in a tall building with a doorman. He had never had a doorman before, or lived in such a large building, and he saw immediately it had been the right thing to do. The elevators were filled with children and strollers and dogs and old people, and men in suits, and women with briefcases, their hair damp in the mornings. It was like moving to a new city. He lived on the eighteenth floor, across the hall from an old couple, Rhoda and Murray, who welcomed him in with a drink the first week he was there. "We've got the best floor," said Murray, who wore thick glasses and used a cane, which he waved about their living room. "I sleep till noon but Rhoda's up every morning at six, grinding that coffee to wake the dead. You have children? You divorced? So what, Rhoda's been divorced, I nabbed her thirty years ago, everyone's divorced now."

"Forget it," Rhoda said, about not having kids. She filled his wineglass (the first wine he'd had in weeks). "My kids are a pain in the butt. I love them, they drive me nuts. All I have are these cashews, who knows how old."

"Sit down, Rhoda. He can eat the cashews and be grateful." Murray had settled into a large chair, his cane placed carefully on the floor beside him. He lifted his own wineglass in Bob's direction.

Rhoda collapsed into the sofa. "Have you met the couple down at the end? One of the little boys has that, what's it called, come on," snapping her fingers, "well, whatever affects the growth of his spine. The mother's a saint, has a wonderful husband. Burgess? Are you related to Jim Burgess? *Really?* Oh, what a trial that was! Guilty, that son of a bitch, but what a trial, we loved watching that trial."

Back in his apartment, he called Jim.

"I know you moved," Jim said.

"You knew?"

"Of course I knew. I walked by your place and there were curtains in the window, it actually looked habitable, so I knew you'd taken off. I got an investigator in our office to find out where you'd gone. And how come you still have an unlisted number? Every time you called our landline and it came up PRIVATE we knew it was you. What's that about?"

It was about not being a Burgess. Back in the Wally Packer days, Pam had said she was sick of getting calls asking if they were related to Jim Burgess. "It's the way I want it," Bob said now.

"You've hurt Helen's feelings. You never call. And you moved without a word. You'll have to tell her you were a mess about some woman, that's what I told her."

"Why didn't you tell her the truth?"

Silence. Then: "What truth? I don't know the *truth* of why you moved, slob-dog."

"Because you upset me, Jim. Jesus. Did you tell her about that?"

"Not yet." Jim sighed through the phone. "Christ. Listen, have you spoken with Susan recently? She sounds very lonely."

"Of course she's lonely. I'm going to invite her down here."

"You are? Susan's never been to New York in her whole life. Well, look, have fun with that. We're going to Arizona to see Larry."

"Then I'll wait until you get back." Bob hung up. The idea that his brother had tracked him down—so momentarily and achingly sweet in its surprise—had been taken away by Jim's tone. Bob sat on his couch and gazed out the window at the view of the river, and he could see small sailboats moving now, a larger boat behind them. He had no memory of life without Jim being the brightness of its center.

4

Mrs. Drinkwater lingered by the door of Susan's bedroom, where Susan stood with her hands on her hips. "Come in," Susan said. "I can't seem to think."

Mrs. Drinkwater sat down on Susan's bed. "In the past, I believe they wore a lot of black in New York. I don't know if that's still true."

"Black?"

"Used to. It's a hundred years since I worked at Peck's, but sometimes a woman came in wanting a black dress, and naturally I supposed it was for a funeral and I'd try and be tactful, but it would turn out she was going to New York. That happened a few times."

Susan picked up an unframed photo that was lying flat on her bedside table. "He's gained weight," she said, handing it to the old lady, "in just two months," and Mrs. Drinkwater said, "My word."

It took her a moment to realize it was Zachary. He was standing at a kitchen counter, almost smiling at the camera. His hair was longer and fell across his forehead. "He looks—" Mrs. Drinkwater stopped herself.

"Normal?" Susan asked. She sat down on the other side of the bed, took the photo back and gazed at it. "That's what I thought when I looked at it. I thought, Holy moley, my son looks normal." She added, "It came in today's mail."

"He looks awful good," Mrs. Drinkwater admitted. "Is he happy, then?"

Susan put the photo back on her bed stand. "Seems to be. His father's girlfriend lives with them. She's a nurse, and maybe a good cook, I don't know. But Zach likes her. She's got kids of her own about his age, I guess they live nearby. They all do things together." Susan looked up at the ceiling. "It's good." She pinched her nose and blinked. Then she looked around the room, her hands in her lap. Finally she said, "I didn't know you worked at Peck's."

"For twenty years. I loved it."

"I'd better go feed the dog." But Susan stayed sitting on the bed.

Mrs. Drinkwater stood. "I'll do it. And I'll scramble a few eggs for supper, how about that?"

"You're very good to me." Susan raised her shoulders and sighed.

"That's all right, dear. Find a black turtleneck and a pair of black slacks and you'll be all set."

Susan looked at the photo again. The kitchen Zach was standing in looked to her more like an operating room, clean-angled with lots of stainless steel. Her son (her son!) looked at the camera, looked at her, with a combination of openness and something that was not shyness but perhaps more an apology. His face, which had been so angular and awkward, was a handsome face now with the extra weight, his eyes large and dark, his jawbone strong, defined. Almost, and it was so bizarre that she had to keep looking and looking, but almost, he resembled a young Jim. The flush of pleasure this had first produced had given way now to a sense of something unbearable—loss, and a glimpse of her past behavior as a mother and wife.

Memory. Open-palmed it passed before her scenes, and then would close, taking away the beginning, the end, the framework these scenes existed within. But in glimpses of herself—shouting at Steve, at Zach— she recognized her own mother, and Susan's face burned with shame.

She had never seen what she saw now: that her mother's fits of fury had made fury acceptable, that how Susan had been spoken to became the way she spoke to others. Her mother had never said, Susan, I'm sorry, I should not have spoken to you that way. And so years later, speaking that way herself, Susan had never apologized either.

And it was too late. No one wants to believe something is too late, but it is always becoming too late, and then it is.

5

In Arizona, Helen and Jim stayed at a resort in the foothills of the Santa Catalina Mountains. Their room looked over a huge saguaro cactus that had one thick green arm turned up and another aimed down; there was also a view of the swimming pool. "Well," Helen said, the second morning they were there, "I know you were disappointed with Larry going to school out here, but it's a beautiful place for us to visit."

"You were disappointed, not me." Jim was reading something on his phone.

"Because it's so far away."

"And because it wasn't Amherst or Yale." Jim was typing on his phone now, his thumbs flying.

"You were the one disappointed about that."

"I wasn't, though." Jim looked up. "I went to a state school, Helen. I don't have a problem with a state school."

"You went to Harvard. The only thing I'm disappointed about is that Larry's not hiking with us today."

"He's working on his paper, like he said. We'll see him again tonight."

Jim clicked his phone shut, then opened it immediately, glanced at it again.

"Jimmy, whatever you're doing, can't that wait?"

"One second. It's this work thing, hold on."

"But the sun's getting higher every minute. And I didn't sleep well, I told you."

"Helen. Please."

"The hike takes four hours, Jimmy. Why don't we find a shorter one?"

"I know the hike is four hours. And it's beautiful and I like it. And you liked it last time. If you'd just give me a second here, we'll go enjoy it again."

By the time they left the hotel it was eleven o'clock and 87 degrees. They parked near the visitor center, then walked up a tarred road for a long time before the trail turned off and led into a dusty path between cactus and mesquite trees, and then they came to the river, which they crossed, stepping on broad, smooth stones. Helen had woken at four in the morning and not returned to sleep. Somehow, at dinner, while Larry's girlfriend, Ariel, went on and *on* about her awful stepfather, Helen must have continued to fill her wineglass with deep red wine, as Ariel tugged on her long hair, talking quickly, all the while Larry looking at her with a childlike reverence. They were sleeping together, or he would not look at her that way; Helen understood this. Why would he choose an idiot to be with? It broke her heart a little.

"She's not so bad" is all Jim said. And that broke her heart a little, too.

Now Helen watched the back of Jim's hiking shoes and followed them. It was very hot and the trail was narrow. A small lizard darted across the path. "Jimmy, how long has it been?" she finally asked.

Jim looked at his watch. "An hour." He drank from his water, she drank from hers.

"I don't know if I can make it all the way to the lakes," she said.

His mirrored sunglasses looked toward her. "No?"

"I feel a little . . . whoopsie."

"Let's see how it goes."

The sun beat down. Helen walked more quickly, up the rocks, past twiggy branches and dried-looking plants. She did not speak but noted, when Jim reached to scratch his calf, that his watch showed another thirty minutes had gone by. And then, as they stepped onto a small ridge, the heat became something alive and fierce and Helen saw it had been chasing her and now had her. Large dark spots appeared in the lower part of her sight. She sank against the stump of a small tree. "Jimmy, I'm going to faint. Help me."

He told her to put her head between her legs, and gave her water to drink. "You'll be okay," he said, and she said no, something was wrong. She was going to throw up. And she was almost two hours away from the parking lot, from the visitor center, from safety. She said, "Please just call someone on your cell phone, please, it will take them a long time to get here." He said he had not brought his cell phone. He gave her more water, told her to drink it slowly, then began leading her back the way they had come; her legs were trembling so much she kept falling. "Jimmy," she whispered, holding her arms out in front of her. "Oh, Jimmy, I don't want to die here." She did not want to die in the desert of Arizona, a few miles from her son—briefly she thought of him being told, nauseating, this practical aspect of death: One died, and their children were told. But Larry would be so sad, and that was how it was, already his grief seemed far away from her.

"You just had a checkup," said Jim. "You're not going to die."

Later she wondered if he had actually said that about the checkup or if she thought it herself; the ludicrousness of a checkup. Bent over, she stumbled while Jim held her. A thin trickle of water was in the riverbed. Jim untied the shirt from around his waist and got the shirt wet and put it on her head. This is how they made their way back through the canyon.

When they arrived on the tarred road Helen felt as happy as a child who'd been lost and had found her way home. They sat on a bench and she held Jim's hand. "Does Larry seem okay to you?" she asked, after she drank most of the water.

"He's in love. In lust. Whatever you want to call it."

"Jimmy, that's a little crass." Helen was lighthearted in her safety.

Jim took his hand from hers and wiped at his forehead. "Fine."

"Let's go." Helen stood up. "Oh, I'm so glad I didn't die up there."

"You weren't going to die," Jim said. He hoisted the knapsack back onto his shoulders.

They missed a turn on the road. Too late, Helen saw that the path off the road—which led to the other road—had been missed, and now they were headed up a hill and around a long curve. And yet neither could say for sure that the path off the road was the right one. Jim said not to worry. This road would eventually lead back to the visitor center. But the sun screamed down, and after walking half an hour they were no closer. There was no water here to soak Jim's shirt in. "Jimmy," she cried.

He poured the little water left in his bottle onto her head and she felt her legs give way as though they no longer belonged to her. Kneeling next to the road, she saw that she was going to lose consciousness and not regain it. She had used everything up just to get out of the desert, to get this far. Jim was walking quickly up the road to look around the corner and she saw his blurry figure disappear. "Jim, don't leave me," she called, and he came back.

"It's a long way." In his voice, she could hear the worry.

She could not understand why he had not brought his cell phone.

Her hands trembled and the spots in her eyes were huge and black. A buzzing like large insects sounded in her ears. The heat was cruel, triumphant, fooling her earlier when they had sat on the bench; waiting in the wings for this couple who thought they had everything.

By the time the trolley van turned the corner and Jim stood waving frantically, Helen had vomited once. The trolley was empty of passengers, and the driver, along with Jim, lifted her onto the backseat beneath the canopy. The driver was used to this. He had Gatorade beneath the seat, and told Jim to have her sip it slowly. She heard the driver say, "You can see why people die on those border crossings."

Jim murmured, "That's good, Hellie. Good girl, sweetheart," as she got the Gatorade into her mouth with his help, not unlike how she had taught the children to use cups when they were babies. But Jim was far away, all was far away—yet there was something, what was it? Her husband was afraid. This tiny piece of knowledge was nothing more than a dust particle hanging in the air. It would disappear, was disappearing—

In the hotel room they closed the shades and got into bed. Helen was very cold now, and she sank into the softness of the quilt; they lay next to each other holding hands. She thought *People who almost die together stay together,* and she thought it was a strange thought to have.

"Where were you?" said Ariel, the last night of their visit.

Ariel.

Helen, who had said, "What a lovely name," could not stand the name. She squinted now in the twilight at Ariel. They were in the parking lot of the hotel, ready to say goodbye. Larry and Jim were on the other side of his car, talking. "Where was I when?" Helen asked this girl, who slept beside her son.

The air felt cold to Helen, and dry.

"When Larry went to summer camp."

Helen, having lived for many years with a defense attorney, felt the familiar sense of a trap being laid. "You'll have to explain yourself," she said evenly. And when the young Ariel did not reply, Helen added, "I simply don't know what you mean."

"I *mean*—where were you? Larry didn't want to go to those places, and you knew it. At least he thinks you knew it. But you let him go. And he was miserable. He thinks it was his father's fault. That Jim insisted he go. But my question is, where were you?"

Oh, the young! They know everything!

Helen was quiet for a long time, long enough for Ariel to look down at her sandaled foot and trace its toe over the gravel.

"Where was I?" Helen said, coolly. "In New York, shopping most likely."

Ariel looked over, giggled.

"No, I mean it. Most likely that's where I was. Shopping and sending off packages to the kids each week, those camp packages filled with candy and brownies and all the stuff the camp tells you not to send."

"Didn't you know Larry was unhappy?"

Helen had known, and now she felt as though Ariel had slipped a thin knife into her chest. Such cruelty. "Ariel, when you have children, you'll find you make decisions according to what you think is best for that child. And we thought it best that Larry not succumb to his homesickness. Now, tell me how your classes are going."

She did not listen as Ariel talked. She thought how sick she had been on the trail a few days ago. She thought how she had tried to continue to please Jim. She thought of the visiting days at Larry's summer camps, how her heart would be broken to see his hopefulness, that he had been preparing his speech of why he should be allowed to come home, and his despondency when he realized it would not work, he would have to stay another four weeks. Why hadn't she insisted he be allowed to come home? Because Jim thought the boy should not be allowed to come home. Because two people can't have entirely different opinions without one of them being final.

Helen wanted to say something to Ariel that would hurt her, and when Ariel, reaching into the car's front seat, handed her a box of cookies she had made that day especially for them, Helen said, "Well, I don't eat chocolate anymore. But they'll be fine for Jim."

6

At the airport baggage claim, Bob could not find Susan. There were people wearing sandals and straw hats, people with coats and small children, teenagers slumped against trolleys, earbuds in their ears while their parents, younger than Bob, looked with worry at the moving luggage belt. Near him a thin gray-haired woman was punching numbers on a cell phone, a handbag tight beneath her arm, a foot tucked protectively around a little suitcase. "Susan?" he said. She looked different.

"You look different," she said, putting the cell phone in her handbag.

He wheeled her little suitcase out to the taxi line.

"Are there always so many people?" Susan asked. "This is like being in Bangladesh. My God."

"When were you last in Bangladesh?" He thought he sounded like Jim, saying that. He added, "Look, we'll have fun, don't worry. And we'll go out to Brooklyn to see Jim, I haven't seen him in ages." Susan was watching the taxi dispatcher, her head moving back and forth as the dispatcher worked the line, blowing his whistle, shouting, opening taxi doors. Bob asked, "What do you hear from Zach?"

Susan reached into her handbag and put on a pair of sunglasses, even though the sky was overcast. "He's okay."

"That's it?"

Susan looked up at the sky.

"I haven't heard from him in a while," Bob said.

"He's mad at you."

"He's *mad*? At me?"

"He's in a family now, and it makes him wonder where you and Jim were all those years."

"He doesn't wonder where his father was all those years?"

Susan didn't answer this. When they got into a cab, Bob slammed the door hard.

He took her to Rockefeller Center. He took her through Central Park, pointing out the young woman who was spray-painted gold. He took her to a Broadway musical. She was like a bashful child, nodding. He gave her his bedroom and slept on the couch. On her second morning she sat at the table, holding her coffee mug with both hands, and asked, "Don't you get scared living this high up? What if there was a fire?"

"I don't think about it," he said. Bob pulled his own chair closer to the table. "Do you remember anything about the accident?" he asked.

She looked at him, surprised. "No," she finally said, in a small voice.

"Nothing?"

Her face was open and innocent, her eyes moved about as she considered this. She spoke tentatively, as though afraid of giving a wrong answer. "I think it was a really sunny day. I think I remember blinding sun everywhere." She pushed back her mug of coffee. "But it could have been raining."

"It wasn't raining. I remember sun too." They had never spoken of this to each other, and Bob looked around his apartment as though he needed to look away from Susan. His apartment was still new enough that it was unfamiliar, the kitchen so clean it sparkled. Jim would not call this a graduate dorm; Bob would not smoke out the window here. He wished he had not mentioned the accident; it was more awkward than if he'd asked Susan for details of her intimate life with Steve. Shame, bone-deep, tightened his arms.

Susan said, "I always thought I'd done it."

"What?" said Bob, turning his face to her.

"Yeah." She looked at him briefly, then down at her hands, which she held together on her lap. "I thought it was why Mom yelled at me so much. She never yelled at the two of you. So maybe I did it, I've often thought that. And since Zach left I've been having these terrible night- mares. I can't remember them when I wake up but they are *awful*. And they sort of, you know, feel like that."

"Susie, you know you didn't. All the times you said to me when we were little, 'It's all your fault, you stupid-head'?"

Susan's eyes seized up with a tenderness of expression. "Oh, Bobby. Of course I said that. I was a scared little kid."

"You didn't mean it all the times you said it?"

"I didn't know what I meant."

"Well, Jim was talking to me about it. He remembers it. He says he remembers it."

"What does he remember?" she asked.

But Bob found he could not say it. He opened his hands on the table. He shrugged. "An ambulance. Police, I think. But he knows you didn't do it. So please don't worry about that."

For a long time the twins sat silently. Beyond the window, the river sparkled. Finally Susan said, "Everything here is so expensive. At home I could buy a sandwich for what a cup of coffee costs here."

Bob stood up. "Let's get going," he said.

In the hallway Murray called, "Hey!," reaching forward to shake hands. Rhoda held on to Susan's arm. "What have you done so far? Don't let him tire you out, people get tired out and what fun is that? To Brooklyn? See that famous brother of yours? Hey, nice to meet you, have a wonderful time!"

On the sidewalk, Susan said, "People like that, I never know what to say."

"Warm, friendly people? Yeah, they're a conversation stopper all right." Again, Bob thought he sounded like Jim. But he couldn't believe how tired she made him.

On the subway she sat without moving, her handbag clutched with both hands on her lap, while Bob swayed from the hand grip he was holding. "I used to take this subway ride every day," he told her, and she didn't answer him. "Hey," he said. "What we were talking about earlier. You didn't do it. Don't worry."

She made no gesture to indicate having heard him, except to have her eyes move to his just briefly. They were aboveground now, and she turned her neck to look out the window of the train. He tried to point out to her the Statue of Liberty, but by the time her eyes followed where he pointed, they had gone by.

———•———

"How's it been?" Helen asked, stepping back from the door. She did not seem herself. Smaller, older, and not as pretty.

"Sorry I haven't been around for a while," Bob said, and Helen said, "I understand. You have a life."

"Slob-dog. You've brought our long-lost sister, how's it going, Susan?" Jim entered the room, tall, very trim. He clapped Bob on the shoulder, gave Susan a quick hug. "You like the city?" he asked her.

Helen said, "Susan, you look terrified."

Susan, asking right away to use the bathroom, sat on the edge of the tub and cried. They had no idea. The problem wasn't the city, which she hated, and which seemed slightly ridiculous, like a crowded state fair that went on for acres, the field poured with concrete, the rides underground instead of above it; it all seemed vaguely tawdry, the urine-smelling steps down to the subway, the litter skittering along the curbs, the smeared droppings of pigeons sliding down the statues, the gold-sprayed girl who stood in the park. No, it was not the city that terrified Susan. It was her brothers.

Who *were* they? How could they live this way? They were not the Bob and Jim from her childhood. Bob, in what was essentially a hotel, his front door nothing more than an opening off a carpeted hallway that hid other people's rooms. And a uniformed guard in the lobby who was there to keep homeless people from stumbling in, and to push the revolving door. It was an awful way to live, not really human. Bob asking if she didn't love the view of the river. What did she care about a river so far below that it seemed viewed through an airplane window? And then, strangest of all, for Bob to raise the silently-promised-never-to-talk-about-it fact of their father's accident in such a place, to raise it at all! Susan was disoriented, physically faint from the assault of this.

Her brothers, even after they had moved from Shirley Falls, were still her brothers. But not now. What Susan was experiencing now, as she blew her nose on toilet paper, was some tilting of the universe. She was utterly alone, attached only to a son who no longer needed her. Look at this house she was in (splashing water on her face, opening the bathroom door to step out), where Jim had raised three children, had dinner parties (Susan imagined this as she walked back to the living room), where he had big family Christmases, where he roamed on weekend mornings in his pajamas, tossing newspapers onto the coffee table, where he had watched television countless nights with his children and wife, here in this house that was no home at all. It was a large piece of furniture. A high-ceilinged museum. And *dark*. Who would live in a place so dark, the wood carved and fancy, the light fixtures like old antiques? Who would live like that?

They were speaking to her, Helen gesturing for her to come upstairs, a tour, Helen was saying, fun to see other people's houses, the dressing room, Helen was saying, she was the only woman in the city whose husband had more clothes than his wife, and they went past rows of suits, like a department store had set itself up, there was a window, as though the clothes needed a view, and a wall that was all one mirror, huge and high. Susan was forced to see herself: the pale-faced woman with the gray hair, her black slacks baggy. But Helen, in the mirror, looked small, compact, neat as a pin, wearing a fitted knit dress and tights, how did she know to dress that way?

Yes, the universe tilted. It was frightening to have the safety of the self give way. To have no father, mother, husband, brothers, and her son not—

"Susan." Helen's voice seemed sharp. "Do you need something to drink?"

———•———

In the back garden Susan and Bob sat next to each other on the wrought-iron bench, each holding a glass of club soda. Helen perched on the edge of a garden chair, her legs crossed, holding her own large glass of wine filled almost to the top. "Jim, sit," she said, because her husband was wandering about, bending to squint at the hosta plants or the shoots of the lilies—he had never cared about anything in the garden—or leaning against the support beam to the deck, or even once going back into the house and coming out empty-handed.

Helen was not sure she had ever been so angry, though of course she must have been. But right now, right here, something was really, really wrong, and all Helen knew was that no one was helping, it was completely—somehow, among four adults—completely up to her to keep this social moment afloat. It was easy to blame Susan, and Helen did. The recessive quality of her posture, the shapeless turtleneck, pilled toward the bottom it was of such poor quality—all this depressed Helen, and there were the quivers of pity that ran through her, too—it fizzed her up inside, she was dizzy with this many-threaded rage. "Jim, would you sit," she said again. He looked at her quizzically, as though the sharpness of her tone startled him.

"Let me get a beer." He went back inside the house.

Staring up at the small green plums that hung on the branches above her, Helen said, "Look at all the plums. Last year there weren't so many, but that's how it is with fruit trees, every other year they're abundant. The squirrels will be happy, plum-stuffed Park Slope squirrels."

The Burgess twins gazed at her blankly from the bench. Bob sipped his club soda politely, his eyebrows raised in a look of passivity. Susan sipped from her own glass, then looked slightly away from Helen, as though her face were saying, I'm not here, Helen, and I hate your big house and your stupid patch of backyard you call a garden, I think it's all vulgar, your big dressing room upstairs, your big grill out here, I hate it all, you rich Connecticut-born consumer, materialist of the modern world.

Helen, feeling this was contained in the face of her sister-in-law, thought the word *Rube*, and then felt very tired deep down inside herself. She did not want to think that, or be that way, and she thought it was awful such a word came to her, and no sooner did she think that than to her horror she thought the word *Nigger*, which had sometimes happened to her before, *Nigger, nigger*, as though her mind had Tourette's syndrome and these terrible things went uncontrollably through it.

"Do you eat them?" Bob asked.

Behind Helen the door opened, and Jim appeared with a bottle of beer. He pulled up a lawn chair. "The squirrels?" he said to Bob. "We grill them," nodding toward the grill.

"The plums. Do you eat the plums."

"They're too bitter," Helen answered, thinking, It is not my responsibility to make them comfortable. But of course it was. "You've lost weight," she said to Bob.

He nodded. "I'm not drinking these days. Much."

"Why aren't you drinking?" Helen heard the accusatory tone in her voice, saw Bob glance at Jim.

"You guys are tan," Susan said.

"They're always tan," Bob said, and Helen hated both of them.

"We were in Arizona visiting Larry, I thought you knew," Helen answered.

Susan turned her gaze away again, and Helen found this most deplorable of all, not to even ask about her nephew just because the woman's own son was a disappointment, had run off from living with her.

"How is Larry?" Bob asked.

"He's lovely." Helen took a large swallow of her wine, felt it go straight to her head, and then there was simultaneously the sound of glass breaking and a phone ringing a tinny ring and Susan standing up saying, "Oh no, oh no, I'm sorry."

Susan's cell phone had gone off, and apparently this had startled her to the point of dropping her glass, and while she rummaged through her bag, finding the phone—bizarrely handing it straight to Jim, who had stood and gone to her—Helen said, "Oh, don't worry, I'll get that cleaned up," thinking how broken glass would now be wedged in tiny pieces throughout the brick pattern of the walkway, and how the gardener, who came weekly this time of year, would be annoyed.

"Charlie Tibbetts," Jim said. "Susan's right here. Wait, she's saying you should just talk to me." Jim walked around the garden, the phone clapped to his ear, nodding, "Yuh, yuh, I hear you," and waved one hand through the air like a conductor leading an orchestra. He finally snapped Susan's phone shut, returned it to her, and said, "That's it, folks. It's over. Zach's a free man. The charges have been filed."

A silence fell. Jim sat back down, drank from his bottle of beer, tilting his head way back.

"What do you mean, 'filed'?" Helen was the one to finally ask.

"It means they're stuck away. If Zach is good, they disappear altogether. The case lost its sizzle. This actually happens all the time, and was what Charlie was hoping for. Except in this case there was political fallout, of course. But the Somali community, the elders, whoever it is they asked, said they'd be okay with it getting filed." Jim shrugged. "Who knows."

Susan said, "But now he'll never come home," and Helen, who had assumed she'd hear an uttering of happiness from Susan, heard the anguish in her voice and saw immediately how this might be the case—the boy would never come home.

"Oh, Susan," Helen murmured, and she rose and went to her sister-in-law, rubbing her back gently.

The brothers sat. Bob kept glancing at Jim, but Jim did not look back.

———•———

On a warm day in July, Adriana Martic walked into Alan Anglin's office and silently handed him papers, which he knew immediately from their size and font were a complaint. "What have we here?" he asked pleasantly, and nodded toward a chair in front of his desk. "Have a seat, Adri."

Adriana sat. After reading a moment, Alan glanced at her. Her long, streaky blond hair was pulled back in a low ponytail, and her face was pale. She had always been a quiet young woman, and she was quiet now as she met his eyes. She did not look away.

He read the complaint in its entirety. It was four pages long, and when Alan set it down on his desk he felt a moistness on his face in spite of the air-conditioned room. His first instinct was to get up and close the door, but the very nature of the complaint made this woman dangerous. She could have been sitting there quietly holding an automatic machine gun in her lap; to be alone with her would be like handing her another magazine of bullets. She was asking for one million dollars in damages.

"Let's take a walk," Alan said, standing up. She stood as well, and he held forth his hand to indicate that she—being a woman—should step through the doorway first.

Outside, the heat was blazing down on the Midtown sidewalk. People walked by wearing sunglasses and carrying briefcases. A homeless man was going through the garbage near the newsstand on the corner. He wore a winter coat, ripped at the pockets.

"How can he wear such a thing in the heat?" Adriana spoke quietly.

"He's ill. Most likely schizophrenic, delusional. They get very cold. It's one of the symptoms."

"I know what schizophrenic is," Adriana said, with a touch of irritation to her voice. "But I didn't know about the body temperature," she added.

He bought two bottles of water from the newsstand, and when she took the one he offered he noted that her fingernails were bitten to the quick; he felt, in a new way, the level of great danger. They sat on a bench in the shade. Around them men and women moved rapidly, in spite of the heat. One old woman walked slowly clutching a plastic

shopping bag in her hand. "Why don't you talk to me?" Alan said pleasantly, turning to Adriana.

She talked. He saw that she was prepared, that she was frightened,
although he was not sure if she was frightened of him or of not being
believed. She had phone texts, voicemails, restaurant receipts, hotel receipts. Emails on a private account. Also emails on the firm's account.
She pulled from her large handbag a folder, looked through papers, then
handed some to him.

He felt the indecency of reading the panicked lines of a man he had
known for years, loved almost as a brother, a man who had made the
mistake of many men (though he would not have thought this of Jim,
but it is often that way), cornered by Adriana's taunting suggestions that
she would contact his wife—Alan closed his eyes briefly at seeing the
word "Helen," then continued reading. Yes, there it was, a threat: *You'd
be foolish to do that, you'd throw your career right out the window, who do
you think you're dealing with here?*

And there was more.

"It will be in the papers," Adriana said calmly.

"We can try and keep that from happening."

"Probably it will happen. You're too big, too famous, this law firm."

"Are you ready to have this in the papers?" he asked. "We have to do
what's right, and you may be correct, it may get into the papers, which
means you, things about you, will be in the papers. You're ready for that?"

She looked down at her high heels, her legs stretched out before her.
She wore no stockings, he saw. It would be too hot, of course. But her
legs were perfect, without veins or splotches, just smooth shins neither
tanned nor too white. Her high heels were brown and toeless. He felt
nauseated.

"Have you spoken about this to anyone? Gone to a lawyer?" He
touched his mouth with the paper napkin that had come with his water.

"Not yet. I wrote the complaint myself."

Alan nodded. "May I ask you to hold off for one more day before
mentioning this to anyone? You and I will talk tomorrow."

She sipped from her bottle of water. "Okay," she said.

———

Jim and Helen were staying at the condo they rented in Montauk. Alan called Dorothy, then he called Jim, then he went to Penn Station and took a train out to Montauk. When he stepped out onto the platform, Jim was there to meet him, and the air was briny and they drove to the beach, where the waves came in lazily and without stopping.

———

"Go," said Rhoda, waving her hand from where she sat on the couch. "Your famous brother can't be bothered to return your call? Go out there and show up at his door."

For years, during his marriage, Bob and Pam had joined Jim and Helen for a week at their place in Montauk each summer. Pam riding a boogie board, shrieking with laughter, Helen lathering her kids with lotion, Jim running three miles down the beach, expecting praise when he got back, and getting it, then jumping into the waves. . . . After Pam left, Bob continued his visits there, going deep-sea fishing with Jim and Larry (poor Larry, always so seasick), then sitting on the balcony in the evening with his drink. Those summer days were a constant in a world that was inconstant. The wide ocean and sand were very different from the Maine coastline, harshly rocked and seaweed-laden, where their grandmother had taken them, potato chips warm from the car ride, the thermos of ice water, the dry peanut butter sandwiches; in Montauk, pleasure was embraced. "Look at the Burgess boys," Helen would say, bringing out a tray of cheese and crackers and cold shrimp. "Free, free, free at last."

Now, for the first time, Jim had not called, or Helen, with the usual checking of dates. "Go, and meet a nice girl," Rhoda said.

"Rhoda's right," Murray counseled from his chair. "New York's terrible in the summer. All the old people sitting on benches in the park. They look like melting candles. The sidewalks smell like garbage."

"I like it here," said Bob.

"Of course you do." Murray nodded. "In all of New York City, you are living on the best floor."

"Go," Rhoda said again. "He's your brother. Bring me back a shell."

———◆———

Bob left messages on Jim's phone. Also Helen's. He heard from neither of them. The last time Bob said, "Come on, call. I don't even know if you're alive." But of course they were alive. He'd have heard from someone if they were not. And so he understood that after years of opening their home and family to him, he was no longer wanted.

A few times he went with friends to the Berkshires, once to Cape Cod. But his heart was contracted with sorrow, and it took effort to have it not show. The last day he was on the Cape he saw Jim, and his whole body seemed to tingle with the suddenness of happiness. The chiseled features, the mirrored sunglasses: In front of the post office, there he was, his arms crossed, reading a sign painted on a restaurant. *Hey!*, Bob almost yelped, happiness flying from him, before the man uncrossed his arms, wiped his face—and it was not Jim at all, but a muscular man with a tattoo of a serpent crawling up his calf.

When he did see his brother, he passed him without knowing it at first. This was in front of the Public Library on Fifth Avenue at Forty-second Street. Bob was to meet a woman for lunch, a blind date set up by a friend; she worked at the library. The day was very hot, and Bob squinted behind his sunglasses. He would have missed Jim altogether if not for the lingering image in his mind's eye that the man he had just passed, wearing a baseball hat and mirrored sunglasses, had looked away with furtiveness. Bob turned and called, "Jim!" The man walked faster, and Bob ran to catch up, pedestrians moving aside. Shrunken-looking inside his suit jacket, Jim said nothing. He stood motionless, his face beneath the baseball cap still except for a twitching of his jaw.

"Jimmy—" Bob faltered. "Jimmy, are you sick?" He took his own sunglasses off, but could not see his brother's eyes behind his mirrored lenses. The chiseled aspect of Jim's face became prominent only when he lifted his chin, Jimlike, with defiance.

"No. I'm not."

"What's going on? Why didn't you answer my calls?"

Jim looked toward the sky, and then behind him, and then toward Bob again. "I was trying to have a nice time in Montauk this year. With my wife." In recalling this moment over the next months, Bob thought that his brother had not looked at him once; the conversation that followed was short and Bob would not be able to recall any of it except for the pleadingness of his own voice, and then the final lines delivered by Jim, whose lips were thin and almost blue, his words slow, deliberate, not loud. "Bob, I have to be really straight here. You have always made me crazy. I'm tired of you, Bob. I am so fucking tired of you. Of your Bobness. I am so— Bob, I just want you gone. Jesus, please go."

In that remarkable way people sometimes have, Bob was able to step into a coffee shop away from the noise of the street and call the woman he was to have lunch with. He spoke calmly, politely: Something had suddenly come up at work, he was terribly sorry, he would call later to reschedule.

After that he wandered the hot streets blindly, his shirt soaked through with sweat, stopping sometimes to sit on a step, smoking, smoking, smoking.

7

By the middle of August, in spite of the heat, the tops of a few maple trees had already turned orange. One could be seen across the street from where Susan and Mrs. Drinkwater were sitting in lawn chairs on the back porch. There was no breeze, and a faint mulchy smell of earth hung in the humid air. The old lady had rolled her stockings down to her ankles, and she sat with her skinny pale legs slightly apart, her dress hitched up past her knees. "Funny how when you're a kid, the heat doesn't seem to bother a bit." Mrs. Drinkwater fanned herself with a magazine.

Susan said that was true, and sipped from her glass of iced tea. Since her trip to New York—since finding out Zachary's charges were filed—Susan had spoken to her son once a week on the telephone. Each time there was the same afterglow of happiness at the sound of his deep, full voice, and then a seizing sadness set in. It was over—the frantic worry after his arrest, the buildup to the demonstration (it seemed so long ago), the catastrophic thought that Zach might go to prison—it was over. Her mind could not get hold of this. She said, picking up the water-beaded glass by her feet, "Zach's working in a hospital. Volunteering."

"My word." Mrs. Drinkwater pushed up her eyeglasses with the back of her hand.

"Not bedpans. He's stocking storage closets with bandages, things like that. I guess."

"But he's with people."

"He is."

From down the street came the sound of a lawn mower starting up. When the sound diminished, as if the mower had gone behind a house, Susan added, "I spoke with Steve today for the first time in years. I told him I was sorry about all the ways I'd been a bad wife. He was awful nice." As she feared would happen, a tear sprang to her eye, slipped out. She wiped it with her wrist.

"That's wonderful, dear. That he was nice." Mrs. Drinkwater removed her glasses and cleaned them with a tissue. "Regrets are no fun. Not at all."

The release of the tear loosened Susan's sadness, and she said, "But *you* can't have regrets about being a bad wife? Sounds to me like you were the perfect wife. You gave up your family for him."

Mrs. Drinkwater nodded just slightly. "Regrets about my girls. I was a good wife. I think I loved Carl more than my girls and I don't think that's natural. I think they felt lonely. Angry." The old lady slipped her glasses back on and was silent for a while, gazing toward the grass. She said, "It's not uncommon, dear, to have one child turn out with difficulties. But to have *two* children turn out that way."

From the shady soil beneath the Norway maple, the dog whimpered in a dream. Her tail thumped once and then she slept peacefully again.

Susan held her cool glass against her neck for a moment. She said, "The Somalians think you should have a dozen children. That's what I heard. They feel sorry for you if you only have two kids." She added, "So having just one must be bizarre, like giving birth to a goat."

"I always thought the point of the Catholic Church was to keep turning out little Catholics. Maybe the Somalians want to keep turning out Somalians." Mrs. Drinkwater turned her huge glasses toward Susan. "But neither of my girls had children, and it makes me feel very bad."

She cupped her hand to her cheek. "Both of them not wanting to be a mother. My word."

Susan gazed down at the toe of her sneaker. She still wore the flat simple sneakers of her youth. She said kindly, "I think there is no perfect way to live," glancing up at the old lady. "If they don't have children, they don't have children."

"No," Mrs. Drinkwater agreed, "there's no perfect way to live."

Susan said, musingly, "When I was in New York, it went through my mind, maybe this is how the Somalians feel. I'm sure it's not, well, maybe a little. But coming here where everything's completely confusing. I didn't know how to use a subway, and everyone was rushing past, because *they* knew. All the things people take for granted, because they're used to it. I felt confused every minute. It wasn't nice, I'll tell you."

Mrs. Drinkwater cocked her head, birdlike.

"My brothers seemed the strangest of all," Susan added. "Maybe when Somalian family members make it over here, the family that's been here awhile—maybe they seem strange too." Susan scratched her ankle. "It's just something I thought."

Steve had said he was more to blame than she was. You're a decent, hardworking person, he'd said. Zach is crazy about you.

Mrs. Drinkwater said, "I wish things never changed from the old days." She looked at Susan. "I just had a memory of Peck's."

"Tell me the memory of Peck's." Susan sipped from her glass of iced tea, not listening. She had seldom gone into Peck's. The boys got their school clothes there, but her own clothes were made by her mother. Susan, standing on a chair in the kitchen for the hem to be done. "Stand *still*," her mother would say. "For *God's* sake."

We did the best we could, Steve said on the phone this morning. Neither of us had an easy time as kids, Susan. Neither of us knew what we were doing. I wouldn't want you blaming yourself, he said.

Mrs. Drinkwater was concluding, "They'd be dressed nicely, the ladies at Peck's. You didn't do your shopping without looking nice. Back then."

Steve's mother, as a child, had been found barefoot and filthy, walking through that small town so far north. Relatives took her in, starting a feud that lasted years, families casting aspersions. Obese, by the time Susan met her, and divorced.

"I have a story," Susan said.

Mrs. Drinkwater turned her chair partly toward Susan. "Oh, I love stories."

"Remember a few years ago in that town up north when the deacon of the church poisoned the coffee at coffee hour and killed a couple people? Remember that? Well, that was in New Sweden, Steve's hometown."

Mrs. Drinkwater fixed her wobbly gaze on Susan. "That was your husband's hometown?"

Susan nodded. "I never thought they were very nice up there. They brought the Swedes over to work in the mills back in the 1800s, you know, because they wanted white people there."

"Not Canucks like me," Mrs. Drinkwater said, cheerfully, shaking her head. "People are funny. I'd forgotten about that. The deacon poisoning the coffee. My word."

"Well, the town's practically gone now. The mills are shut down. And people leave. Like Steve, going over to Sweden."

"Better to leave than stay and poison each other," Mrs. Drinkwater said. "What happened to the deacon? I forget."

"Killed himself."

They sat in comfortable silence, the sun moving behind trees, and the air getting just a little bit cooler. The dog, still asleep, thumped her tail lazily.

"I forgot to tell you," Susan said. "Gerry O'Hare's wife—the police chief I went to high school with—his wife called and asked if I wanted to join her knitting group."

"I hope you said yes, dear."

"I did. I'm a little nervous."

"Oh, phooey," the old lady said.

8

It was the day after Labor Day when Helen came upon Dorothy in a greengrocer's. Helen was at the cash register, purchasing three stalks of sunflowers. The man was wrapping them in paper, and Helen was holding her wallet open when she turned and saw Dorothy. "Hi!" said Helen, for the sight of Dorothy made her miss their old friendship. "How *are* you? Did you just get back from the Berkshires? We spent August in the city, which we haven't done for years, but of course—Jim wanted to get things started." Helen finished paying for the flowers, took them in her arms. "It's exciting for us, but it does seem the end to an era."

"What's exciting for you, Helen?"

Later, Helen would not be able to remember what Dorothy had been buying that day, only that she stood behind Helen in line while Helen said with enthusiasm, "That Jim's going out on his own."

Dorothy said, "What pretty sunflowers, Helen."

Helen would recall in Dorothy's face a combination of suppressed surprise and some pity. That is how Helen remembered it, later (and for the rest of her life), after she discovered that Jim had been asked by Alan to leave the law firm, that a sexual harassment lawsuit had been threatened, alleging that he had partaken in an intimate physical relationship with his employee, used his power and influence to make this employee uncomfortable— It had been covered up quickly, the young woman given a sum of money, the papers not getting hold of it. For five weeks Jim Burgess had gotten dressed each morning, taken his briefcase, kissed Helen at the door, and gone to the Public Library in Manhattan. He told Helen a new policy at the firm required personal calls be taken on their cell phones, so it was important she not call him through the receptionist, and she had naturally agreed. Jim spoke more frequently about not being happy at the firm, and Helen said, "So why not finally go out on your own? With your reputation and skills, you can pick and choose as you like."

He was worried about the expense of running an office. "But we have the money. Let's use some of mine," Helen exclaimed, and she sat with him in the evenings, computing rent and billing services and malpractice and secretarial costs. She called a friend of a friend who was in commercial real estate in Manhattan. An office space on the twenty-fourth floor of a building in downtown Manhattan was available to look at, and if he didn't like that, there were other options. It's true Helen thought Jim was not as excited about his freedom as he should be, given the freedom he said he wanted. She would remember this. And it's true that earlier that spring she had found a long pale hair on his shirt when she was getting the laundry ready for the dry cleaner, that is true too, but what would Helen Farber Burgess think of a long pale hair found on the sleeve of her husband's shirt? She was not a forensic scientist.

In his pants pocket one morning, a few days after meeting Dorothy in the greengrocer's (Jim was out of town, taking a deposition in Atlanta), Helen found the business card of someone advertising herself as a "life coach." *Your life is my job.* Helen sat on the bed. She didn't like the word "job." She didn't like the whole thing. She called her husband on his cell phone. "Oh, she's an idiot," he said. "Some woman looking at the same office space. Handed out her card to the realtor, to anyone."

"A life coach was looking at the same office space you were looking at? How much office space does a life coach need? What is a life coach, for heaven's sake?"

"Hellie, I don't know. Sweetheart, let it go."

Helen stayed sitting on the bed for a long while. She thought how Jim had not been sleeping well, she thought how he had lost weight. She thought that Bob's poor behavior—he seemed to have just stepped away from Jim, the way Zach unpeeled himself from Susan—must have something to do with this. She almost called Bob, but she was insulted by his absence. Finally she picked up the telephone and called the friend-of-a-friend realtor to say she'd like to see the office spaces that Jim had been seeing, and the realtor sounded confused and said, "Mrs. Burgess, your husband hasn't been looking at any office space."

When she called Jim on his cell phone, she was trembling. She heard Jim pause and then say quietly, "We have to talk." In another moment he said more quietly, "I'll be home tomorrow. We'll talk then."

"I'd like you to fly home now. I'd like to talk now," Helen said.

"Tomorrow, Hellie. I have to finish this deposition."

Helen's heart was beating like a bird's, her nose and chin tingling as she hung up. She had the odd sensation that she ought to go and buy bottled water and flashlights and batteries and milk and eggs, as she did when there were hurricane warnings. But she stayed home. She ate a piece of cold chicken while watching television. Waiting for her husband to come through the door.

9

In Maine, more maple trees were turning red, the birch trees showed patches of yellow. The days were warm, but evenings the air became chilly, and as daylight receded people pulled out their wool sweaters. Tonight Abdikarim had pulled on his loose-fitting quilted vest; he was leaning forward, listening to Haweeya and her husband speak; the children were asleep. Their eldest child was in middle school now, and she was a good girl, graceful and obedient. But she brought home descriptions of twelve-year-old girls wearing tank tops with their bosoms showing almost completely, kissing boys in the hallway, or behind the school. Haweeya had understood this day would come, but she had not foreseen her feelings, which were deep and anxious and glum.

"He'll take care of us until we're settled," she kept repeating. Her brother lived in Nairobi, where there was a community of Somalis.

Omad did not want to live in Nairobi. "They hate us there too," he said.

Haweeya nodded. "But you know Rashid and Noda Oya, and many cousins, and our children can remain Somali. Here they can remain

Muslim. But they can't remain Somali. They will be Somali-Americans, and I do not want that."

Abdikarim knew he would not go with them. He had moved as many times now as was possible for him. He had his café, his daughter in Nashville, his grandchildren could soon come to Shirley Falls to visit, or even to live. Abdikarim privately dreamed of this: his grandsons coming and working with him. As for his young wife Asha and their son, pictures were sometimes sent to him, and his heart remained closed. The boy's expression was always elusive, this last time he appeared to be sneering in a way that some of the *adano* boys on Gratham Street sneered, as if they had no one who cared for them, or taught them, and Abdikarim understood Haweeya's fears. He had seen himself how her children were speaking English to their parents, using American expressions to each other. You are mad cool. You are the hot diggity bomb. And of course the longer they stayed the more American they would become. They would be hyphenated people. Somali-American. What a strange thing, Abdikarim thought, to become hyphenated to a country now gratifying itself with the impression that all Somalis were pirates. In the spring, Somali pirates had killed a Chinese boat captain in the Gulf of Aden. This caused pain in the community in Shirley Falls: No one could condone that. But the news reporters had no wish, perhaps no ability, to understand that the fishermen's coastline had been spoiled with toxic waste, that they could not fish as they once had—Americans really did not understand desperation. It was easier, and certainly more pleasing, to view the Gulf of Aden as a lawless place where Somali pirates reigned. A crazy parent, America was. Good and openhearted one way, dismissive and cruel in others. Thinking this, Abdikarim pressed his fingers to his forehead; one could say he treated his living son, Asha's son, the same way. Seeing this, briefly, caused him to feel more benevolent, not to the son but to America. Life was difficult, decisions were made—

"I'll see Margaret Estaver tomorrow," Haweeya was saying. She looked toward Abdikarim, who nodded.

———◆———

Margaret Estaver's office looked like Margaret. Unorganized, and gentle, and welcoming. Haweeya sat watching this woman, whom she had grown to love, whose messy hair was slipping from its clip. Margaret had been looking out the window ever since Haweeya told her the plans. "I thought you liked the stoplights," Margaret finally said.

"I do. I love the stoplights. People obey them. I love the Constitution. But my children—" Haweeya moved her hands. "I want them to be African. They won't be, if we stay here." Haweeya was repeating what she had said for the last half hour. Her brother had a business in Kenya, her husband was agreeing. Repeat and repeat.

Margaret nodded. "I'll miss you," she said.

The breeze caused the leaves outside the window to suddenly rustle, and the partly opened window slammed shut. Haweeya sat up straight, waiting for her heart to slow. Then she said, "I'll miss you too." She had a keen sense of the pain this conversation was causing. "Other people need your help, Margaret. Your work is very important."

Margaret Estaver smiled at her tiredly, leaned over to the window to open it once again. "Sorry about that noise," she said, and propped a book between the sill and the window frame, then turned back to face Haweeya, who was quietly shocked to see that the book used was a Holy Bible.

Haweeya said, "In America, it is about the individual. Self-realization. Go to the grocery store, the doctor's office, open any magazine, and it is self, self, self. But in my culture it is about community and family."

Margaret said, "I know that, Haweeya. You don't need to explain."

"I want to explain. I want my children not to feel—what is the word? —entitled. People here raise their children to feel entitled. If the child feels something, he says what he feels, even if it's rude to his elders. And the parents say, Oh, good, he is expressing himself. They say, I want my child to feel entitled."

"I don't think that's entirely true." Margaret took a deep breath and let it out slowly. "I work with many families in this town, and believe me, lots of kids here, American kids, don't feel entitled or even wanted." When Haweeya did not answer, Margaret conceded, "But I know what you mean."

Haweeya tried to make a joke. "Yes, I am entitled to my opinion." But she saw that Margaret was not in a mood to joke. "Thank you," Haweeya said.

Margaret stood. She looked older than Haweeya thought she was. Margaret said, "You are absolutely right to think of your children."

Haweeya stood as well. She wanted to say, but did not, You would not be alone if you were Somali, Margaret. You would have brothers and sisters and aunts and uncles everywhere with you. You would not go home to your empty rooms each night. But perhaps Margaret did not mind the empty rooms. Haweeya had never been able to figure out exactly what Americans wanted. (Everything, she sometimes thought. They wanted everything.)

10

Oh, Helen, Helen, Helen!

"Why?" she kept whispering as she watched her husband speaking. "Why? Why, Jim?" The man looked at her helplessly. His eyes were small and dry.

"I don't know," he said repeatedly. "Hellie, I don't know."

"Did you love her?"

"No."

The day was a warm one, and Helen got up and closed each window. Then she closed the shutters. "And everyone knows," she said softly, amazed, as she moved back to sit on the edge of the coffee table.

"No, Hellie, they kept it quiet."

"They can't keep something like that quiet. That horrible slut herself tells people."

"No, Hellie. It's part of the settlement. She can't talk about it."

"Oh, you are a fool, Jim Burgess. An absolute stinking fool. A girl like that has friends. Girls *talk*. They talk about the stupid wife. Did you talk about me?"

"God, of course not."

But she saw, she thought, that he had. "Did you tell her I almost died in Arizona because you weren't paying attention to me? Because when I wanted to go back to the hotel that day, you said no?"

He did not answer, only stood with his arms by his sides.

"Every day you walked out of this house and went to the *library*? Every single day you lied to me like that?"

"I was scared, Hellie."

"Did you go to see her?"

"Oh no. God, no."

"Where were you last night?"

"In Atlanta, Helen. Doing a deposition. Helping to finish a case."

"Oh my God, you're lying."

"Hellie. Please. I'm not. Please."

"Where is she?"

"I don't know. I don't even know if she's still at the firm. I don't talk to anyone there except sometimes Alan, since he's distributing my cases."

"But you're lying! If you were in Atlanta last night you must've been with someone from the firm. So either you weren't *in* Atlanta, or you *do* talk to people other than Alan in the firm. And you know perfectly well where she is!"

"There was an associate with me in Atlanta. He didn't mention her because he doesn't even know—"

"I'm going to be sick." In the bathroom she almost allowed him to stroke her hair, but then she was not sick, and so she pushed him away. There was something theatrical to her gestures. She meant them, as she meant everything she said. But the way she moved her arms, the way she said words, had never been needed before, and was foreign. She struggled to be calm, understanding that once it left her she would be wild inside the foreignness—a void of hysteria waited. She stalled.

"I don't understand," she kept saying. Jim remained standing and she told him to sit down. "But not near me. I don't want you near me." Loudly: "I don't want you near me." She withdrew farther into the corner of the couch. She was not saying this to punish him. She did not want him near. She wanted to be away, away. She felt like a spider, contracting. "Oh God," she whispered, feeling herself closer to the wilderness waiting.

"What did I do wrong?" she asked.

He was sitting on the edge of the leather ottoman, his lips almost white. "Nothing."

"That's not true, Jim. I must have done something you never told me about."

"No, no, Hellie."

"Please try and tell me why." She said this nicely, deceiving them both.

He did not look at her. But he began slowly to talk in sentences. He said going to Maine to take care of Zach, which he had failed at, and which Bob had failed at too, had made him feel really angry, furious, like a pipe with rusty water pouring through him.

"I don't understand," she said truthfully.

He said he didn't understand either. But he said he had wanted to wander far away and never come back. Seeing the mess Zach turned into, the emptiness of Bob's life—

"The emptiness of Bob's life?" Helen almost screamed this. "The emptiness of Bob's life made you have a sordid office affair? And Bob's life isn't even empty! What are you *talking* about?"

He looked at her with his small, frightened eyes. "I don't know, Helen. I was supposed to take care of everyone. Growing up. That was my job. And then I left when Mom died, and I wasn't there for Susan or Zach when Steve left, and Bob—"

"Stop. Stop. You were supposed to take care of everyone? Where's the violin, Jim? Is this suddenly news? Do you think I haven't listened to you about this before? Honestly—well, honestly, Jim, I can't *honestly* believe this is what you have to say right now."

He nodded, looking down.

"But keep going," she finally said. She did not know what else to do.

He looked around the room, then back to her. "The kids are all gone."

He put out his arm and moved it through the air to indicate the emptiness of their home. "Things felt so—so awful. And Adri made me feel
important."

And so Helen's crying arrived, long, racking, heaving sobs and sounds,
and Jim went and touched her arm tentatively. Sometimes she cried out
words, or phrases, to indicate that Bob's life was not empty but Jim's,
and Helen had mourned the children going away and never been com-
forted by Jim one bit and she never ever would have thought to go *find
someone to sleep with so she could feel important* and he had ruined everything, how could he not see that he had done that? He rubbed her
arm and said he knew.

And never—never—was he to speak that horrible woman's name
again. Bringing her name into the house! She didn't have children, did
she? No, of course not. She was nothing more than a puddle of urine on
the floor, a woman like that. And Jim said Helen was right, he would
never say the name again, he didn't want to ever say the name again, not
here not anywhere.

That night they fell asleep holding each other, in their nightclothes,
afraid.

Helen woke early, the light was greenish and not full. Her husband
was no longer beside her. "Jim?" He was sitting in the chair by the window, and he turned and looked at her and said nothing. She whispered,
"Jimmy, did that all happen?" He nodded. There were dark patches beneath his eyes.

She sat up and immediately looked for her clothes. She stepped into
the dressing room and pulled on what she had been wearing the day
before, then pulled those clothes off—she would throw them away—and
put on others. Back inside the bedroom she said, "You'll have to tell the
children," and Jim looked stricken and then nodded. Immediately she
said, "I'll tell the children," because she did not want them frightened
and of course they would be terribly frightened, she had never been so
frightened herself.

He said, "Please don't leave me."

She said, "I'm not leaving. You left." What she meant was that he had left the bed, had left her in her sleep. But she said, "I want you gone."

She did not want him gone, but she must have because she kept saying it, even as he put things in a suitcase, she kept saying, "I want you gone. All I want is to be away from you." She could not believe he believed her. She wanted this person, repellent, terrifying, to be gone; that's what she meant. When he stopped and looked at her with blank-faced panic, she said, "Go! Go! I want you gone." She said she hated him. She said she had given her life to him. She said she had trusted him always. She followed him down to the door as she said she had never once betrayed him. She said again she wanted him gone.

She ran up the stairs so as to not hear the click of the grated gate. And then she moved through the house, calling, "Jim! Jim!" She could not believe that he would do that, just go. She could not believe any of it. "Jim," she called. "Jim."

———•———

The Hudson River had barges and tugboats and sailboats moving on it constantly. More compelling to Bob was the way the river changed according to the time of day and of course the weather. In the morning the water was often calm and gray, by afternoon the sun hit it with glory, and on Saturdays the sailboats gathered like a fleet of toys seen from Bob's eighteenth-story window. By evening the sun threw off great gusts of pink and red and the water shone as though it were a painting brought to life, the strokes of color moving and thick and thrilling, and the lights of New Jersey seemed to indicate a foreign shore. All the time he had lived in New York he had been (he now thought) surprisingly uninterested in its history. In Maine he had learned early on about the Abenaki Indians and their trips down the Androscoggin River each spring, planting crops along the way, harvesting them on their way back. But here was the Hudson, and what a history *it* had. Bob bought books, one leading to another, and then he was reading about Ellis Island, which of course he knew about, but not really. (Growing up in Shirley Falls, he knew no one who had relatives that had come to the country through Ellis Island.) He watched documentaries, leaning toward his television to see the mass of people pressed forward, coming on land with such hope and trepidation, because some of them would be turned back— doctors deciding they were blind, or syphilitic, or just mad—and they knew it. When they were allowed through, waved on, these people in jerking motion of black-and-white, Bob felt relief for each one.

Bob himself was emerging into a world where all felt doable. This was unexpected and gradual, but swift, too. As autumn returned the city to its routines, he went about his life unencumbered by the crust of doubt he'd been so used to that he had not known it covered him until it was gone. He had little memory of August, only the sense of the city's grittiness and heat and a roaring of a wind inside him. The unimaginable had happened: Jim was not in his life. At times he woke in agony, and could only think: Jim. But Bob was not a young man, and he knew about loss. He knew the quiet that arrived, the blinding force of panic, and he knew too that each loss brought with it some odd, barely acknowledged sense of release. He was not an especially contemplative person, and he did not dwell on this. But by October there were many days when the swell of rightness, loose-limbedness, and gentle gravity came to him. It recalled to him being a child, when he found one day he could finally color within the lines.

At work, he noticed that people often came to him for help, their eyes receptive. Perhaps it had always been this way. He became used to the doorman nodding, "Hello, Mr. Bob," and Rhoda and Murray open-ing their door, "Bobbeleh! Come in, have a glass of wine." He babysat for the little boys down the hall one night, he walked a neighbor's dog, wa-tered plants for someone gone.

His apartment he kept picked up, and this—more than the fact that he seldom drank and had only one cigarette a day—made him take note: He had changed. He did not know why he hung up his coat, or put the dishes away, or tossed his socks into the hamper. But he understood why his earlier inability to do so had irritated Pam—he did see this now in a different way. Pam, though, was gone for him. Gone with Jim somehow. The two of them seemed to have fallen into a pocket where the self knows to put dark, unpleasant things—and without excessive wine to start his mind wandering, they seemed to stay that way.

He called Susan each week. Always she told him first what Zachary was doing (they had Skyped, and he spoke words of Swedish). She told Bob her fears that Zach's current capacity for happiness proved she'd been a bad mother since he'd never been happy like this with her, but all she wanted, she said, was this health he seemed to now have. Bob answered each worry she expressed, noting that her tone was not that of a woman depressed. She had a knitting club she belonged to—Brenda O'Hare, Gerry's wife, was awfully, awfully nice—and she ate every night with Mrs. Drinkwater; did Bob think she should lower the rent. No, he advised, she had not raised it in years. One day Susan had come across Rick Huddleston from the Office of Racial Anti-Defamation, this was in the grocery store, and he just stared at her like she was evil. Too bad, Bob said. He's a jerk if he did that. That's what I told myself, Susan said. (They were like brother and sister. They were like twins.) Only once did Susan ask if he had heard from Jim, she said she had called him and he never called back. Don't worry about it, Bob said, I don't hear from him either.

Wally Packer had been arrested again. This was for the possession of illegal arms, but he had resisted arrest and threatened a police officer; he faced possible jail time. The twins discussed this, Susan saying, in a resigned way, that there was something unsurprising about it, and Bob agreed. Neither mentioned Jim as they spoke of this, and Bob felt the small breeze of freedom to realize he did not have to talk to Jim about Wally Packer (or anything), did not have to be demeaned by him.

Mostly, he could not have predicted that he would feel the way he did.

In the middle of October, New York was suddenly very warm. The sun streamed down like summertime, and sidewalk cafés filled with people. On his way to work one morning, Bob passed a place where people sat with their coffee and newspapers, and when he heard his name called he did not think anything about it. But it was Pam, standing up, almost knocking over a chair at a table Bob walked by. "Bob! Wait! Oh, shit," because she had spilled her coffee. He stopped.

"Pam. What're you doing here?"

"New shrink. Just saw him. Please, can I walk with you?" She had slapped down some bills on the table, plunked her spilled coffee cup on top of them, and was walking to get to the sidewalk to meet him.

"I'm on my way to work."

"I know that, Bobby. I was just thinking about you. This shrink is really good. He says we have unresolved issues."

Bob stopped walking. "When did you start believing in therapy?"

Pam looked thin and worried. "I don't know. I thought I'd give it a shot. I'm feeling kind of adrift these days. *You've* practically disappeared. Hey, get this." She touched his arm. "Before I went to this shrink, who's pretty good, I went to a woman shrink and she kept calling Shirley Falls 'Shelly Falls,' and I finally said, Why can't you get that straight? And she said, Oh, Pamela, a small mistake, excuse me. And I said, Well, people in Shirley Falls might not think it's a small mistake. What if I said, Oh, your office is on Flatbush Avenue, I got it mixed up with Park Avenue, *saaawwry!*"

Bob stared at her.

"She was an asshole. She kept calling me 'Pamela' and I said my name was Pam and she said that was the name of a girl and I was a woman. Honestly. A dipshit in a red blazer with a huge desk."

"Pam, why are you paying a therapist to talk about Shirley Falls?"

She looked taken aback. "Well, I don't talk about it all the *time*. It comes up because, you know, I miss it or something."

"You live in a huge townhouse and you go to parties with Picassos on the walls, and you miss Shirley Falls."

She looked down the street. "Sometimes."

"Pam. Listen to me." He saw fear drop onto her face. People moved past them on their way to work, briefcase straps slung across their chests, heels clicking on the sidewalk. "Let me ask you one question. After we split up, did you track down Jim and get drunk and tell him he was attractive and tell him stuff you'd been up to when we were still married? Just tell me."

"What?" Her head ducked forward slightly, as though trying to find him. "What?" she asked again. The fear had changed to confusion. "Tell your brother I found him attractive? *Jim?*"

"He's the only brother I have. Yes, Jim. Many people find him attractive. One of the sexiest men of 1993." Bob tried to step back from all the people moving down the sidewalk toward their bus stop or the subway. Pam followed him; they were almost in the street. He told her what Jim had said about her in the hotel in Shirley Falls when they had gone up for the demonstration. "That you made poor confessional choices," he finished.

"You know what?" Pam spread her fingers through her hair. "You listen to this, Bob Burgess. I can't stand your brother. You know why? He's actually kind of like me. Only he's *not* like me because he's hard and successful and manages to find himself new audiences. I'm anxious, a little pathetic, and I can't *find* my audience, which is partly why I like going to this shrink even if I have to pay him to be my audience. But Jim and I—we recognize each other, always have, and in his passive hostile way, he's put me down. He *craves* attention, his need for it is so transparent it makes me sick, and poor Helen puts up with it because she's too stupid to see it. So he demands attention and then keeps people out when he gets it, because wanting attention has nothing to do with *relating* to people, which is kind of what most human beings like to do. And yeah, I had a drink with him. He *got* me to say stuff, because that's what he does. A whole career spent getting people to say what he wants them to, whether it's a confession or a lie. Did I tell him I found him *attractive?* Does that sound like a word I use? Oh, Jim, I've always found you so *attractive.* Are you kidding me? That's the kind of thing Helen, poor rich Connecticut stuffed sofa, would say."

"He said you were a parasite."

"Nice. Nice of you to repeat that."

"Ah, Pam. Who cares what he said?"

"You care! Or you wouldn't be accosting me like this."

"I'm not accosting you. I just wanted to know."

"Well, what *I* want is to tell your brother he has no business screwing around with your head. *He's* the parasite. Feeding off the back of Wally Packer. And then off the back of white-collar criminals. Oh, that's holy work, isn't it?"

She was not crying. She was not close to crying. She was the most Pam he had seen in years. He apologized. He said he would find her a cab.

"Fuck that," she said. She pulled her cell phone from her bag. "I feel like calling him right now. You can hear what I have to say to him." She pointed her cell phone at Bob's chest. "Jim and I aren't really parasites, Bob. We're statistics. Two more baby boomers not doing all the great things for society we thought we'd do. And then we get whiny about it, boo hoo. Yes, I go to dinner parties with Picassos on the wall, and some-times, Bobby—shoot me—I feel sad, because I kind of thought I'd be a scientist tramping around Africa finding parasites and people would think I was *great*. Half-dead people wouldn't die because of me. Hell, I'd save all Somalia! It's called grandiosity, Bobby. As far as I can tell it's a sickness like any other—

"Stay right here. I have some things to say to that motherfucker brother of yours. What's his number? Never mind. I'll call 411. Yes. Man-hattan. Business. A law firm, please. Anglin, Davenport, and Sheath. Thank you."

"Pam—"

"What? My shrink was just saying, just half an hour ago, why did everyone in the family cater to Jim? And I thought, yeah, why? Why hasn't anyone confronted him about how disgusting he's always been to you? He told me that day— Oh, never mind. He can tell you himself what he said about you, how you'd always driven him nuts— Yes, I'd like to speak to Jim Burgess, please. Pam. Pam Carlson."

"Pam, why are you bothering a shrink about—"

She shook her head at him. "Oh, I see. He's unavailable. Well, you have him call me." She gave out her number, furiously, coldly. "What's that?" She cocked her head, put a finger to her other ear, looked at Bob with a deep scowl of puzzlement. "Did you just say, Mr. Burgess no longer works here?"

———◆———

The ride to Park Slope was not long or short, merely a piece of time in which Bob stood pressed against others as the train rumbled beneath the streets of Manhattan and then beneath the East River. Everyone on the train seemed innocent and dear to him, their eyes unfocused with morning reveries that were theirs alone, perhaps words spoken to them earlier, or words they dreamed of speaking; some read newspapers, many listened through earbuds to their own soundtrack, but most stared absently as Bob did—and he was moved by the singularity and mystery of each person he saw. His own mind, had it been peered into, was filled with odd and shocking thoughts, yet he assumed that those around him—tugging on the shoulder straps of their bags, lurching forward as the train stopped in a station, murmuring Sorry for a foot stepped on, the nod of acceptance—had everyday things on their minds, but how did he know, how did he know, the train rocked forward again.

His first thought—or visitation of feeling, for it was not really a thought—once he freed himself from Pam on the sidewalk and tried, without success, to call Jim, then Helen, was that some terrible crime had been committed, that Jim Burgess had secretly murdered someone or was to be murdered, the family fleeing in one of those twisted awful stories that made their way to the front page of a tabloid— The ludicrous aspect of this was not lost on Bob, but the fear of it caused him to love the innocence of, and be gently envious of, the ordinary people around him, who were either dreading or not dreading their day of work, but who were not standing there contemplating their brother's murder. His head was not quite right, he recognized this. More people got off the train, and by the time it pulled into Park Slope only a few people were left in his car, and his quietly exalted state was gone. Whatever was going on with Jim—Bob had a foreboding—was not dramatic, just dismally quotidian. Bob was weary as he walked; even in fantasy his brother demanded the grandiosity Pam had spoken of.

But doubt pricked him, and four blocks from the house he called his nephew Larry, who surprised him by answering, and surprised him more by saying, Oh, Uncle Bob, things are a mess, hold on, I'll call you right back, and then calling back and saying, Yeah, Mom's home, she said you can come over, but they've split up, Uncle Bob, my dad was sleeping with some girl in his office. And then Bob walked quickly, out of breath, turning down the street where his brother lived.

———◆———

Stepping into the house, Bob sensed the difference, though it took a moment to understand it was not just an atmosphere of loss; things were gone. The coats, for example, that always hung in the foyer. There was only one short black coat of Helen's. And the bookshelves in the living room had at least half their books missing. The big flat-screen television was gone.

"Helen, did he take all this stuff with him?"

"He took the clothes he was wearing at the time he came home and told me what had happened with that filthy paralegal. Everything else I threw out."

"You threw out his clothes? His books?" He glanced quickly at his sister-in-law. Her hair was tied back, and the shorter sections by her ears were gray. Her face had the naked look of someone whose glasses were removed, but Helen did not wear glasses, except on her nose when she was reading.

"Yes. I threw out that big TV because he liked it. I brought up the old one from the basement. Anything to do with him is gone from this house."

"Wow." Bob said slowly.

"Wow?" Helen turned and looked at him, as she sat down on the couch. "Don't judge me, Bob."

"Not judging." He held up both hands. The rocking chair was gone. He sat down in an old leather chair that he couldn't remember from before.

Helen crossed her ankles. She seemed quite small. Her shoes were like ballet slippers with little black bows. She wore no jewelry, he noticed, no rings at all. She did not offer him a drink, nor did he ask. "How are you, Helen?" he said, cautiously.

"I'm not even going to answer that."

He nodded. "That's fair. Ah, look. Can I help?"

"Maybe because you were divorced you think you know what this is like, but you don't." She said this without harshness.

"No, no, Helen. I know I don't."

They sat. Helen asked if he would mind closing the shutters. She'd opened them earlier, but really, she was more comfortable with them closed.

Bob got up and did that, then sat down again. He turned on a lamp near him. "Where is he?"

"He's teaching at a swanky little college somewhere. Upstate. I don't know what town, and I really don't care. But if he beds down some student, he'll lose that job too."

"Ah, Jimmy won't do that," Bob said.

"Don't you"—and here Helen leaned forward and whispered furiously—"*fucking* get it?"

Bob had never heard Helen use that word.

"Don't you get it?" she asked, tears glistening in her eyes. "He is not. The person. I thought. He was." Bob opened his mouth to answer, but Helen continued, still leaning toward him. "Do you know who she was? This tramp at his office? She was the girl who lived below you, who kicked her husband out. She said you told her to apply to Jim for her stupid, stupid, stupid job."

"Adriana? Adriana Martic? Are you kidding?"

"Kidding?" Helen's voice quieted, and she sat back. "I'm not kidding even mildly, Bob. Oh-o-oh, not kidding a bit. But why would you send her to Jim, Bobby? Why would you do that?" She looked at Bob with such sincere confusion that he started to say, "Helen—" But she was asking, "Can't you tell a whore when you see one? No, you can't. I always thought Pam had a slut quality too. You have no idea, Bob. You can't, because you're not a woman. But a woman who makes a nice home, who raises children, who keeps herself fit—it's not like it's easy. And then the man wants some cartoon of a sleazy girl that must remind him of high school or something, I don't know, but it hurts, Bob, you can't imagine. And of course you never think it will happen to you. It's why I don't go out. I have friends who would love to come over and hold my hand. I'd rather die, I really would. They're happy, deep down, because they think it can't happen to them. It can."

"Helen—"

"She made him feel important, that's what he said. He gave her advice about her divorce. Thirty-three years old, his *daughter* is almost that age. She kept a record of everything, then turned him in. Does he tell me? Of course not. Instead he lets himself slide farther down the sewer pipe and decides he's headed for hell—no, wait, says he was *in* hell, can you imagine, I'm supposed to feel sorry for Jim Burgess who put himself in hell, he actually acted like that, Bob, like maybe I was supposed to feel sorry for him, always, always, always, about *him*—so he goes off with a *life coach*, Bob, just in case you don't think it's unbelievable enough, and she takes him out to Fire Island, her husband's away, and Jim tells me he's in Atlanta. I found out because she called him here. After he'd gone. Can you believe that? After lying to me for so long, what's another lie?" Helen gazed blankly in front of her. "Nothing. Another lie is nothing. Because everything is nothing."

There was silence for a long while. Then Bob said quietly, more to himself, "Jim did all that?"

"Jim did all that. And probably more. The kids are a mess. They all flew home to help me, but I could see they were scared to death. You want *parents,* Bob, no matter what age you are. They lost the golden image of their father, which is terrifying to them, I couldn't let them see a wretched mother. So I had to act strong and comfort them and send them away and it was just exhausting, you can't know."

"Ah, Helen. I'm sorry."

And he was. He was terribly sorry. He was also unspeakably sad. It was like the universe had cracked in half; Helen and Jim were one unit, they couldn't possibly be two. He felt a sickening pity for their kids, he felt like he had lost what they had lost. But they were younger and it was their parents and it was so much worse— "Oy," he said. "Oy."

Helen nodded. After a moment, she added, reflectively, "I did everything for him."

"You did." Bob saw this clearly. Helen had been picking up Jim's socks right here that day he tossed them onto the floor and the coffee table while Bob was telling about Adriana calling the police on her husband. (Adriana! Bob had felt sorry for her, standing on the sidewalk that morning!) "Oh Christ, Helen, I'm sorry I mentioned Jim's law firm to that woman. It just fell out of my mouth. I should have known she wasn't trustworthy. I kept saying that day I didn't think what she told the police was true."

Helen looked at him vacantly. "What?"

"Adriana. You're right, I should have known she was no good."

Helen smiled sadly. "Oh, Bobby," she murmured. "Don't take that on too. He would have found somebody else. Like the life coach. They're just out there waiting, I guess. I don't know, it's a foreign language to me. I wouldn't even know the words that are used to start an affair."

Bob nodded. "You're a good person, Helen."

"He used to say that." Helen raised a limp hand, dropped it back into her lap. "And it made me happy to hear. God."

Bob looked slowly around the room. Helen had made a beautiful home, been a patient, warm mother, she'd been friendly to the neighbors when Jim walked arrogantly past them. She'd filled the house with plants and flowers, been good to Ana, she'd packed suitcases for their expensive vacations, waited while he played golf, and mostly (Pam was right about this) listened while Jim talked about himself endlessly, how smart he'd been in court that day, how he was the *best* in the business and everyone knew it. . . . She had bought him a drawer full of cuff links, a ludicrously expensive watch, because, he said, he'd always wanted one.

But, still: A home should not be destroyed. People didn't understand this: Homes and families should not be destroyed. He said, "Helen, did Jim tell you why we haven't been speaking for months?"

Helen lifted a hand vaguely. "Some girl you were with, I don't know."

"No. It's because we had a fight."

"I don't care."

"But you need to care. Didn't he tell you about the fight? About what he told me?"

"No. And I don't need to care. I need the opposite. I need to be free of caring."

He told her what Jim had said on the balcony of the hotel when Zachary was missing. "Jim's been living his whole life with that, Helen. The guy killed his father, or he thinks he did, and he was too scared to tell anyone. Helen?"

Her eyes were squinting hard. She said, "Is this supposed to make me feel better?"

"It's to make you see why he's all messed up."

"It makes me feel worse. I've been telling myself that he's had some kind of midlife crisis, but he's been a scheming liar all his life."

"You can't call that lying, Helen. That's fear." He was pleading now, lawyerlike, trying to keep the pleading from his voice. "Any kid will do that, try and get out of something. He was eight years old, Helen. He was a child. Even the law says an eight-year-old is a child. So he did this thing, or he *thinks* he did this thing, and time goes by and he can't tell, because the more time that goes by the harder it is to tell. So he ends up living with fear all his life, like he's going to get found out and punished."

Helen stood up. "Bob. Stop. You're making it worse. Now there isn't one day of my marriage, not one day, that I know was truly mine, with a good and honest husband. I don't know what to do, I have no idea how to get through the days. That's the truth. I'm jealous of dead

people, Bob. I don't even cry, because the sound disgusts me, the pathetic, pitiful sounds I make here alone at night. I have lawyers drawing
up the agreement, and then—I don't know what. I'll move somewhere.
Please go."

"Helen." Bob stood up, one arm reaching forward. "Helen, please.
Feel some pity. You can't leave him. You can't. He's all alone. He loves
you. You're his family. Come on, Helen, you're his wife. Jesus. Thirty
years. You can't just toss it over your shoulder!"

Oh, the poor woman went nuts. She was crazed, or allowed herself
to be crazed, Bob was never—when he thought about it later, as he did
often—sure how much of the outburst she could control. Because she
said some pretty incredible things.

She said (and Bob would whisper "Jesus" every time he recalled it)
that she'd always, deep down, thought the Burgess family was kind of
crappy. Close to trash, really. Hillbilly, rube trash, that god-awful little
house they'd grown up in, Susan being a bitch. Susan had been cold-
hearted to Helen from the moment she'd met her years ago. You know
what Susan gave Helen for Christmas one year? An umbrella!

Helen said Bob must leave, so he went out the door, and he was
halfway down the sidewalk when he heard Helen yell after him, "A *black*
umbrella! *No thank you!*"

11

Bob drove and drove and drove. The car swooped around a curve, up over a hill, down past a creek, through a town of few houses and one gas station. He drove for hours before he saw a sign for the college. For the last many miles the road had been winding and narrow, and on both sides hills rose up, golden in the autumn sun. At times the road went along the top of one of those hills and he could see for miles around him the soft rolling curves of the earth, the varied tones of fields, brown, yellow, green, and spread out above a sky that was endless and blue with white clouds scattered. Its beauty did not touch him.

"Oh Christ," Bob murmured as he drove into the small town of Wilson, where the college was. He spoke aloud to get it straight: "Jim's teaching at this college. Things change. This is not a horror film." But that's how it felt; Bob couldn't shake it. There was something about the little town, the one small main street—there was something bad about it. He felt that hidden eyes were watching him, the lone red rental car going through the empty streets on a Saturday afternoon in Wilson.

He found his brother's apartment not far from the campus. The building was tucked into a hill, and there were many wooden steps that had to be walked up to even reach the front door. Bob buzzed the buzzer and waited, finally hearing the sound of footsteps within.

Jim opened the door partway, leaning against it. There were purplish circles under his eyes, and he wore a sweatshirt with no shirt beneath; his neck was corded and his collarbone jutted out. "Hey," Jim said, raising a hand laconically. Bob followed him up the stained carpeted stairway, watching his brother's feet in dirty socks, and his jeans that were too loose. Passing a door on the second landing, Bob heard a staccato foreign language coming from inside, and there was an acrid smell of sweetened garlic and spices; the smell was insidious. Jim looked back over his shoulder and pointed upward: Keep going.

In his apartment, Jim sank down onto a green plaid couch and nodded toward a chair in the corner. Bob sat tentatively. "Want a beer?" Jim asked.

Bob shook his head. The apartment seemed to have little light, in spite of the large window behind the couch where Jim sat. Jim's face seemed gray.

"It's pretty awful, huh." Jim opened a Band-Aid box next to a lamp, and brought out a joint. He licked his fingers.

"Jimmy—"

"How are you, brother of mine?"

"Jimmy, you're—"

"I hate it here, I have to say. In case you were going to ask." Jim held up a finger, put the joint between his thin lips, found a lighter in his pocket, and lit, dragged, and held. "Hate the students," he said, still holding in the smoke, "hate the campus, hate this apartment"—exhaling now—"hate the—whoever they are, Vietnamese, I guess—downstairs who start that fucking smell of grease and garlic at six in the morning."

"Jimmy, you look like shit."

Jim ignored this. "Creepy place, Wilson. Football game today. But you never see anyone. The faculty live out in the hills, students in their dorms, fraternity houses." He took another hit on the joint. "Horrible place."

"That smell coming from downstairs is just sickening."

"Yuh. Yuh, it is."

Jim looked cold. He rubbed one arm and crossed his legs. He leaned his head back onto the couch, exhaled, stared at the ceiling for a moment, then picked his head up and looked back at his brother. "Nice to see you, Bobby."

Bob leaned forward. "Jesus, Jimmy. Listen to me."

"Listening."

"What are you doing here?" It was the stubble on Jim's face that made it gray.

"Running away," Jim said. "What do you think I'm doing here? I figured, sweet campus, smart kids, new chance. But I don't know how to teach, that's the truth of it."

"Do you like any students?"

"I hate the students, I told you. Wanna know something funny? They don't even know who Wally Packer is, not really. They go, Oh, yeah, I know that song. They think he's practically like Frank Sinatra; they have no idea about the trial. They don't even know who O. J. Simpson is. Most of them don't. They were babies when that was happening. Don't know, and they don't care. They're very, very privileged kids, Bob. The sons of the captains of industry. That's who they are. One guy on the faculty told me this is where the corporate guys send their kids, knowing they'll still come home Republican."

"How did you even get this job?"

Jim shrugged, smoked more of the joint. "Some dude here Alan knows had surgery and took a leave or something. Alan fixed it up for me."

"Do you do that a lot?" Bob nodded toward the joint in Jim's hand. "'Cause you're kind of skinny for a pothead."

Jim shrugged again.

"What—you're doing more than that? You've never— Oh God, Jim. Is this something you started with your new now-I'm-going-to-crack-up life?"

Jim waved a hand tiredly.

"You're not doing coke or anything, are you? You might just think about your heart."

"My heart. Yeah. I might just think about my heart."

Bob stood up, went and looked in the refrigerator. There was beer, a quart of milk, and a jar of olives. He came back to where Jim was. "Well, they should know who O.J. is now. He's back in jail. Or released for the moment, I guess. But going back to prison for good." He sat down slowly in the chair. "Along with your friend Wally."

"Yep. Yep, that's true." Jim's eyes were getting red around the rims. "But no Wilson student gives a shit."

"I don't think anyone gives a shit," Bob said.

"No, I think you're right."

After a moment Bob asked, "So have you heard from Wally?"

Jim nodded. "He's on his own with this."

"Think he'll go to prison? I haven't paid much attention."

Jim nodded. "He will."

It was a sad moment. There are sad moments in life, and this was one of them. Bob thought of his brother in his tailored suits and expensive cuff links, speaking into the microphones on the front steps of the courthouse at the end of each day. The glee of the acquittal. And now the defendant was headed, possibly, probably, after all these years, to prison, for being careless, reckless, obstreperous. And here was his defender, Jim Burgess, sitting skinny and unshaven in a small apartment out in the woods with awful smells of acrid garlicky something seeping through the walls—

"Jim."

His brother raised his eyebrows, tapped out the roach in an ashtray, preserving it carefully in its little baggie before putting it back into the Band-Aid box.

"I want you to leave this place."

Jim nodded.

"Tell them you can't stay. I'll tell them."

Jim said, "I've been thinking about things."

Bob waited.

"And one of the things that is so clear to me, so strikingly clear—and trust me, not much is clear, but one thing is: I don't have any idea what it's like to be black in this country."

"Excuse me?"

"I mean it. And neither do you."

"Well, of course not. Jesus. Did I ever claim to? Did *you* ever claim to?"

"No. But that's not the point."

"What's the point, Jim?"

Jim looked confused. "I forget." Then he suddenly leaned forward. "Listen to this, my brother from Maine. Listen to this. When you meet a stranger and get introduced, you're not supposed to say, Nice to meet you. That's vulgar. Too familiar, lacking class." He sat back. "You're supposed to say, How are you?" Jim nodded. "Bet you didn't know that."

"I didn't."

"Well, that's because we're bozos from Maine. The truly high-class people of this country know that when you meet someone you say, How are you? And they *laugh* at those who say, Nice to meet you. That's what I've learned at this school."

"God," Bob said. "Jimmy, you're starting to scare me."

"It should scare you."

Bob stood and walked to the door of Jim's bedroom. Clothes were strewn about, the bureau drawers were open, the bed was so unmade that part of its mattress showed. Bob turned back. "How many weeks till the end of the semester?"

Jim looked at him with his reddened eyes. "Seven." He sat forward. "That sexual harassment stuff—it just wasn't true. It's true we had sex. That's true. But it's not true she was scared of me, or scared of losing her job. *I* was the one scared."

"Of what?" Bob asked.

"Of what?" Jim threw up one hand. "Of this! Of losing Helen! But I didn't think Adriana was going after a million dollars. I didn't think I'd lose my job."

"Is that what she got?"

"She got five hundred thousand. They all start by asking for a million. I have to pay it, you know. Comes out of the equity of my share of the firm." Jim sat with his arms on each side of him, his chest looked thin. He gave a small shake of his head that seemed to indicate indifference. "She lived in your building in Brooklyn. The girl you felt sorry for."

"I know that. I was the one who suggested your—"

Jim waved a hand. "She'd have come there anyway. She was looking for money, she applied to all the big places. Anyway, she was a tough negotiator, it turns out. That's what she walked away with."

"You weren't scared you'd lose your job? That never went through your head? How could that not go through your head, Jim? You're a lawyer."

"Bobby, you're a touching fellow. I mean that, don't get mad. You think like a child. Like things are supposed to make sense. People say, Oh, that was so stupid of him, when some congressman tries to hit on a guy in a bus-station bathroom. Well, yeah. 'Course it was."

Bob looked in the closet, found a suitcase and brought it out.

Jim didn't seem to notice. He said, "Some of us are secretly in love with destruction. That's what I think. Honestly? From the moment I heard about Zach throwing that pig's head, I just knew deep down I was fucked. *Your cheatin' heart will tell on you.* Could not get that song out of my head. But man, all my life—and especially when Zach fucked up, and the kids had all gone off so the house was empty, and that stupid fucking meaningless job at the firm—I thought: Dead man going down. Just a matter of time." Jim looked as though this speech had exhausted him. He closed his eyes, moved a hand tiredly. "I could not keep it up."

"You got to get out of here, Jimmy."

"You keep saying that. Where do you think I'm going to go?"

Bob's cell phone rang. "Susan," he said. He listened. Then he said, "That's great. That's wonderful. I'll drive up. Yeah, really. I'm bringing Jim. I'm with him now in Wilson. He's a mess and he looks like shit, so be prepared." He clicked his phone shut and said to his brother, "We're going to Maine. Our nephew's coming home. Day after tomorrow. He'll get off a bus in Portland and all three of us will be there. Get it? Family."

Jim shook his head, rubbed his face. "Did you know Larry's always hated me? I made him stay at sleepaway camp when he wanted to come home."

"That was a long time ago, Jim. He doesn't hate you."

"Nothing's a long time ago."

"Give me the name of the chairman," Bob said.

"Woman," Jim said. "Chairwoman. Chairperson. Chair-who-gives-a-fuck."

12

And so the Burgess brothers drove to Maine from Upstate New York, along winding roads, past run-down farmhouses and farms not so run-down, past small houses and large houses with three cars in front, or a snowmobile, or a boat covered with tarp. They stopped for gas and got back on the road. Bob drove. Jim sat next to him, slumped down, sometimes fast asleep, or else staring out the passenger window.

"Thinking of Helen?" Bob asked.

"Always." Jim sat up straighter. "And I don't want to talk about it." After a few moments he added, "I can't believe I'm headed to Maine."

"You've said that a few times. It's better than the hole I found you in. And being in motion is good."

"Why?"

"Because of the sway of embryonic fluid, or something. Something like that."

Jim looked out the window again. They passed more fields, gas stations, little strip malls, antiques stores, the road went on and on. Every house they passed seemed isolated and desolate to Bob, and when Jim said, "Some guy in the German Department said I'd like it here because Upstate New York looks like Maine," Bob said he didn't think it looked like Maine at all, and Jim said, "I don't either."

They crossed into Massachusetts and the clouds were low and the trees scrubbier, the fields they passed were untamed and calming. "Jim. So you remember him?"

Jim looked at Bob, as though from far away. "Who?"

"Our father. Who art in heaven."

Jim moved in his seat, shifted his legs so his knees pointed more in the direction of Bob. After a few moments, he said, "I remember he took me ice fishing. He told me to watch a little orange ball floating on a tiny circle of water in the middle of ice. He said if the ball dipped down, we had a fish. We never got a fish. I can't remember his face, but I remember that little orange ball."

"What else?"

"Sometimes in the summer when it was hot he'd spray us with the hose, do you remember that?"

Bob did not.

"Sometimes he'd sing."

"Sing? Was he drunk?"

"Oh God, no." Jim looked at the ceiling of the car, shaking his head. "Only a Puritan from New England would think you had to be drunk to sing. No, Bob, I think he just liked to sing once in a while. Like 'Home on the Range,' I think."

"Did he yell at us?"

"I don't remember that he did."

"So he was—what was he like?"

"I think he was kind of like you." Jim said this thoughtfully, his hands now pressed beneath his knees. "I don't know what he was *like*, of course, I don't have enough memories, but lots of time I've thought—you know, Bob, you have your own brand of, sort of, goofiness, and I've thought you might have taken after him." Jim was silent for many minutes while Bob waited. Then Jim said, "If Pam had come back and asked you, begged you, to take her back, would you have?"

"Yes. She never asked. But you don't want to wait too long."

"Helen's really mad."

"Yuh, she is. She is really mad. Of course she is."

Jim said quietly, "In case you haven't noticed, people get hard-hearted against the people they hurt. Because we can't stand it. Literally. To think *we* did that to someone. *I* did that. So we think of all the reasons why it's okay we did whatever we did. Does Susan know what's going on?"

"I told her. After I saw Helen. I told her I was coming to find you in Wilson."

"Susan never liked Helen."

"She's not blaming Helen. How can anyone blame Helen?"

"I've tried. She has tons of money, you know. From her father. And she kept it tucked away and separate so it passes on to the kids. So I wouldn't get any if she died. Just straight to the kids. Her father wanted it that way." Jim stretched his legs out. "Actually, it's not that uncommon with family money."

"Exactly."

Jim said, "That's about all I've come up with, charges against Helen. The fact that I hated my stupid job doing stupid white-collar stupid crime is not her fault. She's been urging me to leave there for years, she knows it's not what I liked to do. And I don't want to talk about this. One more thing, I think the night with the life coach did her in."

"Jim. If you have any other outside events, don't confess them. That's my advice, okay?"

"What am I going to do, Bob? I have no family."

"You have family," Bob said. "You have a wife who hates you. Kids who are furious with you. A brother and sister who make you insane. And a nephew who used to be kind of a drip but apparently is not so much of a drip now. That's called family."

Jim fell asleep, his head leaning forward almost to his chest.

———◆———

Susan came out to meet them as they pulled into the driveway. She hugged Jim with a tenderness that Bob had not known she contained. "Let's get you inside," she said. "I'm sleeping on the couch tonight. Jim, you can have my room. You need to shower and shave. And I have a cooked meal waiting."

She bustled them about in a way that surprised Bob. He tried to catch Jim's eye, but Jim just looked stunned while Susan found him towels and one of Zach's old razors. Bob was staying in Zach's room, and Susan directed him in there with his bags. When Bob heard the shower running, he said, "I'll be back. I'm going to take a drive."

Margaret Estaver was standing on the sidewalk in front of her church, talking with a tall, dark-skinned man. Bob pulled up to the curb, got out, saw her face open with gladness as he approached. She spoke to the man, who nodded at Bob, and who seemed, as Bob got closer, to be vaguely familiar. "This is Abdikarim Ahmed," Margaret said, and the man extended his hand and said, "Good to meet you, good to meet you." His eyes were dark, intelligent; his teeth, as he smiled, were uneven and stained.

Margaret said, "What do you hear from Zachary?" Bob glanced at Abdikarim; he might have been one of the men in court for Zach's hearing, Bob couldn't be sure.

The man said, "He is good? With his father? Will he come home? He can come home now, I think."

"He's coming home tomorrow," Bob said. He added, "Don't worry, though. He's cleaned up his act. Better behaved." He said the last two words loudly, which is how people talked to foreigners or deaf people, he realized. Margaret rolled her eyes at him.

"Coming home," the man said, looking very pleased. "Very good, very good." He shook hands again. "Very good to meet you. May the boy be well." He nodded, and walked away.

When he was out of earshot, Margaret said, "He's been the advocate for Zach."

"That man?"

Bob followed her to her office. He would always remember how she reached to turn on a lamp and the room became bathed in light as the autumn darkness fell against the windows. He could never place the moment—though it could have been that moment, the lamp's light holding the warmth of Abdikarim, and somehow, too, the warmth of Shirley Falls—when he understood that his future was with her. They did not speak for long, nor did they speak of each other. She wished him luck with Jim, and with Zachary's arrival, and he said she would hear all about it, and she said Yes, and did not walk him to his car.

"He's a mess," his sister murmured, nodding toward the living room. "He's called her three times and she won't pick up. But Zach just emailed that he's really excited, and he's awful glad you'll be there. So *that* part's good at least."

Bob went into the living room and sat across from Jim. "Here's what you do," Bob said. "Go to Park Slope and sleep on the stoop until she lets you in."

"She'll call the police." Jim had his fist on his chin, staring at the rug.

"Let her. It's still your house, isn't it?"

"She'll get a restraining order."

"You didn't hit her, did you? Jesus."

Jim looked up at that. "Come on, Bob. No. I never threw her fucking clothes out the window either."

"Okay," said Bob. "Okay."

———•———

In the morning Mrs. Drinkwater stood at the top of the stairs, eavesdropping. "My word," she mouthed silently, for there was a lot getting said as these three kids—she thought of them as kids, could hear in their voices the lilt with which they spoke, especially Susan, as if being without spouses or children brought them back to their own childhood—discussed Zachary's future (he might go to college) and Jim's crisis (he had messed up everything, it seemed, only one of his daughters would still talk to him) and Susan's own life (she might take a painting class one night a week—this part especially surprised Mrs. Drinkwater, she had no idea Susan wanted to paint).

A kitchen chair scraped back, and Mrs. Drinkwater almost turned to go back to her room, but then water ran in the sink, and stopped, and they were talking again. Bob was telling Susan that someone he worked with knew a woman who was raised poor and always bought her clothes at Kmart, and then she married a really rich guy and still, after all these years of being married to a rich man, bought her clothes at Kmart. "Why?" said Susan, just as Mrs. Drinkwater was wondering the same thing. "Because it's familiar," Bob answered.

"I'd get myself some beautiful clothes if I was married to a wealthy man," Susan said.

"You think that," her brother said. "But you might not."

A pause arrived that was long enough for Mrs. Drinkwater to consider retreating. Then Susan's voice: "Jimmy, do you want Helen back? Because when Steve left, my friends said all the stuff people say: Oh, you're better off without him, all that. And as much as I went around stacking up his faults, I'd have let him come back. I wished he'd come back. So if you want her back, I think you should beg."

"I think you should beg," Bob said.

Mrs. Drinkwater almost fell down the stairs, leaning forward. She wanted to call out, I say you beg too, but discretion stopped her. It was their time together.

"You don't like Helen," Jim said.

And Susan answered, "Don't do that, Jim. She's fine. Don't turn this on me. Maybe you weren't totally comfortable being married to a rich WASP, but that's not Helen's fault." Susan added, "For the longest time I didn't even know *I* was a WASP."

Bob's voice: "When did you find out?"

"When I was twenty."

"What happened when you were twenty?"

"I went out with a Jewish guy."

"You did?" This was Jim's voice.

"I didn't know he was Jewish."

"Oh, well. Thank God for that. You're excused."

Mrs. Drinkwater thought Jim was being sardonic; she liked Jim. She'd liked him years ago when she saw him on television each night.

"How'd you find out he was Jewish?" Bob asked.

"It came up. He said somebody just thought of him as a Jew-boy, and I thought, Huh, he must be Jewish. I didn't care. Why would I care? But then he started calling me Muffy, and I said, Why are you calling me Muffy?, and he said, Because that's what WASP girls are called. Finally I figured it out."

"What happened to him?" Bob asked.

"He graduated. Went back to Massachusetts, where he was from. The next year I met Steve."

"Susie has a history," said Jim. "Who knew."

A scraping chair again, the sound of dishes being stacked. "You guys, I'm so nervous I feel sick to my stomach. What if Zach doesn't like me when he sees me?"

"He *loves* you. He's coming home." This was Bob's voice, and Mrs. Drinkwater went back to her room.

13

They sat in the bus station, which was not the Portland bus station of
their youth but a newer one stuck in what seemed to be the middle of a
huge parking lot. Through the large windows could be seen a few taxi
drivers, sitting in their cars—not yellow—waiting for the buses to come
in. "Why didn't Zach take a bus to Shirley Falls?" Jim asked. He sat
slumped in his plastic chair, not looking around.

"Because he'd have to change buses here, and wait for hours, and
that bus gets in to Shirley Falls really late," Susan said. "So I offered to
come get him here."

"Of course you did," Bob said. He was thinking of Margaret. How he
would tell her all of this. "Susie, don't freak out if he's awkward and
doesn't hug you. He probably feels very grown up these days. I'm expecting he'll shake my hand. Just don't be disappointed, is all I'm saying."

"I've thought of all that," Susan said.

Bob stood. "I'm getting a cup of coffee from that vending machine.
You want anything?"

Susan said, "No, thank you." Jim said nothing.

If either one saw him go to the ticket counter, they did not mention it. There were buses going to Boston, New York, Washington, and also to Bangor. Bob came back with his coffee. "Did you see the taxi drivers? A couple are Somali. In Minneapolis, some couldn't get hired because they didn't want to take people that have alcohol."

"How would they know if someone had alcohol?" Susan asked. "And is it any of their business? I mean, if they want a job so bad."

"Susie-Q, Susie-Q. Keep these opinions to yourself. Your son is able to come home because of one Abdikarim." Bob raised his eyebrows and nodded. "Seriously. The guy who testified at his hearing. He's very re-spected in the Somali community. He took a real interest in Zach—campaigned for him with the elders. If he hadn't, the DA probably wouldn't have filed the case, and you'd be facing a trial right now. I talked to him yesterday."

Susan couldn't take this in. She kept frowning at Bob. "That Somali man did that? Why?"

"I just told you. He liked Zach, he reminds him of his son he lost years ago, back home."

"I don't know what to say."

Bob shrugged. "Well, you know. Keep it in mind. And eventually we need to educate Zach."

Throughout this conversation Jim was quiet. When he stood up, Susan asked where he was going. "To the bathroom. If you don't mind." He walked across the station, stooped and thin.

Susan and Bob watched him. "I'm awful worried about him," Susan said, her eyes staying on the back of her brother.

"You know, Susie—" Bob put his coffee onto the floor by his feet. "Jim told me he did it. That I didn't."

Susan waited, looking at him. "Did wha— *That?* Seriously? Oh, wow. But of course he didn't. You don't think it's true, do you?"

"I don't think we'll ever know."

"But he thinks he did?"

"He seems to think he did."

"When did he tell you?"

"When Zach was missing."

They watched Jim come back to them across the station. He did not seem tall, as he always had, but old-looking, and gaunt, in his long coat. "You guys talking about me?" He sat down between them.

"Yes," they said in unison.

Over the loudspeaker came the announcement that the bus for New York City was now boarding. The twins glanced at each other, then at Jim. Jim's jaw twitched. "Get on the bus, Jimmy," Susan said gently.

"I don't have a ticket. I don't have any of my stuff, and the line's too—"

"Get on the bus, Jim." Bob flipped the ticket to his brother. "Go. I'll leave my phone on. Go."

Jim sat.

Susan slipped her hand beneath his elbow, and Bob took his other arm; all three stood up. As if he were a prisoner between them they walked him to the door. Susan, watching him move to the waiting bus outside, had a sudden stabbing of despair—as though Zach was leaving her again.

Jim turned. "You say hi to my nephew," he said. "You tell him I'm glad he's back."

They stood while he boarded the bus. Through the tinted windows he wasn't visible. They waited until the bus had pulled away, then went back to their plastic chairs. Bob finally said, "You sure you don't want coffee?"

Susan shook her head.

"How much time?" he asked, and Susan said ten minutes. He touched her knee. "Don't worry about Jimmy. He's got us, if it comes to that," and Susan nodded. He understood they would probably never again discuss the death of their father. The facts didn't matter. Their stories mattered, and each of their stories belonged to each of them alone.

"There it is." Susan hit his arm. Through the station window they saw the bus, like a friendly oversize caterpillar, pull into the lot. The wait by the door was interminable, then swift, because all of a sudden Zachary was there: hair falling over his forehead, tall, and shyly grinning, Zach.

"Hey, Mom." And Bob stood back while his sister hugged her son, they hugged and hugged, swaying slightly back and forth. People stepped around them politely, some smiling quickly as they passed by. Then Zach hugged Bob, and Bob felt a sturdiness to the young man. When he pulled away he held Zach by his shoulders and said, "You look *great.*"

In fact, of course, he was very much Zach. A sprinkle of acne ran across the top of his forehead, visible as he ran his hand again and again through his hair. And while he had gained weight, he still gave the appearance of awkward skinniness. What was different was how his face flickered with emotion. "Weird, man. Weird, right? So weird," he kept saying as they walked to the car. What Bob had not counted on—and probably Susan hadn't either—was the fact that he talked. And talked. He talked about people paying lots of taxes in Sweden, his father had explained this, but then people had everything they wanted. Hospitals, doctors, perfect fire stations, clean streets. He talked about people living closer together, taking care of each other a lot more than here. He talked about how pretty the girls were, you wouldn't believe it, Uncle Bob. Gorgeous girls just everywhere, at first he felt like a loser, but they were always nice to him. Was he talking too much? He asked this.

"Heavens, no," Susan said.

But the house caused him to hesitate, Bob saw that. Scratching the dog's head, looking around, Zach said, "It's all the same. But it's not."

"I know," Susan said. She leaned against a chair. "You're not obligated to be here, honey, you can go back any time you want."

Zach scraped his hand through his hair, gave his mother his goofy grin. "Oh, I want to be here. I'm just saying it's *weird.*"

"Well, you can't stay here forever," Susan said. "It wouldn't be natural. And nobody young stays in Maine anymore. There aren't any jobs."

"Susie," Bob said. "You're sounding crispy. If Zach goes into geriatric medicine, he can work here forever."

"Hey, *you* guys, what happened to Uncle Jim?"

"He's busy," said Bob. "Real busy, we hope."

———•———

Night had fallen hours earlier across the Eastern Seaboard. Across the coastal town of Lubec, Maine, the sun set first, then the town of Shirley Falls, then quickly down the coastline: Massachusetts, Connecticut, New York; dark for hours by the time the bus carrying Jim Burgess pulled into the cavernous Port Authority, dark as he stared out a taxi window riding across the Brooklyn Bridge. Abdikarim had completed his day's final prayer, and was considering Bob Burgess, who must be home with the dark-eyed boy, the boy who, in fact, turning to his mother, had just said, "Man, we have to paint this room." Bob had gone downstairs to let the dog outside, and stood now on the porch in the cold. The sky had no moonlight, no stars. He could not believe how dark it was. He thought of Margaret, with wonderment, and with a heart that understood its fate. He had never—never—expected to return to Maine. For a few moments he felt shivers of apprehension: thick sweaters worn day after day, snow kicked from boots, cold rooms entered. He had run from this, and so had Jim. And yet, what lay before him did not seem strange, and life was like that, he thought. About Jim there was no thought—only the rushing sweep of sensation as large as the dark sky. He called to the dog and went inside. When Bob fell asleep on Susan's couch he held in his hands—held on to it all night—his phone, set on vibrate, in case Jim needed him, but the phone remained unmoving and unblinking and it stayed that way as the first pale light crept unapologetically beneath the blinds.

Acknowledgments

The author wishes to thank the following people who were enormously helpful in the writing of this book: Kathy Chamberlain, Molly Friedrich, Susan Kamil, Lucy Carson, Benjamin Dreyer, Jim Howaniec, Ellen Crosby, Trish Riley and Peter Schwindt, and Jonathan Strout, as well as the many, many people who were so generous with their time in helping to bring forth an understanding of an immigrant population.

ABOUT THE AUTHOR

ELIZABETH STROUT is the author of the *New York Times* bestseller *Olive Kitteridge,* for which she was awarded the Pulitzer Prize; the national bestseller *Abide with Me;* and *Amy and Isabelle,* winner of the *Los Angeles Times* Art Seidenbaum Award and the *Chicago Tribune* Heartland Prize. She has also been a finalist for the PEN/Faulkner Award and the Orange Prize in London. She lives in Maine and New York City.

Elizabeth Strout is available for select readings and lectures. To inquire about a possible appearance, please contact the Random House Speakers Bureau at 212-572-2013 or rhspeakers@randomhouse.com.

ABOUT THE TYPE

This book was set in Fairfield, the first typeface from the hand of the distinguished American artist and engraver Rudolph Ruzicka (1883–1978). Ruzicka was born in Bohemia and came to America in 1894. He set up his own shop, devoted to wood engraving and printing, in New York in 1913 after a varied career working as a wood engraver, in photoengraving and banknote printing plants, and as an art director and freelance artist. He designed and illustrated many books, and was the creator of a considerable list of individual prints—wood engravings, line engravings on copper, and aquatints.